"This is a riveting, brilliant novel. The language sings, the concepts are original and engrossing."

—Charles de Lint

"*King Rat* goes down as sweetly as week-old garbage, to leave the reader eyeing speculatively the manhole covers of Soho and Battersea. A knotted, toothy, thought-provoking read."

—M. John Harrison

"China Miéville blends a lot of good, solid folkloric material with a good deal of contemporary urban paranoia and Drum and Bass music, the multilayered richness of which the Piper seeks to use for his own ends. It's ambitious, to be sure, and involved at times—it would help to know something about Cockney rhyming slang, the layout of London and its environs, and jungle music—but the book can easily be enjoyed by anyone with a love of good, gritty make-believe. *King Rat* is a strong first novel in the quirky sub-sub-genre of subterranean fairy tales that, with such recent good books as Lisa Goldstein's *Dark Cities Underground* and Neil Gaiman's *Neverwhere*, looks less cute and more promising by the minute."

—*The Onion*

"For lovers of modern urban tales, China Miéville's *King Rat* could be a serious contender to rival Neil Gaiman's *Neverwhere*, Peter Crowther and James Lovegrove's *Escardy Gap*, and anything by Charles de Lint.... A richly imagined and detailed tapestry, *King Rat* is a unique blend, with a pinch of the Brothers Grimm and a dash of Tolkien. A fine meld of the exotic and rare, dark and mysterious, that becomes a wholly mesmerizing and original voice that's impossible to ignore."

—*Charleston Post & Courier*

"[Miéville's] prose melds James Herbert's nihilistic violence with the metropolitan paranoia of Martin Amis, circa *London Fields*, and he shows a talent for authentic dialogue and cinematic set pieces. Most striking, perhaps, is the meticulously crafted topography of a brooding London peopled by despondent youth and bizarre night creatures and rife with the rhythms of Drum 'n' Bass."

—*The Times* (London)

"*King Rat*: a story so compelling you almost haven't time to notice how fine the writing is: a dark myth reinvented for our time and for London in particular with great wit, style, and imagination."

—Ramsey Campbell

"[An] extraordinary debut novel...China Miéville is a remarkably eloquent new writer who has produced genuine magic here."

—*Locus*

TOR®

A TOM DOHERTY ASSOCIATES BOOK

NEW YORK

KING RAT

CHINA MIÉVILLE

This is a work of fiction. All the characters and events portrayed in this novel are either fictitious or are used fictitiously.

KING RAT

Copyright © 1998 by China Miéville

This book is printed on acid-free paper.

Book design by Victoria Kuskowski

First published in England by Macmillan, 1998.

A Tor Book
Published by Tom Doherty Associates, LLC
175 Fifth Avenue
New York, NY 10010

www.tor.com

Tor® is a registered trademark of Tom Doherty Associates, LLC.

LIBRARY OF CONGRESS CATALOGING-IN-PUBLICATION DATA

Miéville, China.
  King Rat / China Miéville.
   p. cm.
  "A Tom Doherty Associates book."
  ISBN 0-312-89073-7 (hc)
  ISBN 0-312-89072-9 (pbk)
  I. Title.
PR6063.I265K56 1999
823'.914—dc21   99-26657
                                                      CIP

Printed in the United States of America

0 9 8 7 6

TO MAX

ACKNOWLEDGMENTS

Thank you to everyone who read this in the early stages. All my love and gratitude go to my mother, Claudia, for all her support, always: and to my sister, Jemima, for her advice and feedback.

Deep love and thanks to Emma, of course, for everything.

My heartfelt thanks to Max Schaefer, who gave me invaluable criticisms, hours of word-processing help, and great friendship during a generally rubbish year.

I can never thank Mic Cheetham enough. I am incredibly lucky to have her on my side. And thanks to all at Macmillan, particularly Peter Lavery, and at Tor, particularly Brian Cholfin and Jenna Felice.

I owe too many writers and artists to mention, but respect is especially due to Two Fingers and James T. Kirk for their novel *Junglist*. They blazed a trail. Many thanks also to Iain Sinclair for generously letting me keep the metaphor I accidently stole from him. Jake Pilikian introduced me to Drum and Bass music and changed my life. Big up to all the DJs and Crews who provided a soundtrack. Awe and gratitude especially to A Guy Called Gerald for the sublime *Gloc:* old, now, but still the most terrifying slab of guerrilla bass ever committed to vinyl. Rewind.

A LONDON SOMETIN' . . .
TEK 9

I can squeeze between buildings through spaces you can't even see. I can walk behind you so close my breath raises goose-flesh on your neck and you won't hear me. I can hear the muscles in your eyes contract when your pupils dilate. I can feed off your filth and live in your house and sleep under your bed and you will never know unless I want you to.

I climb above the streets. All the dimensions of the city are open to me. Your walls are my walls and my ceilings and my floors.

The wind whips my overcoat with a sound like washing on a line. A thousand scratches on my arms tingle like electricity as I scale roofs and move through squat copses of chimneys. I have business tonight.

I spill like mercury over the lip of a building and slither down drainpipes to the alley fifty feet below. I slide silently through piles of rubbish in the sepia lamplight and crack the seal on the sewers, pulling the metal cover out of the street without a sound.

Now I am in darkness but I can still see. I can hear the growling of water through the tunnels. I am up to my waist in your shit, I can feel it tugging at me, I can smell it. I know my way through these passages.

I am heading north, submerged in the current, wading, clinging to walls and ceiling. Live things scuttle and slither to get out of my way. I weave without hesitation through the dank corridors. The rain has been fitful and hesitant but all the water in London seems eager to reach its destination tonight. The brick rivers of the underground are swollen. I dive under the surface and swim in the cloying dark until the time has come to emerge and I rise from the deeps, dripping. I pass noiselessly again through the pavement.

Towering above me is the red brick of my destination. A great dark mass broken with squares of irrelevant light. One glimmering in the shadow of the eaves holds my attention. I straddle the corner of the building and ease my way up. I am slower now. The sound of television and the smell of food seep out of the window, which I am reaching toward now, which I am rattling now with my long nails, scratching, a sound like a pigeon or a twig, an intriguing sound, bait.

PART ONE

GLASS

ONE

The trains that enter London arrive like ships sailing across the roofs. They pass between towers jutting into the sky like long-necked sea beasts and the great gas-cylinders wallowing in dirty scrub like whales. In the depths below are lines of small shops and obscure franchises, cafés with peeling paint and businesses tucked into the arches over which the trains pass. The colors and curves of graffiti mark every wall. Top-floor windows pass by so close that passengers can peer inside, into small bare offices and store cupboards. They can make out the contours of trade calendars and pin-ups on the walls.

The rhythms of London are played out here, in the sprawling flat zone between suburbs and center.

Gradually the streets widen and the names of the shops and cafés become more familiar; the main roads are more salubrious; the traffic is denser; and the city rises to meet the tracks.

At the end of a day in October a train made this journey toward King's Cross. Flanked by air, it progressed over the outlands of North London, the city building up below it as it neared the Holloway Road. The people beneath ignored its passage. Only children looked up as it clattered overhead, and some of the very young pointed. As the train drew closer to the station, it slipped below the level of the roofs.

There were few people in the carriage to watch the bricks rise around them. The sky disappeared above the windows. A cloud of pigeons rose from a hiding place beside the tracks and wheeled off to the east.

The flurry of wings and bodies distracted a thickset young man at the rear of the compartment. He had been trying not to stare openly at the woman sitting opposite him. Thick with relaxer, her hair had been teased from its tight curls and was coiled like snakes on her head. The man broke off his furtive scrutiny as the birds passed by, and he ran his hands through his own cropped hair.

The train was now below the houses. It wound through a deep groove in the city, as if the years of passage had worn down the concrete under the tracks. Saul Garamond glanced again at the woman sitting in front of him, and turned his attention to the windows. The light in the carriage had made them mirrors, and he stared at himself, his heavy face. Beyond his face was a layer of brick, dimly visible, and beyond that the cellars of the houses that rose like cliffs on either side.

It was days since Saul had been in the city.

Every rattle of the tracks took him closer to his home. He closed his eyes.

Outside, the gash through which the tracks passed had widened as the station approached. The walls on either side were punctuated by dark alcoves, small caves full of rubbish a few feet from the track. The silhouettes of cranes arched over the skyline. The walls around the train parted. Tracks fanned away on either side as the train slowed and edged its way into King's Cross.

The passengers rose. Saul swung his bag over his shoulder and shuffled out of the carriage. Freezing air stretched up to the great vaulted ceilings. The cold shocked him. Saul hurried through the buildings, through the crowds, threading his way between knots of people. He still had a way to go. He headed underground.

He could feel the presence of the population around him. After days in a tent on the Suffolk coast, the weight of ten million people so close to him seemed to make the air vibrate. The tube was full of garish colors and bare flesh, as people headed to clubs and parties.

His father would probably be waiting for him. He knew Saul was coming back, and he would surely make an effort to be welcoming, forfeiting his usual evening in the pub to greet his son. Saul already resented him for that. He felt gauche and uncharitable, but he despised his father's faltering attempts to communicate. He was happier when the two of them avoided each other. Being surly was easy, and felt more honest.

By the time his tube train burst out of the tunnels of the Jubilee Line it was dark. Saul knew the route. The darkness transformed the rubble behind Finchley Road into a dimly glimpsed no-man's-land, but he was able to fill in the details he could not see, even down to the tags and the graffiti. Burner. Nax. Coma. He knew the names of the intrepid little rebels clutching their magic markers, and he knew where they had been.

The grandiose tower of the Gaumont State cinema jutted into the sky on his left, a bizarre totalitarian monument among the budget groceries and hoardings of Kilburn High Road. Saul could feel the cold through the windows and he wrapped his coat around him as the train neared Willesden station. The passengers had thinned. Saul left only a very few behind him as he got out of the carriage.

Outside the station he huddled against the chill. The air smelled faintly of smoke from some local bonfire, someone clearing his allotment. Saul set off down the hill toward the library.

He stopped at a takeaway and ate as he walked, moving slowly to avoid spilling soy sauce and vegetables down himself. Saul was sorry the sun had gone down. Willesden lent itself to spectacular sunsets. On a day like today, when there were few clouds, its low skyline let the light flood the streets, pouring into the strangest crevices; the windows that faced each other bounced the rays endlessly back and forth between themselves and sent it hurtling in unpredictable directions; the rows and rows of brick glowed as if lit from within.

Saul turned into the backstreets. He wound through the cold until his father's house rose before him. Terragon Mansions was an ugly Victorian block, squat and mean-looking for all its size. It was fronted by the garden: a strip of dirty vegetation frequented only by dogs. His father lived on the top floor. Saul looked up and saw that the lights were on. He climbed the steps and let himself in, glancing into the darkness of the bushes and scrub on either side.

He ignored the huge lift with its steel-mesh door, not wanting its groans to announce him. Instead he crept up the flights of stairs and gently unlocked his father's door.

The flat was freezing.

Saul stood in the hall and listened. He could hear the sound of the television from behind the sitting room door. He waited, but his father was silent. Saul shivered and looked around him.

He knew he should go in, should rouse his father from slumber, and he even got as far as reaching for the door. But he stopped and looked at his own room. He sneered at himself in disgust, but he crept toward it anyway.

He could apologize in the morning. *I thought you were asleep, Dad. I heard you snoring. I came in drunk and fell into bed. I was so knackered I wouldn't have been any kind of com-*

pany anyway. He cocked an ear, heard only the voices of one of the late-night discussion programmes his father so loved, muffled and pompous. Saul turned away and slipped into his room.

Sleep came easily. Saul dreamed of being cold, and woke once in the night to pull his duvet closer. He dreamed of slamming, a heavy beating noise, so loud it pulled him out of sleep and he realized it was real, it was there. Adrenaline surged through him, making him tremble. His heart quivered and lurched as he swung out of bed.

It was icy in the flat.

Someone was pounding on the front door.

The noise would not stop, it was frightening him. He was shaking, disorientated. It was not yet light. Saul glanced at his clock. It was a little after six. He stumbled into the hall. The horrible *bang bang bang* was incessant, and now he could hear shouting as well, distorted and unintelligible.

He fought into a shirt and shouted: "Who is it?"

The slamming did not stop. He called out again, and this time a voice was raised above the din.

"Police!"

Saul struggled to clear his head. With a sudden panic he thought of the small stash of dope in his drawer, but that was absurd. He was no drugs kingpin, no one would waste a dawn raid on him. He was reaching out to open the door, his heart still tearing, when he suddenly remembered to check that they were who they claimed, but it was too late now, the door flew back and knocked him down as a torrent of bodies streamed into the flat.

Blue trousers and big shoes all around him. Saul was yanked to his feet. He started to flail at the intruders. Anger waxed with his fear. He tried to yell but someone smacked him in the stomach and he doubled up. Voices were reverberating everywhere around him, making no sense.

" . . . cold like a bastard . . . "

"... cocky little cunt ..."

"... fucking glass, watch yourself ..."

"... his son, or what? High as a fucking kite, must be ..."

And above all these voices he could hear a weather forecast, the cheery tones of a breakfast television presenter. Saul struggled to turn and face the men who were holding him so tight.

"What the fuck's going on?" he gasped. Without speaking, the men propelled him into the sitting room.

The room was full of police, but Saul saw straight through them. He saw the television first: the woman in the bright suit was warning him it would be chilly again today. On the sofa was a plate of congealed pasta, and a half-drunk glass of beer sat on the floor. Cold gusts of air caught at him and he looked up at the window, out over houses. The curtains were billowing dramatically. He saw that jags of glass littered the floor. There was almost no glass left in the window-frame, only a few shards around the edges.

Saul sagged with terror and tried to pull himself to the window.

A thin man in civilian clothes turned and saw him.

"Down the station now," he shouted at Saul's captors.

Saul was spun on his heels. The room turned around him like a funfair ride, the rows of books and his father's small pictures rushing past him. He struggled to turn back.

"Dad!" he shouted. "Dad!"

He was pulled effortlessly out of the flat. The dark of the corridor was pierced by slivers of light spilling out of doors. Saul saw uncomprehending faces and hands clutching at dressing-gowns, as he was hauled toward the lift. Neighbors in pajamas were staring at him. He bellowed at them as he passed.

He still could not see the men holding him. He shouted at them, begging to know what was going on, pleading, threatening and railing.

"Where's my dad? *What's going on?*"

"Shut up."

"What's going on?"

Something slammed into his kidneys, not hard but with the threat of greater force. "Shut up." The lift door closed behind them.

"What's happened to my *fucking dad*?"

As soon as he had seen the broken window a voice inside Saul had spoken quietly. He had not been able to hear it clearly until now. Inside the flat the brutal crunch of boots and the swearing had drowned it out. But here where he had been dragged, in the relative silence of the lift, he could hear it whispering.

Dead, it said. *Dad's dead.*

Saul's knees buckled. The men behind him held him upright, but he was utterly weak in their arms. He moaned.

"Where's my dad?" he pleaded.

The light outside was the color of the clouds. Blue strobes swirled on a mass of police cars, staining the drab buildings. The frozen air cleared Saul's head. He tugged desperately at the arms holding him as he struggled to see over the hedges that ringed Terragon Mansions. He saw faces staring down from the hole that was his father's window. He saw the glint of a million splinters of glass covering the dying grass. He saw a mass of uniformed police frozen in a threatening diorama. All their faces were turned to him. One held a roll of tape covered in crime scene warnings, a tape he was stretching around stakes in the ground, circumscribing a piece of the earth. Inside the chosen area he saw one man kneeling before a dark shape on the lawn. The man was staring at him like all the others. His body obscured the untidy thing. Saul was swept past before he could see anymore.

He was pushed into one of the cars, light-headed now, hardly able to feel a thing. His breath came very fast. Somewhere along the line handcuffs had been snapped onto his wrists. He shouted again at the men in front, but they ignored him.

The streets rolled by.

They put him in a cell, gave him a cup of tea and warmer

clothes: a gray cardigan and corduroy trousers that stank of alcohol. Saul sat huddled in a stranger's clothes. He waited for a long time.

He lay on the bed, draped the thin blanket around him.

Sometimes he heard the voice inside him. *Suicide*, it said. *Dad's committed suicide.*

Sometimes he would argue with it. It was a ridiculous idea, something his father could never do. Then it would convince him and he might start to hyperventilate, to panic. He closed his ears to it. He kept it quiet. He would not listen to rumors, even if they came from inside himself.

No one had told him why he was there. Whenever footsteps went by outside he would shout, sometimes swearing, demanding to know what was happening. Sometimes the footsteps would stop and the grill would be lifted on the door. "We're sorry for the delay," a voice would say. "We'll be with you as soon as we can," or "Shut the fuck up."

"You can't keep me here," he yelled at one point. "What's going on?" His voice echoed around empty corridors.

Saul sat on the bed and stared at the ceiling.

A fine network of cracks spread out from one corner. Saul followed them with his eyes, allowing himself to be mesmerized.

Why are you here? the voice inside whispered to him nervously. *Why do they want you? Why won't they speak to you?*

Saul sat and stared at the cracks and ignored the voice.

After a long time he heard the key in the lock. Two uniformed policemen entered, followed by the thin man Saul had seen in his father's flat. The man was dressed in the same brown suit and ugly tan raincoat. He stared at Saul, who returned his gaze from beneath the dirty blanket, forlorn and pathetic and aggressive. When the thin man spoke his voice was much softer than Saul would have imagined.

"Mr. Garamond," he said. "I'm sorry to have to tell you that your father is dead."

Saul gazed at him. That much was obvious surely, he felt like shouting, but tears stopped him. He tried to speak through his streaming eyes and nose, but could issue nothing but a sob.

He wept noisily for a minute, then struggled to control himself. He sniffed back tears like a baby and wiped his snotty nose on his sleeve. The three policemen stood and watched him impassively until he had controlled himself a little more.

"What's going on?" he croaked.

"I was hoping you might be able to tell us that, Saul," said the thin man. His voice remained quite impassive. "I'm Detective Inspector Crowley, Saul. Now, I'm going to ask you a few questions . . . "

"What happened to Dad?" Saul interrupted. There was a pause.

"He fell from the window, Saul," Crowley said. "It's a long way up. I don't think he suffered any." There was a pause. "Did you not realize what had happened to your dad, Saul?"

"I thought maybe something . . . I saw in the garden . . . Why am I *here*?" Saul was shaking.

Crowley pursed his lips and moved a little closer. "Well, Saul, first let me apologize for how long you've been waiting. It's been very hectic out here. I had hoped someone might come and take care of you, but it seems no one has. I'm sorry about that. I'll be having a few words.

"As to why you're here, well, it was all a bit confused back there. We get a call from a neighbor saying there's someone lying out front of the building, we go in, there you are, we don't know who you are . . . you can see how it all gets out of hand. Anyway, you're here, long and short of it, in the hope that you can tell us your side of the story."

Saul stared at Crowley. "My *side*?" he shouted. "My side of what? I've got home and my dad's . . . "

Crowley shushed him, his hands up, placating, nodding.

"I know, I know, Saul. We've just got to understand what happened. I want you to come with me." He gave a sad little smile as he said this. He looked down at Saul sitting on the bed; dirty, smelly, in strange clothes, confused, pugnacious, tear-stained and orphaned. Crowley's face creased with what looked like concern.

"I want to ask you some questions."

TWO

Once, when he was three, Saul was sitting on his father's shoulders, coming home from the park. They had passed a group of workmen repairing a road, and Saul had tangled his hands in his father's hair and leaned over and gazed at the bubbling pot of tar his father pointed out: the pot heating on the van, and the big metal stick they used to stir it. His nose was filled with the thick smell of tar, and as Saul gazed into the simmering glop he remembered the witch's cauldron in *Hansel and Gretel* and he was seized with the sudden terror that he would fall into the tar and be cooked alive. And Saul had squirmed backwards and his father had stopped and asked him what was the matter. When he understood he had taken Saul off his shoulders and walked with him over to the workmen, who had leaned on their shovels and grinned quizzically at the anxious child. Saul's father had leaned down and whispered encouragement into his ear, and Saul had asked the men what the tar was. The men had told him about how they would spread it thin and put it on the road, and they had stirred it for him as his father held him. He did not fall in. And he was still afraid, but not as much as he had been, and he knew why his father had made him find out about the tar, and he had been brave.

A mug of milky tea coagulated slowly in front of him. A bored-looking constable stood by the door of the bare room. A rhythmic metallic wheeze issued from the tape-recorder on the table. Crowley sat opposite him, his arms folded, his face impassive.

"Tell me about your father."

Saul's father had been racked with a desperate embarrassment whenever his son came home with girls. It was very important to him that he should not seem distant or old-fashioned, and in a ghastly miscalculation he had tried to put Saul's guests at their ease. He was terrified that he would say the wrong thing. The struggle not to bolt for his own room stiffened him. He would stand uneasily in the doorway, a grim smile clamped to his face, his voice firm and serious as he asked the terrified fifteen-year-olds what they were doing at school and whether they enjoyed it. Saul would gaze at his father and will him to leave. He would stare furiously at the floor as his father stolidly discussed the weather and GCSE English.

"I've heard that sometimes you argued. Is that true, Saul? Tell me about that."

When Saul was ten, the time he liked most was in the mornings. Saul's father left for work on the railways early, and Saul had half an hour to himself in the flat. He would wander around and stare at the titles of the books his father left lying on all the surfaces: books about money and politics and history. His father would always pay close attention to what Saul was doing in history at school, asking what the teachers had said. He would lean over his chair, urging Saul not to believe everything his history teacher told him. He would thrust books at his son, stare at them, become distracted, take them back, flick through the pages, murmur that Saul was perhaps too young. He would ask his son what he thought about the issues they discussed. He took Saul's opinions very seriously. Sometimes these discussions bored Saul. More often they made him feel uneasy at the sudden welter of ideas, but inspired.

"Did your father ever make you feel guilty, Saul?"

Something had been poisoned between the two of them when Saul was about sixteen. He had been sure this was an awkwardness that would pass, but once it had taken root the bitterness would not go. Saul's father forgot how to talk to him. He had nothing more to teach and nothing more to say. Saul was angry with his father's disappointment. His father was disappointed at his laziness and his lack of political fervor. Saul could not make his father feel at ease, and his father was disappointed at that. Saul had stopped going on the marches and the demonstrations, and his father had stopped asking him. Every once in a while there would be an argument. Doors would slam. More usually there was nothing.

Saul's father was bad at accepting presents. He never took women to the flat when his son was there. Once when the twelve-year-old Saul was being bullied, his father came into the school unannounced and harangued the teachers, to Saul's profound embarrassment.

"Do you miss your mother, Saul? Are you sorry you never knew her?"

Saul's father was a short man with powerful shoulders and a body like a thick pillar. He had thinning gray hair and gray eyes.

The previous Christmas he had given Saul a book by Lenin. Saul's friends had laughed at how little the aging man knew his son, but Saul had not felt any scorn—only loss. He understood what his father was trying to offer him.

His father was trying to resolve a paradox. He was trying to make sense of his bright, educated son letting life come to him rather than wresting what he wanted from it. He understood only that his son was dissatisfied. That much was true. In Saul's teenage years he had been a living cliché, sulky and adrift in *ennui*. To his father this could only mean that Saul was paralyzed in the face of a terrifying and vast future, the whole of his life, the whole of the world. Saul had emerged, passed twenty unscathed, but his father and he would never really be able to talk together again.

That Christmas, Saul had sat on his bed and turned the little book over and over in his hands. It was a leather-bound edition illustrated with stark woodcuts of toiling workers, a beautiful little commodity. *What Is To Be Done?* demanded the title. What is to be done with you, Saul?

He read the book. He read Lenin's exhortations that the future must be grasped, struggled for, molded, and he knew that his father was trying to explain the world to him, trying to help him. His father wanted to be his vanguard. What paralyzes is fear, his father believed, and what makes fear is ignorance. When we learn, we no longer fear. This is tar, and this is what it does, and this is the world, and this is what it does, and this is what we can do to it.

There was a long time of gentle questions and monosyllabic answers. Almost imperceptibly, the pace of the interrogation built up. *I was out of London*, Saul tried to explain, *I was camping. I got in late, about eleven, I went straight to bed, I didn't see Dad.*

Crowley was insistent. He ignored Saul's plaintive evasions. He grew gradually more aggressive. He asked Saul about the previous night.

Crowley relentlessly reconstructed Saul's route home. Saul felt as if he had been slapped. He was curt, struggling to control the adrenaline which rushed through him. Crowley piled meat on the skeletal answers Saul offered him, threading through Willesden with such detail that Saul once more stalked its dark streets.

"What did you do when you saw your father?" Crowley asked.

I did not see my father, Saul wanted to say, *he died without me seeing him*, but instead he heard himself whine something inaudible like a petulant child.

"Did he make you angry when you found him waiting for you?" Crowley said, and Saul felt fear spread through him from the groin outward. He shook his head.

"Did he make you angry, Saul? Did you argue?"

"I didn't see him!"

"Did you fight, Saul?" A shaken head, no. "Did you fight?" No. "Did you?"

Crowley waited a long time for an answer. Eventually he pursed his lips and scribbled something in a notebook. He looked up and met Saul's eyes, dared him to speak.

"I didn't see him! I don't know what you want . . . I wasn't there!" Saul was afraid. When, he begged to know, would they let him go? But Crowley would not say.

Crowley and the constable led him back to the cell. There would be further interviews, they warned him. They offered him food which, in a fit of righteous petulance, he refused. He did not know if he was hungry. He felt as if he had forgotten how to tell.

"I want to make a phone call!" Saul called as the men's

footsteps died away, but they did not return and he did not shout again.

Saul lay on the bench and covered his eyes.

He was acutely aware of every sound. He could hear the tattoo of feet in the corridor long before they passed his door. Muffled conversations of men and women welled up and died as they walked by; laughter sounded suddenly from another part of the building; cars were moving some way off, their mutterings filtered by trees and walls.

For a long time Saul lay listening. Was he allowed a phone call? he wondered. Who would he call? Was he under arrest? But these thoughts seemed to take up very little of his mind. For the most part he just lay and listened.

A long time passed.

Saul opened his eyes with a start. For a moment he was uncertain what had happened.

The sounds were changing.

The depth seemed to be bleeding out of all the noises in the world.

Saul could still make out everything he had heard before, but it was ebbing away into two dimensions. The change was swift and inexorable. Like the curious echoes of shrieks which fill swimming pools, the sounds were clear and audible, but empty.

Saul sat up. A loud scratching startled him: the noise of his chest against the rough blanket. He could hear the thump of his heart. The sounds of his body were as full as ever, unaffected by the strange sonic vampirism. They seemed unnaturally clear. Saul felt like a cut-out pasted ineptly onto the world. He moved his head slowly from side to side, touched his ears.

A faint patter of boots sounded in the corridor, wan and ineffectual. A policeman walked past the cell, his steps unconvincing. Saul stood tentatively and looked up at the ceiling. The network of cracks and lines in the paint seemed to shift uneasily, the shadows moving imperceptibly, as if a faint light were being moved about the room.

Saul's breath came fast and shallow. The air felt stretched out taut and tasted of dust.

Saul moved, reeled, made dizzy by the cacophony of his own body.

Above the stripped-down murmurings, slow footsteps became audible. Like the sounds Saul made, these steps cut through the surrounding whispers effortlessly, deliberately. Other steps passed them hurriedly in both directions, but the pace of these feet did not change. They moved steadily toward his door. Saul could feel vibrations in the desiccated air.

Without thought, he backed into a corner of the room and stared at the door. The feet stopped. Saul heard no key in his lock, but the handle turned and the door swung open.

The motion seemed to take a long long time, the door fighting its way through air suddenly glutinous. The complaints of the hinges, emaciated with malaise, stretched out long after the door had stopped moving.

The light in the corridor was bright. Saul could not make out the figure who stepped into his cell and gently closed the door.

The figure stood motionless, regarding Saul.

The light in the cell performed only a rudimentary job on the man.

Like moonlight it sketched out nothing but an edge. Two eyes full of dark, a sharp nose and pinched mouth.

Shadows were draped over the face like cobwebs. He was tall but not very tall; his shoulders were bunched up tight as if against the wind, a defensive posture. The vague face was thin and lined; the long dark hair was lank and uncombed, falling over those tight shoulders in untidy clots. A shapeless coat of indiscriminate gray was draped over dark clothes. The man plunged his hands into his pockets. His face was turned slightly down. He was looking at Saul from beneath his brows.

A smell of rubbish and wet animals filled the room. The man stood motionless, watching Saul from across the floor.

"You're safe."

Saul started. He had only dimly seen the man's mouth move, but the harsh whisper echoed in his head as if those lips were an inch from his ear. It took a moment for him to understand what had been said.

"What do you mean?" he said. "Who are you?"

"You're safe now. No one can get to you now." A strong London accent, an aggressive, secretive snarl whispered right in Saul's ear. "I want you to know why you're here."

Saul felt dizzy, swallowed spit made thick with phlegm by the atmosphere. He did not, he did not understand what was happening.

"Who are you?" Saul hissed. "Are you police? Where's Crowley?"

The man jerked his head in what might have been dismissal, shock, or a laugh.

"How did you get in?" demanded Saul.

"I crept past all the little boys in blue on tippy-toe. I slid hugger-mugger under the counter and I *sneaked* my way to your little queer ken. Do you know why you're here?"

Saul nodded dumbly.

"They think . . . "

"The constables think you killed your daddy, but you didn't, I know that. Granted, you'll have a fine time getting them to Adam and Eve that . . . but I do."

Saul was shaking. He sank onto the bunk. The stench which had entered with the man was overpowering. The voice continued, relentless. "I've been watching you carefully, you know. Keeping tabs. We've a lot to talk about, you know. I can . . . do you a favor."

Saul was utterly bewildered. Was this some casualty off the streets? Someone ill in his head, too full of alcohol or voices to make any sense? The air was still taut like a bowstring. What did this man know about his father?

"I don't know who the fuck you are," he started slowly. "And I don't know how you got in . . . "

"You don't understand." The whisper became a little

harsher. "Listen, matey. We're out of that world now. No more people and no more people things, get it? *Look at you,*" the voice harsh with disgust. "Sitting there in your borrowed duds like a fool, waiting patiently to get took before the Barnaby. Think they'll take kindly to your whids? They'll bang you up till you rot, foolish boy." There was a long pause. "And then I appear, like a bloody angel of mercy. I spring your jigger, no problem. This is where I live, get it? This is the city where I live. It shares all the points of yours and theirs, but none of its properties. *I go where I want.* And I'm here to tell you how it is with you. Welcome to my home."

The voice filled the small room, it would not give Saul space or time to think.

The shadowy face bore down on Saul. The man was coming nearer. He moved in little spurts, his chest and shoulders still tight, he approached from the side, zigzagged a little, came a little closer from another direction, his demeanor at once furtive and aggressive.

Saul swallowed. His head was light, his mouth dry. He fought for spit. The air was arid and so full of tension he could almost hear it, a faint keening as if the sound of the door hinge had never died away. He could not think, he could only listen.

The stinking apparition before him moved a little out of the shadows. The filthy trenchcoat was open, and Saul caught sudden sight of a lighter gray shirt underneath, decorated with rows of black arrows pointing up, convict chic.

The angle of the man's head was proud, the shoulders skulking.

"There's nothing I don't know about Rome-vill, you see. Nor Gay Paree, nor Cairo, nor Berlin, nor no city, but London's special to me, has been for a long time. Stop looking at me and wondering, boy. You're not going to get it. I've crept through these bricks when they were barns, then mills, then factories and banks. You're not looking at people, boy. You should count yourself lucky I'm interested in you. Because I'm doing you a big favor." The man's snarling monologue paused theatrically.

This was madness, Saul knew. His head spun. None of

this meant anything; it was meaningless words, ludicrous, he should laugh, but something in the curdled air held his tongue. He could not speak, he could not mock. He realized he was crying, or perhaps his eyes were just watering in the stagnant atmosphere of the room.

His tears seemed to annoy the intruder.

"Stop moaning on about your fat dad," he spat. "That's all over, and you've more important things to worry about."

He paused again.

"Shall we go?"

Saul looked up sharply. He reached his voice at last.

"What are you *talking* about? What do you mean?" He was whispering.

"Shall we go? I said. It's time to scarper, it's time to split, to quit, to take our leave." The man looked about him conspiratorially, and hid his mouth behind the back of his hand in a melodramatic stage whisper. *"I'm breaking you out."* He straightened up a little and nodded his head, that indistinct face bobbing enthusiastically. "Let's just say your path and mine cross at this point. It's darkmans outside already, I can smell it, and it looks like they've forgot about you. No Tommy Tucker for you, it seems, so let's bow out gracefully. You and I've got business together, and this is no place to conduct it. And if we wait much longer they'll have banged you up as a member of the parenticide club and eaten the key. There's no justice there, I know. So let me ask you *one more time* . . . shall we go?"

He could do it, Saul realized. With a terrified amazement he realized he was going to go with this creature, was going to follow this man whose face he could not see into the police station, and the two of them would escape.

"Who . . . what . . . are you?"

"I'll tell you that."

The voice filled Saul up and made him faint. The thin face was inches from his, silhouetted by the bare bulb. He tried to see through the obfuscating darkness and discern clear features, but the shadows were stubborn and subtle. The words mesmerized him like a spell, as hypnotic as dance music.

"You're in the presence of royalty, mate. I go where my subjects go, and my subjects are everywhere. And here in the cities there're a million crevices for my kingdom. I fill all the spaces in-between.

"Let me tell you about me.

"I can hear the things left unsaid.

"I know the secret life of houses and the social life of things. I can read the writing on the wall.

"I live in old London town.

"Let me tell you who I am.

"I'm the big-time crime boss. I'm the one that stinks. I'm the scavenger chief, I live where you don't want me. I'm the intruder. I killed the usurper, I take you to safekeeping. I killed half your continent one time. I know when your ships are sinking. I can break your traps across my knee and eat the cheese in your face and make you blind with my piss. I'm the one with the hardest teeth in the world, I'm the whiskered boy. I'm the Duce of the sewers, I run the underground. I'm the king."

In one sudden movement he turned to face the door and sloughed the coat from his shoulders, unveiling the name stencilled crudely in black on the back of his shirt, between the rows of arrows.

"I'm King Rat."

THREE

A long way off to the south, somewhere in the heart of the city, a siren sounded mournfully. The smell of smoke still clung faintly to the air. It mingled with exhaust fumes and the whiff of rubbish, all made chill and even refreshing by the night.

Above the black bags and deserted streets rose the walls of North London; above the walls the slate roofs; and, above the slates, two figures: one standing astride the apex of the police station roof like a mountain climber, the other crouching in the shadow of the aerials.

Saul wrapped his arms tightly around himself. The unlikely figure of his savior loomed above him. He was sore. His borrowed clothes had rubbed against concrete many times during his escape, till his skin was scraped raw and bleeding, imprinted with a bas-relief of cotton weave.

Somewhere in the guts of the building under his feet was the cell he had recently vacated. He supposed that the police had discovered him missing by now. He imagined them scurrying about frantically, searching for him, looking out of windows and filling the area with cars.

Back in that cell, the grotesque figure calling itself King Rat had impaled Saul with his grandiloquent and preposterous declamations, taking his breath away and rendering him dumb. Then he had paused again, and hunched those bony shoulders defensively. And again that invitation, as casual as from a bored lover at a party.

"Shall we go?"

Saul had hovered, his heart shaking his body, eager to follow instructions. King Rat had sidled up to the door and gently tugged it open, silent this time. In a sudden movement he had poked his head into the tight crack between door and frame, and twisted his head exaggeratedly in both directions, then reached a hand behind him without looking back and beckoned to Saul. Something magic had come to take him away, and Saul had crept forward with guilt and hope and excitement.

King Rat had briefly turned as he approached and, without warning, swept him up over his shoulder in a fireman's lift. Saul had let out a bark of surprise before King Rat crushed his body against him, driving the air from him and hissing: "Shut it."

Saul lay still as King Rat stalked forward with ease. He jounced up and down as the stinking figure paced out of the room. Saul listened.

His head was flat against the other's back. The smell of dirt and animal suffused him. He heard a very faint whine as the door was pushed further open. He closed his eyes. The light of the police-station corridor shone red through his eyelids.

King Rat's thin shoulder dug into Saul's stomach.

Through the flesh of his belly he felt King Rat pause, then pad forward without the slightest sound. Saul kept his eyes shut tight. His breath came in starts. He could hear the low hubbub of people nearby. He felt the wall press into him. King Rat was hugging the shadows.

From somewhere in front of them came footsteps, brisk and inexorable. The wall scraped along Saul's side as King Rat swiftly sank into a crouch and froze. Saul held his breath. The footsteps came closer and closer. Saul wanted to shriek his guilt, his presence, anything to break the unbearable tension.

With a tiny breeze and a moment of warmth, the footsteps passed by.

The gray shape moved on, one arm coiled tight around Saul's legs. King Rat was weighed down under Saul's motionless body like a grave-robber.

King Rat and his cargo passed silently through the halls. Again and again footsteps approached, voices, laughing. Each time Saul held his breath, King Rat was still, as people passed by impossibly close, near enough to touch, without seeing him or his burden.

Saul kept his eyes closed. Through his lids he could see changes in darkness and light. Unbidden, his mind drew a map of the station, rendering it a land of these stark and sudden oppositions. *Here be monsters*, he thought, and felt ridiculously close to giggling. He became acutely aware of sounds. The echoes he heard aided his helpless cartography, waxing and waning as the rooms and corridors through which he was carried grew and shrank. Another door creaked open, and Saul was held still.

The echoes hollowed out, changed direction. The bobbing of his body increased. He felt himself borne upwards.

Saul opened his eyes. They were on a narrow flight of gray stairs, musty and sterile and badly lit. Muffled sounds came from above and below. His rescuer carried him up several flights, past floor after floor of filthy windows and doors, eventually coming to rest and ducking his body for Saul to dismount. Saul struggled off the bony shoulder and looked about him.

They had reached the top of the building. On his left was a white door through which the tapping of a keyboard could be heard. There was nowhere else to go. On all other sides was dirty wall.

Saul turned to his companion. "What now?" he whispered.

King Rat turned back to face the stairs. Directly in front of him was a big greasy window, high above the little entresol where the stairs had changed direction. As Saul stared, the gray figure cocked his head, sniffed the expanse of air between himself and the window ten feet away. In a burst of feverish motion he locked his hands onto the banister and sprang astride it, right foot planted below the left, perfectly still and poised on the sloping plastic. He seemed to bunch up his shoulders, contracting muscles and sinews relentlessly one by one. He paused for a moment, the sharp, obscure face contorted in a grin or a grimace, then he burst forward in a silent flurry of limbs, for a moment filling the gap between mezzanine and ceiling. He flew through the air, grasped the handles of the window and set his feet on the edge of the tiny sill. And as suddenly as he had moved he was quite still, a bizarre shape spreadeagled on the glass. His trenchcoat was the only thing in motion, swinging gently.

Saul gasped, clapped his hand over his mouth, glanced fearfully over his shoulder at the nearby door.

King Rat was sinuously unwinding. His long limbs disentangled and his left hand scrabbled quietly at the window lock. With a click and a gust of cold, the window opened. His right hand still poised on the sill, the weird apparition twisted his body, pulling it bit by bit out of the narrow opening. He made himself impossibly thin as he squeezed through the vertical strip of darkness that was all the window was built to admit. His passage was as enchanted as that of a genie from a lamp, clinging as tight to the outside frame as he had within, poised on a few centimeters of wood five stories above the earth, until those unclear eyes were staring at Saul from beyond the filthy glass.

Only King Rat's right hand remained inside the police station. It beckoned to Saul. Outside the dark figure breathed mist onto the pane, then wrote with the index finger of his left hand. He wrote in looking-glass script so the words appeared the right way around to Saul.

NOW YOU he wrote, and waited.

Saul tried to clamber onto the banister. He scrabbled ineffectually as his legs slid toward the floor. He clung desperately and started to haul himself up again, but the weight of his body tugged at him. He was beginning to pant.

He stared up at the thin figure in the window. That bony hand still stretched out toward him. Saul descended to the mezzanine. Flattening his body as low as it would go on the window-ledge, the other swung his hand down, following Saul, reaching toward the floor. Saul looked up at the tiny opening under the window-frame: it was no more than nine inches wide. He looked down at himself. He was broad, a little fleshy. He spread his hands about his girth, looked up at the window again, looked at the thing waiting for him outside, shook his head.

The hand stretched toward him clawed the air impatiently, clutched fitfully at nothing. It would not take no for an answer. Somewhere below them in the building, a door slammed and two voices entered the stairwell. Saul stared over the banister, saw feet and the tops of heads two floors below. He jumped back out of sight. The men were rising toward him. The hand still clutched at him; outside, that shady face was twisted.

Saul positioned himself underneath the hand, stretched his arms up and leapt.

Strong fingers caught him around his left wrist, locked tight, dug into his flesh. He opened his mouth to cry out, caught himself, hissed. He was hauled silently through the air, all thirteen stone of blood and flesh and clothes. Another hand slid around his body, a booted foot locked efficiently underneath him. How was his sinewy benefactor holding on? Saul twisted through the air, saw the window approach him. He turned his head to one side, felt his shoulders and chest lock in the tight space. Hands slid over his body, finding purchase, easing his passage into the outside world. He was slipping through the window now, his stomach pressing painfully against the lock fixed on the frame, but moving much too smoothly through that narrow gash and out into the shock of cold air.

Impossibly, he was delivered.

Wind buffeted him. Warm breath tickled his neck.

"Cling on," came the hissed order, as Saul was pulled into the air. Saul clung. He wrapped his legs around King Rat's thin waist and threw his arms over those bony shoulders.

King Rat stood on the tiny ledge, his boots clinging precariously to the paint. Saul, who was much the bigger, perched on his back, frosty with terror. King Rat's right hand held the window-frame; his left hand was locked into an absurdly tiny crack above his head. Over them rose an expanse of sheer brickwork four or five feet high crowned with a strip of plastic guttering. Above that the roof, its slates too steep to be seen.

Saul turned his head. His stomach pitched like an anchor. Five floors below him was the rubbish-strewn concrete of a freezing alley. The shock of vertigo made Saul feel sick. His mind shrieked at him to put his feet on ground. *He can't possibly hold on!* he thought. *He can't possibly hold on!* He felt the lithe body shift under him and he nearly screamed.

Dimly Saul heard the voices from the stairwell approach the window, but they suddenly receded as he felt himself moving again.

King Rat lifted his right hand from the window-frame, and reached up to wrap his fingers around a nail rusted into the wall, its purpose long forgotten. His left hand moved now, creeping swiftly along invisible paths in the brick and mortar to stop suddenly and grip at a seemingly arbitrary spot in the surface. Those fingers were acute to unseen clues and potentials in the architecture.

The booted feet stepped free of the ledge. Saul was twisted to one side as King Rat swung his right foot up above his shoulder, suspending himself and his burden from only clenched white knuckles. His feet scraped at the wall, investigating like octopus tentacles, till they found purchase and locked on some minor aberration, some imperfection of the brick.

King Rat reached up with his right hand, grasping; then his left, then his right, this time gripping the rim of the black plastic gutter that marked the border between brick and slate. It creaked dolefully but, unperturbed, he tugged at it with both hands. He pulled his knees up into his stomach, his feet planted firmly against the brick, hung poised for a moment, then pushed out with his thighs like a swimmer.

Saul and King Rat somersaulted through the air. Saul heard himself wail as the wall, the alley below, the lights of buildings, streetlamps and stars spun around his head. The guttering cracked as King Rat clung to it, his hands the center of the circle his body described. He released his grip, his feet met the sloping roof slates, he bent low to muffle the sound and, twisting his body, flung himself flat on the roof itself. Hardly pausing, he scrambled on up the tiles like a spider, with Saul holding so tight to him it felt as if he would never come loose.

King Rat scampered on all fours up the slate incline, his heavy boots making no sound. Like a tightrope-walker the surreal figure then crept swiftly along the apex of the roof toward the chimneys, and a looming tower block beyond. Terror had cemented Saul to his body, his fingers twisted into the fabric of the stinking trenchcoat with the tenacity of rigor mortis. But King Rat prised him loose with ease and swung him off his shoulders, depositing him shivering in the shadow of the chimney.

And there Saul lay.

He shivered there for several minutes, with the unclear shape of the thin man who did impossible things standing above him, ignoring him. Saul could feel a part of himself going into shock, shaking with a terrible cold out of all proportion to the night wind.

But the spasm passed, the threat receded.

Something in the insanity of the night calmed him. What was the point of being afraid? he wondered. He had suspended all common sense half an hour before and, with that gone, he was free simply to immerse himself in the charged night.

Gradually Saul stopped gasping. He unfolded. He looked

up at King Rat, who stood staring at the vast tower block above them.

Saul braced himself with his hands, then, holding his breath, he rose to his feet, one planted on each side of the building's vertex, wobbling with gusts of vertigo. He steadied himself with his left hand against the chimney stack and relaxed a little. King Rat twitched his eyes over him momentarily, then sauntered a few feet further away, balancing on the apex of the roof.

Saul looked out over the London skyline. A swell of euphoria gathered in him and crescendoed, he swayed and yelped with incredulous laughter.

"It's *unbelievable*! What the *fuck* am I doing up here?" He swivelled his head to stare at King Rat, who again stood regarding him with those imprecise eyes. King Rat gestured briefly over the chimney's bulk, and Saul turned, realizing that those eyes had not been fixed on him at all. The side of the tower block beyond was studded with lights.

"Look at them," King Rat said. "In the windows."

Saul looked and saw, here and there, minuscule figures bustling past, each reduced to a snatch of color and motion. In the center of the building one patch of shade remained still: someone leaning out of their flat window, looking over the hillocks and knolls of slate on which Saul and King Rat stood, brazen in their night-time camouflage.

"Say goodbye to that now," King Rat said.

Saul turned his head to face him, quizzical.

"That geezer there, stopping and staring, that's as close as you ever got to this before now. The place he's looking at now— no, he's not looking at it, he's caught a *glimpse*, a *hint*, it's teasing him out of the corner of his eye—that's your gaff now, me old son." Emotion was disguised in King Rat's bass snarl, but he seemed satisfied, as if with a job well done. "The rest of it, that's just in-between for you now. All the main streets, the front rooms and the rest of it, that's just filler, that's just *chaff*, that ain't the real city. You get to *that* by the *back* door. I seen you in the windows, at night, at the close of the lightmans. Staring out, playing look-but-don't-touch. Well, you've touched it now. All the vacant lots and all—that's your stomping ground now, your pad, your burrow, Saul. That's London.

"You can't go back *now*, can you? You stick with me, boy. I'll see you're alright."

"Why me?" said Saul slowly. "What do you want from me?" he stopped, remembering, for what seemed the first time in hours, why he had been in the police station. "What do you know about my father?"

King Rat turned and stared at Saul, those features, already so obscured, now invisible in the moonlight. Without taking his eyes from Saul, he slowly sank until he sat straddling the roof ridge like a horseman.

"Slide over here, cove, and I'll tell you the story. You aren't going to like it."

Saul lowered himself carefully, facing King Rat, and pulled himself forward until he was only a couple of feet away from him. If anyone could see them, Saul realized, they must look like two schoolboys, ungainly figures from a comic strip, sitting with their legs swinging. Saul's exhilaration had dissipated with as little warning as it had arrived. He was swallowing with anxiety. He was remembering his father. This was the key to everything, he thought; this was the catalyst, the legend that would make sense of the surreality which had caught him up in its gusts.

King Rat spoke, and just as it had in the police cell, his voice took on a rhythm, a dislocating monotony like a bagpipe drone. The sense and meaning of what he said crept into Saul's head as much by insinuation as by conscious understanding.

"This here Rome-vill, London, that's my manor, but I been around wherever my little courtiers found grain and rubbish to Tea Leaf. And they did my *bidding*, because I'm their king. But I was never alone, Saul; that's never how it was. Rats believe in their Godfers, chuck out *broods*, the more mouths to filch, the better.

"What do you know about your mother, Saul?"

The question took him by surprise. "I . . . her name was Eloise . . . She was, uh, a health visitor . . . She died when I was born, something went wrong . . . "

"Seen any Beechams?"

Saul shook his head in confusion.

"Beechams: pictures, photos . . . "

"Of course . . . she's short and dark, pretty . . . What's this about? Where are you going?"

"Sometimes, me old China, sometimes there are *black sheep*, ne'er-do-wells, if you clock me. I'd lay good money you and your dad were snarling at each other's throats sometimes, am I right? Didn't get on like you might have hoped? Well, do you really think rats aren't the same?

"She was always the gentry mort, your ma. Took to your daddy a whole lot, and he to her. What a beauty she was, luscious, who'd have passed that up?" King Rat finished his sentence with a flourish, twisted his head and looked at Saul from around the corner of his face.

"Your ma made a choice, Saul. Health visitor! That was a cheeky little joke. Set a thief to catch a thief, they say, isn't it, and so, likewise, with her. Walk into a place, one sniff of the I Suppose, and your ma knew exactly how many rats was in there, and where. Recidivist, traitor, they called her, but I suppose that's the power of love . . . "

Saul was incredulous, staring and staring at King Rat.

"She wasn't built for the likes of you. You bumped her off on arrival. You're a big strong lad, sonny, stronger than you probably think. There's a lot you can do you don't know about. I bet you gawped out of all those night-time windows longer and harder than any of your mates. I think you've been scrabbling to get into this city for real for a long time.

"You want to know who did the deed on your old man, I know. That's what you call petulance, that is, that bod smashed out front, in the garden.

"The one who did that . . . he was after you. Your old dad just got in the way.

"You're a special boy, Saul, got special blood in your veins, and there's one in the city who'd like to see it spilled. Your mum was my sister, Saul.

"Your mum was a rat."

FOUR

With that insane allegation hanging in the air, King Rat rocked back onto the flesh of his arse and fell silent.

Saul shook his head and struggled between incredulity and excitement and disgust.

"She was . . . what?"

"A . . . fucking . . . *rat*." King Rat spoke slowly. "She crept out of the sewers because she fell for your dad. More tragic than Romeo and Juliet. And her of royal blood, too, but still she went. Couldn't get shot of me, though. I used to come see her on the nows and thens; she'd tell me to sling my hook. Wanted all that behind her, but with her new nose she stank to herself. Couldn't shake birthright, you know. Blood's thicker than water, and rat blood's the thickest of all."

Somewhere in the tar-black below, a patrol car lurched out of the pound spewing blue light.

"And since your mum got put in the ground, I've been keeping a little eye out for you: trying to keep you out of trouble. What's family for, Saul? But it looks like things have caught up. Can't outrun your blood, Saul. Looks like you've been rumbled, and your dad had to take a fall."

Saul sat still and gazed over King Rat's shoulder. The words, the deadly understatement delivered with something like a flourish, unlocked a door inside him. He could see his father in a hundred images. And, like a backdrop to all the frozen moments he recalled, Saul could see a powerful fat body pitching in slow motion through the night air, the mouth a distended yawn of shock and terror, eyes rolling in frantic search for safety, thinning hair flickering like candlelight, jowls trembling with gravity's sudden shift, paddling ineffectually with those thick limbs, jagged scintillas of glass whirling around him as he flew toward the dark lawn, its soil frost-hardened like tundra.

Saul's throat caught, and he let out a tiny sound of grief. His tears amazed him with their speed, flooding his vision instantly.

"Oh Dad . . . " he sobbed.

King Rat was incensed.

"Leave it out now, leave it *out*, will you give it a fucking *rest*?"

His hand snapped out and he slapped Saul lightly across the face.

"Hey. *Hey*. Fucking enough."

"*Fuck off!*" Saul found a voice between sniffing, weeping and wiping his nose on the sleeve of the police-issue jumper. "Just *stop* for a minute. Just leave me alone . . . "

Saul relapsed into tears for his father. He beat himself on the head in his loneliness, screwed up his eyes as if he were being tortured, moaned rhythmically as he pummelled his forehead.

"I'm sorry Dad I'm sorry I'm sorry . . . " he crooned between his quiet cries. His words were garbled and confused in isolation and terrible inchoate anger. He wrapped his arms around his head, desperate and alone up on the roof.

Through the gap between his arms, he saw that King Rat was no longer sitting before him, that he had risen without a sound and had somehow reached the other end of the roof, where he stood looking out over London, facing away from Saul whose sadness angered him so much. Saul's body moved with sobs, as he stared from behind his hands at the strange figure perched between two outcroppings of brick, King Rat. His uncle.

Saul wriggled backwards, still weeping, until he felt the damp pressure of the chimney on his back. He looked over his shoulder and saw a place where two chimney stacks met near the roof edge, leaving a space between them, a rooftop cubbyhole into which he crept with a quick contortion. He curled up in this little space, insulated from the sky and the sickening drop on all sides, out of the sight of King Rat. He was so tired, exhaustion had soaked into his bones. He lay on his side in the cramped, sloping chamber he had found and covered his head with his hands. He cried some more until his tears became mechanical, like a child who has forgotten what he is weeping for. Saul lay there on the slate slope under the chimneys, without food inside him, in someone else's ruined clothes, lonely and utterly confused, until, amazingly, he slept.

When he woke, the sky was still dark, with only a faint fringe of dun in the east. There was no time for a luxurious morning state for Saul, no slow stretches or confusion, no slow remembrance of where he was and why. He opened his eyes onto red brick, and realized with a shudder of claustrophobia that he was surrounded, that curled up around him was King Rat. He started, pulled himself upright out of that passionless, utilitarian embrace. King Rat's eyes were open.

"Morning, boy. Bit parky in the small hours. Thought we'd share a bit of warmth to help you kip."

King Rat uncoiled and rose, stretching each limb individually. He grabbed the top of the high chimney and hauled himself up with his arms, his legs dangling. He looked slowly from one side to the other, surveying the dim urban sprawl, before hawking noisily and spitting a gob of phlegm down the chimney. Only then did he relax his arms and lower himself to the roof again. Saul struggled to his feet, slipping on the slope. He wiped rheum and rubbish from his face.

King Rat turned to him. "We never finished our little chat. We was . . . *interrupted* last night. You've an awful lot to learn, matey, and you're looking at teacher, like it or not. But first off, let's make ourselves scarce." He laughed: a filthy, throaty bark that tickled Saul's ear. "They were going hell for leather for you last night. No sirens, mind—didn't want to warn you off, I reckon, but they were frantic: cars and constables running around like the blue-arsed proverbials, in a right old state, and all the time there I am playing at peek-a-boo over their gables." He laughed again, the noise of it, like all he issued, sounding as if it were just inches from Saul's ear. "Oh yes, I am a most accomplished thief." He said this final line with stilted gusto, as if delivering lines in a play.

He scampered to the edge of the roof, impossibly sure-footed on its steep angle. Clinging onto the guttering, he scouted some distance around the edge, until he found what he was looking for. He turned and gestured for Saul to follow him. Saul edged along the roof ridge on all fours, afraid to expose himself to the wicked-looking gray slate. He reached the spot directly above King Rat, and there he waited.

King Rat bared his teeth at him. "Slide down," he whispered.

With both hands, Saul gripped the little concrete ridge he was straddling, and slowly swung his leg over until his whole body was spreadeagled on the slope above King Rat. At this point his arms rebelled and would not release him. He swiftly changed his mind about his actions, and attempted to haul himself back across the roof ridge, but his muscles were stiff with terror. Trapped on the slippery surface, he panicked. His brittle fingers lost their grip.

For a long, sick-making moment he was sliding toward his death, until he met King Rat's strong hand. He was halted sharply, plucked from the roof and swung up and over in a terrifying hauling motion before being dropped hard onto a steel fire escape below.

The noise of his landing was muffled and insubstantial. Above him grinned King Rat. He still hung onto the edge of the roof with his left hand, his right extended over the stairs where he had deposited Saul. As Saul watched, he released himself, and fell the short distance to the iron mesh of the platform, his big rough boots landing without a sound.

Saul's heart was still racing with fear, but his recent undignified precipitation galled him.

"I . . . I'm not a fucking sack of potatoes," he hissed with spurious bravado.

King Rat grinned. "You don't even know which way's up, you little terror. And until you've a bit of learning in your Loaf, that's exactly what you are."

The two crept down the steps, past door after door, descending to the alley.

Dawn came fast. King Rat and Saul made their way through the crepuscular streets. Afraid and excited, Saul half expected his companion to repeat his escapades of last night, and he glanced from side to side at drainpipes and garage roofs, the entrances to rooftop passageways. But this time they remained earthbound. King Rat led Saul through deserted building sites and car parks, down narrow passages masquerading as culs-de-sac. Their route was chosen with an instinct Saul did not understand, and they did not pass any early morning walkers.

The dark dwindled. Daylight, wan and anemic, had done what it could by seven o'clock.

Saul leaned against the wall of an alley. King Rat stood framed by its entrance, his right arm outstretched, just touching the bricks, the daylight beyond silhouetting him like the lead in a *film noir*.

"I'm starving." said Saul.

"Me too, sonny, me too. I've been starving for a long time." King Rat leaned out of the alley. He was peering at a nondescript terraced row of red brick. Each roof was topped with a dragon rampant: little flurries of clay enthusiasm now broken and crumbled. Their features were washed out by acid rain.

That morning the city seemed made up of backstreets.

"Alright then," murmured King Rat. "Time for tucker."

King Rat, a figure skulking like a Victorian villain, stepped carefully from his point of concealment. He lifted his face to the air. As Saul watched, he sniffed loudly twice, twitched his nose, turned his face a little to one side. Gesturing for Saul to follow him, King Rat scampered down the deserted street and ducked into a gash between two houses. At the far end was a wall of black rubbish bags.

"Always follow your I Suppose." King Rat grinned briefly. He was crouched at the end of the narrow alleyway, a hunched shape at the bottom of a brickwork chasm. The surrounding walls were inscrutable, unbroken by windows.

Saul approached.

King Rat was tearing at a plastic sack. The rich smell of rot was released. King Rat plunged his arm into the hole, and fumbled inside in an unsettling parody of surgery. He pulled a polystyrene box from the wound. It dripped with tea-leaves and egg yolk, but the hamburger logo was still evident. King Rat placed it on the ground, reached inside the bag again, and pulled out a damp crust of bread.

He thrust the sack aside and reached for another, ripped it open. This time his reward was half a fruitcake, flattened and embedded with sawdust. Chicken bones and crushed chocolate, the remnants of sweetcorn and rice, fish-heads and stale crisps, the bags yielded them all, disgorged them into a stinking pile on the concrete.

Saul watched the mound of ruined food grow. He put his hand over his mouth.

"You have *got* to be joking," he said, and swallowed.

King Rat looked up at him.

"Thought you was peckish."

Saul shook his head in horror, his hand still clamped firmly over his mouth.

"When was the last time you puked?"

Saul furrowed his brow at the question. King Rat wiped his wet hand on his trenchcoat, adding to the camouflage-pattern of stains hidden in its dark gray. He poked at the food.

"You can't recall," he said, without looking at Saul. "You can't recall because you've never done it. Never spewed nothing. You've been ill, I'll bet, but not like other Godfers. No colds or sneezing; only some queer sickness making you shiver for days, once or twice. But even then, not a sign of puke." He finally met Saul's eye, and his voice dropped. He hissed at him, something like victory in his voice. "Got the notion? Your belly won't rebel. No sicking up Pig's, no matter how plastered, no sweet sticky chocolate bile on *your* pillow the night after Easter, no hurling seafood across the tiles, no matter *how* dodgy the take-away. *You've got rat blood in your veins. There's nothing you can't stomach.*"

There was a long moment of silence as the two stared at each other.

King Rat continued.

"And there's more. There's no grub you don't *want*. Said you were starving. I should coco; it's been a while. Well here we go. Sitting comfortably? I'm going to teach you what it is to be rat. Look at all this scran your uncle sorted you out with. Said you were starving. Here's breakfast."

King Rat picked up the fruitcake without taking his eyes from Saul. He raised it slowly to his mouth. Moist chunks dropped from his hand, sultanas made juicy from their long marinating in black plastic. He bit into it, crumbs bursting out of his mouth as he exhaled in satisfaction.

He was right. Saul could not remember a time when he had thrown up. He had always eaten a lot, even for his frame, and had never been able to sympathize with people put off their food. Stories about maggots told over risotto left him unmoved. He had never suffered after too much sugar or fat or alcohol. This had never occurred to him before; he sympathized with others when they complained that something made them feel sick, never stopping to ask what it meant or if it was true.

Now he was sloughing off those layers of habit. He stood watching King Rat eat. The wiry figure would not take his eyes from him.

It had been hours and hours since Saul had last had food. He investigated his own hunger.

King Rat continued chewing. The stench of slowly collapsing food was overwhelming. Saul gazed at the leftovers and remnants heaped in front of the bags, the flecks of mold, the bite marks, and the dirt.

He began to salivate.

King Rat kept eating.

When he opened his mouth wet chunks of cake were visible. "You can eat pigeon-meat scraped off a car-wheel," he said. "This here's good scran."

Saul's stomach growled. He squatted before the pile of food. Gingerly, he picked out the unfinished burger. He sniffed it. It was long cold. He could see where teeth had torn through the bun. He brushed at it, cleared it of grime as best he could.

It was damp and clammy, still shiny with spit where it had been bitten.

Saul put it near his mouth. He let his mind play over the filth of the dustbin, waited for his stomach to turn. But it did not.

His mind still rang with admonishments heard long ago—*don't touch, it's dirty, take it out of your mouth*—but his stomach, his stomach remained firm. The smell of the meat was enticing.

He willed himself to feel ill. He strove for nausea.

He took a bite. He wriggled his tongue into the meat, pushed apart the fibers. He probed, tasting the dirt and decay. Lumps of gristle and fat split open in his mouth, mixed with his saliva.

The burger was delicious.

Saul swallowed and did not feel ill. His hunger, piqued, demanded more. He took another bite, and another, eating faster and faster all the time.

He felt something slipping away from him. He drew his strength from the old cold meat, food that had surrendered to people and decay, and now to him. His world changed.

King Rat nodded and ate on, grabbed handfuls and shoved them into his mouth without looking at them.

Saul reached for a slimy chicken wing.

In the street, only twenty feet away, children were appearing in outsized school uniforms. The bricks and the bags kept Saul and King Rat hidden. They looked up as the children passed, paused briefly in their breakfast.

They were silent while they ate. When they had finished, Saul licked his lips. The taste of filth and carrion was very strong in his mouth, and he investigated it, still wondering that it did not turn his stomach.

King Rat nestled into the bags and pulled his coat about him. "Feeling better now?" he asked.

Saul nodded. For the first time since his sudden release, he felt calm. He could feel the acids of his stomach getting to work inside him, breaking down the old food he had eaten. He felt molecules scurrying out of his gut, carrying strange energy from the ruins of other people's suppers and breakfasts. He was changing from the inside out.

My mother was like this creature, he said to himself, *this skulking thing. My mother was like this thin-faced vagrant with magical powers. My mother was a spirit, it seems, a dirty spirit. My mother was a rat.*

"You can't go back, you know." King Rat looked at Saul from under his eyelids. Saul had long given up trying to make sense of his features. The light would not fall full on King Rat's face, no matter where he stood or lay. Saul glanced at him again, but his eyes found no purchase.

"I know it," he said.

"They think you did your pa, and they'll do you for that. And now you've slung your hook from their old Bucket they'll have your guts for garters."

The city had been made unsafe. Saul felt it yawn before him, infinitely vaster than he had imagined, unknowable and furtive.

"So, so . . . " said Saul slowly. *So what is London?* he thought. *If you can be what you are, what's London? What's the world? I've had it all wrong. Do werewolves and trolls lurk under bridges in the parks? What are the boundaries of the world?*

"So . . . what do I do now?"

"Well, you aren't going back, so you got to bing a waste forward. I've to teach you how to be rat. You got a lot going for you, sonny. Hold your breath and squeeze in tight, freeze like a statue . . . you're invisible. Move just right, dainty on your toes, you'll make nary a sound. You can be like me. As far as you're concerned, up's no longer out of bounds, and down's nothing to fear."

It didn't matter anymore that he didn't understand. Unbelievably, King Rat's words took away Saul's trepidation. He felt himself grow strong. He stretched out his arms. He felt like laughing.

"I feel like I can do anything," he said. He was overwhelmed.

"You can, my old son. You're a ratling boy. Just got to learn the tricks. We'll cut your teeth. You and me together, dynamite. We've a kingdom to win back."

Saul had risen to his feet, was staring out into the street beyond. At King Rat's words he turned slowly and looked down at the thin figure cocooned in black plastic.

"Back?" he said levelly. "Back from who?"

King Rat nodded. "Time," he said, "for a word in your shell-like. Much as I hate to piss on your chips, you're forgetting something. You're in another country now because your old man did the six-story swan-dive"—King Rat blithely ignored Saul's aghast stare— "and he did that, the old codger, in lieu of you. There's something out there wants your head, chal, and you'd be wise not to forget it."

Saul wobbled to his knees. "Who?" he whispered.

"Well now, that's the biggy, isn't it? That's *the* question. And therein lies a story, a twisting rat-tale."

PART TWO

THE

NEW CITY

F I V E

Fabian was trying to call Natasha but he could not reach her. She had taken her phone off the hook. The news about Saul's father was spreading among his friends like a virus, but Natasha had immunized herself for a little while longer.

It was just after midday. The sun was bright but as cold as snow. The sounds of Ladbroke Grove filtered along the backstreets to the first floor of a flat on Bassett Road. They slid through the windows and filled the front room, a susurrus of dogs and paper-sellers and cars. The sounds were faint; they were what passed for silence in the city.

In the flat a woman stood motionless in front of a keyboard. She was short and her face was severe, with dark eyebrows that met above a scimitar nose. Her long hair was dark, her skin sallow. Her name was Natasha Karadjian.

Natasha stood with her eyes closed and listened to the streets outside. She reached out and pressed the power button on her sampler. There was a static thud as her speakers clicked into life.

She ran her hands over the keys and the cursor. She had stood motionless for a minute or two now. Even alone she felt self-conscious. Natasha rarely let people watch when she created her music. She was afraid they would think her precious, with her silent preparations and her closed eyes.

She tapped out a message on a clutch of small buttons, twisted her cursor control, displayed her musical spoils on the LCD display. She scrolled through the selection and plucked a favorite bassline from her digital killing jar. She had snatched it from a forgotten Reggae track, sampled it, preserved it, and now she pulled it out and looped it and gave it another life. The zombie sound travelled the innards of the machine and out through wires, through the vast black stereo against her wall, and burst out of those great speakers.

The sound filled her room.

The bass was trapped. The sample ended just as the bassplayer had been about to reach a crescendo, and expectation was audible in the thudding strings as they reached out for something, for a flourish . . . then a break, and the cycle started again.

This bassline was in purgatory. It burst into existence with a recurring surge of excitement, waiting for a release that never came.

Natasha nodded her head slowly. This was the breakbeat, the rhythm of tortured music. She loved it.

Again her hands moved. A pounding beat joined the bass, cymbals clattering like insects. And the sound looped.

Natasha moved her shoulders to the rhythm. Her eyes were wide as she scanned her kills, her pickled sounds, and she found what she wanted: a snatch of trumpet from Linton Kwesi Johnson, a wail from Tony Rebel, a cry of invitation from Al Green. She dropped them into her tune. They segued smoothly into the rolling bass, the slamming drums.

This was Jungle.

The child of House, the child of Raggamuffin, the child of Dancehall, the apotheosis of black music, the Drum and Bass soundtrack for a London of council estates and dirty walls, black youth and white youth, Armenian girls.

The music was uncompromising. The rhythm was stolen from Hip Hop, born of Funk. The beats were fast, too fast to dance to unless you were wired. It was the bassline you followed with your feet, the bassline that gave Jungle its soul.

And above the bassline was the high end of Jungle: the treble. Stolen chords and shouts that rode the waves of bass like surfers. They were fleeting and teasing, snatches of sound winking into existence and sliding over the beat, tracing it, then winking away.

Natasha nodded her satisfaction.

She could feel the bass. She knew it intimately. She searched instead for the sounds at the top, she wanted something perfect, a leitmotif to weave in and out of the drums.

She knew the people who ran the clubs, and they would always play her music. People liked her tracks a lot, gave her respect and bookings. But she felt a vague dissatisfaction with everything she wrote, even when the sensation was shot through with pride. When she finished a track she did not feel any purgation of relief, only a slight unease. Natasha would cast around, ransacking her friends' record collections in an attempt to find the sounds she wanted to steal, or would make her own on her keyboard, but they never touched her like the bass. The bass never evaded her; she needed only to reach out for it, and it would drop out of her speakers complete and perfect.

The track was nearing a crescendo now: *Gwan,* exhorted a sampled voice, *Gwan gyal.* Natasha broke the beat, teasing the rhythm out, paring it down. She stripped flesh from the tune's bones and the samples echoed in the cavernous ribcage, in the belly of the beat. *Come now . . . we rollin' this way, rudebwoy . . .* She pulled her sounds out one by one, until only the bass was left. It had ushered the song in; it ushered it out again.

The room was silent.

Natasha waited a while until the city silence of children and cars crept into her ears again. She looked around at her room. Her flat contained a tiny kitchen, a tiny bathroom and the beautiful big bedroom she was in now. She had put her meager collection of prints and posters in the other rooms and the hall; the walls here were quite bare. The room itself was empty except for a mattress on the floor, the hulking black stand which housed her stereo, and her keyboard. The wooden floor was criss-crossed with black leads.

She reached down and put the receiver back on the phone. She was about to wander into the kitchen, when the doorbell sounded. Natasha crossed the room to the open window and leaned out.

A man was standing in front of her door, looking straight up at her eyes. She had a brief impression of a thin face, bright eyes and long blond hair, before she ducked back into the room and headed down the stairs. He had not looked like a Jehovah's witness or a troublemaker.

She walked through the dingy communal hall. Through the rippled glass of the front door she could see that the man was very tall. She pulled the door open, admitting voices from the next house and the daylight that was flooding the street.

Natasha looked up into his narrow face. The man was about six feet four, dwarfing her by nearly a foot, but he was so slim he looked as if he might snap in half at the waist any moment. He was probably in his early thirties, but he was so pale it was difficult to tell. His hair was a sickly yellow. The pallor of his face was exaggerated by his black leather jacket. He would have looked quite ill were it not for his bright blue eyes and his air of fidgety animation. He started to grin even before the door was fully open.

Natasha and her visitor stared at each other, he smiling, she with a guarded, quizzical expression.

"Brilliant," he said suddenly.

Natasha stared at him.

"Your music," he said. "Brilliant."

The man's voice was deeper and richer than she would have thought possible from such a slender frame. It was slightly breathless, as if he were rushing to get his words out. She stared up at him and her eyes narrowed. This was much too weird a way of starting a conversation. She was not having it.

"What do you mean?" she said levelly.

He smiled apologetically. His words slowed down a little.

"I've been listening to your music," he said. "I came past here last week and I heard you playing up there. I tell you, I was just standing there with my mouth open."

Natasha was embarrassed and amazed. She opened her mouth to interrupt but he continued.

"I came back and I heard it again. It made me want to start dancing in the street!" He laughed. "The next time I heard you stop halfway through, and I realized someone was actually playing while I listened. I'd thought it was a record. It was such an exciting thought that you were actually up there making it."

Natasha finally spoke.

"This is really . . . flattering. But did you knock on my door just to tell me that?" This man unnerved her with his excited grin and breathy voice. It was only curiosity that stopped her shutting the door. "I've not got a fan club yet."

He stared at her and the nature of his smile changed. Until that moment it had been sincere, almost childish in its excitement. Slowly his lips closed a fraction and hid his teeth. He straightened his long back and his eyelids slid halfway down over his eyes. He leaned his head slightly to one side, without taking his eyes off her.

Natasha felt a wave of adrenaline. She looked back at him in shock. The change which had come over him was extraordinary. He stared at her now with a look so sexual, so casually knowing, that she felt vertiginous.

She was furious with him. She shook her head a little and

prepared to slam the door. He held it open. Before she could say anything, his arrogance had gone and the old look was back.

"Please," he said quickly. "I'm sorry. I'm not explaining myself. I'm flustered because I've . . . been plucking up courage to talk to you.

"You see," he continued, "what you're playing is beautiful, but sometimes it feels a little bit—don't get angry—a bit unfinished. I sort of feel like the treble isn't quite . . . working. And I wouldn't say that to you except I play a little bit myself and I thought maybe we could help each other out."

Natasha stepped backward. She felt intrigued and threatened. She always stonewalled about her music, refusing to discuss her feelings about it with any except her very closest friends. The intense but inchoate frustrations she felt were rarely verbalized, as if to do so would give them form. She chose to keep them at bay with obfuscation, from herself as much as from others, and now this man seemed to be unwrapping them with an unnerving casualness.

"Do you have a suggestion?" she said as acidly as she could. He reached behind him and picked up a black case. He shook it in front of her.

"This might sound a bit cocky," he said, "and I don't want you to think I reckon I can do better than you. But, when I heard your playing, I just knew I could complement it." He undid the clasp of the case and opened it in front of her. She saw a disassembled flute.

"I know you might think I'm crazy," he pre-empted hurriedly. "You think what you play is totally different to what I play. But . . . I've been looking for *bass* like yours for longer than you could believe."

He spoke earnestly now, his eyebrows furrowed as he held her gaze. She stubbornly stared back, refusing to be overawed by this apparition on her doorstep.

"I want to play with you," he said.

This was stupid, Natasha told herself: even if this man was not arrogant beyond belief, you could not play the flute to Jungle. It was so long since she had stared at a traditional instrument she felt a gust of *déjà vu*: images of her nine-year-old self banging the xylophone in the school orchestra. Flutes meant enthusiastic cacophonies at the hands of children or the alien landscape of classical music, an intimidating world of great beauty but vicious social exclusivity, to which she had never known the passwords.

But to her amazement, this lanky stranger had impressed her. She wanted to let him in and hear him play his flute in her room. She wanted to hear him play over some of her basslines. Discordant indie bands had done it, she knew: My Bloody Valentine had used flutes. And while the result had left her as dead cold as the rest of that genre, surely the alliance itself was no more unlikely than this one. She realized that she was intrigued.

But she was not simply going to stand aside. She had a reputation for being intimidating. She was not used to feeling so disarmed, and her defenses flared.

"Listen," she said slowly. "I don't know what you think qualifies you to speak about my tracks. Why should I play with you?"

"Try it once," he said, and again that sudden change flooded his features, the same curled smile on the edge of the lips, the same heavy-lidded nonchalance about the eyes.

And Natasha was suddenly furious with this pretentious little art-school wanker, livid where a moment ago she had been captivated, and she leaned forward and up on tiptoes, until her face was as close to his as it would go, and she raised one eyebrow, and she said: "I don't think so."

She closed the door in his face.

Natasha stalked back up her stairs. The window was open. She stood next to it, close to the wall, looking down at the street without putting herself in view. She could see no sign of the man. She walked slowly to her keyboard. She smiled.

OK, you cocky fucker, she thought. *Let's see how good you are.*

She turned the volume down slightly, and pulled another rhythm out of her collection. This time the drums came crashing out of nowhere. The bass came chasing after, filling out the snare and framing the sound with a funky backdrop. She threw in a few minimal shouts and snatches of brass, looped a moment of trumpet, but the treble was subdued; this was an offering to the man outside, and it was all about rhythm.

The beats looped once, twice. Then, sailing up from the street came a thin snatch of music, a trill of flute that mimicked the looping repetition of her own music, but elaborated on itself, changed a little with every cycle. He was standing below her window, his hastily assembled instrument to his lips.

Natasha smiled. He had made good on his arrogance. She would have been disappointed if he had not.

She stripped the beat down and left it to loop. She stood back and listened.

The flute skittered over the drums, teasing the beat, touching just enough to stay anchored, then transporting itself. It suddenly became a series of staccato flutterings. It lilted between drum and bass, now wailing like a siren, now stuttering like Morse code.

Natasha was . . . not transfixed, perhaps, but impressed.

She closed her eyes. The flute soared and dived; it fleshed out her skeletal tune in a way she could never achieve. The life in the live music was exuberant and neurotic and it sparked off the revivified bass, the very alive dancing with the dead. There was a promise to this tension.

Natasha nodded. She was eager to hear more, to feed that flute into her music. She smiled sardonically. She would admit defeat. So long as he behaved, so long as there were not too many of those knowing looks, she would admit that she wanted to hear more.

Natasha paced silently back down the stairs. She opened the door. He was standing a few feet back, his flute to his lips, staring up at her window. He stopped as he saw her, and lowered his hands. No trace of a smile now. He looked anxious for approval.

She inclined her head and gave him a sideways look. He hovered.

"OK," she said. "I'll buy it." He finally smiled. "It's Natasha." She jerked her thumb at herself.

"Pete," the tall man said.

Natasha stood aside, and Pete passed into her house.

SIX

Again Fabian tried Natasha's number, and again she was engaged. He swore and slammed his receiver down. He turned on his heel, paced pointlessly. He had spoken to everyone who knew Saul except for Natasha, and she was the one who mattered most.

Fabian was not gossiping. As soon as he had heard about Saul's father he had got on the phone, almost before he was aware of what he was doing, and begun to spread the news. At some point he had rushed out to buy a paper, before starting again on the phone. But this was not gossip. He felt a powerful sense of duty. This, he believed, was what was needed of him.

He pulled on his jacket, tugged his thin dreadlocks into a ponytail. Enough, he decided. He would go to Natasha, tell her in person. It was a fair journey from Brixton to Ladbroke Grove, but the thought of the cold air in his face and lungs was beguiling. His house felt oppressive. He had spent hours on the phone that morning, the same phrases again and again—*Six floors straight down . . . The filth won't let me talk to him*—and the walls had soaked up the news. They were saturated with the old man's death. Fabian wanted space. He wanted to clean out his head.

He shoved a page of newspaper into his pocket. He could recite the relevant story by heart: *News in brief. A man died in Willesden, North London, yesterday, after falling through a sixth-floor window. Police will not say if they are treating the death as suspicious. The man's son is helping them with their enquiries.* The screaming accusation of the last sentence stung him.

He left his room for the filthy hall of the shared house. Someone was shouting upstairs. The dirty, ill-fitting carpets irritated him always; now they made him feel violent. As he struggled with his bike, he glanced at the unwashed walls, the broken banisters. The presence of the house weighed down on him. He burst out of the front door with a sigh of relief.

Fabian treated his bike carelessly, letting it fall when he dismounted, chucking it against walls. He was rough with it. He yanked himself onto it now with unthinking brutality, and swung out into the road.

The streets were full. It was a Saturday and people were thronging the streets, coming to and from Brixton market, determined on their outward journey and slow on the way back, laden down with cheap, colorful clothes and big fruit. Trains rumbled, competed with the sounds of Soca, Reggae, Rave, Rap, Jungle, House, and the shouting: all the cut-up market rhythm. Rudeboys in outlandish trousers clustered around corners and music shops, touched fists. Shaven-headed men in tight tops and AIDS ribbons made for Brockwell Park or The Brixtonian café. Food wrappers and lost television supplements tugged at ankles. The capricious traffic lights were a bad joke: pedestrians hovered like suicides at the edge of the pavement, launched themselves across at the slightest sign of a gap. The cars made angry noises and sped away, anxious to escape. Impassive, the people watched them pass by.

Fabian twisted his wheels through the bodies. The railway bridge passed above him; some way ahead the clocktower told him it was mid-morning. He rode and walked intermittently past the tube station, wheeled his bike across Brixton Road, and again over Acre Lane. There were no crowds here, and no Reggae. Acre Lane stretched out wide. The buildings that contained it were separate, sparse and low. The sky was always very big over Acre Lane.

Fabian jumped back onto his bike and took off up the slight incline toward Clapham. From there he would twist across into Clapham Manor Street, wind a little through back-streets to join Silverthorne Road, a steep sine-wave of minor industrial estates and peculiarly suburban houses tucked between Battersea and Clapham, a conduit feeding directly into Queenstown Road, across Chelsea Bridge.

For the first time that day Fabian felt his head clear.

Early that morning a suspicious policeman had answered Saul's phone, had demanded Fabian's name. Outraged, Fabian had hung up. He had rung up Willesden police station, again refusing to give his name, but demanding to know why policemen were answering his friend's phone. Only when he acquiesced and told them who he was would they tell him that Saul's father had died, and that Saul was with them—again that disingenuous phrase—helping with enquiries.

First he felt nothing but shock; then quickly a sense of a monstrous error.

And a great fear. Because Fabian understood immediately that it would be easy for them to believe that Saul had killed his father. And, as immediately, he knew without any equivocation or doubt that Saul had not. But he was terribly afraid, because only he knew that, because he knew Saul. And there was nothing he could tell others to help them understand.

He wanted to see Saul; he did not understand why the

officer's voice changed when he demanded this. He was told it would be some time before he could speak to Saul, Saul was deep in conversation, his attention wholly grabbed, and Fabian would just have to wait. There was something the man was not telling him, Fabian knew, and he was scared. He left his phone number, was reassured that he would be contacted as soon as Saul was free to speak.

Fabian sped along Acre Lane. On his left he passed an extraordinary white building, a mass of grubby turrets and shabby Art Deco windows. It looked long deserted. On the step sat two boys, dwarfed by jackets declaring allegiance to American Football teams neither had ever seen play. They were oblivious to the faded grandeur of their bench. One had his eyes closed, was leaning back against the door like Mexican cannon-fodder in a spaghetti Western. His friend spoke animatedly into his hand, his tiny mobile phone hidden within the voluminous folds of his sleeve. Fabian felt the thrill of materialist envy, but battened it down. This was one impulse he resisted.

Not me, he thought, as he always did. *I'll hold out a bit longer. I won't be another black man with a mobile, another troublemaker with "Drug Dealer" written on his forehead in script only the police can read.*

He stood up out of his seat, kicked down and sped off toward Clapham.

Fabian knew Saul hated his father's disappointment. Fabian knew Saul and his father could not speak together. Fabian had been the only one of Saul's friends who had seen him turn that volume by Lenin over and over in his hands, open it and close it, read the inscription again and again. His father's writing was tight and controlled, as if trying not to break the pen. Saul had put the book in Fabian's lap, had waited while his friend read.

To Saul, This always made sense to me. Love from the Old Leftie.

Fabian remembered looking up into Saul's face. His mouth was sealed, his eyes looked tired. He took the book off

Fabian's lap and closed it, stroked the cover, put it on his shelf. Fabian knew Saul had not killed his father.

He crossed Clapham High Street, a concourse of restaurants and charity shops, and slid into the backstreets, wiggling through the parked cars to emerge on Silverthorne Road. He started down the long incline toward the river.

He knew that Natasha would be working. He knew he would turn into Bassett Road and hear the faint boom of Drum and Bass. She would be hunched over her keyboard, twiddling dials and pressing keys with the concentration of an alchemist, juggling long sequences of zeros and ones and transforming them into music. Listening and creating. That was what Natasha spent all her time doing. When she was not concentrating on source material behind the till of friends' record shops, serving customers in an efficient autopilot mode, she was reconstituting it into the tracks she christened with spiky one-word titles: *Arrival; Rebellion; Maelstrom.*

Fabian believed it was Natasha's concentration which made her so asexual to him. She was attractive in a fierce way, and was never short of offers, especially at clubs, especially when word got around that the music playing was hers; but Fabian had never known her to seem very interested, even when she took someone home. He felt blasphemous even thinking of her in a sexual context. Fabian was alone in his opinion, he was assured by his friend Kay, a cheerful dope-raddled clown who drooled lasciviously after Natasha whenever he saw her. The music was the thing, Kay said, and the intensity was the thing, and the carelessness was the thing. Just like a nun, it was the promise of what was under the habit.

But Fabian could only grin sheepishly at Kay, absurdly embarrassed. Amateur psychologists around London, Saul included, had wasted no time deciding he was in love with Natasha; but Fabian did not think that was the case. She infuriated him with her style-fascism and her solipsism, but he supposed he loved her. Just not in the way Saul meant it.

He twisted under the filthy railway bridge on Queenstown Road now, fast approaching Battersea Park. He was riding an incline, racing toward Chelsea Bridge. He took the round-about with casual arrogance, put his head down and climbed toward the river. On Fabian's right, the four chimneys of Battersea Power Station loomed into view. Its roof was long gone, it looked like a bombed-out relic, a blitz survivor. It was a great upturned plug straining to suck voltage out of the clouds, a monument to energy.

Fabian burst free of South London. He slowed and looked into the Thames, past the towers and railings of steel that surrounded him, keeping him snug on Chelsea Bridge. The river sent shards of cold sunlight in all directions.

He scudded over the face of the water like a pondskater, dwarfed by the girders and bolts ostentatiously holding the bridge together. He hung poised for a moment between the South Bank and the North Bank, his head high to see over the sides into the water, to see the black barges that never moved, waiting to ferry cargo long forgotten, his legs still, freewheeling his way toward Ladbroke Grove.

The route to Natasha's house took Fabian past the Albert Hall and through Kensington, which he hated. It was a soulless place, a purgatory filled only with rich transients drifting pointlessly through Nicole Farhi and Red or Dead. He sped up Kensington Church Street toward Notting Hill and on through to Portobello Road.

It was a market day, the second in the week, designed to wrest money from tourists. Merchandise that had cost five pounds on Friday was now offered for ten. The air was thick with garish cagoules and backpacks and French and Italian. Fabian cussed quietly and inched through the throng. He ducked left down Elgin Crescent and then right, bearing down on the Bassett Road flat.

A gust of wind stained the air brown with leaves. Fabian swung into the street. The leaves boiled around him, stuck to his jacket. Pared-down trees lined the tarmac. Fabian dismounted while still in motion, walked toward Natasha's flat.

He could hear her working. The faint thumping of Drum and Bass was audible from the end of the street. As he walked, wheeling his bike beside him, Fabian heard the sound of wings. Natasha's house teemed with pigeons. Every protuberance and ledge was gray with plump, stirring bodies. A few were in the air, hovering nervously around the windows and gables, settling, dislodging their peers. They shifted and shat a little as Fabian stopped at the door directly below them.

Natasha's rhythm was loud now, and Fabian could hear something unusual, a clear sound like pipes, a recorder or a flute, bursting with energy and exuberance, shadowing the bass. He stood still and listened. The quality of this sound was different from that of samples, and it was not trapped in any loops. Fabian suspected it was being played live. And by something of a virtuoso.

He rang the bell. The electronic boom of the bass stopped cold. The flute faltered on for a second or two. As silence fell, the company of pigeons rose en masse into the air with the abruptness of panic, circled once like a school of fish and disappeared into the north. Fabian heard footsteps on the stairs.

Natasha opened the door to him and smiled.

"Alright, Fabe," she said, reaching up to touch her clenched right fist to his. He did so, at the same time bending down to put an arm around her and kiss her cheek. She responded, though her surprise was evident.

"Tash," he whispered, in greeting and in warning. She heard it in his voice, pulled back holding his shoulders in her hands. Her face sharpened in concern.

"What? What's happened?"

"Tash, it's Saul." He'd told the story so often today he'd become an automaton, just mouthing the words, but this time it was difficult all over again. He licked his lips.

Natasha started. "What is it, Fabe?" Her voice cracked.

"No no," he said hurriedly. "Saul's fine. Well, I guess . . . He's in with the pigs."

She shook her head in confusion.

"Listen, Tash . . . Saul's dad . . . he died." He rushed on before she could misunderstand. "He was killed. He was lobbed out of a window two nights back. I think . . . I think the police reckon Saul did it." He reached into his pocket and brought out the scrunched-up news story. Natasha read it.

"No," she said.

"I know, I know. But I suppose they heard about him and the old man having arguments and that, and . . . I dunno."

"No," said Natasha again. The two of them stood quite still, staring at each other. Eventually Natasha moved. "Look," she said, "come in. We'd better talk. There's this bloke here . . . "

"The one playing the flute?"

She smiled slightly. "Yeah. He's good, isn't he? I'll get rid of him."

Fabian closed the door behind him and followed her up the stairs. She was some way ahead of him and, as he approached her inner door, he heard voices.

"What's happening?" It was a man's voice, muffled and anxious.

"A friend's in a bit of bother," Natasha was saying. Fabian entered the sparse bedroom, nodded in greeting at the tall blond man he saw over Natasha's shoulder. The man had his mouth slightly open, was fingering his ponytail nervously. In his right hand was a silver flute. He looked up and down at the two in the doorway.

"Pete, Fabian." Natasha waved her hand vaguely between the two in a cursory introduction. "Sorry, Pete, but you're going to have to split. I have to talk to Fabe. Something's come up."

The blond man nodded and hurriedly gathered his things together. As he did so, he spoke rapidly.

"Natasha, do you want to do this again? I felt like we were . . . really getting into it."

Fabian raised his eyebrows.

The tall man squeezed past Fabian without taking his

eyes off Natasha. She was clearly distracted, but she smiled and nodded.

"Yeah. For sure. Do you want to leave me your number or something?"

"No, I'll come by again."

"Do you want my number, then?"

"No. I'll just come by, and if you're not in, I'll come by again." Pete stopped in front of the stairs and turned back. "Hope I see you again, Fabian," he said.

Fabian nodded abstractedly, then looked into Pete's eyes. The tall man was gazing at him with a peculiar intensity, demanding a response. The two were locked for a moment, until Fabian acquiesced and nodded more pointedly. Only then did Pete seem satisfied. He descended the stairs, followed by Natasha.

The two were speaking, but Fabian could not make out any words. He frowned. The front door slammed shut and Natasha returned to the room.

"He's a bit of a weirdo, isn't he?" Fabian asked.

Natasha nodded vehemently. " 'Strue, man, do you know what I mean? I threw him out at first, he was kind of getting leery."

"Trying it on?"

"Kind of. But he was going on and on about wanting to play with me, and I was intrigued, and he started playing outside. He was good so I let him back in."

"Suitably humbled, yeah?" Fabian grinned briefly.

"Damn right. But he plays . . . he plays like a fucking angel, Fabe." She was excited. "He's the original nutter, you're right, I know, but there's something very right about his playing."

There was a short silence. Natasha tugged at Fabian's jacket and pulled him into the kitchen. "I need a coffee, man. You need a coffee. And I need to know about Saul."

In the street stood the tall man. He stared up at the window, the flute limp in his hand. His clothes twisted in the wind. He was even paler in the cold, in front of the dark trees. He was quite motionless. He watched the tiny variations of light as bodies moved in and out of the sitting room. He cocked his ear slightly, pulled his fringe out of his eyes, twisted a lock of hair in his fingers. His eyes were the color of the clouds. He raised the flute slowly to his lips, played a brief refrain. A little group of sparrows wheeled out from the branches of a tree, circled him. The man lowered his flute and watched as the birds disappeared.

SEVEN

Two eyes stained yellow by death gaped stupidly. All the imperfections of the human body were magnified by utter stillness. Crowley ran his eyes over the face, took note of the wide pores, the pockmarks, the hairs sprouting from nostrils, the patch of stubble under the Adam's apple that the razor had missed.

The skin folded up under the chin and became a tightly wound coil, a skein of flesh wrung out to dry. The body was chest-down, limbs uncomfortable, and the head was facing the ceiling, twisted around nearly 180 degrees. Crowley stood and pushed his hands into his pockets to disguise their trembling. He turned and faced his entourage, two burly officers whose faces were identical portraits of disbelieving revulsion, scarcely more mobile than their fallen comrade's.

Crowley paced through the small hall to the bedroom.

The flat was full of busy people, photographers, pathologists. Fingerprint dust sat in the air in flat layers, like geological strata.

He peered around the frame of the bedroom door. A suited man crouched on the floor before a figure sitting with splayed legs, leaning against a wall. Crowley looked at the seated man and made a small disgusted noise, as if at rotten food. He stared into the ruinous mess of the other's face. Blood was smeared across the wall. The dead man's uniform was saturated with it, stiff like an oilskin coat.

The suited doctor removed his tentative fingers from the bloody mess, and glanced behind him at Crowley.

"You are . . . ?"

"DI Crowley. Doctor, what *happened* here?"

The doctor gestured at the slumped figure. His voice was utterly detached, exhibiting the defensive professionalism Crowley had seen before at unpleasant deaths.

"Ah, this chap, Constable Barker, yes? Well . . . he's been hit in the face, basically, very fast and very hard." He stood, ran his hands through his hair. "I think he's come here to the front of the room, opened the door and been walloped with a . . . a bloody *piledriver* which sent him into the wall and onto the floor, at which point our assailant has borne down on him and cracked him a few more times. Once or twice with his fists, I think, then with a stick or a club or something, lots of long thin bruises across the shoulders and neck. And the line of damage here . . . " He indicated a particular trough in the bone-flecked pulp of the face.

"And the other?"

The doctor shook his head, and blinked several times. "Never seen that before, to be honest. He's had his neck broken, which sounds straightforward enough, but . . . well, my God, you've seen him, yes?" Crowley nodded. "I don't know . . . do you have any idea how strong the human neck is, Inspector? It's not so very difficult to break a neck but someone has *turned his the wrong way round* . . . And they've had to dislocate all the vertebrae completely, so that tension in the flesh doesn't send the head back round to the front. So they didn't just turn his head round, they pulled *upwards* while they were doing it. You're dealing with someone very, *very* strong, and, I shouldn't wonder, with some sort of karate or judo or something."

Crowley pursed his lips. "There's no real sign of struggle, so they were fast. Page opens the door and has his neck done in half a second, makes a little noise. Barker moves to the door of the bedroom, and . . . "

The doctor looked at Crowley in silence. Crowley nodded his thanks and rejoined his companions. Herrin and Bailey were still staring at the implausible figure of Constable Page.

Herrin looked up as Crowley approached. "Jesus fucking Christ, sir, it's like that film . . . "

"*The Exorcist*. I know, Constable."

"But like all the way round, sir . . . "

"*I know*, Detective, now give it a rest. We're leaving."

The three ducked under the twists of tape which sealed the flat, and made their way down through the bowels of the building. Outside, a large patch of grass was still surrounded with the same tape that closed off the flat above. Vicious droplets of glass still littered the earth.

"It doesn't seem possible, sir," said Bailey, as they approached the car.

"What do you mean?"

"Well, I saw Garamond when he came in. Quite a big bloke but no Schwarzenegger. And Jesus, he didn't look capable of . . . " Bailey spoke quickly, still deeply shocked.

Crowley nodded as he swung the car round. "I know you're never supposed to let yourself make judgments about who's 'the type' and who's not, but I've got to admit, Garamond's shocked me. I thought, 'Fine, no problem. Argues with the dad, struggle, shoves him out the window, in shock, goes to bed.' Bit odd that, I admit, but when you're drunk and freaked out, you do odd things.

"But I certainly didn't have him down for the little Houdini he turned out to be. And as for this . . . "

Herrin was nodding vehemently.

"How did he *do* that? Door open, cell empty, no one sees him, no one hears a thing."

"But all this," continued Crowley, "this is a real . . . *surprise*." He gobbed the word out with disgust. He spoke slowly, his quiet voice halting momentarily between each word. "What I interviewed last night was a scared, confused, fucked-up little man. Whatever escaped from the station was some sort of *master criminal*, and whatever killed Page and Barker was . . . an animal."

He thinned his eyes and gently thumped the steering wheel. "But everything about this is weird. Why did none of the neighbors hear anything going on between him and the dad? His camping story checks out?" Herrin nodded. "We can put him in Willesden at about ten, Mr Garamond hit the ground at about ten-thirty, eleven. Someone should've heard it. How's it going with the rest of the family?"

"Series of blanks," said Bailey. "Mum's long dead, you know, and she was an orphan. His dad's parents are dead, there's no uncles, an aunt in America no one's seen for years . . . I'm moving on to his mates. Some of them have already been calling in. We'll go chase them up."

Crowley grunted assent as they pulled in at the station. Colleagues slowed as he walked past, gazed at him unhappily, wanting to say something about Page and Barker. He preempted them by nodding sadly, then moved on. He had no desire to share his shock.

He returned to his desk, sipping the crap from the coffee machine. Crowley was losing his grasp on what was going on. It was disquieting him. The previous evening, when he had discovered that Saul had walked out of his cell, he had been filthy angry, livid—but he had made the right noises, done the right things. There'd been some major fuck-up obviously, and he would have serious words with a few people, just as the governor had had words with him. He had sent men out delving into Willesden's darkness; Saul could not have got far. As a precaution, he had sent Barker to join Page in the boring task of watching over the crime scene, just in case Saul should be so stupid as to return home.

Which it seemed he had done. But not the Saul he had interviewed, he would not believe that. He accepted that he made mistakes, could misjudge people, but not like that, he could not believe it. Something had demented Saul, given him the strength of the unhinged, and changed him from the person Crowley had interviewed into the devastating assassin who had brought such carnage to the small flat.

Why had he not run? Crowley could not understand. He shoved his fingers into his eyes, kneaded them till they ached. Saul had returned, he pictured it, disorientated and stumbling, to the flat; to atone, perhaps, to try to remember, perhaps; and when he opened the door on the men in uniform he should have run, or fallen to the floor crying, denied all knowledge, snivelled.

Instead he had reached out toward Constable Page, taken his head in his hands and torn it around in less than a second. Crowley winced. His eyes were closed but that was no respite from the brutal image. *Saul had quietly closed the door behind him, had turned to Constable Barker who was surely gazing at him in momentary confusion, had punched him back five feet, following the suddenly limp body, and beaten his face systematically into a broken, bloody, shattered thing.*

Constable Page was a stupid stocky man, quite new to the force. He was talkative, forever telling idiot jokes. They were often racist, although his girlfriend, Crowley knew, was of mixed race. Barker was a perpetual footsoldier, had been a constable for too long, but would not get the message and change his career. Crowley had not known either of the men well.

There was an unpleasant somberness about the station: not so much shock as a tentative uncertainty about how to react. People were unused to death.

Crowley put his head in his hands. He did not know where Saul was, he did not know what to do.

EIGHT

Greasy-looking clouds slid above the alley in which King Rat and Saul sat digesting. Everything seemed dirty to Saul. His clothes and face and hair were smeared with a day and a half's muck, and now dirt was inside him. As he drew sustenance from it, it colored what he could see, but he looked around at his newly tarnished world as if it were a cynosure. It held no horror for him.

Purity is a negative state and contrary to nature, Saul had once read. That made sense to him now. He could see the world clearly in all its natural and supernatural impurity, for the first time in his life.

He was conscious of his own smell: the old acridity of alcohol splashed on these clothes long ago, the muck from the gutter of the roof, rotting food; but something new underneath it all. A taste of animal in his sweat, something of that scent which had entered his cell with King Rat two nights ago. Maybe it was in his mind. Maybe there was nothing beyond the faint remnants of deodorant, but Saul believed he could smell the rat in him coming out.

King Rat leaned back against the rubbish sacks, staring at the sky.

"It occurs," he said presently, "that thee and me should scarper. Full?"

Saul nodded. "You've got a story to tell me," he said.

"I know it," said King Rat. "But I can't exercise myself on that particular just yet. I've to teach you to be rat. Your eyes aren't even open yet; you're still such a mewling little furless thing. So . . . " He got to his feet. "What say we retire? Grab a bit of tucker for the underground." He pushed handfuls of leftover fruitcake into his pockets.

King Rat turned to face the wall behind the rubbish sacks. He moved to the right-angle of brick where the wall met one side of the narrow alley, wedged himself within it in his impossible way, and began to scale the wall. He teetered at the top, twenty feet up, his feet daintily picking between rusting coils of barbed wire as though they were flowers. He squatted between them and beckoned to Saul.

Saul approached the wall. He set his teeth and jutted out his lower jaw, confrontational. He pushed himself into the corner space, as hard as he could, feeling his flesh mold itself into the space. He reached up with his arms. *Like a rat*, he thought, *squeeze and move and pull like a rat*. His fingers gripped the spaces between bricks and he hauled himself up with a prodigious strength. His face ballooned with effort, his feet scrabbled, but he was progressing up the wall in his own undignified fashion. He let out a growl, and heard an admonitory hissing from above him. He pushed his right arm up again, the dank smell of rat-sweat more evident than ever beneath his arms. His legs failed him, he quivered and fell, was caught and pulled into the thicket of crumbling wire.

"Not so bad, ratling boy. Isn't it a marvel what you can

do with a scrap of decent grub in your belly? You were right up near the top."

And Saul felt pride at his climbing.

Below them was a little courtyard hemmed in on all sides by dirty walls and windows. To Saul's new eyes the robust dirt of the enclosure was almost too vibrant to look at. Every corner teemed with the spreading stains of decay; this weak spot of the city had been convincingly annexed by the forces of filth. A disconcerting line of dolls gently moldered where they had been placed, their backs to the wall, eyes on the pewter-colored plug in the corner of the courtyard. A manhole.

King Rat exhaled through his nose triumphantly.

"Home," he hissed. "Into the palace."

He leapt from the top of the wall, landing in a crouch over the manhole, surrounding it. He made no sound as he came to rest on the concrete. His coat drifted down around him, surrounding him like an oily puddle. He looked up and waited.

Saul looked down and felt the old fears. He steeled himself, swallowed. He willed himself to jump, but his legs had locked into a fearful squat, and he grew exasperated as he readied himself to land beside his uncle. He breathed in, once, twice, very deeply, then stood, swung his arms and launched himself at the shape waiting for him.

He saw grays and reds of bricks and concrete lurch around him in slow motion, he moved his body, prepared his landing, as he saw King Rat's grin approach him at speed; then the world jolted hard, his eyes and teeth juddered in his face, and he was down. His knees pushed all the air out of his stomach, but he smiled with exhilaration as he overcame his spasming belly and sucked air into his lungs. He had flown, had landed ready. He was shedding his humanity like an old snakeskin, scratching it off in great swathes. It was so fast, this assumption of a new form inside.

"You're a good boy," said King Rat, and busied himself with the metal in the ground.

Saul looked up. He saw figures move behind the windows above, wondered if anyone could see them.

King Rat's London snarl had assumed a didactic tone. "Pay attention, ratling. This here is the entrance to your ceremonial abode. The all of Rome-vill is yours by rights, you're royalty. But there's a special palace, the rat's own hidey-hole, and you bing a waste there through these portholes." He indicated the metal cover. "Observe."

King Rat's fingers scuttled over the iron disc like a virtuoso typist's, investigating its surface. He turned his head from side to side, cocked it briefly, then suddenly tensed his body and slipped his fingers into infinitesimal gaps between the seal and its shaft. It was like sleight of hand: Saul could not see what had happened, or how the fingers had fit, yet they were there, pulling, in the gaps.

The manhole cover twisted with a yelp of rust. There was a rush of dirty wind as King Rat pulled it free.

Saul stared into the pit. The swirling winds of the courtyard yanked at the rich-smelling wisps of vapor emerging from the hole. The sewer was gorged with darkness; it seemed to overflow, seeping out of the open concrete and obscuring the ground. The organic scent of compost billowed out. Just visible, a ladder driven into the subterranean brick plunged out of sight. Where it was riveted to the wall, metal had oxidized and leached out profusely, making the sewer bleed rust. The sound of a thin flow of water was amplified by the yawning tunnels, making for a bizarre booming trickle.

King Rat looked at Saul. He clenched his hand into a fist, extended a pointing index finger, and his hand described an elaborate twisting path through the air, playfully circling, till it spiralled down and came to rest pointing into the sewer. King Rat stood at the edge of the thin circle. He stepped out over the hole and dropped through the pavement. There was a tiny echoing damp sound.

King Rat's voice emerged from underground.

"Down you come."

Saul squeezed his hips through the hole.

"Put a lid on it," said King Rat from below, and laughed briefly. Saul fumbled with the metal cover. He was half in, half out of the sewer. He sank under the weight of the metal. He held it above his head and descended. The light disappeared.

Saul shivered in the cold of the sewer. His feet clapped on the metal. He stumbled as his feet hit wetness. He backed away from the ladder and rubbed himself in the darkness. Air gusted and hissed; freezing water flooded his shoes.

"Where are you?" he whispered.

"Watching," came King Rat's voice. It moved around him. "Wait. You'll see. You've never tried this, laddie, so hold your horses. The darkmans is nothing to you."

Saul stood still. His hands were invisible before him.

Shapes moved in front of him. He thought they were real until the corridors themselves began to emerge from the darkness and he realized that those other fleeting, indistinct forms were born in his mind. They were dispelled as Saul began to see.

He saw the muck of the drains. He saw the energy it contained spilling out, a gray light that showed no colors but illuminated the damp tunnels. Before him a study in perspective, the shit- and algae-encrusted walls of the shaft meeting in the distance. Behind him and to his right more tunnels, and everywhere the smell, rot and feces, and the pungent smell of piss, rat piss. He wrinkled his nose, his hackles rising.

"No worries," said King Rat, a figure saturated in shadows, drenched in them, a mass of darkness. "Some cove's staked a claim and made a mark, but we're *royalty*. His territory doesn't mean fuck to us."

Saul looked about him. A thin rivulet of dirty water seeped by at his feet. His every movement seemed to set off an explosion of echoes. He stood in a twisting brick cylinder seven feet in diameter. From everywhere came the noises of streaming water and falling stones, and organic sounds of squeaks and scratches, peaking, dying out and being replaced, sounds far away being written over by those nearby, a palimpsest of noise.

"I want to see you leg it, staying mum as you like," said King Rat. He startled Saul. His voice wandered through the tunnels, exploring every corner. "I want to see you shift your arse, climb sharpish. I want to see you swim. School is in."

King Rat turned to face the same direction as Saul. He pointed into the charcoal gray.

"We're off thataway. And we're off sharpish. So pull your finger out and keep up. Ready, my old lad?"

Saul shivered with excitement, the cold irrelevant now, and crouched in a starter's position.

"Come on, then," he said.

King Rat turned and bolted.

Saul did not feel his legs moving as he followed. The rapid, faint beat of footsteps he heard was his own; King Rat was soundless. Saul could feel his nose twitching and he felt like laughing.

He panted with exhilaration. King Rat was an ill-defined blur before him, his coat flapping vaguely in the noisome wind. Tunnels passed by on either side, water spattered him. King Rat disappeared suddenly, cutting sharply left down a smaller tunnel where the water pressure was greater, swirling insistently around Saul's legs. He pulled his legs up out of the stream.

King Rat turned his head for a second, a flash of pale flesh. He crouched as he ran and pulled to a sudden halt. He waited briefly while Saul caught him up, then ducked into a claustrophobic shaft barely three feet high. Saul did not hesitate, but dove in after him.

Saul's breath and the sound of his flesh on the brick came bouncing back at him, as loud and intimate as if they existed only in his head. He stumbled, mud smearing his legs, careering along the tube in a messy, effective fashion.

His nose hit wet cloth. King Rat had stopped suddenly.

Saul peered over King Rat's shoulder.

"What is it?" he hissed.

King Rat jerked his head. He raised his hand, pointing perfunctorily.

Something moved in the flat, leaden light. Two small creatures edged backwards and forward uneasily in the brick warren. They crept a few ineffectual inches in one direction, then in another, without once taking their eyes from the figures before them.

Rats.

King Rat was quite still. Saul hovered, bewildered.

One rat stood on either side of the dirty water. They moved in concert, forward together, backwards together, a tentative dance, staring at King Rat.

"What's happening?" whispered Saul.

King Rat did not answer.

One of the rats scuttled forward and sat up on its hind legs, six feet in front of King Rat. It paddled its front legs aggressively, squeaked, bared its teeth. It returned to all fours and crept a little further forward, baring its teeth, clearly afraid but apparently angry, contemptuous.

The rat appeared to spit.

King Rat suddenly barked in outrage and lurched forward, his arm outstretched, but the two rats had bolted.

King Rat picked himself silently out of the muck and continued along the tunnel.

"Hey, *hey*, hold on," said Saul in amazement. King Rat kept moving. "What the fuck was that all about?"

King Rat kept moving.

"What's going on?" shouted Saul.

"*Stow it!*" screamed King Rat without turning. He crept on. "Not now," he said more quietly. "That's the seat of my sorrow. Not now. Just you wait till I get you home."

He disappeared around a corner.

Saul became lulled by the sewers. He kept King Rat in his sights, losing himself in the damp brick convolutions. More rats passed them, but no more taunted them as the first two had seemed to do. They stopped when they saw King Rat, and then quickly ran.

King Rat ignored them, winding through the complex at a constant quick trudge.

Saul felt like a tourist. He investigated the walls in passing, reading the mildew on the bricks. He was hypnotized by his own footsteps. Time passed as a succession of brick tributaries. He was ignorant of the cold and intoxicated by the smell. Occasional growls of traffic filtered through the earth and tar above, to yawn through the cavernous sewers.

Presently King Rat stopped in a tunnel through which the two explorers had to crawl. He turned to face Saul, a trick which looked impossible in the tiny space. The air was thick with the smell of piss, a particular piss, a strong, familiar smell, the smell which permeated King Rat's clothes.

"Righto," murmured King Rat. "So have you clocked your whereabouts?" Saul shook his head. "We're at the crossroads of Rome-vill, the center, my very own conjunction, under King's Cross. Hold your tongue and prick up your ears: hear the trains *growling*? Got the map in your bonce? *Learn the way*. This is where you've to get to. Just follow your I Suppose. I've marked out my manor nice and strong, you can sniff it out from anywhere underground." And Saul felt suddenly sure that he *could* find his way there, as easy as breathing.

But he looked around him, and could see only the same bricks, the same dirty water as everywhere else.

"What," he ventured slowly, "is here?"

King Rat pushed his finger against his nose and winked.

"I set myself down anywhere I bloody fancy, but a king wants a palace." As he spoke, King Rat was busying himself with the bricks below him, running a long fingernail between them, creating a rising worm of dirt. He traced a jagged square of brick whose uneven sides were a little less than two feet long. He dug his fingernails under the corners and pulled what looked like a tray of bricks out of the floor.

Saul whistled with amazement at the hole he had uncovered. The wind played over the newly opened hole like a flute. He looked at the bricks King Rat held. They were an artifice, a single concrete plug with angled edges under the thin veneer of brick, so that it sat snug and invisible in the tunnel floor.

Saul peered into the opening. A chute curved away steeply out of sight. He looked up. King Rat was hugging the lid, waiting for Saul.

Saul swung his legs over the lip of the chute, and breathed its stale air. He pushed himself forward with his bum and slid under the tight curve, greased with living slime.

A breakneck careering ride and Saul was deposited breathless into a pool of freezing water. He spluttered and gobbed, emptying his mouth of the taste of dirt and squeezing his eyes clear. When he opened them, he stopped quite still, water dripping from his open mouth.

The walls stretched out away from each other so suddenly and violently it was as though they were afraid of one another. Saul sat in the cold pool at one end of the chamber. It swept out, a three-dimensional ellipse, like a raindrop on its side, ninety feet long, with him dumbstruck at the thin end. Reinforced brick ribs striped the walls of the chamber and arched overhead: cathedral architecture, thirty feet high, like the fossilized belly of a whale long entombed under the city.

Saul stumbled from the pool, took a few short steps forward. To either side the room dipped a little, creating a thin moat drawing its water from the pool into which the chute had deposited Saul. Every few feet, just above the moat, were the circular ends of pipes disappearing, Saul supposed, into the main sewer above.

Before him there was a raised walkway, which climbed an incline until at the opposite end of the chamber it was eight feet from the floor, and there was the throne.

It faced Saul. It was rough, a utilitarian design sculpted with bricks, like everything under the ground. The throne room was quite empty.

Behind Saul something hit the water. The report leisurely explored the room. King Rat came to stand behind Saul.

"Ta very much, Mr. Bazalgette."

Saul turned his head, shook it to show that he did not understand. King Rat scampered up the walkway and curled into the chair. He sat facing Saul, one leg thrown over a brick-work arm. His voice came as clear as ever to Saul's ears, although he did not raise it.

"He was the man with the plan, built the whole maze in the time of the last queen. People owe him their flush crappers, and me . . . I can thank him for my underworld."

"But all this . . . " breathed Saul. "This room . . . why did he build this room?"

"Mr. Bazalgette was a canny gent." King Rat snickered unpleasantly. "I had a few whids, burnt his lugholes, told him a few tales, sights I'd seen. We had a conflab about him and his habits, not all of which were unknown to me." King Rat winked exaggeratedly. "He was of the opinion that these tales should remain undisclosed. We came to an arrangement. You'll not find this here burrow, my cubby-hole, on any plans."

Saul approached King Rat's throne. He squatted on all fours in front of the seat.

"What are we doing here? What do we do now?" Saul was suddenly weary of following like a disciple, unable to intervene or shape events. "I want to know what you want."

King Rat stared at him without speaking.

Saul continued. "Is this about those rats?" he said. There was no answer.

"Is this about the rats? What was that about? You're the king, right? You're King Rat. So command them. I didn't see them showing any tribute or respect. They looked pretty pissed off to me. What's this about? Call on the rats, make them come to you."

There was no sound in the hall. King Rat continued to stare.

Eventually he spoke. "Not . . . yet."

Saul waited.

"I won't . . . yet. They're still . . . *narked* . . . with me. They'll not do what I tell them just yet."

"How long have they been . . . narked?"

"Seven hundred years."

King Rat looked a pathetic figure. He skulked with his characteristic combination of defensiveness and arrogance. He looked lonely.

"You're . . . not the king at all, are you?"

"*I am the king!*" King Rat was on his feet, spitting at the figure below him. *"Don't dare talk to me like that! I'm the King, I'm the one, the cutpurse, the thief, the deserter chief!"*

"So *what's going on?*" yelled Saul.

"Something . . . went . . . wrong . . . Once upon a time. Rats've long memories, see?" King Rat thumped his head. "They don't forget stuff. They keep it all in the noggin. That's all. And *you're involved*, sunshine. This is all tied up with the one that wants you dead, the cove that bumped off your fucking dad."

Fucking dad, said the echoes for a long time afterwards.

"What . . . who . . . is it?" said Saul.

King Rat looked balefully at him with those shadow-encrusted eyes.

"The Ratcatcher."

PART THREE

LESSONS

IN RHYTHM
AND HISTORY

Almost as soon as Fabian had left, Pete had appeared. His alacrity was suspicious. In another mood it would have pissed Natasha off, but she felt like forgetting about Saul, just for a short time.

She and Fabian had sat up late in her small kitchen. Fabian always commented on Natasha's rather self-consciously minimalist approach to decor, complaining that it made him feel uneasy, but that night they had other things on their minds. The faint strains of Drum and Bass filtered through from the stereo next door.

The next morning Natasha rose at eight, regretting the cigarettes she had shared with Fabian. He rolled out of the sleeping-bag she had lent him, when he heard her stir. They had no more words to say about Saul. They were numb and tired. Fabian left quickly.

Natasha wandered out of the kitchen dripping night-clothes, pulling a shapeless sweater over her shoulders. She turned on the stereo, slipped the needle onto the vinyl on the turntable. It was the best of last year's compilations, now some months old, rendering it an ancient classic in the fast-mutating world of Drum and Bass.

She ran her hands through her hair, pulling brutally at the tangles.

Pete rang the bell. She guessed it was him.

She was tired but she let him in. As she drank her coffee, she leaned against the counter and peered at him. She considered him ugly, his pale skin and thin limbs. He was hardly a style guru, either. The world of Jungle could be elitist. She smiled slightly at the thought of the rudeboys and hard-steppers in the club AWOL being presented with this under-sunned apparition, complete with flute.

"How much do you know about Drum and Bass?" she asked.

He shook his head. "Not much, really . . . "

"I can tell. When you played yesterday it was impressive, but I've got to tell you it's a *weird idea* playing flutes or shit like that to Jungle. If it's going to work, we're going to have to figure it out carefully."

He nodded, his face comical with concentration. Natasha almost wished for a repeat of his extraordinary performance of the previous day, his sudden knowing smile. The alternative was so cringing, so desperate to please, that it all but nauseated her. If this day didn't go well, she decided, she wasn't having any more of it.

She sighed. "I'm not cutting anything with you without you knowing something about the music. Just because General fucking Levy gets a single in the top ten, and some art-school wankers start writing about Jungle, and the next thing you know anything with a backbeat's 'Jungle.' Even Everything But The fucking Girl!" She folded her arms. "Everything But The Girl aren't Jungle, alright?"

He nodded. It was clear he had never heard of Everything But The Girl.

She closed her eyes and bit back a grin.

"Right. There's a lot going on in Jungle: there's intelligent Jungle, there's Hardstep, Techstepping, Jazz Jungle . . . I like 'em all, but I can't cut Hardstep tracks. All the darkness edges. You want Hardstep, go to Ed Rush or Skyscraper or something, OK? I cut tunes more like Bukem, DJ Rap, stuff like that." Natasha was enjoying herself enormously, lecturing him, watching his eyes dart frantically around. He had no idea what she was talking about.

"DJs have started bringing musicians to gigs; Goldie brings in a drummer, and stuff like that. Some people don't like it, they reckon Jungle should be digital or nothing. I'm not down with that, but I got no immediate plans to be dragging you on stage either. What I'm interested in is maybe playing with you for a while and sampling some of your flute for the top end. Loop it and cut it and stuff."

Pete nodded. He was fumbling with his case, assembling his flute.

Saul woke in the throne room under the city. He sat curled up in the cold, below the unmoving shape of King Rat, stiff on his throne. As soon as Saul's eyes opened, King Rat stood up. He had been waiting for Saul to awake.

They ate and left the chamber by the brick ladder which crept up behind the throne, emerging by means of another hidden door into the main sewer. Saul followed King Rat through the tunnels, and this time he paid attention to his location, his movements, he created a map in his head, he tracked himself.

The water rushed around them as drizzle hit the urban sprawl above and poured into their recesses. It slid around the bricks, transporting a sudden deluge of oil. The walls here were coated with fat, thick with translucent white residue.

"Restaurants," hissed King Rat as he plunged on, and Saul picked up his feet to avoid the slippery muck. He could smell it as he ran past, the stench of old frying and stale butter. It made him hungry. He ran a finger along the wall as he moved, sucked the glutinous mess he had picked up, and laughed, still amazed and excited by his hunger for old food.

Saul could hear things frantically escaping their path. The corridors were thick with rats, nibbling at the walls and the abundant edible detritus, fleeing as they approached. King Rat hissed and the path ahead of them cleared.

The two of them quit the underground, emerging into a Piccadilly backstreet, behind a great stinking pile of food waste, gastronomic effluent spewed out by London's finest.

They ate. Saul devoured a crushed concoction of old cold fish in some rich sauce, King Rat wolfing broken tiramisu and polenta cake.

And then up onto the roofs, King Rat ascending by a stairway of iron piping and broken brick. As soon as he had used it, its purpose became clear. Saul saw through vulgar reality, discerned possibilities. Alternative architecture and topography were asserting themselves. He followed without hesitation, slipping behind slate screens and running unseen over the skyline.

They barely spoke. Periodically, King Rat would stop and stare at Saul, investigate his motions, nod or indicate to him a more effective way to climb or hide or jump. They picked their way over banks and behind publishing houses, sly and invisible.

King Rat whispered obscure descriptions under his breath. He waved at the buildings they passed and murmured at Saul, hinted at the dark truth concerning the scratchmarks on the walls, the hollows that broke up lines of chimneys, the destination of the cats that scattered at their approach.

They wove in and out of central London, climbing, creeping, moving behind houses and between them, over offices and under the streets. Magic had entered Saul's life. It didn't matter anymore that he didn't understand.

This was a million miles from the tawdry world of conjuring tricks. His life was in thrall to another hex, a power which had crept into his police cell and claimed him, a dirty, raw magic, a spell that stank of piss. This was urban voodoo, fueled by the sacrifices of road deaths, of cats and people dying on the tarmac, an I Ching of spilled and stolen groceries, a Cabbala of road signs. Saul could feel King Rat watching him. He felt giddy with rude, secular energy.

They ate. They raced north beyond King's Cross and Islington, the light already hinting that it would soon leave. They passed Hampstead, Saul still not tired, gorging himself from time to time from backstreet rubbish bins. They skirted briefly into Hampstead Heath, out of the intricate paved world. They doubled back and found their way through small parks and along ignored bus routes to the borders of the financial world, the City.

Saul and King Rat stood behind a café on the corner of High Holborn and Kingsway. Away in the east was the forest of skyscrapers where so much money was made. A huge squat building stood before them, a financial Gormenghast, a hulk of steel and concrete which seemed to exude like a growth from the buildings around it. It was impossible to define where it began and ended.

Away in Ladbroke Grove, Pete peered over Natasha's shoulder. She indicated the tiny gray screen on her keyboard as the beats cascaded out of the speakers. She was tweaking the treble, playing with sounds. Pete's pale eyes flitted from screen to speaker to flute.

Fabian emerged from Willesden police station, cursing with disbelief. He slipped into patois, into American slang, into profanities.

"*Bambaclaht* motherfucker shithead *blahdclaht* white-bread pig chickenshit piss-artist *fuckers*."

He wrestled with his jacket and stormed toward the tube station. The police had arrived to pick him up without warning, had not let him take his bike.

He still muttered obscenities in his rage. He flounced up the hill to the underground.

Kay stood under Natasha's window, wondering what she had done to her music, where she'd got the flute sound from.

"I don't think he knows anything, sir," said Herrin. Crowley nodded in vague agreement. He was not listening. *Where are you, Saul?* he thought.

Who's the Ratcatcher? Saul wondered. *What wants to kill me?* But King Rat had mooched into melancholia after he had mentioned the name, and would say nothing more. Time enough for that, he had said. I don't want to scare you.

King Rat and Saul saw the sun turn red over the Thames. Saul found himself scrambling without fear up the vast wires of the Charing Cross railway bridge, looking out over the river. He hugged the metal. Trains wriggled below like illuminated worms.

South, and they careered secretly through Brixton, bore west for Wimbledon.

King Rat told more and more stories about the city as they passed. His assertions were wild and poetic, unreal, senseless. His tone was as casual as a cabby's.

The tour seemed to end quite suddenly, and they wound back toward Battersea. Saul was exhilarated. His body throbbed with exhaustion and power. *The city's mine*, he thought. He felt headstrong and intoxicated.

They came to a manhole in a deserted car park and King Rat stood aside. Saul wiped the dust from the metal disc. He fumbled with it, pushed his fingers around it. He felt strong.

His muscles were taut from the continual effort of the day, and he rubbed them in a motion that would have been narcissistic were it not for his obvious amazement. He twisted at the metal, felt his pores open with sweat and dirt then clog them, invigorating him.

The cover squealed momentarily and burst from its housing.

Saul barked in triumph and ducked into the darkness.

The music coming from Natasha's window was by Hydro, Fabian realized. He had calmed somewhat in the time it had taken for him to reach Ladbroke Grove. The sky boiled in time to the beats.

He hammered on the door. Natasha came to him, opening the door, her small grin frozen by his scowl.

"Tash, man, you ain't going to fucking believe it. Just keeps getting weirder."

She stood aside for him. As he came up the stairs he heard Kay's laconic assertions.

" . . . go down there once or twice a month, you know, and all Goldie and shit and them come there sometimes . . . Hey, Fabian, whassup man?"

Kay sat on the edge of the bed and peered up at him. Pete sat somewhat stiffly in a chair brought in from the kitchen.

Kay's amiable face was devoid of concern, blind to Fabian's mood. He sat with the same vague, open smile while Natasha caught up and entered the room. Pete was clearly uncomfortable, but he sat with his eyes unblinking on Fabian until Natasha arrived.

Fabian paused before speaking.

"I just spent the afternoon with the fucking pigs dem. They been giving me serious shit for nuff time, all fucking day, 'What can you tell us about Saul?' I told the motherfuckers time and fucking again, I don't know *shit*."

Natasha sat cross-legged on the mattress.

"They still think Saul did in his dad?"

Fabian laughed theatrically.

"Oh, Tash, man, no no no, not anymore, that's *nothing*, that's the least of anyone's worries." He sucked his teeth and pulled a battered newspaper out of his bag, waved it in front of them. The story was thumbed, the ink smeared. "You won't get much from that," he said as they tracked it with their eyes. "Only the bare bones. Lemme give you the real deal.

"Saul's gone. He escaped."

Fabian laughed unpleasantly at Kay's and Natasha's dumbfounded expressions. He pre-empted their exclamations.

"Not yet, man, there's more. Two police got killed at Saul's dad's flat, smashed up bad. And it looks . . . they reckon Saul did it. They're fucking *bananas* to find him. They'll come for you all, your turn soon. With all the fucking questions."

No one spoke.

The strains of Hydro were alone in filling the room.

TEN

King Rat was gone.

Saul brooded. He felt gorged on the supernatural and surreal.

He was crouched behind King Rat's throne. He had lain down there after the epic journey around London, sated and exhausted. That night he had oozed in and out of sleep and when he awoke, King Rat had gone.

Saul had risen and meandered around the room. He listened to the sound of dripping and distant howls.

King Rat had pinned a grubby piece of paper to the throne.

BACK SOON, it said. STAY PUT.

Alone, Saul felt unreal.

It was difficult to believe that he existed independently of King Rat, that King Rat was not a figment of his imagination, or Saul of his. Saul felt the stirrings of panic.

Alone, he was suddenly sick of King Rat's evasion. *What was the Ratcatcher?* he wanted to know. King Rat would not say. Their run across the city had been largely silent. With King Rat by his side, Saul had acquiesced, was complicit in the cover-up; he had been busy listening to the rat in him wake up.

But alone, he realized that it had been a long time since he had thought of his father's death. That he had been remiss in his mourning. His father's death was the fulcrum. Understand that and he would know what wanted to kill him, he would know why the rats would not obey their king.

With King Rat by his side, Saul had seen a new city. The map of London had been ripped up and redrawn according to King Rat's criteria. Alone, Saul was suddenly afraid that the city no longer existed.

Stay put? he thought. *Fuck that.*

Saul climbed out of the room and into the sewer.

Wind swept through the tunnels. Saul stood perfectly still and listened. He could not hear King Rat anywhere. He replaced the door to the hidden exit and moved gingerly away.

As he left the side tunnel which concealed the ways in and out of the throne room, the strong smell of King Rat's piss dissipated. Three rats hovered outside the tunnel, moving nervously, regarding him. He was unafraid but uncertain. He stopped and watched.

One of the three scampered forward a little and shook its head in a shockingly human motion.

Saul took off through the sewers, trembling with trepidation. Alone, the sewer was a different world from the one that King Rat had shown him, but Saul was not afraid. He walked through an olfactory patchwork, and the smells of piss told him stories. The rat who pissed here was aggressive and quick to anger; the one who pissed here was a follower; the one here ate too much, and his favorite food was chicken.

Saul could feel the city above him. He felt lines and directions pull at him. He followed the geomantic tugging.

From behind him, Saul heard a pattering. He turned, and in the gray non-light he saw three rats following him. He stopped still and watched them. They halted six feet from him and shifted, without taking their eyes from him. As he watched two more rats jumped from a pipe that jutted into the tunnel, and joined their fellows.

Saul backed up a little and the rats followed, keeping their distance. One of them squeaked loudly and the others joined in, a discordant cacophony which was taken up throughout the tunnels nearby. Small feet scampered from all directions toward him. The squealing reverberated around Saul's head.

More rats began to froth around him, out of the side tunnels and the surrounding dark. They came in twos and threes and tens, and although he did not fear them the sheer number was overwhelming. There was no light to glint off the hundreds of eyes which ringed him; they remained only little points of blackness in the general gloom, foci in the simmering mass of bodies which had filled the tunnel around him.

The squealing continued. It filled his head.

Suddenly, through his trepidation Saul felt a burst of excitement. He was confused by the sensation, it felt alien and out of place. And he realized that it was not his excitement at all, but that of the rats, that he understood their shrill communication, that he could feel what they felt.

He was awash with vicarious emotions.

Saul trembled and turned. There was nothing to distinguish what was before him from what was behind, everywhere was filled with the tiny eyes and bodies of the rats. The rats' voices were tremulous, cosseting, pleading.

Saul fled the pressure of the sound, flooded by panic. He turned and leapt over the mass of bodies, which parted under him, little islands of clear sewer appearing under his feet as he landed, tails being whisked out of the way. The voices were suddenly plaintive. They followed him.

Saul ran through the tunnels and the rats scampered after him. Ahead of him he saw a wall-mounted ladder. He leapt up, caught it. The rats jumped, scratching at the bottom rail. Saul felt a surge of relief as he looked down into their inscrutable faces.

He climbed and forced open the metal cover, peeping out through the crack. The exit was fringed with high grass. Saul climbed out of the depths and emerged in a hollow between shadowy bushes. He was in a deserted park. Above the distant hum of traffic there were closer sounds of birds. Saul saw water before him, a twisted lake with islands.

Trees framed his field of vision. He saw a shape over the arboreal boundary: a huge gilded dome surmounted with a shaving of crescent moon. London's central mosque, burnished by the streetlamps. To the south he saw the thin stiletto of Telecom Tower. He was in Regent's Park.

Saul circled the boating lake and slipped silently through the hedgerows and trees and railings.

Saul clambered out into the dark city.

He walked south to Baker Street. Lights waved wildly over the faces of the buildings as cars swung by. Headlights pinned him in their glare as a battered van swept toward him and past. Saul's heart raced for a long time after it had gone.

He turned onto Marylebone Road.

People bore down on him from all directions. It took him a moment to realize that they also moved away on past him, that they were simply walking along the street. Saul's breath shook a little as he exhaled. He pushed his hands into his pockets and set off west.

The first man to pass him was dressed in a blazer and jeans, his rugby shirt tucked in, cuddling his distended belly. He glanced momentarily at Saul before his eyes flickered back ahead of him.

Look at me! Saul shouted in his head. *I'm a rat! Can you tell? Can you smell?* The man must have detected the stench which hung around Saul's clothes, but was it so much worse than that which colored the passing of a drunk? The man did not turn to investigate Saul, who stopped and stared after him. He turned and gazed at the next person approaching him, a young Asian woman in a short tight dress. She smoked as she passed him. She did not spare him a glance.

Saul laughed, giddy. He was passed from behind by a short black man, from in front by a group of singing teenagers, and then a very tall man with glasses, from behind by a man in a suit who walked, then jogged, then walked to his destination.

No one minded Saul.

Ahead of him the broken stream of night traffic rose, cut across Edgware Road. It returned briefly to earth then rebounded, flying again. This was the Westway, the vast raised road which swept above London. A thousand tons of impossibly suspended asphalt, it soared off over Paddington and Westbourne Grove, with the city spattered out forever on all sides. In the west, over Latimer Road, it twisted into an intricate mess of raised ramps and exits. It extricated itself from this tangle and continued, finally returning to earth outside Wormwood Scrubs prison.

Saul stared at the Westway. It passed Ladbroke Grove station, where Natasha lived. The rules of the city no longer concerned him. The prohibition against pedestrians on the Westway did not apply to rats.

He ducked between the sparse cars and scampered onto the central reservation, racing up the incline, skirting the barrier with vehicles buzzing past him on both sides.

Below him he heard faint shouts from the mustard-colored estates. Dirty winking lights swept away from him. The drivers could not see him. He was a dark figure, utterly inured to the cold, his back bent, his arms grasping the barriers, pulling himself along. He moved like a cartoon villain on speed, a fast, exaggerated skulking.

Four great squat blocks reached up like stubby fingers around the Westway: brown tower blocks overlooking him with uneven points of light. The sound of traffic was a rhythmic, constant crescendo, flows without ebbs, never dying away.

Isolated in the center of this wide road, Saul could not see the streets below him. He could not gaze into windows or over the edge of the Westway at late-night walkers. He was alone with the anonymous cars and the horizon. The whole city had become horizon punctuated by fat towers.

To his left, the raised tracks of the Hammersmith and City tube line shadowed the Westway, only a few feet away. A train rattled past. With a rush of adrenaline, Saul pictured himself racing across the road and leaping out, catching it as it went by and straddling it like a rodeo rider, but he felt a sudden, certain intimation that he could not make that jump, not yet, and he stood still as the train headed on to Ladbroke Grove.

He followed its passage on the Westway until he could see Ladbroke Grove station hovering in the air to his left. It was so close that he could probably leap across onto the platform itself. Saul peered into the headlights to his right, and bundled himself across the road, passing like a discarded coat in the wind before the windscreens of startled drivers. He flattened himself against the barrier and leaned over.

Just beyond the station, Ladbroke Grove still throbbed with the beats of ghetto-blasters. A group of youth leaned, studiously cool, outside the closed Quasar building. They did their best to intimidate the passers-by. Late-night grocers leaned out of their doors and chatted to each other, to customers, to the mini-cab drivers. The streets did not throng, but they were hardly empty. From his precarious hide, Saul watched.

Unnoticed he clambered over the barrier and held it behind his back, leaning out over the streets. He enjoyed his own insouciance.

It was an easy jump to the drainpipe opposite, barely four feet, and he accomplished it without a sound. He descended to the wedge of low roofing between the station and the raised road, and slid into the Westway's looming shadow. He clambered over mildewed eaves. *Three days ago,* he thought as he jumped to the ground, *I was heavy and human. And now,* he thought as he moved out of the graffitied darkness toward Ladbroke Grove itself, *I'm rat and I can travel how I like. I woke up so fast.*

He made no effort to hide himself, even swaggering a little, and the groups of young men who clotted the pavement eyed him but let him pass, their noses wrinkling in his wake. He walked through conversations in accented English, in Arabic and in Portuguese.

He turned into Bassett Road and trotted up to Natasha's house. Her lights were off. He cursed and turned on his heel, pacing away to a tree opposite her window. He leaned against it and folded his arms, debating whether or not to wake her.

Saul had no illusions. He could never go back, he had become a rat. There was no way into that world again. But he had lived there once and he missed his friends.

As he stood trying to make up his mind, a slouching figure made its way down the street. With a sudden thrill, Saul recognized the stumbling gait. As the man approached Natasha's house and slowed, Saul cupped his hands over his mouth and hissed, "Kay."

Kay jumped and looked all around him in confusion. Saul hissed again. Kay stared straight at him for a moment and panned his eyes around, comically nervous.

Saul stepped out of the cover of the tree.

"Jesus, Saul man, you gave me a heart attack!" said Kay as he slumped with relief. "You were fucking *invisible* under that tree, and your voice has gone all weird . . . " He stopped short suddenly, shook his head and put his hands to his face.

"Shit, man!" he hissed, looking wildly around him. "What's gone on? How the fuck are you? I just heard about all your shit! Jesus! What's happened?"

Saul had reached him, and he slapped his shoulder and gripped his hand.

"Seriously, Kay, you wouldn't fucking believe it. I'm not fobbing you off, man, it's just . . . I don't even understand it myself."

Kay's face had screwed up.

"What is that stink, man? Is that you? I mean no offense, man, but . . . "

"I'm . . . hiding out."

"Where? The fucking sewers?" Saul said nothing and Kay's eyes widened. "Fuck me! You *aren't*? I wasn't *serious* . . ." Saul cut him off.

"Yeah, well, you heard about me getting out of the cell? I got to hide, man, the police think I killed my dad."

Kay stared at him for a moment.

Saul was aghast. "No I fucking didn't. Jesus, do you have to ask me that?"

All the talk of chase and crime and capture was making him nervous, and he backed into the darkness under the tree, pulling Kay with him.

"So what are you doing?" said Kay.

"Oh . . . " Saul was vague. "I've got to find something to prove I didn't do it." He could not explain that he could never go back.

"What about the two cops?" Saul stared at Kay blankly. "The ones who bought it in your flat."

Saul stared at him in mounting horror.

"Didn't you *know*?"

"So what fucking happened?" Saul shook his lapels. Kay backed away, wrinkling his nose.

"I don't know, I don't know. Fabian came up to Tash's waving a newspaper around. The police have been interviewing him all day, said the two watching your flat got beat up and died. They've got you pegged for it, man."

Kay had no malice. He could see that Saul knew nothing of the crime, and felt only concern, no more suspicion.

"Do you . . . know . . . do you know who . . . " he continued.

"No, but I think I know someone who does. *Shit!*" Saul ran his hands through his hair. "Shit, they'll be going ballistic for me now! Shit!"

He's going to tell me, he thought, overcome with rage. *No more petulant silences. When I find King Rat he's got to tell me who's doing this and why, and fuck all this fobbing me off.*

He turned back to Kay.

"What's going on, man? Why you here?"

Kay pointed up the road.

"I was in the pub with Tash and Fabe and this geezer Tash has started cutting some tracks with. It's a lock-in . . . we're all talking about you, man." He grinned weakly. "I realized I left my bag at Tash's, and she give me her keys. I'm going back in a minute. You want to come?" Saul hesitated and Kay began to urge him. "Come on, man, everyone's worried fucking *sick* over you, man. Fabe's terrible."

Saul thought of Fabian and felt a wave of nostalgia. His friendships felt shockingly distant. He wanted to come to the pub, but he was suddenly terrified. He had nothing in common with these people anymore, though he wanted them desperately; he missed them. What could he say to them, tell them? And the police . . . they were already questioning them. After this latest killing, could he risk incriminating them?

"I . . . can't, Kay. I'm wanted, man, and I can't be hanging around in pubs and stuff. I got to keep moving. But . . . will you tell them that I'm missing them and I promise I'll try to see them. And Kay . . . tell them if they don't hear from me for a bit they can't worry . . . I'm sorting things out. OK? Will you tell them that?"

"Are you sure you won't come back?"

Saul shook his head.

Kay acquiesced with a sideways nod. "So . . . at least tell me what's going *on*. How the fuck d'you get out of prison?"

Saul even laughed a little.

"It was only a cell, and . . . I really can't explain now. I'm really sorry."

"How are you looking after yourself?"

"Kay . . . I can't, alright? Please stop, man. I can't explain it."

"But are you OK?" Kay was concerned. "You don't sound all that good. Like I say, your voice is all . . . weird, and you smell . . . like . . . "

"I *know*, but I can't talk about it. I promise I'm looking after myself. I have to go, man. I'm sorry. Give them all my big love." He touched him briefly on the shoulder and walked into the dark, turning to wave.

Kay stood under the tree, waving back. His eyes peered intently as Saul left the circle of shadow and found other darkness beside the front walls of houses.

"Take care, man," Kay said, too loud, from behind him.

Saul was lost to his sight.

Kay stood for a moment under the tree before walking slowly to Natasha's front door and letting himself in. He was deeply confused. Something was obviously very wrong with Saul, but he could not tell what. The man had turned into some kind of Ninja, for one thing; walk five feet away from him and he turned invisible. And his voice . . . husky and somehow . . . *close up*.

It had unnerved Kay, made him a little afraid. It was clear that Saul did not know anything about the dead policemen, but Kay found himself wondering whether he was somehow involved without knowing it. There was certainly a touch of the psychopath about him tonight: his eyes all dark, his voice and manner intense, and that smell . . . ! The man must be living in pigshit. Could he really be dossing in the sewers? How would you even get into them?

He was afraid for his friend.

He found his bag in the unlit sitting room and left the flat, locking the door behind him. He was eager to tell the others of his meeting. At least Saul was . . . well alive, if not OK.

He stepped out into the street and turned left, still shaking his head in confusion. Something emerged from a patch of darkness behind him and moved in fast. Kay heard nothing. Metal twirled briefly and something long and hard cracked him on the back of his head. Kay emitted a gasp of air as he fell forward, was caught, dead-weight, hanging like a corpse, before he hit the pavement.

Blood welled up and dribbled onto his bag, trickling inside, staining the covers of records by Ray Keith and the Omni Trio.

ELEVEN

Saul saw the fat pillars of the Westway loom out at him again.

He turned right, skirting the great dark thoroughfare, wandering slowly west. He did not know where to turn. He turned his eyes to the ground, seeking a manhole. Perhaps he should hide himself from view, seek out King Rat again. He did not know if he could find his way back through the sewers to the throne room. He did not want to see the rats. They had unnerved him with their pleading. They wanted something of him.

A few late walkers passed him by. Saul wanted to stop, to sit and think for a while, to eat. He was not tired. He thought suddenly of the policemen who had died in his flat, and he winced.

He was gravitating toward the tangled concrete of the Westway's mid-air junction, a confusion of sweeping curves which hung above the earth like an imminent threat. Below the skeins of steel and tarmac the council had provided enclosures for basketball and football, a climbing wall and chin-up bars. During the day the area was full of the shouts of young players oblivious to the concrete above and around them, swooping in all directions with functional grandeur, a found stadium occluding direct light, obscuring the sky.

Saul wandered into the darkness between the pitches. He looked up at the underside of the Westway itself. The traffic above sounded very far away.

He meandered into the passageways between chain-link fences and football fields. The wind was still under the roadway. He stood and listened to it buffet the edges of the secluded ground.

There was another sound.

A faint, quick scampering echoed quietly between the pillars.

Saul turned and moved his head sharply as something circled him. He backed away. Panic bubbled up inside him. *The Ratcatcher!* he thought, and ran for the faint glow of the streetlamps.

He spun around on his heel, desperately looking for a way out of the darkness. Something flitted across his vision, a black body that swung down from the shadows above him, from the crevices in the underside of the Westway. It swung around him, too quick for his eye to follow, free of gravity's constraints, moving in all directions through the air. Saul's breath came fast as he turned and ran.

Something sailed out of the air above him and flew overhead in a perfect parabola, with a grace and speed that eclipsed any gymnast or circus performer alive. The dark mass curved over the Earth and came to rest, landing lightly twenty feet in front of him. The crouching form sprang upright, splaying legs and arms suddenly like a jack-in-the-box.

A tall, fat man swayed before Saul, his arms and legs spread wide as if anticipating an embrace.

Saul braked and backed away, turning suddenly and running back into the darkness from which he had come. He tried to remember to hide, to become a rat, but terror had frozen his cunning.

As he ducked behind a tennis court, the fleeting shape passed, flying over the net, and the man was there before him again, arms outstretched. A thin cord suspended from somewhere above recoiled from the swing, and brushed against Saul as it returned along its flight path.

Saul changed direction and disappeared behind a climbing frame. He heard something hissing behind him. Saul gasped as he ran, his rat-strength pushing him faster than he had ever moved before. His skin crawled with fear. Ahead of him he glimpsed threadbare trees. There was a thin gap between two of the wire fences, beyond which was the garden to a housing estate.

He raced for the slit and careered along it, making very little sound, when something caught his ankle and he swung like a felled tree toward the concrete.

He was yanked away from the ground before he hit and he hung for a moment in the air. Thin ropes were stretched across his path, tied to the chain links on either side. One had swept away his foot, and another had caught him across the chest. He cursed frantically and struggled to stand, tugging at the rope which had somehow entangled itself around his ankle. He plowed forward and saw spindly shapes before him: more ropes, a thicket of them across his path. How had he not seen them before?

He struggled to climb over them, but they confused him; some tied so loosely they came away in his hand and wrapped themselves around him, others so tight they vibrated like a bass string as they repulsed him. He fell again, caught in this cat's cradle. He could not move. He hung suspended at a forty-five-degree angle, head downwards, four feet from the ground.

Saul heard a footstep behind him. He jerked his head, disentangling himself frantically, swivelled in the midst of his mesh to face the way he had come, his back to the morose shrubs he had sought.

The man stood at the entrance to the little passageway.

Light from the far-off lamps struggled to illuminate him, glinting faintly on his skin. He wore nothing but a pair of black cut-off shorts on his lanky legs. He seemed unaffected by the cold. The man had very dark skin and a massive belly jutting over his belt, but arms and legs that were ridiculously long and thin, every muscle standing firm with every movement. His stomach was distended, globular but taut as a bubble. It hardly rippled as he moved slowly toward Saul. Saul saw a thick coil of filthy white rope wound around his left shoulder.

"Don't give me no more trouble, pickney, or me gwan mash you up."

The voice was scratchy and sharp, vibrant with Caribbean intonation. It sounded close in his ear, as King Rat's did.

The man moved in little bursts. He paced quickly forward a few feet, then stopped to investigate Saul, moved forward again. As he approached, he unwound the rope from his shoulder.

Saul shook violently to free himself from the tangles of rope, seemed only to pull them tighter around him. He began to screech.

The man was upon him, fetched him a vicious slap across the cheek that stopped Saul's cry instantly. His head rocked. He was dizzy and his face throbbed.

"Me tell you fe shut your *mouth*, bwoy!" The man kissed his teeth.

Saul's head wobbled forward and he blinked hard. The man was bending over him. Saul was deeply afraid. He put up his hands, tried to push them through the ropes to ward off the attack he was sure was coming. He thrashed in his bonds and opened his mouth to scream again.

The man reached down as fast as a snake and pushed his fingers into Saul's mouth. Saul tried to bite down, but the man spread his fingers and with inhuman strength forced Saul's mouth open. Saul's captor tugged at the rope draped over his shoulder with his free hand. He wound it around Saul's head once, twice, stuffed it into his mouth like a gag.

He muttered to himself in patois.

As he spoke, the man yanked the rope tight and wound it expertly around Saul's head again, obscuring the lower half of his face. Saul mewed frantically from behind this mask as his eyes darted from side to side.

The man pulled at Saul's arms, twisting the rope around them and pulling tight, securing them behind Saul's back. He tugged Saul free of the little alley. Saul stumbled and ran forward till his feet were jerked out from under him and he fell. He had reached the end of the rope which bound him. He slid back across the concrete. The man was reeling him in.

Saul was pulled to his feet and turned to face his captor. With his mouth blocked, Saul breathed frantically through his nose, sputtering flecks of snot onto his bindings. Black eyes stared into his own, which were wet with fear.

"You come with me fe see ratty. There some bad obeah loose now."

He twirled the rope suddenly over Saul's head like a film cowboy. The coils slid down through the air and wound around Saul's body. The man spun him on the spot, tightening the bonds, letting out slack to constrict him like a top. He bent and ran the rope on down Saul's legs, until his whole body was obscured in a shroud of grubby white cord.

Only Saul's eyes could move. He could feel a hammering in his arms and legs as his heart struggled to push blood past the obstructions cutting into his flesh.

The man bit through the rope and tied the end at Saul's feet. He stood before Saul and looked down at him, nodded.

"No more nonsense and hollering now, innit?"

Saul began to pitch forward but the man caught him and, to Saul's sudden horror, rolled him through the air and onto his back. He pulled Saul into position as effortlessly as King Rat had done. Saul felt like fluff. The man took more rope from his shoulder and wrapped it around his captive several times, attaching him more firmly. Saul was helpless on those broad flat muscles, his eyes facing backward. His legs were twisted up into a tight bend. He was suspended from the man's shoulders and waist, the rope cutting into his captor's skin, seemingly painlessly. Saul bobbed in a terrifying and undignified fashion as his abductor raced suddenly through the darkness.

He rushed through the underworld below the Westway at a rate of knots, his route violent and oscillating. The hidden byways receded before Saul's eyes. The man beneath him lurched suddenly and Saul saw the dark horizon drop around him. They were airborne. Saul's eyes widened and he gave a muffled yell, spit slithering down his chin behind the ropes.

They flew through the air, paused and swung backward, then around, a pendulum ten feet from the ground. They were suspended, clinging to a rope, Saul realized. The man began to climb.

He moved easily, the curve of his back suggesting that he was using both feet and hands. The pace was utterly smooth. The sports grounds disappeared below them and, as they swung from side to side, vistas of West London peeked in and out of Saul's vision. The occasional roar of traffic was closer now.

They reached the top of the rope. Saul was facing away from the highway, out over badly lit sidestreets. The man clung to the barrier and scampered along the side of the Westway. Saul's stomach drummed with fear. There was nothing below his feet. He saw the streets below curve a little closer to him, and he saw the dim light catch on a filament, a thread passing up from the chimney of a house fast approaching.

They were opposite the house now, and he caught another glimpse of the thin line of light. It was close by, twisting toward him.

Suddenly he was falling.

But the ground stopped rushing toward him, and he bobbed in the air. He was facing directly down, the Westway growling a few feet above and behind him. The filament he had seen was another rope, tied at one end to the roof and another to the railings of the great road above. The man was descending the rope now, headfirst, hand over hand, bouncing unnervingly as he slid fast toward the intricate darkness of the roofscape.

Saul prayed that the rope was strong.

And then they were down, and Saul was swung around. He heard a loud snap, and when the man turned again Saul saw that he had broken the rope behind them, obscured their passing.

They were off over the tops of houses, another raised race across London. The man swung himself around obstacles, scampering over the slates even faster than King Rat.

Blocks fleeted away below them. Behind them Saul saw the monolithic Westway shrinking.

The man leapt forward and bounced perilously over a road that blocked his path. Saul realized with terror that they were on another rope tied horizontally between buildings, but this time moving *on top of it*, tightrope-walking faster than Saul could run.

The air was buffeted out of him by the quick motion of his captor and the constricting ropes on his chest. Below them Saul saw a solitary walker moving nervously through the backstreets, oblivious to the mad funambulism above him.

With a jump the dark man left the rope, landed on the opposite roof, snapped the trail behind them.

They moved like this at a crazy speed over the streets, traversing a network of ropes already laid. They passed through grassland and into an estate, leaping along flat roofs and scampering insanely fast down sheer bricks. Saul was convulsed with terror, unable to see what his captor was doing.

They raced down a bank of scrub onto a railway line, and rushed along the wooden sleepers. Saul watched the tracks curve away behind them.

Again their passage was interrupted as the dark man climbed the side of a bridge that passed over the railway and the canal that skirted it. They swept through an industrial estate, a collection of low, shabby buildings and motionless forklift trucks. Saul was hypnotized by the breakneck progress over the houses. He had been caught, he did not know by whom, and he did not know what was to happen to him.

The noise of the city became oddly distant. They had entered a yard full of ruined cars crushed flat, piles of them like geological features: strata of old Volvos and Fords and Saabs. The cars teetered around them, leaving only narrow alleys through which to pass.

They wound through these walkways.

Suddenly the man stopped and Saul heard another's voice: a strange, vain, musical voice colored with a European accent he could not specify.

"You did find him, then."

"Yeah, man. Caught the lickle bleeder down south from here, not far you know."

There was no more speaking. Saul suddenly felt the ties that bound him slipping, and he fell in a heap to the dust. He was still wrapped tight in his own rope swaddling. The fat man picked him up and carried him in his arms like a bride.

Saul caught a glimpse of the newcomer: thin and very pale, with red hair, a sharp hawkish nose and wide eyes. Saul was borne toward his destination, a huge steel container like a vast skip ten feet high, over which loomed a yellow structure something like a crane.

His eyes flitted about as he was carried, he saw the cars all flattened around him, and he realized that this was a car-crusher, that the lid of the dark container would bear down on whatever was inside, and squeeze it, press it like a flower into two dimensions. And as he was borne inexorably toward it Saul's eyes widened in horror and he began to struggle, to shout through his gag.

He flopped pathetically in the man's arms, tried to roll out of his grip, but the man held him firm and kissed his teeth in disgust, did not break his stride, no matter how Saul emitted frantic humming protests and jack-knifed. The man hauled Saul over his shoulder, Saul staring for a moment into the insane-looking eyes of the redhead behind them. Saul was held, bending and unbending at the waist pathetically, till the tall man heaved him upwards and he sailed over the edge of the ominous gray container . . . hung silent and still for a moment . . . fell, passing into the shadow of its metal walls, feeling the air cool and still, slamming into the pitted floor.

He landed hard on the shards of metal and glass which littered the dark.

Only because he was a rat was he not unconscious or dead, he decided, as he lay moaning. He struggled to sit upright, trickles of blood discoloring the cords which held him. Something approached him, footsteps clanging on the metal floor, and he tried to turn, and fell again, banging his head, only to feel himself grabbed around the shoulders and pulled upright. He opened his eyes and stared into a face glaring balefully at his, a dark face, darker than the shadows in the deadly car-crusher, a face boiling with anger, teeth gritted hard, scoring lines around the mouth, and the familiar stink of old wet animals and rubbish made acrid with anger.

King Rat looked at him and spat in his face.

TWELVE

The spittle slid down around Saul's nose. His gaze was bouncing off the walls of the crusher, vibrating back and forth, trapped. King Rat stared at him unflinching and angry. Why was he angry, Saul wondered frantically, the thoughts crowding around each other in his head. What was happening? They'd both been caught by the Ratcatcher, that was why they were here, about to be crushed, so why was King Rat still? He wasn't trapped like Saul. Why did he not leap out of the container and save them, or flee?

With his breath fast and ugly in his ears, Saul saw the suspended weight of the lid hovering above them, hideous with potential energy, full of pent-up momentum. King Rat was trying to hold Saul's eyes, was muttering something, but in his panic Saul stared briefly at his uncle, then up at the lid, back down and up again, waiting for it to descend.

King Rat shook him and growled, a quiet bellow of rage.

"What by *damn* do you reckon you're *playing at*? Off I go for my constitutional, on the lookout for some victuals, leave you akip like a babe, and what happens? You up and *piss off*."

Saul shook his head frantically and King Rat impatiently yanked at the rope around his face, tearing it free. Saul sputtered, breathed deeply, spraying mucus and spit and a little blood at King Rat.

King Rat did not move, did not wipe himself clean.

Instead he slapped Saul in the face.

Saul felt so abused, so sore and bloodied, the sting of it was nothing to him, but his anger and confusion overflowed. He exhaled, and the breath turned into a long shout, a yell of incoherent frustration. He wriggled and felt his muscles bunch up against his bonds.

"What are you doing?" he yelled.

King Rat pushed his hand over Saul's mouth.

"Stow your parley, you little fucker. Don't come the misunderstood. Don't *ever* be fucking off on your tod, got it?" He was motionless, staring at Saul, pushing him hard with his hand, driving his point home. "Care to share the whys and wherefores of your little exhibition, eh?"

Saul's voice emerged muffled from behind King Rat's hand.

"I wanted to look about, that was all; wasn't looking for trouble. I've been learning, haven't I? No one saw me, and I climbed like . . . you would've been proud."

"Enough of your crap!" King Rat bellowed. "Trouble's got its eyes peeled for you, sonny. There's a roughneck out there wants you *dead*! Like I told you, you're wanted, you're prey, someone's out for your hide . . . and mine."

"So fucking tell me what's going on," spat Saul, suddenly jutting his chin into King Rat's face. There was a long silence. "You go on and on, talking in riddles like you think you stepped out of a fucking fable, and I don't have time to wait for you to tell me what the moral of it is! Something's after me? Fine. *What*? Tell me, explain to me what *the fuck* is going on, or shut up."

The silence returned, stretched out.

"He's right, rattymon. He have to know wha'appen. You can't keep him in the dark. He can't protect himself."

The voice of the man who had carried him from the Westway dropped from above, and Saul glanced up to see him crouched like a monkey on the corner of the car-crusher. As he watched, the redhead appeared, arriving suddenly next to the black man, with his legs dangling into the container, as if he had jumped up from below and landed perfectly on his bum.

"And who are *they*?" said Saul, jerking his head at the watchers. "I thought the Ratcatcher had caught me. I'm walking along and suddenly that geezer's got me trussed up, tripped up. I thought he was going to crush me in this thing."

King Rat did not look up at the men sitting on the rim above, even as one of them spoke.

"Not just Ratcatcher, you know, bwoy. The one want you, him the Ratcatcher and the Birdcatcher and the Spidercatcher and the Batcatcher and the Humancatcher and *all tings catcher*."

King Rat slowly nodded.

"So tell me," said Saul. "Listen to your mate. I need to fucking know. And get me out of these!"

King Rat reached into an inside pocket and pulled out a flick-knife. It emerged from its case with a *snikt*, and he shoved it under Saul's bonds and pulled. The ropes fell away. King Rat turned his head and paced to the far end of the container. Saul opened his mouth to speak, but King Rat's voice emerged from the darkness, pre-empting him.

"I want nary word fucking one to emerge from your gob, boy. I'll give you the whole spiel then, my old son, if that'll quell your hankering."

Saul could dimly see that he had turned to face him. The three men now faced him in a row: the two above—one squatting, one swinging his legs like a child—and the one below glowering in the corner.

Saul pushed the ropes away from him and backed into the opposite corner, pulled up his knees like protection for his brutalized body, listened.

"Meet my mates," said King Rat. Saul looked up. The man who had caught him was still motionless on his haunches.

"Me name Anansi, pickney."

"Me old China Anansi," interjected King Rat. "The gent who most likely saved your skin from the ruffian out there on the hunt for you."

Saul knew the name Anansi. He remembered sitting in a hushed circle, surrounded by other tiny bodies all sucking lukewarm milk out of tiny bottles, listening to his Trinidadian teacher tell the class about Anansi the spider. He could not remember any more.

The redhead was standing now, balancing without effort on the thin metal edge. He gave an exaggerated bow, sweeping one arm out behind him. He wore suit trousers in burgundy, tightly pressed and perfect, a stiff white shirt and dark braces, a floral tie. His clothes were immaculate and stylish. Again he spoke in that peculiar accent, a composite of all the European intonations Saul could think of.

"Loplop presents Loplop," he said.

"Loplop, aka Hornebom, Bird Superior," said King Rat. "We go back a long way, not all of it friendly. When I saw you'd slung your hook, I called on this pair of coves. You put us to a lot of strife, sonny. And you want the story of the Ratcatcher."

"Spidercatcher," said Anansi softly.

"Birdcatcher," spat Loplop.

King Rat's voice held Saul still. King Rat settled back.

"We've all had our admirers, you know, your uncles 'Nans and Loplop and I. Loplop chased a painter for a while, and I was always partial to a snatch or two of verse. If you know some poesy you might know this story already, acos I told it once before to another, and he wrote it down for the Godfers—a child's story he called it. I didn't mind. He can call it what he wants. He knew it was for honest.

"I haven't always lived in the Smoke, you know. I've lived all over. I was here when London was born, but it was measly pickings for a long time, so I took my flock and jumped ship long time gone. Your ma was entertaining herself elsewhere while I bing a waste to Europa for a shufti with the faithful, going hell for leather over land in packs with me at the head, my coat sleek. One twitch of my tail and the massed ranks of Rattus went west, east, wherever I gave the word. We run through the dewse-a-vill, through the fields of France, the high-pads of Belge, through the flatlands near Arnhem, and on through to Germany—not that those were the names they used.

"Next thing you know we're looking around, bellies on the growl. We've found a place where John Barleycorn's been *most* generous . . . The crops are high and golden, ripe and ready and fit to burst. We took a Butcher's. 'Yes,' I says, 'this'll do,' and on we trog, slower now, on the skedge for a place to set us down.

"Through a forest, tight-clumped together under me the boss-man, afeared of nowt, on the hoof through lightmans and darkmans. By a river we found us a town, not too gentry a gaff, mind, but with silos that fair creaked at the seams, and knockabout houses with a hundred holes, nesting nooks, eaves and cellars, a hundred little corners for a knackered rat to rest a Crust.

"I gave the word. In we marched. The populace dropped their bags, gobsmacked and agog. Next thing they've lost their marbles, running around hither and thither, and letting loose with such a damned caterwauling . . . ! We were an impressive phalanx: we spewed in and didn't stop till the whole town was chock with me and my boys and girls. We herded the squealing civvies into the square, and they stood clutching their pathetic duds and children. We were bushed, been on the go a long time, but we pulled ourselves up proud in the sun and our teeth were magnificent.

"They tried to give us the heave-ho, flailing around with torches ablaze and paltry little shovels. So we bared our teeth, sank them in deep, and they ran screaming like yellow-bellied ponces, disappearing as quick as you like. We had the square to ourselves. I called the troops to order. 'Right,' I says, 'quick march. This town is ours. This is Year One: this is the Year of the Rat. Spread out, make your mark, set the stage, find your places, eat your fill, anyone gives you any gyp, send them to me.'

"An explosion of little lithe bodies, and the square's empty.

"Rats in the rub-a-dubs, the houses, the kazis, the dews-a-vill, the orchards. We gave them what for. I did walkabouts, with nary a word said, but all and sundry knew who ran things. Any burgher raised a hand against one of my own, I took them down. People soon clocked the rules.

"And that was how the rats came to Hamelin."

"Saul, Saul, you should've seen us. Good times, chal, the best. The town was *ours*. I grew *fat* and *sleek*. We fought the dogs and killed the cats. The loudest sound in that town was rats talking, chattering and making plans. The grain was *mine*, the gaffs were *mine*; the tucker they cooked, we took our cut *first*. It was all *mine*, my Kingdom, my finest hour. I was the King-pin, I made the rules, I was Copper and jury and Barnaby and, when occasion demanded, I was Finisher of the Law.

"It turned famous, our little town, and rats flocked to us, to join the little Shangri-La we put together, where we ruled the roost. I was the boss-man.

"Until that Ruffian, that bastard, that peripatetic fucking minstrel, that stupid tasteless shit with his ridiculous duds, the prancing nancy, until he strolled into town.

"First I knew of it, one of my girls tells me there's a queer cove with the mayor, furtive at the gates, dressed in a two-tone coat. 'Hallo,' says I, 'they're about to have a go. They think they've a trick up the sleeve.' I settled back to piss on their parade, and it all went a little sorry.

"There was a note.

"Music, something in the air. Another note, and I prick up my ears to hear what's going on. Little sleek brown heads appear from holes all over town.

"Then the third note sounds, and apocalypse begins.

"Suddenly I could hear something: a body scraping tripe from a bowl, a huge bowl. I could see it! I heard apples tumbling into a press, and my Plates start moving forward. I could hear someone leaving cupboards ajar, and I knew the jigger had been sprung on *the Devil's own pantry* . . . the door was wide open, and I could fair *sniff* the scran inside, and I had to find it, and I had *to eat it all.*

"I started forward and I could hear a rumble, a shaking, a scamper of a hundred million little feet and I saw the air around me heaving with my little minions, all shouting for joy. They could hear the food too.

"I do a leap from the gables into the Frog. Splashdown in a stream of rats, all my little boys and girls, my lovers and my soldiers, big and fat and small and brown and black and quick and old and slow and frisky and *all of them,* all of us after that *food.*

"And as I troop ravenous onward, I suddenly feel queer horror in my gut. I was using my nous, and I saw there wasn't no food where we were going.

" 'Stop,' I shrieks, and *no one listens.* They just bump my bum from behind to get past. 'Don't,' I yell, and that starving stream just parts around me, rejoins.

"I felt that hunger waxing, and I scamper over and sink me Hampsteads fast into the wood of a door, hard as you like, holding myself back with my good strong gob. My pegs are dancing, they want that music, that food, but my mouth's holding strong. I feel my mind go slack and I gnaw some more, locking my jaw . . . but disaster strikes.

"I take a bite from the door. My mouth snaps free and, before you can say knife, I'm in the stream of my subjects, my brainbox weaving in and out of hunger and joy for the tucker I can all but taste—and the despair, I'm King Rat, I know what's happening to me and my kind, and no one will listen. Something dire's in the offing.

"On we march, willy-nilly, and from the corner of my eye I can see the people leaning out the windows, and the bastards are clapping, cheering, giving it all that. We're trotting in time, all four legs stately and sharpish to that . . . *abominable* piping, tails swaying like metronomes.

"I can see where we're headed, a little journey to the suburbs I've taken more times nor I can think, on a beeline for the grain silos beyond the walls. And there behind the silos, bloated after the showers, hollering like the sea, roaring and pelting down through the dews-a-vill, wide and rocky, filthy with swirling muck and mud and rain, is the river.

"There by the bridge I catch sight of the swine playing his flute in his fatuous duds. His Loaf bobs up and down, and I clock a revolting grin all over his North while he plays. The first ranks of rats are at the bridge now, and I can see them troop calmly to the edge, nary a hint of disquiet, eyes still narrowed on that lovely mountain of scran they're headed for. I can see them getting ready and I'm screaming at them to stop, but I'm pissing in the wind, it's a done deal.

"They step off the stone walls of the bridge into the water.

"The most almighty cacophony of squeals starts up from below the bridge, but none of the sisters and brothers can hear it. They're still listening to the dance of the sugarplums and bacon rind.

"The next in line jump on their comrades, and more and more—the Fisherman's is seething. I can't bear it, I can hear the screams, every one a blade in my gut, my boys and girls giving up the ghost in the water, fighting to keep their Crusts over the waves, good swimmers all but not built for this. I can hear wails and keens as bodies are swept downriver, *and still my goddamn fucking legs keep moving.* I pull back through the ranks, trying to turn round, going a little slower than the others, feeling them pass me, and the squire on the bridge looks at me, that infernal flute still clamped to his gob, and he sees who I am. I can see him see I'm King Rat.

"And he smiles a little more, and bows to me as I march on past onto the bridge and into the river."

Loplop hissed and Anansi breathed something to himself. The three were locked into themselves, all staring ahead, all remembering.

"The Fisherman's was icy, and the touch of it cleared the

bonce of nonsense. Every splash was quick-echoed by a screech, a wail as my poor little minions fight to keep their I Supposes in the air, thinking *What the fuck am I doing here?* and busy dying.

"More and more bodies jumping in to join them, more and more fur becoming waterlogged, feeling the tug of the river, slipping below the caps, raking their claws every which way in panic, tearing each other's bellies and eyes, and dragging brothers and sisters into the freezing cold under the air.

"I kicked my pegs to get away. There was a frantic mass of us kicking up froth, an isle of rat bodies, fighting and killing to climb atop, the foundations dying and disappearing below.

"Water plugged my lugs. All I can hear is the in-out of my breath, panicked and disjointed, gulping and retching and breathing in bile. The waves are smashing me around, tossing me against rocks, and on all sides rats are dying in thousands and thousands. I can just make out the noise of the flute. It's stripped of magic here in the Fisherman's, just a whining noise. I can hear the splashes of more rats leaping in the water to die; it's endless and merciless. Screams and choking are everywhere; stiff little bodies bob past me like buoys in hell's harbor. This is the end of the world, I think, and the stinking water fills my lungs, and I sink.

"Everywhere are corpses.

"They move with the swell, and through my half-closed eyes I can just clock them, all around me, suspended under the water, above me as I sink and below me too, blobs of brown approaching. And there in the murk, as the last bubbles of air spew out of me, I can see the charnel house under the river, the killing fields, those sharp black rocks an abattoir for ratkind, pile upon pile of cadavers, little skinless babies and old gray males, fat matron rats and pugnacious youth, the fit, the ill, an endless mass of death shifting with the torrent above.

"And I alone stared this holocaust in the face."

Drowned rats seemed to hover before Saul as he listened. His ears pounded as if his lungs fought for air.

King Rat's voice came back, and the dead tone which had crept into his descriptions had gone.

"And I opened my eyes and said, 'No.'

"I kicked suddenly, and left that cataclysm behind. I didn't have no air, don't forget, so my lungs were screaming murder, whipping me one stroke for every heartbeat, and I climbed out of the quiet into the light, and I could hear the cries through the river above me, and I moved out and away, and finally pushed my face into the air.

"I sucked it in like an addict. I was eager.

"I turned my Crust and it was still going on, the deaths still continuing, but the spume was a sight lower by now and there was no more ratkind falling out of the sky. I saw the man with his flute walk away.

"He didn't see me watch him.

"And I decided, as I watched, that he had to die.

"I dragged myself out of the river, and laid myself down under a stone. The cries of the dying continued for a while, and then they went out, and the river swept all the evidence away behind it. And I lay and breathed and swore revenge for my Rat Nation.

"The poet called me a Caesar, who lived to swim across. But that wasn't my Rubicon. That was my Styx. I should've gone. I should be a drowned rat. Maybe I am. I've thought of that. Maybe I never made it, and maybe it's just hate that seeped into my bones that keeps me up and scrapping.

"I got some small satisfaction, the first part only, from the bastard sons and daughters of Hamelin. The stupid, stupid fuckers tried to put one over on the Piper and I had the pleasure of watching the gurning *cunts,* who'd clapped as we took our leave, screaming in the alleys, stuck like glue while their *Kinder* pranced away to the tune of the flute. And I had the small joy of smiling when the queer cove made the mountain split open for those little Godfers, and they skipped on in. Because those little Dustbins went to *hell,* and they hadn't even died, and they hadn't even done any wrong, and their bastard parents knew that.

"That was some pleasure, like I say.

"But it was that damnable minstrel himself I wanted. He was the real culprit. He's the one who has a certain *reckoning* due."

Saul shivered at the viciousness of King Rat's tone, but he stopped himself from remonstrating about the innocence of the children.

"He sucked all the birds out of the sky and taunted me, till I grew mad in my impotence." Loplop was speaking in the same dreaming tone as King Rat. "I fled to Bedlam, forgetting myself, thinking myself nothing but a madman who thought himself King of Birds. For a long time I rotted in the cage, till I remembered and burst away again."

"Him clear all the scorpion and my lickle pickneys from the palace in Baghdad. Him call me in with him piccolo, and my mind was gone, and him rough me, mash me up, hurt me bad. And all the lickle spiders them saw." Anansi spoke softly.

The three were emasculated, casually stripped of power by the Piper. Saul remembered the contempt, the spitting of the rats in the sewer.

"That's why the rats don't obey you," he murmured, looking at King Rat.

"When Anansi and Loplop were caught, some lived to see them suffer, saw Loplop lose his mind, saw Anansi tortured. They bore witness to the martyrdom of the monarchs. It was plain for every Jack with eyes to see.

"My rats, my troops, they saw nothing. Every one was taken. And drowning leaves no marks, no scars or stripes to illustrate engagement. Word spread to the towns and dews-a-vill around that King Rat had run, left his people to the swollen river. And they dethroned me. Stupid shits! They've not got the nous to live without me. It's *anarchy*, no control. We should *run* the Smoke, and instead it's chaos. And I've been without my crown more nor half a thousand years."

When he heard this, Saul thought of the entreating, pleading rats who circled him below the pavements. He said nothing.

"Anansi and Loplop, they still rule, bloodied maybe, bowed and cowed, but they've got their kingdom. *I want mine.*"

"And if," said Saul slowly, "you can defeat the Piper, you think the rats will come back to you."

King Rat was silent.

"He roams around the world," said Loplop flatly. "He has not been here for a hundred years, since he cast me into the bird-cage. I knew he had returned when I called all my birds to me a night not long ago, and they did not come. There is only one thing can make them deaf to my command: the damnable pipe."

"Sometimes the spiders rush away from me like them do another's bidding. The Badman back in town, fe true, and him want the rattymon bad this time."

"None's ever escaped, you see, sonny, except me," said King Rat. "He let Loplop and Anansi go, after shaming them, letting them clock who's the bossman, he reckons. But me, he wanted my hide. *I'm the one that got away.* And for seven hundred years he's been trying to make good his mistake. And when he found I had a nephew, he came looking for you. He's on the skedge for you now. Anything to square accounts."

Anansi and Loplop looked at each other, looked down at Saul.

"What is he?" breathed Saul.

"Him greed," said Anansi.

"Covetousness," said Loplop.

"He exists to own," said King Rat. "He has to suck things in to him, always, which is why he's so narked at me for having pulled a disappearing trick. He's the spirit of narcissism. He's to prove his worth by guzzling all and sundry in."

"Him can charm anything," said Anansi.

"He's congealed hunger," said Loplop. "He's insatiable."

"He can choose, see?" said King Rat. "Will I call the rats? The birds? The spiders? Dogs? Cats? Fish? Reynards? Minks? Kinder? He can ring anyone's bell, charm anything he fancies.

Just choose and he plays the right tune. Owt he chooses, Saul, except nor one thing.

"He can't charm you, Saul.

"You're rat and human, more and less than each. Call the rats and the person in you is deaf to it. Call to the man and the rat'll twitch its tail and run. He can't charm you, Saul. You're double trouble. You're my deuce, Saul, my trump card. An ace in the hole. You're his worst nightmare. He can't play two tunes at once, Saul. He can't charm you.

"No, you he just wants to kill."

No one spoke. Three pairs of unclear eyes transfixed Saul.

"But no need to panic, sonny. Things are going to change around here," King Rat suddenly spat. "See, my mates and me are pissed off. We've had enough. Loplop owes the Piper for his brain-box that was Tea-Leafed off him. Anansi here got tortured, still feels it sore in all his pegs—and in front of his own people. And me . . . I owe the fucker because he stole my nation and I want it back."

"Revenge," said Loplop.

"Revenge," said Anansi.

"Revenge is right," said King Rat. "Piper-man fucker better steel himself for some animal magic."

"The three of you . . . " said Saul. "Is that how many there are? To take him."

"There are others," said Loplop, "but not here, not to do the job. Tibault, King of the Cats, he's trapped in a nightmare, a story told by a man called Yoll. Kataris, Queen Bitch, who runs with the dogs, she's disappeared, no one knows where."

"Mr. Bub, Lord of the Flies, him a shifty murderer and me can't work with him," said Anansi.

"There are others but we're the ones, the hard core, the sufferers, who've scores to settle," said King Rat. "We're bringing the war back to him. And you can help us, sonny."

THIRTEEN

What woke Kay was the drumbeat of blood in his head. Each stroke that landed on the back of his skull sent vibrations of pain through the bone.

His eyes cracked a seal of rheum. He opened them and saw nothing but black. He blinked, tried to focus on the vague geometry he could glimpse in the shadows. He felt that something stretched away in front of him.

Kay was freezing. He groaned and raised his head, a motion accompanied by a crescendo of aches, rolled his neck and tried to move. His arms hurt and he realized they were stretched out above him, held fast, and stripped of clothing. He opened his eyes more and saw coils of thick dirty rope around his wrists, disappearing into the gloom above him. He was suspended, his weight dragging him hard, pulling the skin of his armpits taut.

He tried to twist his body, to investigate his position, but he was suddenly constrained, his feet refusing to obey. He shook his groggy head and looked down. He saw that he was naked, his cock shriveled and tiny in the cold. He saw the same rope around his ankles, spreading his legs. He was caught tight in a petrified star-jump, he was an X hovering in the dark, the pain in his wrists and ankles and arms beginning to register. Gusts of wind pulled at him, raised goosebumps.

Kay winced, blinked hard, tried to work out where he was, lowered his eyes again to his feet. As the cold air began to cut through the muck of pain in his head he became aware of the dim diffuse light around him. Shapes clarified in the shadow below his dangling toes: sharp lines, concrete, bolts, wood. Railway tracks.

Kay's head wobbled up. He tried to throw it behind him, to see over his shoulder.

He gave a yell of shock which bounced back and forward in its enclosed environs.

Behind him, illuminated by half-hearted little bulbs dribbling beige light, stretched an underground platform covered in dust and small pieces of rubbish. The darkness before him stopped sharp above Kay's head, where the bricks of the tunnel began. Those bricks arced down on both sides of him. To his right was a wall, to his left the platform edge. The ropes which bound him stretched out to that arch, wound around huge nails driven roughly into the old brickwork.

He hung cruciform at the entrance to the tunnel, from where the trains emerged.

Kay's scream echoed around and around him.

He shook ineffectually, tried to wriggle from his bonds. His fear was complete. He was utterly vulnerable, suspended nude in the path of the locomotives.

He screamed and screamed, but no one came.

He twisted his head around as far as he could. Kay's eyes frantically skipped from surface to surface, searching for some clue to tell him where he was. The trimmings of the station were black; the line above the poster spaces—all empty—was black. This was the Northern Line. At the edge of his limited field of vision he saw the curved edge of an underground sign, the tell-tale red circle bisected by a blue line containing the name of the station. He pulled his head over, ignoring the pain in his neck and skull, trying to push his shoulder out of the way with his chin, desperate to see where he was. As he vibrated to and fro the sign moved in and out of his view. He caught glimpses of the two words it contained, one above the other.

gton ent . . . ington scent . . . rnington rescent . . .

Mornington Crescent. The ghost station, the strange zone between Euston and Camden Town on the decrepit Northern Line: the odd, poky little tube stop which had been closed for repairs sometime in the late Eighties and had never opened again. Trains would slow down as they passed through, so as not to create a vacuum in the empty space, and passengers would glimpse the platform. Sometimes posters would apologize and promise a swift resumption of service, and sometimes obscure pieces of equipment to cure ailing underground stations lay scattered on the abandoned concrete. Often there was nothing, just the signs proclaiming the name of the station in the faint light. It lived a half-life, never being finally laid to rest, haunted by the unlikely promise that it would one day open for business again.

Behind him Kay heard footsteps.

"Who's there?" he yelled. "Who's that? Help me!"

Whoever it was had been standing on the platform, out of his sight when he had tried to turn round. Kay's head was twisted as violently over his left shoulder as he could manage. The steps approached him. A tall figure strolled into view, reading something.

"Alright, Kay?" said Pete without looking up. He chuckled as he read. "My God, they're not averse to a bit of pretension, this bunch, are they?" He held up what he was reading and Kay saw it was *Drum 'n' Bass Massive 3!*, a CD Kay had just bought. Kay fought to speak but his mouth was suddenly dry in terror. " 'Rudeness MC sends shouts to: the Rough an'

Ready Posse, Shy FX,' blah blah blah, 'an' Boys from da North, da South, da East, da West, remember . . . It's a London Something! Urban-style ghetto bass!' " Pete looked up, grinning. "This is drivel, Kay."

"Pete . . . " Kay finally croaked. "What's going on? Get me down, man! How did I get here?"

"Well, I needed to ask you some questions about something. I'm concerned about something." Pete moved off, still reading. In his other hand he held Kay's bag. He replaced the CD and brought out another. " 'Jungle versus the Hardsteppers.' Cor! I've got a lot of lingo to learn if I'm going to get in with Natasha, haven't I?"

Kay licked his lips. He was sweating even as he shivered. His skin felt slick with terror.

"How did you get me here, man?" he moaned. "What do you want?"

Pete turned to him, replaced the CD, squatted down on the platform to his left. His flute, Kay saw, was thrust through his belt like a saber.

"It's early yet, Kay, probably not yet five o'clock. The Northern Line doesn't start for a while. Just thought I'd let you know. And, yes, what I wanted . . . well. When I came out of the pub I headed for Natasha's flat as well, a little after you, wanted to have a word or something. See what you got up to. I've been very interested in all these stories I keep hearing about your mate who's in trouble, and I wanted to maybe get you on your own—see what you could tell me about him.

"Then, as I come toward you, downwind, I smell a *very particular scent*, one that someone wore once who I'm trying to track down. And it occurs to me that maybe your mate knows the bloke I'm after!" He smiled reasonably and put his head on one side.

"So. You did bump into your mate last night, didn't you?"

Kay swallowed. "Yeah . . . but Pete . . . let me down . . . please. I'll tell you all about it if you'll just . . . please, man . . . this is really freaking me out."

Kay's mind was racing. He could not think for the pain in

his head. Pete was mad. He swallowed again. He had to make him take him down, he had to do it now. Kay could not formulate his thoughts clearly, so overwhelming was the adrenaline rush brought on by fear. He was trembling violently.

Pete nodded.

"I'm not surprised it's freaking you out, Kay. Where's your mate?"

"You mean Saul? I don't know, man, I don't know. Please . . . "

"Where's Saul?"

"Just get me fucking down!"

Kay's control broke and he began to cry.

Pete shook his head thoughtfully.

"No. You see, you haven't told me where Saul is yet."

"I don't know, I swear I don't know! He, he, he said he was . . . " Kay thought desperately for something to tell Pete, something that might save him. *"Please let me go!"*

"Where's Saul?"

"The sewers! He said something . . . he stank. I asked where'd he been, and he was on about the sewers . . . " Kay's waist twisted, legs yanking violently at the strong cord.

"Now *that's* interesting," said Pete, leaning forward. "Did he say anything about *where* in the sewers? Because I've often suspected that . . . this guy I'm after uses them."

Kay was sobbing.

"Nah, man, he didn't say nothing else . . . please . . . please . . . he was weird, his voice was weird, he stank . . . he wouldn't tell me anything . . . *Please let me down!"*

"No, Kay, I *won't* let you down," Pete's voice was suddenly shockingly vicious. He rose and stalked toward him. "Not yet. You see, I want to know *everything you know* about your friend Saul, because it's important to me. I want to know *everything,* Kay, capeesh?"

Kay gabbled, tried to think of what he knew. He screamed about sewers, repeated that Saul had stunk, that he was hiding in the sewers. He ran out of anything to say. He whimpered and twisted where he hung.

Pete had been taking notes, nodding with interest now and then, writing carefully in a little notebook.

"Tell me about Saul's life," he said without looking up.

Kay talked about Saul's father, the fat socialist they had all laughed at; about Saul's brief, disastrous attempt to move in with a girlfriend; his return home, temporary he said, always temporary for the next two years. Kay kept talking, about Saul's friends, about his social life, Jungle, the clubs, and as Kay spoke tears rolled down his cheeks. He was pathetically eager to please. He whimpered with each breath. He had no more to say and he was afraid, because Pete seemed pleased with him when he told him about Saul, and all Kay could think of was that he must keep Pete happy. But he truly had no more to say.

Pete sighed and put the pad in his pocket. He glanced at his watch.

"Thanks, Kay," he said. "I guess you're wondering what this all means, what I'm up to. I'm afraid I won't tell you that. But you've helped me a lot. The sewers, huh? I thought as much, but you don't really want to go wading around in shit unless you're quite sure you have to, do you? It's not really my *turf*, know what I mean? I'll have to get him out." He grimaced light-heartedly.

"Maybe . . . maybe . . . you . . . can . . . let . . . me . . . go . . . " Kay forced the words out past chattering teeth. His body was shaking with little sobs, and every word of Pete's chilled him.

Pete looked at him and smiled.

"No," he said after a moment's hesitation. "I don't think so."

Kay's screams began again, went shooting off down the tunnel he faced, bounced around him. He threatened, cajoled, pleaded, and Pete ignored him, and continued speaking in his conversational tone.

"You don't know me, Kay. I can do a trick." He pulled the flute from his belt. "See this?" Kay continued begging. "I can play this, make anything I want come to me. Play the right notes and I can get you the cockroaches around us, the mice, anything close enough to hear. *And it feels so good to make them come to me.*" He crooned the last sentence, and at the sound of that cloying wetness, that fucked-up sugary tone, Kay retched.

"And I was looking at these tunnels and thinking how much they looked like wormholes," Pete continued. "If I played this, what do you think I might call?"

Pete put the flute to his lips and began to play, a strange, droning tune, a hypnotic dirge that wailed flatly over Kay's garbled exhortations.

Kay gazed into the mouth of the tunnel.

Behind him the melody continued, and Kay could hear the slap of feet as Pete danced to his own tune.

The wind jerked around Kay, pushed into his face from somewhere far off.

Deep in the darkness before him something growled.

Kay hung like an obscene toy, nude and chubby in the yawning darkness of the underground.

The wind pushed on with more resolve, and the growl sounded again. Kay shrieked in despair, felt himself relax in terror, sag in his bonds, felt piss run down his legs. The tune continued.

There was a sound like steel whiplashing as the tracks buckled and moved under the oncoming weight. The wind began to hit Kay now, began to push his hair out of his face. Scraps of paper and dirt came whirling out of the blackness, surrounding him, sticking to him; grit filled his eyes and mouth and he fought and spat to clear himself of debris, consumed by a ghastly desperation to see.

The growling ebbed and flowed, became a clattering, began to drown out the disinterested flute. A great presence rushed toward him.

Lights had appeared in the distance, two dirty white lights that seemed to *crawl* toward him, seemed determined never to arrive. It was only the wind and noise that moved at speed, he reasoned desperately, but even as he decided that, he saw how much closer those lights suddenly were, and Kay wriggled and fought and screamed prayers to God and Jesus.

He was in a tornado now as the lights suddenly *rushed* toward him. The howl and rumble echoed around the tube with a strange raging melancholy, an empty roar. The track was visible as glistening threads illuminated by those lights. The filthy off-white of the first Northern Line train of the day became evident before him, the driver's glass front still a black slit. *He must see me*, thought Kay. *He'll stop!* But the great flat surface moved ineluctably forward at a horrible speed, pushing the air out, clogging the wind with dirt. The speed was *intolerable*, thought Kay, just *stop*, but the lights kept coming, there was no let-up, the howl of the tunnel had become a charnel roar, the lights were dazzling, they blinded him, he looked up as he screamed, still hearing the flute, always the flute behind him, he looked up at the reflections varnished onto the windscreen, caught a glimpse of his ridiculous little body spreadeagled like a medical specimen, then saw through that, through the wide-open mouth of his reflection, into the incredulous gaze of the driver who bore down on him, disbelief and horror smeared across his face, those eyes aghast, *Kay could see the whites of the other man's eyes . . .*

The glass front of the train burst open like a vast blood-blister. The first Northern Line train of the day arrived at Mornington Crescent station and plowed to an unscheduled halt, dripping.

PART FOUR

BLOOD

Days came and went in the city. In the sewers, on the rooftops, under the canal bridges, in all the cramped spaces of London, King Rat and his comrades held councils of war.

Saul would sit and listen as the three unlikely figures murmured together.

Much of what they said made no sense to him: references to people and places and occurrences that he could not fathom. But he understood enough of the growled discussion to know that, despite their grandiose declarations of hostilities, neither King Rat nor Loplop nor Anansi had any idea how to proceed.

The prosaic truth was that they were afraid. Sometimes the arguments became heated, and accusations of cowardice would flurry between the three. These accusations were true. The circular discussions, the half-plans, the protestations of anger and pugnacity, all were stymied by the fact that the three knew that in any confrontation one of them would be doomed.

As soon as the Piper got his flute to his lips, or even pursed his lips to whistle, or perhaps even hummed, one of them would be commandeered, one of them would be taken over to the other side. His eyes would glaze and he would start to fight against his allies, his ears stuffed with the enticing sounds of food and sex and freedom.

Anansi would hear sluggish fat flies blundering near his mouth, and the skittering of lovelorn feet approaching him over towering webs to mate. That was what he had heard in Baghdad, as the Piper had thrashed him mercilessly.

Loplop knew that he would hear the snapping of threadlike filaments as the roots of grass were pushed aside and juicy worms groped blindly into the light, toward his bill. He would hear the rush of air as he felt himself swoop above the city, the come-hither calls of the most beautiful birds of paradise.

And King Rat would once again hear the doors of the pantries in hell swinging open.

None of the three wanted to die. It was a mission which involved certain destruction for one. The sheer force of animal self-preservation seemed to preclude their willingness even to risk the odds of one in three. There was to be no sentimental self-sacrifice in this fight.

Saul was vaguely aware that he was a vital component in this argument, that ultimately he was the weapon which would have to be deployed. It did not yet frighten him, as he could not begin to take it seriously.

Some days, Loplop and Anansi would disappear. Saul remained with King Rat.

Every time he walked or climbed or ate, he felt stronger. He would look down over London as he scaled the side of a gas tower and think *How did I get up here?* with exhilaration. Their journeys across London became rarer, more sporadic. Saul was frustrated. He was moving faster and more quietly. He wanted to roam, to make his mark—literally, sometimes, as he had discovered the pleasure of pissing his strong-smelling piss against walls and knowing that that corner was now *his*. His piss was changing, just like his voice.

King Rat was always there when Saul woke. After the initial exhilaration of a new existence at right-angles to the world of people he had left behind, Saul was disheartened by the speed with which his days blurred. Life as a rat was dull.

The individual moments still thrilled him with adrenaline, but those moments no longer coalesced.

He knew King Rat was waiting. His ferocious whispered arguments with his comrades became the focal point of Saul's life. In gravelly hisses and fluting tones the three bickered furiously over whether Anansi's webs would hold the Piper, and how best to wrest his flute away from him, and whether spiders or birds would constitute better cover. King Rat grew furious. He was alone; he could contribute no troops to any battle. The rats had snubbed him and ignored his commands.

Saul became quieter, learning more about the three creatures who constituted his circle.

He was alone on a roof, one night, sitting with his back to an air-conditioning vent, while King Rat scoured the alley below for food, when Anansi crept over the side of the building before him. Saul was still in his shadows and Anansi looked straight at him for a moment, then cast his eyes around the roof.

I'm getting better at this, thought Saul, with idle pride. *Even he can't see me now.*

Anansi sneaked forward under dark red clouds which rolled around each other, belching themselves into and out of existence. They threatened rain. Anansi squatted on the roof, stripped to the waist, as always, despite the cold. He reached into his pocket and drew out a glittering handful, a shifting mass of little buzzing bodies. He smeared the insects into his mouth.

Saul's eyes widened in fascination, even as he grimaced. He was not surprised by what he saw. He thought he could hear the humming of mother-of-pearl wings obscured by Anansi's cheeks, till those cheeks tensed and he saw Anansi suck hard, not chewing, but pursing his lips and working his mouth as if he sucked the juice from a big gobstopper.

There was the faintest of crunching sounds.

Anansi opened his mouth and poked out a tongue rolled into a tight U. He exhaled sharply, as if through a blowpipe, and a cascade of chitin shot out across the roof, scattering near Saul's feet; the desiccated body parts of flies and woodlice and ants.

Saul rose to his feet and Anansi started a little, his eyes widening momentarily.

"Wha'appen, pickney," he said evenly, gazing at Saul. "Me never see you there. You a quiet lickle bwoy."

Loplop was harder to surprise. He would appear suddenly from behind chimney stacks and rubbish bins, ruffling his foppish coat behind him. His passage was always invisible. Occasionally he would look up and yell "Oy!" into the firmament, and a pigeon, or a flock of starlings, or a thrush, would wheel suddenly out of the clouds, obeying his call, and perch nervously on his wrist.

He would peer at the bird, then briefly up at Saul or whoever observed him, and smile in satisfaction. He would glance back at the bird, imperious suddenly, and bark a command at it, upon which it would seem to cringe and give obeisance, bobbing its head and bowing. And then Loplop would become a good and just king all of a sudden, with no time for such puerile displays of power, and he would murmur reassuringly to his subject, and jettison it, watching it disappear with a look of noble benediction.

Saul believed that Loplop was still a little mad.

And King Rat, King Rat was the same: cantankerous and cockney and irritable and otherworldly.

Kay did not reappear with Natasha's keys, and she was forced to wake her downstairs neighbor, with whom she left a spare set.

It was just like Kay to meander off and forget that he had them, and she waited for him to call with his cheerful apology. He did not call. After a couple of days she tried his number, and his flatmates said they had not seen him for ages. Natasha was heartily pissed off. After another couple of days she had a new set cut and resolved to charge him when he re-emerged.

The police did seek her out. She was taken to the station and interviewed by a quiet man named Crowley, who asked her several times in several different ways if she had seen Saul since his disappearance. He asked her if she thought Saul capable of murder. He asked her what she had thought of Saul's father, whom she had never met, and what Saul thought of him. He asked her what Saul thought of the police. He asked what she thought of the police.

When they let her go she returned home seething, to discover a note on her door from Fabian, who was waiting for her in the pub. She fetched him back to her house where they smoked a joint and, to the sound of Fabian's abrupt giggles, composed a Jungle track on her sequencer using loads of samples from *The Bill*. They christened the song *Fuck You Mister Policeman Sir!*.

Pete was coming around more and more. Natasha was waiting for him to make a move on her, something which seemed to happen with the majority of blokes she hung out with for any length of time. He did not, which was a relief to her, as she was completely uninterested and did not want to have to deal with his embarrassment.

He was listening to more and more Drum and Bass, was making comments that were more and more astute. She sampled his flute and wove it into her tunes. She liked the sound it made; there was a breath of the organic about it. Normally, for the main sounds at the top end she would simply create something with her digital powers, but the soullessness those noises possessed, a quality she often revelled in, was beginning to alienate her. She enjoyed the sounds of his flute, the tiny pauses for breath, the hint of vibration when she slowed it down, the infinitesimal imperfections that were the hallmark of the human animal. She sent the bass to follow the flute track.

She was still experimenting, still laying plenty of tracks without him. After a time she focused her flute experimentation on one track. Sometimes they would play together, she snapping down a drum track, a bass line, some interjections, and he would improvise over the top. She recorded these sessions for ideas, and a notion formed in her mind of how they could play together: a session of Jazz Jungle, the newest and most controversial twist to the Drum and Bass cannon.

But for now she concentrated on the track she had christened *Wind City*. She returned to it day on day, tweaking it, adding layers to the low end, tickling the flute, looping it back on itself.

She had a clear idea of the feeling she sought, the neurotic beats of Public Enemy, especially on *Fear Of A Black Planet*, the sense of a treble constantly looking over its own shoulder. She took the harmony of the flute and stretched it. Repetition makes listeners wary of a statement, and Natasha made the flute protest too much, coming back in and back in on its purest note, till that purity became a testimony of paranoia, no sweet sound of innocence.

Pete loved what she was doing.

She would not let him hear the track until it was finished, but occasionally she would give in to his pesterings and play him a snippet, a fifteen-second phrase. The truth was that although she feigned exasperation, she enjoyed his rapturous reception.

"Oh, Natasha," he said as he listened, "you *really* understand me. More than I think you think you do."

Crowley was still haunted by the scene of the Mornington Crescent murder.

There had been something of a news blackout, a halfway house of secrecy whereby the unknown victim's death had been reported but the intricacies withheld. There was a vain and desperate hope that by mulling over the unbelievable facts in private, by containing them, they could be understood.

Crowley did not believe it would work.

The crime was not connected to his own investigation, but Crowley had come to examine the scene. The unearthly circumstances surrounding the murder reminded him of the peculiarities of Saul's disappearance and the murder of the two police officers.

Crowley had stood on the platform, the train still waiting there some hours after a hysterical driver had reported something which made no sense. A brief examination of the scene told the police that the driver's "floating man" had been suspended by rope to the tunnel entrance. Frayed cord dangled from the brick. The few passengers had been cleared out and the driver was with a counsellor elsewhere in the station.

The front of the train was encrusted with blood. There was very little of the body left to identify. Dental records had been rendered useless by the crushing, inexorable onrush of metal and glass onto the victim's face.

There was no escaping this crime, it lay all around him, on the platform, spattering the walls, carbonized on the live rail, smeared by gravity the length of the first carriage. No cameras had recorded the passing of criminal or victim. They had come and gone invisibly. It was as if the metal stakes and bloodied stubs of rope, the ruined flesh, had been conjured up spontaneously out of the dark tunnels.

Crowley exchanged words with the investigating detective, a man whose hands still shook since his first arrival at the scene an hour or more previously. Crowley had only tenuous reasons to connect the crime to his own investigations. Even the savagery was wrong. The murder of the policemen had seemed an act of huge rage, but a spontaneous act, brutally efficient. This was an imaginative piece of sadism, ritualistic, like a sacrifice to some dangerous god. It was designed to strip the victim of dignity and any vestige of power. And as he thought that, Crowley wondered if the man—they had found flesh that told them it was a man—had been awake and conscious as the train had arrived, and he screwed up his face, felt briefly sick with horror.

And yet, and yet, despite the differences, Crowley felt himself linking the crimes in his mind.

There was something in the infernal *ease* with which life had been taken, a sense of power which seemed to permeate the murder sites, the sure and absolute knowledge that none of these victims, for so much as one second, had the slightest chance of escape.

He asked the shaking Camden detective to contact him were there any developments at all, hinting at the connections he might be able to make.

Now, days later, Crowley still visited Mornington Crescent when he slept, its walls chaotically resprayed, abattoir chic, the red carpet laid down, ghastly organic decor.

He was convinced that the three (four?) murders he investigated contained secrets. There was more to the story, there was much more than they knew. The facts were damning, but still he wanted to believe that Saul had not committed the crimes. He sought refuge in a firm if nebulous belief that *something big was going on*, something as yet unexplained, and that whatever Saul was doing, he was not somehow responsible. Whether being absolved by the sudden onset of madness, or another's control, or whatever, Crowley did not know.

FIFTEEN

For a long time Pete had been asking Natasha to take him to a Jungle club. She found his pesterings irritating, and asked why he could not just go by himself, but he made noises about being a newcomer, being intimidated (which was, in all fairness, entirely reasonable given the atmosphere at many clubs). His hectoring stayed just on the right side of whining.

He made one or two good excuses. He did not know where to go, and if he were to follow *Time Out*'s appalling recommendations, he would end up a lonely figure at a hardcore Techno evening or some such fate. Natasha, by contrast, knew the scene, and could walk into any of the choicest evenings in London without paying. Just cashing in favors, calling in accounts set up in the early days of the music, by knowing the names and the faces, talking the talk.

Something was rumbling in the Elephant and Castle. The

AWOL posse were getting together with Style FM in a warehouse near the railway line. Everyone was going to be there, she started to hear. A DJ she knew called Three Fingers phoned her and asked her to come along, bring a tune or two; he'd play them. She could spin a few if she wanted.

She wasn't going to take him up on that, but maybe just turning up wasn't such a bad idea. It was a month since she'd last been out on a serious night, and Pete's clamoring made for a decent excuse to move. Three Fingers put her "plus whoever" on his guest list.

Fabian immediately said he would come. He seemed pathetically grateful for the idea. Kay remained incommunicado and, for the first time since he had disappeared a week or more previously, Natasha and Fabian felt the beginnings of trepidation. But for the moment that was forgotten as they made preparations for the foray into South London.

Pete was ecstatic.

"Yes yes yes! Fantastic! I've been waiting for this for ages!"

Natasha's spirit sank as she saw herself being shoehorned into the role of Junglist Nanny.

"Yeah, well, I don't want to disappoint you or anything Pete, but so long as you know I'm not *looking after* you there or anything. Alright? We get there, I listen, you dance, you leave when you want, I'm leaving when I want. I'm not there to *show you around*, d'you know what I'm saying?"

He looked at her strangely.

"Of course." His brow furrowed. "You've got some odd ideas about me, Natasha. I don't want to cadge off you all evening, and I'm not going to . . . to leach any of your cool, OK?"

Natasha shook her head, irritated and embarrassed. She *was* concerned that having a pencil-necked, white-bread geek padding after her was going to do her credentials as an up-and-coming Drum and Bass figure no good at all. She had only been vaguely conscious of the thought, and having it pointed out with frank good humor made her defensive and snappy.

Pete was grinning at her.

"Natasha, I'm going because I've found a new kind of

music I never knew existed, and it's one which—for all I don't *look the part*—I think I can use, and I think I can probably make. And I presume so do you, because you haven't stopped recording me yet.

"So don't worry about me making you look less than funky in front of your mates. I'm just going to hear the music and see the scene."

After the last bout of arguing, Anansi had disappeared. Loplop had remained in the area for another day or two, but had ultimately followed the spider into obscurity.

King Rat had slumped into a foul mood.

Saul hauled himself into the sewers, careful not to spill the bag of food he carried. He picked his way through the tunnels. It was raining in the streets above, a steady dribble of filthy, acid-saturated water which raced into the tunnels, swirled around Saul's legs, tried to pull him down, a stream nearly two feet high, fast-moving and dilute, the usual warm compost smell mostly dissipated.

King Rat had done nothing about finding food, and Saul, impatient with his self-pity, had left the throne room and gone scavenging. King Rat's leash on him was loosening. The neurotic hold he had kept for so long was almost gone. As his mood grew worse, his determination to keep Saul in his sights weakened.

Saul knew what this meant. His worth for King Rat was not measured by blood. He had not been rescued because he was a nephew, but because he was useful; because his peculiar birthright meant he was a threat to the power of the Piper. As the campaign against the Piper dissolved in petty fights and squabbles, cowardice and fear, Saul's existence meant less and less to King Rat. Without a plan of attack, how could he deploy his chosen weapon?

As Saul picked his way through the saturated tunnels he heard a sound. In a crevice in the concrete stood a waterlogged rat, her babies blind and squealing in the darkness behind her.

She stood uncertainly on the gray lip, overlooking the rush

of water. She was only six inches or so above the rising stream, and the comfortable hollow in which she lived was on the verge of becoming a water-sealed tomb. She looked up across the tunnel. On the far side from where she stood was another hole, an accidental passageway slanting up away from the depths.

The rat raised herself on her hind legs when she smelled Saul, and she let forth a peculiar cry.

She bobbed up and down in the darkness, avoiding looking him in the face, yet clearly aware of his presence. Again the she-rat made a sound, a lengthy screech, purged of the sneer which usually colored rats' voices.

He stopped just before her and hoisted his plastic bag over his shoulder.

The rat was pleading with him.

She was begging him for help.

The tone of the squeal was beseeching, and Saul was reminded of the profusion of rats who had followed him a fortnight previously, rats which had seemed animated by hunger and desperation, and which had been eager to show him *respect*.

Not here, was the sentiment pouring out of the bedraggled rat as she cringed below him. *Not here, not here!*

Saul reached out to her and she hopped onto his hand. A cacophony of infantile rat squeaks poured out of the holes in the concrete, and Saul plunged his hand further into the depths of the rotting stone. Little bodies were pushed onto his hand, where they lay squirming. He closed his fingers gently into a protective cage and drew out his hand, on which the little family lay shivering as the water level rose.

He crossed the tunnel and placed them on the ledge where the mother could pull the babies out of danger. She backed away from him bobbing her head, the pitch of her sounds changed, her fear gone.

Boss, she said to him, *Boss*, before turning and pulling her family out of sight into the darkness.

Saul leaned against the soaking wall.

He knew what was happening. He knew what the rats wanted. He did not think King Rat would like it.

By the time he arrived at the entrance to the throne room, the water was moving faster and the level kept on rising. He fumbled under the surface for the brick plug hiding the chute, pulled it open with a sudden explosive burp of air, and slipped through the cascade of water into the dark room below, pulling the door closed behind him.

He landed in the pool, splashed briefly onto his arse, before standing and walking onto the dry bricks. Behind him water dribbled into the room and down the wall from the imperfectly fitting brick entrance, but the chamber was so large and the hidden sluices so efficient that the moat around the room's central island of raised brickwork became only a little fatter. It would take days of ceaseless rain truly to threaten the air in the throne room.

King Rat sat brooding on his grandiose brick seat.

Saul glared at him. He delved into the plastic bags.

"Here," he said, and threw a paper package across the room. King Rat caught it in one hand, without looking up. "Bit of falafel," said Saul; "bit of cake, bit of bread, bit of fruit. Fit for a king," he added provocatively, but King Rat ignored him.

Saul sat cross-legged at the base of the throne. His own package contained much the same as King Rat's, with the emphasis skewed toward the sugary components of the meal. Saul's sweet tooth had survived his passage to rat-hood. The extra richness which rot lent to fruit was a pleasure he was still indulging in as often as possible.

He dug into the bag and pulled out a peach whose surface was one seamless bruise. He ate, gazing all the time at the morose King Rat.

"I'm fucking sick of this," he finally snapped. "What is up with you?"

King Rat turned to stare at him.

"Shut your trap. You don't know buggery about it."

"You *stink* of self-pity, you know that?" Saul gave a sudden laugh. "You don't see me acting up like this, and if anyone's got reason to be . . . *moody* . . . it's me. First off, you rip me out of my life and turn it into some kind of fucking . . . bad dream . . . So fuck it, alright, I'll do that, and I did a decent enough job didn't I? And now, just when I've got to grips with the rules of my life as Saul, Prince Rat, you get all morose and change the channel. What the fuck is going on? You . . . *galvanize* me, get me ready, for fuck knows what, and then you just slump. What am *I* supposed to do?"

King Rat was staring at him contemptuously, ill at ease.

"You've no clue what you're spouting, you little gobshit . . . "

"Don't tell me that! Jesus! *What the fuck do you want me to do?* Is my role here to fucking get you spurred again? Am I supposed to shake you up? Get you going again? Well fuck off! If you want to sit there on your rat arse and mope, then fine. And spider-features and Loplop can join you, you're as bad as each other. But I'm fucking off!"

"Got any *suggestions*, you mouthy little cunt?" hissed King Rat.

"Yeah, I have. You fuckers have got to be less *chicken*. That's what this is about. You're all scared, and you're scared because you all want a plan which makes sure your own arse isn't on the line. Well, it's not going to happen! You all reckon the Piper is such a bad fucker that you've got to take him, that this is the Final Battle—so long as none of you does the actual fighting. And while we're on that subject, I get the *distinct fucking impression* that it was me who was supposed to do the fighting for you, but you're all still chickenshit because you can't quite work out how to deploy me without any danger of recoil or whatever. Well count me the fuck out!" Saul had worked his way into a righteous anger.

"The Piper wants *you* dead too!" hissed King Rat.

"Yeah, so you say. Well, unlike you, maybe I'm going to do something about it!" There was a long silence. Saul waited a moment, then spoke again.

"The rats want me to take over."

There was a long silence as King Rat slowly swung his head to look at him.

"What?"

"The rats. In the sewers. Sometimes in the streets, or wherever. Whenever you're not around. They come to me, hover, kow-tow, and they squeak, and I'm beginning to make sense of what they're on about. They want me to take over. They want me to be the boss."

King Rat was rising, standing on the throne.

"You little ingrate. You little Tea-Leaf . . . you little shit, you bastard, I'll tan your hide, it's mine, mine, you understand, mine . . . "

"So take a stand, you fucking has-been!" Saul was standing, glaring at him, his face just below King Rat's, their spittle forming a crossfire. "They don't want you back. And they're not going to have you back until you . . . redeem yourself. That seems to be the morality of this fucking terrain."

Saul turned and stormed to the exit. "I'm going out. I don't know when I'll be back, but I don't expect you to care, because you don't think you can use me at the moment. While I'm gone I recommend you think carefully about *doing* something. Use Loplop, use Anansi, get hold of them and *track the motherfucker down*. When you're willing to get off your arse, maybe we can talk." He turned to face King Rat. "Oh, and don't worry about your Magic Kingdom. I don't *want* to be Rat King, not now, not ever, so I wouldn't stress it. I'm going to find my mates or something. I'm bored of you."

Saul turned and swung out of the room, was briefly coated in filthy water, and passed into the sewers.

While Saul stalked through the subterranean realms above him, King Rat stood quivering with rage, his hands tugging fitfully at his overcoat. Eventually his motions ceased and he seated himself.

He brooded.

He jumped up again, purposeful for the first time in days.

"OK, sonny, point taken. So let's talk about *bait*," he murmured to himself.

He rushed out of the room, suddenly moving as he had when Saul first saw him, sinuous and mysterious, fast and chaotic.

He passed quickly, silently through the layers of the earth, while Saul still struggled to find his bearings. King Rat emerged into a dark street. On the other side, figures passed in and out of the puddle of lacklustre lamplight, keeping their eyes fixed in front of them.

He stood quite still, his hidden eyes twitching imperceptibly. He looked around him. His eyes crawled up the wall before him. He stalked forward, one foot rising in a slow arch, curving back down to earth in an exaggerated parabola, his upper body bobbing slightly. He looked up, spread his arms wide, gripped the brick wall like a lover. Silently, he scaled the side of the building, his boots finding impossible purchase, his hands gripping invisible imperfections. He drew his hands back, contracting the muscles of his arms, fixing his attention on the dark below the eaves.

His arms uncoiled, shot out. Something fluttered desperately and a family of dirty pigeons burst from the shadow, disturbed from their sleep. They disappeared into the air behind him. He withdrew his hand and brought with it one of the birds, caught and held tight, its wings trying to stretch open, unable to escape him.

King Rat lowered his face toward his captive. It stopped struggling as he brought his face closer. He held it very tight to him, stared deep into its eye.

"You don't have Jack to fear from me, little cove," he hissed. The bird was still, waiting. "I want you to do me a favor. Go find your boss-man, spread the word. King Rat wants Loplop. Have him track me down."

King Rat released his scout. It lurched into the air, wheeled and swept off over London. King Rat watched it go. When he couldn't see it anymore, he turned his back and disappeared into the dark city.

SIXTEEN

It was the first time since his solo stroll along the Westway that Saul had been alone for so long. His ire was dwindling, threatening to snuff out, and he fed it carefully, maintained it. It gave him a righteous rush.

He wanted out of the claustrophobic sewers, wanted a taste of cold air. Judging by the ebb of water around his legs, the rain outside had let up. He wanted to emerge before it had fully dissipated.

Saul trusted to instinct in his rambles through the brick underworld. The rules of the sewers were different, the distinctions and boundaries between areas blurred. Above ground he knew where he was, and decided where he was going. Under the pavement he felt only a vague tugging to move from one part of the tunnel network to another, a buzzing of the troglodytic radar apparently lodged in his skull, and he would follow his nose. He did not know if he had visited any particular patch of sewer before; it was irrelevant. He knew it all. It was only the environs of the throne room which were particular, and all roads in the underworld seemed to lead there eventually.

He ducked under low bricks, pushed his way through tight tunnels.

Saul heard the patter of feet around him, isolated squeals of excited rats. He saw a hundred little brown heads peeking from chinks in the bricks.

"Hi rats," he hissed as he moved.

Ahead of him he saw the ruined metal of a ladder, old and corroded, dribbling its constituent parts into the stream of rainwater. He grasped it, felt it crumble beneath him, scrambled up it before it disintegrated entirely. He pushed at the cover, to poke his head into Edgware Road.

It was the end of twilight. The street was busy with Lebanese patisseries, mini-cab firms and cut-price electrical repair shops, dirty video stores and clothing warehouses with hand-drawn signs advertising their wares. Saul looked over the top of a building site across the road. Away in the west the fringe of the sky was still a beautiful bright blue, shading to black. At the base of the skyline the edges of the buildings looked unnaturally sharp.

Saul slid gently through the hole in the pavement, nonchalant in the knowledge that he could move without being seen or heard, so long as he kept in the shadows, obeyed the rules. Subtly he oozed through the opening, waiting for a gap in the flow of pedestrians, arching his eyebrows, rolling out of the hole in the ground with the smell.

He reached back to replace the manhole cover, and heard a mass of hisses. Peering over the edge, Saul looked into the eyes of dozens of rats, perched precariously on the rotting ladder.

He regarded them. They gazed at him.

He grunted and pulled the cover over the opening, but

not fully, leaving a slit of darkness, to which he put his mouth and whispered, "Meet me over by the bins."

In a quick, odd motion Saul bobbed to his feet. He stuck his hands in his pockets, sauntered along the street past the clumps of people. They noticed him suddenly, moved aside and apart for him, frowning at his smell. Behind him a brown bolt shot out of the sewers, followed by another, then a sudden mass. One of the proprietors noticed and shrieked, and all attention focused on the manhole. By then the flow had almost finished and the rats had melted into the interstices of the city, made themselves invisible.

Saul continued walking at the same pace as the street erupted into pandemonium behind him. People snatched themselves away from the hole in the ground.

"Who the fuck left that open?" came one yell, along with a mass of Arabic.

Saul slid into the darkness at the edge of the street. The rats had disappeared now and public-spirited citizens were gingerly shoving the metal cover back into position. Saul turned slowly and leaned against a wall, ostentatious, if only for his own benefit. He inspected his nails.

A few feet away to his right was a mass of bins, some tumbling into each other and spilling bags, the whole smelling faintly of baklava, sullied of course by filth. There was a rustling from the bags. A honey-stained head poked up from the black plastic mass. More heads appeared around it.

"Got yourself some food, then?" hissed Saul out of the corner of his mouth. "That's good."

There was a faint screeching from the bins in reply.

A few feet away, in the world of the patisseries, those who had collaborated on resealing the sewers were laughing, unsettled. They were sharing cigarettes and looking around nervously, in case the rats came back.

Saul moved over to the dustbins.

"Alright, squad," he said quietly. "Show me what you can do. First alley on the left, quick march, quiet as . . . mice? Fuck it, I suppose so. Rank yourselves *nice* for me."

There was a sudden explosive burst and a hundred brown torpedoes bolted from cover. Saul watched as they disappeared up drains, behind walls, into the darkness which dribbled down from the eaves of the buildings, into the holes between bricks. The bins were suddenly vacant and still.

Saul turned slowly on one heel in a deliberate motion. He dragged his feet, picking them up, dropping them, walking ponderously along the street. He looked down at his chest as he moved. Saul was thinking.

He felt as if he had lost all capacity for urgency.

Saul wondered what he was trying to achieve. Was this revenge? Boredom? A dare?

He was becoming King Rat. Was he? Was that what he was doing? He was not sure at all. He had not asked the rats to follow him, but he wanted to see what he could do with them.

He was aware that he should fear the Piper, that he should think, form a plan, but he could not, not now. He felt untrustworthy, confused, full of betrayal. He would show King Rat. King Rat who had not chased him, not tried to stop him, not urged him to come back.

He did not know what he was about to do, he did not know where he would go, when he would return. But then the very emptiness he felt was a liberation. For a long time he had felt full of guilt about his father, full of his father's disappointment. Then he had been full of King Rat, full of trepidation and amazement.

Now he was empty, all of a sudden. He felt very alone. He felt light, as if he might evade gravity with every step. As if he had pissed after a day holding it in, or had put down a massive burden he had forgotten he carried. He felt he could blow away in the wind, and he had to keep moving. And each movement, for the first time he could remember, the first time ever, was entirely his own.

There was a screaming from the alley just ahead of him, and he swore and rushed to the corner. He swung around the edge of brick and stared into the shadows. A few feet from the Edgware Road a young woman was lying in the delivery entrance of a shop. She had a dirty face and dirty brown hair. She sat huddled in a greasy blue sleeping-bag, pulling it up tight around her. Her face was shot through with horror, her mouth stretched as if it would split her cheeks. Her voice had run dry. She did not see Saul. She could not take her eyes from the wall before her.

A cascade of rats spewed and bubbled over the edge. The stream was almost soundless, marked only by a low white noise of scratching.

The sleeping-bag slipped slowly from the woman's hands, and they stayed as they were, frozen, framing her face. Rats simmered around her, looked up at Saul, made sounds of supplication, sought approval. They parted as he strode toward the terror-stricken woman.

She did not look at him, still unable to look anywhere except at the deluge of scuttling bodies. There were more rats there than Saul had seen in the sewers. They had been joined by compatriots from the houses around them. Saul glanced up at them, then turned to the woman.

"Hey, hey," he said gently, and kneeled before her. "Don't panic, shhhhh . . ."

The woman's eyes flickered briefly to him and she found her voice.

"Oh my *God* do you *see* them they're *coming for me* Jesus Christ . . ."

She spoke in a strangled screech. It sounded as if there were no air in her lungs, as if it were only fear that was giving her a voice.

Saul grabbed her face in both hands and forced her to look at him. Her eyes were green and open very wide.

"Listen to me. You won't understand this, but don't worry. Shhh, shhh, these rats are *mine*. They won't hurt you, do you understand?"

"But the rats are here to *get me* and they're going to *get me* and . . ."

"*Shut up!*" There was silence, for a second. "Now

watch." Saul held her head still and slowly moved his aside, until the woman could see the rats which waited in the shadows and, as her eyes widened again and the muscles around her mouth went taut, Saul threw his head back briefly and hissed, "Disappear!"

There was a flurry of feet and tails. The rats vanished.

The alley was silent.

Bewilderment crept into the creases on the woman's face. She looked from side to side as Saul moved away from her. She craned her neck and peered nervously around her. Saul sank to his haunches next to her, sat back against the door. He looked to his right and saw the lights of Edgware Road, only ten feet away. Again he thought: these things take place so close to the real city, and no one can see them. They take place ten feet away, somewhere in another world.

Next to him the woman turned. Her voice quivered.

"How did you do that?" She spoke too loudly still.

"I told you," he said. "They're my rats. They'll do what I tell them."

"Is it like a *trick*? Like trained rats? Don't they scare you?"

As she spoke her eyes wavered from side to side. Her voice was unnaturally loud and abrupt. Her panic was over too quickly. She spoke to him as though she were a child. Saul suddenly understood that this woman was probably mentally ill.

Don't treat her like a child, he thought warily. *Don't patronize her.*

"The rats don't scare me, no," he said carefully. "I understand them."

"They frightened the shit out of me. I thought they were out to get me!"

"Yeah, well I'm sorry about that. I didn't know anyone was here when I sent them into the alley."

"It's *amazing* that you can *do* that, I mean make rats do what you want!" She grinned quickly.

There was silence. Saul looked around him but the rats remained hidden. He turned back to his companion. Her eyes were darting around like flies.

"What's your name?" he asked.

"Deborah."

"I'm Saul." They smiled at each other. "Now that you know the rats are mine," he said slowly, "would you still be scared of them?"

She looked at him questioningly. Saul sighed for a long time. He did not know what would happen next. He did not really know what he was doing. He was enjoying his words, rolling every one around his mouth. It was the first time since meeting Kay that he had spoken to a human being. He revelled in every sentence. He did not want the conversation to end.

"I mean, I could bring them out again."

"I don't know, I mean, aren't they dirty and stuff?"

"Not my lot. And if I tell them not to, they won't touch you."

Deborah twisted her face up. She was grinning, a sickly frightened grin.

"Oh you know I don't *know* I mean I don't *know* . . . "

"Don't be scared, now. Look. I'll call them out, and show you they do what I want." He turned his head slightly. He could smell the rats. They waited just out of sight, quivering. "Heads up," he said firmly, "heads only."

There was a stirring in the debris and a hundred little heads poked up, like seals in the waves, sleek skulls under greased-back fur.

Deborah shrieked and put her hand over her mouth. Her head shook, and Saul saw that she was laughing.

"It's *amazing* . . . " she said through her fingers.

"Down," said Saul, and the heads disappeared.

Deborah laughed delightedly.

"How do you *do* it?"

"They have to do what I say," said Saul. "I'm the boss, as far as they're concerned. I'm their prince." She looked at him in consternation. Saul felt irresponsible. He wondered if he was damaging her further. What she needs is reality, he thought, but the realization came firmly to him that this was reality, whether anyone liked it or not. And he wanted to keep talking to her.

"Are you hungry, Deborah?" She nodded. "Well, why don't I get you some food?" He jumped up and crept into Edgware Road, returned some seconds later with two pastries, intricate things encrusted with pistachios and icing sugar, which he put in Deborah's lap.

She bit into one, licked her lips. She was obviously hungry.

"I was asleep," she said, honey muffling her voice. "I heard the rats in my sleep and they woke me up. Oh, it's OK. I'm glad I'm awake. I wasn't sleeping very well, actually, I was dreaming horrible things."

"Wasn't waking to a plague of rats a horrible thing?"

She laughed jerkily.

"Only at first," she said. "Now I know they do what you tell them I don't mind so much. It's very cold." She had finished the pastries. She had eaten very fast.

There was a faint scratching. The rats were becoming impatient. Saul barked a brief order to be quiet and the sound ceased. *It feels so easy,* he thought, *so simple to take control like this.* It didn't even excite him.

"Do you want to go to sleep, Deborah?"

"What do you *mean*?" Her voice was suddenly suspicious, even afraid. She almost whined in her trepidation, and bundled herself up into her sleeping-bag. Saul reached out to reassure her and she shrank away from him in horror and he realized with a sinking feeling that she had heard such a line before, but spoken with different intent.

Saul knew that the streets were brutal.

He wondered how often she had been raped.

He moved his hands away, held them up in surrender.

"I'm sorry, Deborah, I didn't mean anything. I'm just not tired. I'm lonely, and I thought we could go for a wander." She still looked at him with terrified eyes. "I won't . . . I'll go, if you want." He did not want to leave. "I want to show you around. I'll take you anywhere you want to go."

"I don't *know* I don't know what you want to *do* . . . " she moaned.

"Don't you want to *do* something?" he said desperately. "Aren't you *bored*? I swear I won't touch you, won't do anything, I just want some company . . . "

He looked at her and saw her wavering. He put on a silly expression, a clownish sad face, sniffed theatrically, nauseating himself.

Deborah laughed nervously.

"Please," he said, "let's go."

"Oh . . . *OK* . . . " She looked pleased, even though nervous.

He grinned at her reassuringly.

He felt ill at ease, shockingly clumsy. Even the simplest mannerism cost him huge effort. He was relieved that he had not frightened her away.

"I'll take you up to the roofs, if you want, Deborah, and I'll show you the *quick* way of getting around London on foot. Can I . . . " He paused. "Can I bring the rats?"

SEVENTEEN

Bring them, bring the rats, she said, after a little persuasion. It was obvious that, despite her fear, she was fascinated. Saul gave a long whistle and the rats appeared again, eager to show willing.

He did not know how it was he commanded them. It seemed to make no difference what words he used, or if he whistled, or gave a brief shout. He could not think an order for it to be obeyed, he had to make a sound, but the rats seemed to understand him through an empathy, not through language. He invested the sound he made with the spirit of an order for it to be obeyed.

He made the rats line up in rows, to Deborah's delight. He made them move forward and backwards. When he had shown off and made the rats ridiculous, taking away Deborah's fear, she would even touch one. She stroked it nervously as Saul murmured deep in his throat, held the rat in thrall so it would not panic, bite or run.

"No offense or anything, Saul, but you *smell*, you know," she said.

"It's where I live. Smell it again; it's not as bad as you think at first."

She leaned over and sniffed him, wrinkled up her nose and shook her head apologetically.

"You'll get used to it," he said.

When she had lost her fear he suggested that they move. She looked nervous again, but nodded.

"Which way?" she said.

"Do you trust me?" Saul said.

"I *think* so . . . "

"Then hold onto me. We're going up, straight up the walls."

She did not understand at first, and when she did she was terrified, refused to believe that Saul could carry her. He reached out to her gently, slowly so as not to intimidate her, and when he was sure she did not mind being touched, he lifted her easily, held her with his arms outstretched, feeling his muscles snap hard with rat-strength. She laughed delightedly.

He felt like a superhero.

Ratman, he thought as he held her. Doing good with his bizarre rat-powers. Helping the mentally ill. Carrying them around London faster than shit through a sewer. He sneered at himself.

"See. I told you I could carry you. Let me put you on my back."

"Mnnnn . . . " Deborah swung her face from side to side like a flattered child, smiling a little. "MnnnnOK."

"Great. Let's go." The rats scampered a little closer, hearing the dynamism in Saul's voice.

Deborah still looked at them nervously every time they moved, but she had forgotten most of her fear.

Saul bent down and offered her his back. She stepped out of the sleeping-bag.

"Shall I take this?" she said, and Saul shook his head.

"Just hide it. I'll bring you back here."

Deborah gingerly clambered onto Saul's back, and he was struck once again by the fact that it was only her tenuous grip on reality that meant she would do as he suggested. Approach most people with the offer to piggyback them across the roofs and he would not have met with such a willing response.

The irony, of course, being that she was right to trust him.

He rose to his feet and she shrieked as if she was on a fairground ride.

"Gentle, *gentle!*" she yelled, and he hissed at her to keep her voice down.

He strode into the passage, and all around him he heard the pattering of hundreds of rat feet. *This is how I changed worlds*, he thought, *carried to my new city on the back of a rat. What goes around comes around.*

He stopped below a window, its sill nine feet above the pavement.

"See you up top," he hissed at the rats, who disappeared in a flurry, as before. He heard the scrape of claws on brick.

Saul jumped up and grasped the window, and Deborah shouted, a yell which did not die away but ballooned in terror as her fingers fought for purchase on his back. His feet swung above the ground, the toes of his prison-issue shoes scraping the wall.

He called for her to shut up, but she would not, and words began to form in her protest.

"Stopstopstop," she wailed and Saul, mindful of discovery, hauled himself at speed up into the space by the window, flattened himself against the glass, reached up again, determined to pull Deborah out of earshot before she could order him down.

He scrambled up the building. Not yet as fast as King Rat, but so smooth, he thought to himself as he climbed. Terror had stopped Deborah's voice. *I knew that feeling*, thought Saul, and smiled. He would bring this to a close as fast as he could.

Her weight on his back was only a minor irritation. This was not a hard wall to climb. It was festooned with windows and cracks and protuberances and drainpipes. But Saul knew that to Deborah it was just so much unbreachable brick. This building had a flat roof contained by rails, one of which he grasped now and tugged at, raising himself and his cargo up onto the skyline.

He deposited Deborah on the concrete. She clawed at it, her breath ragged.

"Oh now, Deborah, I'm sorry to scare you," he said hurriedly. "I knew you wouldn't let me if I told you what I was going to do, but I swear to you, you were safe, always. I wouldn't put you in danger."

She mumbled incoherently. He dropped to her side and gently put a hand on her shoulder. She flinched and turned to him. He was surprised at her face. She was quivering, but she did not look horrified.

"How can you *do that*?" she breathed. All around them on the roof the concrete began to swarm with rats, struggling to prove their eager devotion. Saul picked Deborah off her side and put her on her feet. He tugged at her sleeve. She did not take her eyes from him but allowed herself to be pulled over to the railing around the roof. The light was entirely leached from the sky by now.

They were not so very high; all around them hotels and apartment blocks looked down on them, and they looked down on as many again. They stood at the midpoint of the undulations in the skyline. Black tangles of branches poked into their field of vision, over in Regent's Park. The graffiti were thinner up here, but not dissipated. Here and there extravagant tags marked the sides of buildings, badges pinned in the most inaccessible places. *I'm not the first to be here*, thought Saul, *and the others weren't rats*. He admired them hugely, their idiot territorial bravery. To scale that wall and spray *BOOMBOY!!!* just there, where the bricks ran out, that was a courageous act. *It's not brave of me*, he thought. *I know I can do it, I'm a rat.*

Deborah was looking at him. From time to time her eyes flitted away toward the view, but it was him she was conscious of. She looked at him with amazement. He looked back at her. He was awash with gratitude. It was so good, so nice to talk to someone who was not a rat, or a bird, or a spider.

"It must be *amazing* to be able to do what all the rats do," she said, studying their massed ranks. They stood a little way behind, quiet and attentive, fidgeting a little when unobserved but hushing when Saul turned to gaze at them.

Saul laughed at what she said.

"Amazing? I don't fucking think so." He could not resist bitching, even though she would not understand. "Let me tell you about rats," he said. "Rats do nothing. All day. They eat any old crap they can find, run around pissing against walls, they shag occasionally—or so I'm led to believe—and they fight over who gets to sleep in which patch of sewer. Sure, they *think* they're the reason the world was invented. But they're *nothing*."

"Sounds like people!" said Deborah and laughed delightedly as if she had said something clever. She repeated it.

"They're *nothing* like people," Saul said quietly. "That's a tired old myth."

He asked her about herself and she was vague about her situation. She would not explain her homelessness, muttering darkly about not being able to handle something. Saul felt guilty but he was not that interested. Not that he did not *care*: he did, he was appalled at her state and, even alienated from her city as he was, he felt the old fury against the government so assiduously trained into him by his father. He cared deeply. But at that moment he wanted to talk to her not for herself particularly but because she was a person. Any person. As long as she kept talking and listening, he was not concerned about what she might say. And he asked her about herself because he was hungry for her company.

He heard a sudden sound of flapping, something like

heavy cloth. He felt a brief gust of wind in his face. He looked up, but there was nothing.

"I tell you what," he said. "Never mind rats being amazing. Do you want to come back to my house?"

She wrinkled her nose again.

"The one that smells like that?"

"No. I was thinking of going back to my real place for a bit." He sounded calm, but his breath came short and fast at the thought of returning. Something in her remarks about rats had reminded him of where he came from. Cut off from King Rat, he wanted to return, touch base.

He missed his dad.

Deborah was happy to visit his house. Saul put her on his back again and set off, with the rats in tow, across the face of London, across a terrain that had quickly become familiar to him.

Sometimes Deborah buried her face in his shoulder, sometimes she leaned back alarmingly and laughed. Saul shifted with her to maintain his balance.

His progress was not as rapid as King Rat's or Anansi's, but he moved fast. He stayed high, loath to touch the ground, a vague rule he remembered from a children's game. Sometimes the platform of roofs stopped short and he had no option but to plunge down the brick, by fire escape or drain or broken wall, and scurry across a short space of pavement before scrambling up above the streets again.

Everywhere around him he heard the sound of the rats. They kept up with him, moving by their own routes, disappearing and reappearing, boiling in and out of his field of vision, anticipating him and following him. There was something else, a presence he was vaguely aware of: the source of that flapping sound. Time and again he sensed it, a faint flurry of wind or wings brushing his face. His momentum was up and he did not stop, but he nursed the vague sense that something kept up with him.

Periodically he would pause for breath and look around him. His passage was quick. He followed a map of lights, keeping parallel to Edgware Road, shadowing it as it became Maida Vale. He followed the route of the 98 bus, passed landmarks he knew well, like the tower with an integument of red girders which jutted out above its roof, making a cage.

The buildings around them began to level out; the spaces between towers grew larger. Saul knew where they were: in the stretch of deceptively suburban housing just before Kilburn High Road. *Terra cognita*, thought Saul. Home ground.

He crossed to the other side of the road so fast that Deborah was hardly aware of it. Saul took off into the dark between main roads, bridging the gap between Kilburn and Willesden, eager to return home.

They stood before Terragon Mansions. Saul was afraid.

He felt fraught, short of breath. He listened to the stillness, realized that the escort of rats had evaporated soundlessly. He was alone with Deborah.

His eyes crawled up the dull brick, weaving between windows, many now dark, a few lit behind net curtains. There at the top, the hole through which his father had plummeted. Still not fixed, pending more police investigation, he supposed, though now the absence was disguised by transparent plastic sheets. The tiny fringe of ragged glass was still just visible in the window-frame.

"I had to leave here in a hurry," he whispered to Deborah. "My dad fell out of that window and they reckon I pushed him."

She gazed at him in horror.

"Did you?" she squeaked, but his face silenced her.

He walked quietly to the front door. She stood behind him, hugging herself against the chill, looking nervously about. He caressed the door, effortlessly and silently slipping the lock. Saul wandered onto the stairs. His feet made no sound. He moved as if dazed. Behind him came Deborah, in fits and starts, her ebullience gone with his. She dragged her feet as if she were whining, but she made no sound.

The door to his apartment was criss-crossed with blue tape. Saul stared at it and considered how it made him feel. Not violated or outraged, as he would have supposed. He felt oddly reassured, as if this tape secured his house from outsiders, sealing it like a time capsule.

He tugged gently at it. It came away in his hand, airy and ineffectual, as if it had been waiting for him, eager to give itself up. He pushed the door open and stepped into the darkness where his father had died.

EIGHTEEN

It was cold, as cold as the night when the police had arrived. He did not turn on the lights. What filtered up from the streets was enough for him. He did not waste time, pushed open the door of the sitting room and entered.

The room was bare, had been stripped of possessions, but he noticed that only in passing. He stared at the jagged window full on. He dared it to unsettle him, to sap his strength. It was just a hole, he thought, wasn't it? Wasn't it just a hole? The plastic billowed back and forth with a noise like whips cracking.

"Saul, I'm scared . . . "

He realized belatedly that Deborah could hardly see. She stood at the threshold to the room, hesitant. He knew what she could see, his obscure form against the dark orange of the distant streetlamps. Saul shook himself in anger. He had been using her with such ease he had forgotten that she was real. He strode across the room and hugged her.

He wrapped himself around her with an affection she poured back into him. It was not sexual, though he sensed that she expected it to be, and might not have minded. But he would have felt manipulative and foul and he *liked* her and pitied her and was so, so grateful to her. They held each other and he realized that he was trembling as much as she. Not all rat yet, then, he thought ruefully. *She's afraid of the dark*, he thought. *What's my excuse?*

There was a book in the middle of the floor.

He saw it suddenly over her shoulder. She felt him stiffen and nearly shrieked in terror, twisting to see whatever had shocked him. He hurriedly hushed her, apologized. She could not see the book in the dark.

It was the only thing in the room. There was no furniture, no pictures, no telephone, no other books, only that.

It was not coincidence, Saul thought. They had not *missed that* when they cleared out the flat. Saul recognized it. An ancient, very fat red-bound A4 notebook, with snatches of paper bursting from its pages; it was his father's scrapbook.

It had appeared regularly throughout Saul's life. Every so often his father would drag it out from wherever he hid it and carefully cut some article from the paper, murmuring. He would glue it into the book, and as often as not write in red biro in the margin. At other times there was no article at all; he would just write. Often Saul knew these bouts were brought on by some political occurrence, something his father wanted to record his pontifications on, but at other times there was no spur that Saul could fathom.

When he was little the book had fascinated him, and he had wanted to read it. His father would let him see some things, articles on wars and strikes, and the neat red notes surrounding them. But it was a private book, he explained, and he would not let Saul examine it all. *Some of it's personal*, he explained patiently. *Some of it's private. Some of it's just for me.*

Saul removed himself from Deborah and picked it up. He opened it from the back. Amazingly, there were still a very few pages not yet full. He flicked backwards slowly, coming to the last page that his father had filled. A light-hearted story from the local paper about a Conservative Party fundraising event which had suffered a catalog of disaster: failing electricity, a double booking and food poisoning. Next to it, in his father's carefully printed letters, Saul read, "There is a God after all!!!"

Before that, a story about the long-running strike at the Liverpool docks, and in his father's hand: "A morsel of information breaches the carefully maintained Wall of Silence! Why the TUC so ineffectual?!"

Saul turned the page backwards, grinned delightedly as he realized that his father had been pondering his *Desert Island Discs* selection. At the top of the page was a list of old Jazz tunes, all with careful question-marks, and below was the tentative list. "One: Ella Fitzgerald. Which one??? Two: 'Strange Fruit.' Three: 'All The Time In The World,' Satchmo. Four: Sarah Vaughan, 'Lullaby of Birdland.' Five: Thelonius? Basie? Six: Bessie Smith. Seven: Armstrong again, 'Mack the Knife.' Eight: 'Internationale.' Why Not? Books: Shakespeare, don't want the Bloody Bible! *Capital? Com. Manifesto?* Luxury: Telescope? Microscope?"

Deborah knelt beside Saul.

"This was my dad's notebook," he explained. "Look, it's really sweet . . . "

"How come it's here?" she asked.

"I don't know," he said after a pause. He kept turning the pages as he spoke, past more cuttings, mostly political, but here and there simply something which had caught his father's eye.

He saw small tales about Egyptian tomb-robbers, giant trees in New Zealand, the growth of the Internet.

Saul began to pull back clumps of pages now, going back years at a time. There was more writing in the earlier years.

7/7/78: Trade Unions. *Must read old arguments!* Had a
long argument with David at work about Union today. He
going on and on about ineffectual and etc. etc. and I
rather letting myself down, just seemed to sit there saying
Yes but solidarity vital! He wasn't having any of it. Must
reread Engels on Trade Unions. Have vague memories of
being rather impressed but could be fooling myself. Saul
still very sulky. Don't know what's going on there at all.
Remember seeing book about Teenagers and Problems,
though can't remember where. Must track it down.

Saul felt awash with the same hopeless love he had felt
when he had shown Fabian the book his father had bought
him. He was going about it all wrong, the old man, but all he
wanted to do was understand. Maybe there was no right way
to do it. *I was wrong too,* he thought.

Back, back, he moved through the years. Deborah cud-
dled into him for warmth.

He read about the time his father had had an argument
with one of his history teachers over the best way to present
Cromwell.

No, fair enough, maybe can't be talking about Bour-
geoisie to group of ten-year-olds but shouldn't be gloss-
ing over him! Terrible man, yes (Ireland, and etc. etc.)
but must make clear nature of Revolution!

He read a reference to one of his father's girlfriends—
"M." He could not remember her at all. He knew his father
had kept such affairs out of the house. He did not think his
father had had any romantic involvement at all in the last six
or seven years of his life.

He read about his own fifth birthday party. He remembered it: he had been given two Indian head-dresses, and in
retrospect a thrill of worry had passed around the adults, concerned at his reaction, but he had been elated. To have not one

but *two* of the beautiful feathered things . . . He remembered the joy.

Saul was seeking the first reference to himself, maybe a mention of his dead mother, who had been carefully excised from his father's ruminations. A date caught his eye: 8/2/72, the only entry from the year of his birth, the birth itself apparently not recorded. There was no cutting attached to the entry. Saul's brow furrowed as he read the first few words.

> We are a few weeks on now from the attack, which I don't really want to talk about. E. is very strong, Thank God. Many fears, of course, alleys and etc. etc., but overall she is getting better daily. Kept asking her was she sure, I thought we should go to the Police. Don't you want him caught? I asked her and she said No I just don't want to see him again. Can't help thinking this is a mistake but it must be her decision of course. Am trying to be what she needs but God knows it is hard. Worst at night, of course. Don't know whether better to comfort/cuddle or not touch and she doesn't seem to know either. Definitely the worst times, tears etc. Am beating about the bush. Fact is, E. had test and is pregnant. Can't be sure of course but have looked at timing carefully and looks very likely that it is his. Discussed abortion but E. can't face it. So after long hard talks have decided to go ahead. No record, so no one need know. Hope everything turns out alright. I'll admit, I'm afraid for child. Haven't yet worked out my own reaction. Must be strong for E.'s sake.

Saul's chest had gone quite hollow.

Somewhere Deborah was saying something to him.

Oh, he felt stupid.

He saw what he had lost.

Stupid, stupid boy, he thought, and at the same time he was thinking: *You needn't have worried, Dad. You were strong as* fuck.

Tears came cold to his eyes and he heard Deborah again.

Look at what you lost, he thought. *She died!* he thought suddenly. *She died, and still he did right by me. How could he? I killed her, I killed his wife! Every time he looked at me, wasn't he looking at the rape? Wasn't he looking at the thing that killed his wife?*

Stupid boy, he thought. Uncle *Rat? When were you going to think that one through?* he thought.

But more than anything he could not stop wondering at the man who had raised him, had tried to understand him, and had given him books to help him understand the world. Because when he had looked at Saul, somehow he did *not* see murder, or his lost wife, or the brutality in the alley (and Saul knew just how that attacker had appeared, as if from nowhere, out of the bricks, as he himself moved). Somehow, when he looked at Saul he looked at his son, and even when the air between them had poisoned and Saul had exercised all his studied teenage insouciance not to care, the fat man had still looked at him and seen his son, and had tried to understand what was wrong between them. He had had no truck with the awful, bloody vulgarity of genes. He had built fatherhood with his actions.

Saul did not sob, but his cheeks were wet. Wasn't it odd and sad, he thought a little hysterically, that it was only on learning that his father was not his father, that he realized how completely his father he had been?

There's a dialectic for you, Dad, he thought, and grinned fleetingly.

It was only in losing him that he regained him, finally, after so many dry years.

He remembered being carried on those broad shoulders to see his mother's stone. He had killed her, he had killed his father's wife, and his father had set him down gently and given him flowers to put on her grave. He wept for his father, who had been given his wife's murderer, the child of her rapist, and who had decided to love him dearly, and had set out to do it, and had succeeded.

And somewhere he kept telling himself how stupid a boy he was. A new thought was occurring to him. *If King Rat lied about this*, he reflected, and the thought trailed off like a sequence of dots . . .

If he lied about this, the thought said, *what else did he lie about?*

Who killed Dad?

He remembered something King Rat had said, a long time ago, at the end of Saul's first life. "I'm the intruder," he had said. "I killed the usurper."

In the succession of words the sense had been drowned, had been another surreal boast, a crowing, bullish aggrandizement without meaning. But Saul could see differently now. A cold stone of fury settled in his gut and he realized how much he hated King Rat.

His father, King Rat.

NINETEEN

The door to the flat opened.

Saul and Deborah had been huddled together on the floor, she murmuring nervous words of support. They looked up at the same moment, at the gentle creak of hinges.

Saul scrambled silently to his feet. He was still clutching the book. Deborah rocked herself, tried to rise. A face peered around the rim of the door.

Deborah clung to Saul and gave a tiny whimper of fear. Saul was primed like an explosive, but as his eyes made light of the darkness his tension ebbed a little, and he stood confused.

The face in the doorway was beaming delightedly, long blond hair falling in untidy clumps around a mouth stretched wide in childish joy. The man stepped forward into the room. He looked like a buffoon.

"I *thought* I heard someone, I *thought* so!" he exclaimed.

Saul straightened a little more, his brow furrowed. "I've been waiting here night after night, saying no, go home, it's ridiculous, he won't come *here*, of all places, and now here you are!" He glanced at the book in Saul's hand. "You found my reading material, then. I wanted to know all about you. I thought that might tell me a bit."

He looked a little closer at Saul's red eyes and his own face widened.

"You didn't know, did you?" His smile of pleasure was broader than ever. "Well. That does explain a few things. I thought you were rather quick to join your so-called father's murderer." Saul's eyes flickered. *Of course*, he thought, giddy with grief, *of course*. The man was eyeing him. "I thought blood must have been thicker than water but, of course, why on Earth should he have told you?" He rocked back on his heels, stuck his hands in his pockets.

"I've needed to talk to you for a long time. The rumors have been flying about you, you know! You've been famous for years! So many places, so many leads, so many possibilities . . . I've been *all over*, chasing impossible crime . . . You know, any time I heard about some weird break-in, some murder, something that doesn't fit the bill, something people couldn't have done, I'd run to investigate. The police can be very helpful with information." He grinned. "So many dead ends! And then I came here . . . " The man grinned again. "I could just *smell* him, and I knew I'd found you, Saul."

"Who *are* you?" Saul finally breathed.

The man smiled pleasantly at him but did not answer. He seemed to see Deborah for the first time.

"Hi! My God, what a night you must be having!" He strolled forward as he laughed. Deborah clung still to Saul. She gazed at the man with guarded eyes. "Anyway," he continued easily, reaching out his hand toward her, "I'm afraid I'm not interested in you."

He snatched her wrist and wrenched her out of Saul's grasp. Too late, Saul realized that the urbane man had taken her, his head moved slowly down to look where she had been even as his mind screamed at him to look up, to move.

He dragged his head up through the thick air.

He saw the man close his left hand in Deborah's hair, Saul reached out in horror, determined to intervene, but the man who was still smiling broadly glanced down at her briefly and sent his other fist slamming into the underside of her chin just as she opened her mouth to scream, and the impact split the skin and bone of her jaw and snapped her mouth closed so fast that blood spurted out from between her lips where she bit deep into her tongue. The scream died before it appeared, mutating into a wet exhalation. Even as Saul's slow, slow feet took him toward her the man swivelled on his toes and pulled her body around from the nape of the neck where he held her, built up momentum, spun fast and buried her face in the side of the door-frame.

He released her and turned back to Saul.

Saul shrieked in anguish and disbelief, stared past the man at Deborah's carcass, which slid down the door-frame and tumbled back into the room. It was twitching as nerve endings died. Her flattened and distorted face stared blindly up at Saul as she danced in a posthumous fit, her heels pattering on the floor like a monsoon, blood and air bubbling out of her exploded mouth.

Saul bellowed and flung himself at the man with all his rat-strength.

"I'll eat your fucking heart!" he screamed.

The tall man sidestepped the flurry of blows easily, still grinning broadly. He pulled his fist back leisurely and sent it into Saul's face.

Saul saw the blow coming and moved away from it, but he was not fast enough and it snapped into the side of his skull, sending him reeling. He spun round, hit the floor hard. A shrill sound hurt his head. He turned to look at the man, who stood with his lips pursed, whistling a jaunty, repetitive air. He glared at Saul and his eyes flickered dangerously. Without pause, the tune he was whistling changed, became less organized, more insidious. Saul ignored him, tried to crawl away. The whistling stopped short.

"So it's true," the Piper hissed, and his urbane voice had metamorphosed into something unstable. He looked as if he was about to be sick, and he looked enraged. "Dammit, neither man nor rat, can't shift you. How *dare you how dare you* . . ." His eyes were wild and sick-looking.

"I can't *believe* how stupid you are coming here, rat-boy," said the Piper as he approached him. He shook with effort and his voice righted itself. "Now I'm going to kill you and string your body up in the sewers for your father to find, and then I'm going to play for him and make him dance and dance, and eventually when he's *really* tired I'm going to kill him."

Saul pulled himself up, stumbled out of his way, sent a lumbering kick at the Piper's balls. The Piper grabbed his foot, pulled up very fast, sending him thumping onto his back and pushing the wind out of him. All the while he kept talking, amiable and animated.

"I'm the Lord of the Dance, I'm the Voice, and when I say jump, people jump. Except you. And I have you here about to die. You're a fucking *abortion*. If you don't dance to my tune, you don't belong in this world. Twenty-five years in the planning, and here's the rat's secret weapon, the supergun, the half-and-half." He shook his head and wrinkled his nose sympathetically. He kneeled next to Saul who struggled for breath, tried to hold his head up.

"I'm going to kill you now."

A high-pitched screech made them both look up. Something burst the plastic sheet shrouding the window with an improbable pop, shot through the tattered window of the flat, a figure, careering through the air toward the Piper, shoving into his body with an impact that took him flying away from Saul's supine body. Saul struggled up, saw an immaculately suited man trying to strangle the Piper, who convulsed, sending his adversary flying back across the room.

It was Loplop, with terror in his eyes, screaming at Saul to come on, grabbing him and running for the window, until a short clear sound stopped him cold. Saul turned and saw the Piper's puckered lips as he rose, whistling. A liquid tune, repetitive and simple. Loplop was stiff. Saul saw a look of wonder cross his face as he turned to face the Piper, his eyes alive and ecstatic.

Saul backed away, felt the wall behind him. He could see Deborah's corpse behind Loplop, see the stain of blood oozing liberally onto the floor. To his left was the Piper, moving forward now, still whistling. Before him was Loplop, stepping toward him, his eyes not seeing, his arms outstretched, his feet moving in rhythm to the Piper's bird song.

Saul tried to get past Loplop, could not, felt his throat underneath those fingers. The Bird Superior fell on him and began to squeeze the air out of him, all the while holding his own entranced face up to catch the music. He was not heavy but his body was as stiff as metal. Saul beat at him, twisted, tugged at his fingers. Loplop was impervious, unaware. As blackness began to creep in at the edges of his vision, Saul saw the Piper in the corner of the room, rubbing his throat, and the rage pushed blood back into Saul's face, even past Loplop's cruel talons, and he spread his arms wide, cupped his hands exactly as his father had warned him not to in the swimming pool, *even if you're just playing, Saul,* and he slammed his hands down, clapping with all his strength, around Loplop's ears.

Loplop shrieked and snapped up, arcing his back, his hands quivering. Saul's rat-strength had driven air deep into those aural cavities, shattering the delicate membranes and sending bubbles rushing in like acid through the ruptured flesh. Loplop shook in agony.

Saul rolled out from under him. The Piper was upon him again, and he wielded the flute like a club. Saul could only roll a little out of his way and feel it crush his shoulder rather than his face. He dodged again and this time his chest was struck, and the pain took his breath away.

Behind him Loplop stumbled away from the wall, fumbled blindly, as if his other senses had gone with his hearing.

The Piper gripped the flute in both hands, straddled Saul and pinned his arms to the floor with his knees, raised the flute like a ceremonial dagger, ready to drive the stubby object into Saul's chest. Saul screamed in terror.

Loplop still shrieked, and his voice mixed with Saul's. The dissonance made the air shake and something in the vibrations made Loplop turn and kick the flute from the Piper's clenched hands. The Piper bellowed in rage and reached for it. Loplop pulled Saul from under the tall man's legs, and hauled him to the window. Still Loplop shrieked, and the sound did not stop as he leapt onto the sill of the ruined window. He was still shrieking as he grabbed Saul with his right hand and stepped out into the darkness.

Saul could not hear his own despairing yell through Loplop's incessant keening. He closed his eyes and felt air swirl around him, waited for the ground, which did not come. He opened his eyes a little and saw a confusion of lights, moving very fast. He was falling still . . . the only sound was Loplop's wail.

He opened his eyes fully and he saw that the constriction around his chest was not terror but Loplop's legs, and that the ground was shooting not toward him but parallel to him, and that he was not falling but flying.

His head faced backwards, so he could not see Loplop as they flew. The Bird Superior's legs, elegant in Savile Row tailory, wrapped around him below his armpits. Terragon Mansions receded behind them. Saul saw a thin figure standing in the punctured plastic shadow of his father's flat, somehow heard a faint whistling over Loplop's cries.

In Willesden's dirty darkness the trees were obscure, a tangle of fractal silhouettes from which there now burst pigeons and sparrows and starlings, startled out of their sleep by the compulsion of the Piper's spell. They swirled like rubbish for a moment, and then their movements became as precise and sudden as a mathematical simulation.

They converged on the Piper, imploding from all sectors of the sky toward his hunched shoulders, and then en masse they rose again, suddenly clumsy, trying to fly in concert, dragging the Piper's body through the air with them.

"The fucker's following us!" Saul screeched in fright. He realized as he spoke that Loplop could not hear him, that all that stopped Loplop from joining his subjects in transporting the Piper was the fact that Saul had deafened him.

Saul rocked alarmingly in Loplop's tight embrace. The streets lurched below them. They oscillated uncertainly between the skies and the freezing earth. Loplop's wails were now turning to moans; he crooned to comfort himself. Behind them a writhing clot of birds dragged the Piper through the air after them. As birds fell away, exhausted or crushed, others rushed to their place, dug their claws into the Piper's clothes and flesh, pulling against each other, bearing him on in a butterfly's drunken rush.

The Piper was gaining on them.

The moon glinted briefly on water and railway tracks far below. Loplop began to spiral out of the sky.

Saul shook the legs that held him, shouted at him to continue, but Loplop was close to fainting, and the screaming in his head was all he could hear. Saul caught glimpses of a vast roadway and an undulating red plain below them, but they were snatched from his field of vision as Loplop's body spun. The Piper was closing in, shedding his entourage like a ragged man shedding clothes.

They fell. Saul caught glimpses of a network of railtracks spreading out like a fan, and then that red field again, the tight-packed roofs of a hundred red buses. They were spiralling toward Westbourne Park station, where bus routes and railways converged on a hill, under the yawning gloom of the Westway.

They swept into that shade and crashed to the ground. Saul was thrown from Loplop's grasp. He rolled over and over, came to a stop, covered in dust and dirt. Loplop lay some feet away, hunched up in a strange position, his arms wrapped around his head, his arse thrust into the air, his knees on the ground.

They were beside the dark entrance to the bus terminus. A little way off was the yard, full of the buses Saul had seen from the air. In the cavernous building before him were hundreds more. They were packed tight, an intricate puzzle set up and solved day after day; there was a strict order in which they could leave the garage. Each was surrounded by its fellows, no more than two feet away on any side, a maze of the ridiculous-looking vehicles.

Loplop's suit was muddy and ruined.

Moving unsteadily through the sky came the Piper. Saul stumbled across the threshold into the vaulted chamber, dragging Loplop behind him. He ducked out of sight behind the nearest bus, which constituted one of the red labyrinth's external walls. He shook Loplop's leg, pulled him toward him. Loplop flopped a little and lay still. He breathed heavily. Saul looked around frantically. He could hear the storm of wings which heralded the Piper's arrival, and above it the thin whistle of the Lord of the Dance himself. There was a gust of air as the Piper was swept down into the cold hall, spewing feathers in his wake.

The whistling stopped. Instantly the birds dispersed in panic, and Saul heard a thud as the Piper landed on the roof of a nearby vehicle. For a minute, there was no sound apart from the escaping birds, then footsteps approached across the buses' roofs.

Saul let go of Loplop's legs and flattened himself against the bus beside him. He crawled sidewise, striving for quietness. He felt feral instincts awaken in him. He was dead silent.

The bus was an old Routemaster, with an open platform at the back. Saul made his way silently into this opening, as the footsteps above him grew nearer. They moved slowly, up and down over the roofs, punctuated by little leaps as the Piper crossed the ravine between two vehicles.

Saul backed slowly up the stairs without a sound as the footsteps approached. Then again there was a jump, and the landing made him shudder with the vibration as the Piper leapt onto Saul's bus and strode across its roof.

The bus was in darkness. Saul moved backwards continually, his hands reaching out to touch the rows of seats on either side. He grasped the steel poles as if the bus was moving, steadying himself. His mouth hung open stupidly. He gazed at the ceiling, his eyes following the steps above. They crossed in a long diagonal, toward where he and Loplop had landed. Then they reached the edge and Saul's heart lurched into his mouth as the Piper's body flew past a window on his left. He froze, but nothing happened. The Piper had not seen him. Saul crouched silently, crept forward, came up from underneath the window-frame, pushed just enough of his head into the open to see, his hands framing his face, his eyes big, like a Chad graffitied on a wall.

Below him, the Piper was leaning over Loplop. He was touching him with one hand, his stance like a concerned bystander who finds someone sitting in the street and crying. The Piper's clothes were shredded from all the tiny bird claws, and they ran red.

Saul waited. But the Piper did not attack Loplop, just left him in his misery and bloody silence. He stood and slowly turned. Saul ducked down and held himself quite still. His mind suddenly began to replay the grotesque two-step he had seen the Piper perform with Deborah and he felt weak and enraged, and disgusted with himself, and scared. He breathed fast and urgent, with his face down on his knees, hunched on the top floor of the bus, in the dark.

And then he heard a whistling, and it came from the passenger entrance below. He felt the enormous welling of energy in his arms and legs that fear gave him.

The Piper's voice called up to him, as amiable and relaxed as ever.

"Don't forget I can smell you, little ratling." Feet began to mount the stairs and Saul scuttled backwards toward the front of the bus. "What, do you think you can live and sleep and eat in a sewer and I wouldn't smell you? Honestly, Saul . . . "

A dark figure appeared at the top of the stairs.

Saul rose to his feet.

"I'm the Lord of the Dance, Saul. You still don't get it, do you? You really think you're going to get away from me? You're dead, Saul, because you *just will not dance to my tune.*"

There was fury in his voice as he said that. The Piper stepped forward, and the weak light of the garage hit him. It was enough for Saul's rat eyes.

The Piper's face was a ghastly white, ruthlessly stripped of color. His hair had been tugged from its neat ponytail by a thousand frantic little claws, and it swept around his face and under his chin and around his throat as if it would strangle him. His clothes were pulled and stripped and tugged and unraveled and stretched in all directions, a collectivity of tiny injuries, and everywhere blood spattered him, streaked his milky face. His expression belied his ruined skin. He stared at Saul with the same relaxed, amiable gaze he had first levelled, the same banal cheerfulness with which he had greeted Saul, dispatched Deborah, the calm which had only disappeared for one moment when he could not make Saul dance.

"Saul," he said, in greeting, and held out his hands.

He walked forward.

"I'm not a sadist, Saul," he said, smiling. He held out his hand as he walked, and when it touched one of the steel poles that rose between seat and ceiling, he gripped it, then grasped it with his other hand. He began to twist it, his body straining and shaking violently with the effort, and the steel slowly bent and tried to stretch, snapped loudly. He did not take his eyes from Saul, nor did his expression change, even as he strained. He yanked at the broken end and the pole broke again, came away in his hand, a twisted cudgel of shining metal.

"I'm not eager to hurt you," he continued, resuming his pace. "But you are going to die, because you *won't dance* when I tell you to. So you're going to die now." The slender club swung down with a flash like an electric arc, and Saul hissed as he saw it move, jerked under the shining thing with a rodent's nervous grace. The club tore great gouts of stuffing into the air as it eviscerated a seat with its ragged tip.

The Piper's strength was awesome and unstoppable, dwarfing the tight rat muscles that reclaimed food had awoken in Saul, his new power that he was so proud of. He rolled away from the club and scuttled backwards to the front end of the bus. He thought of Deborah and rage choked him. His rat-side and his humanity oscillated violently, buffeted by the great storm of his anger. He wanted to *bite out the Piper's throat* and then he wanted to *beat* him, to *smash* his head, pummel him methodically with his fists and then he wanted to *claw at his stomach*, he wanted to gut him with his sharp claws. And he could do none of these things, because he was not strong enough, and the Piper would kill him.

The Piper straightened a little, paused and grinned at Saul. "Enough," he said and lunged straight forward, his weapon held like a spear. Saul screeched in fear and rage and frustration as his bestial reflexes carried him to the side of the brutal thrust.

There was no way past the Piper, that was clear as he jumped, and he pulled his legs up tight under him and brought them down on the seat beside him, and he drove them up again like pistons, kicking hard away from the seat, out to the side, punching at the glass next to him, stretching his body out like a diver, feeling the window fall around him in a million pieces, taking bits of his skin with it as it fell.

He flew through the air between the bus and its neighbor, another of the same route, that had preceded it into the maze. Saul's body passed fifteen feet above the ground, and then another wall of glass disintegrated under his ferocious rat fists and his arms and shoulders disappeared into the next bus before his feet had even left the last one, and the explosive collapse of the first window, still loud in his ears, segued into the next, and he was through, rolling off the seat, glass shards showering him like confetti.

He could still hear a spattering sound from outside, as little nuggets of glass hit the ground. He stood, shaking, ignored his ripped skin and deep bruises. He ran for the stairs at the back of the bus. From behind him he heard a strange sound, a roar of irritation, exasperation raised to the point of rage. There was a further loud crashing, and in the curved mirror at the top of the stairs he saw another window shatter, saw the Piper burst the glass feet-first and land sitting on a seat, his head craned to watch Saul. He swung up immediately, no more talk, and raced after Saul.

Saul careened down the stairs and out of the rear of the bus, running through the dark alleys between the sides of the great red vehicles, losing himself in the maze. He stopped, crouching, and held his breath.

From a way away he heard feet running, and a voice shouting, "What the fuck is going on?" *Oh Christ*, thought Saul. *The fucking guard*. Saul's heart was beating like a Jungle bassline.

He could hear the guard's leaden steps somewhere close by, and he could clearly hear the man's wheezing and panting. Saul stood quite still, tried to listen beyond the sounds of the guard, to hear any movement the Piper might make.

There was nothing.

An overweight, middle-aged man in a gray uniform emerged suddenly into the gap between buses in which Saul stood. The two men stood still for a moment, gazing stupidly at each other. They moved simultaneously. The guard approached with a truncheon raised, opened his mouth to shout, but Saul was on him, underneath the sluggish truncheon, pushing it out of his opponent's hand. He pinned the man's arm behind him, held his mouth closed and hissed in his ear.

"There is a very bad man in here. He will kill you. Leave *right now*."

The guard's eyes were blinking violently.

"Do you understand?" hissed Saul.

The guard nodded vehemently. He was looking around

frantically for his truncheon, deeply scared by the ease with which he had been disarmed.

Saul released him and the man bolted. But as he reached the end of the little bus-street, the sound of the flute pierced the air around them and he froze. Instantly Saul ran to him, slapped his face hard twice, pushed him, but the man's eyes were now ecstatic, fixed with a quizzical, overjoyed look over Saul's shoulder.

He moved suddenly, pushing Saul aside with a strength he should not possess, and skipped like an excited child deep into the red maze.

"Oh fuck, *no!*" breathed Saul, and overtook him, shoved him back, but the man kept moving, simply pushing past Saul without once looking at him. The flute was closer now, and Saul grabbed him in a bear hug, held him, tried to block his ears, but the man, impossibly strong, elbowed him in the groin and punched him expertly in the solar plexus, knocking the wind out of Saul and doubling him over in a crippling reflex prison. He could only stare desperately, willing himself to breathe, as the man disappeared.

Saul pulled himself up and hobbled after him.

In the heart of the bus maze was an empty space. It was a strange little room of red metal and glass, a monk's hole barely six feet square. Saul found his way toward the center, rounded a corner and was there, at the outskirts of the square.

Before him stood the Piper, flute to his lips, staring at Saul over the shoulder of the guard, who pranced ridiculously to the shrillness of the flute.

Saul grabbed the man's shoulders from behind, and hauled him away from the Piper. But the guard spun around and Saul saw that a shard of glass was embedded deep in one of his eyes and thick blood had welled all over his face. Saul shrieked and the Piper's playing stopped dead. The guard's expression took on a puzzled cast; he shook his head, raised his hand experimentally toward his face. Before he could touch his eye, silver flashed behind him and he dropped like a stone. A pool as dark and thick as tar began to spread very quickly from his broken head.

Saul was quite still.

The Piper stood before him, wiping his flute clean.

"I had to let you know, Saul, what I can do." He spoke quietly and did not look up, like a teacher who is very disappointed but is trying not to shout. "You see, I feel that you don't really believe what I can do. I feel that you think because *you* won't listen to me, no one else will. I wanted to show you *quite how hard* they listen, see? I wanted you to know. Before you die."

Saul leapt straight up.

Even the Piper stared, momentarily stupid with amazement, as Saul grabbed one of the surrounding buses' big wing-mirrors, pivoted in his flight, and swung his feet through the top front window. Then the Piper was there behind him, his flute thrust aggressively into his belt. No attempt to hide this time, Saul just hurled himself through windows again, leaping the gap to the next bus, bursting into its top deck. He picked himself up and leapt again, refusing to hear his screaming limbs and skin. Again and again, always followed, always hearing the Piper behind him, the two of them pushing through layer after layer of glass, littering the ground below, a fantastically fast and violent passage through the air, Saul desperate to reach the edge of the maze, eager to take this into open ground.

And then there it was. As he girded himself to leap through another window, he realized that what he could see through it was not just a bus two feet beyond, that he was looking out at a window in the garage wall itself, and through that at a house, a long way off. He smashed free of the last bus and leapt onto the window-ledge, halfway up the bricks. Between him and that house a gash was cut through London soil, a wide chasm filled with railway lines. And between Saul and those railway lines was nothing but a high fence of steel slats and a long drop.

Saul could hear the Piper still following him, great heavy crashes and vibrations rocking the massed ranks of buses. Saul kicked out the final window. He braced himself, jumped out and clutched at the dull metal barrier below. He landed across it, his weight shaking it violently. He clung to it tight, let his balance adjust. Scuttled a little forward, looked back at the ripped-out window. The Piper appeared, looked out. He had stopped grinning. Saul fled down the sheer metal, his descent something between an exercise in rat agility, a controlled slide, and a fall.

He looked up momentarily and saw the Piper trying to follow. But it was too far for him: he could not grasp that fence, he could not crawl like a rat can crawl.

"Fuck it!" he screamed, and snatched his flute to his lips. And as he played, all the birds began to return. They flocked once again to his shoulders.

The railway lines curved out of sight in both directions. Above him Saul could see buildings which seemed to jut out over the valley, seemed to loom over him. He ran, following the tracks to the east. He snatched a glimpse behind him, and saw the birds settling on the dark figure who stood in the window-frame. Saul lurched hopelessly on, and nearly sobbed with delight when he heard a tight metallic snap, a restrained rattling, and he knew that a train was approaching. He looked behind him and saw its lights.

He moved sideways a little, making room, running alongside the tracks. *Come on!* he willed it, as the two lights he could not help but think of as eyes slowly drew nearer. Above them he saw the scarecrow figure of the Piper approaching him.

But now the train was nearby and Saul was smiling as he ran, as his sores and his ripped skin pulled against each other.

Even as the Piper swung close enough for Saul to see his face, the tube train hurtled past Saul and he accelerated as it slowed for a bend, and as it passed him he threw himself at the back of the final carriage, grappling with it like a judo wrestler, jostling for position, thrusting his fingers deep into crevices and under extrusions of metal.

He pulled himself to the top and spread his arms wide, clinging tight to the edges of the roof as the train began to increase its speed. Saul swivelled on his stomach until he faced backwards, stretched his neck and looked up into the Piper's enraged face, bobbing up and down in the air, contorted even as he continued to play, borne aloft by a canopy of dying birds in this slit through the city, this roofless tunnel—but there was nothing the Piper could do to catch Saul now.

And as the train pulled away even faster, Saul saw him become a flying ragdoll, and then a speck, and then he couldn't see him anymore, and he looked instead at the buildings around him.

He saw light and motion inside them, and he realized that people were *alive* that night, making tea and writing reports and having sex and reading books and watching TV and fighting and expiring quietly in bed, and that the city had not cared that he had been about to die, that he had discovered the secret of his ancestry, that a murderous force armed with a flute was preparing to kill the King of the Rats.

The buildings above him were beautiful and impassive. Saul realized that he was very tired and bleeding and in shock, and that he had seen two people die that night, killed by a power that didn't care if they lived or died. And he felt a disturbance in the air behind him, and he put his head down and let his breath out in a great sob as the approaching tunnel swept up rubbish and sucked it in behind the train, as a sudden warm wind hit him like a boxer's glove, and all the diffuse city light went out and he disappeared into the earth.

PART FIVE

SPIRITS

Fabian shook his head, scrunched up his dreadlocks into vicious little bunches. His head ached terribly. He lay on his bed and pulled faces at the mirror just visible on his desk.

Lying some way off was his "work in progress," as his tutor insisted on calling it. The left two-thirds of the huge canvas were a garish panoply of metallic spray-paints and bright, flat acrylic; the right third was covered in ghost letters, faint pencil lines and charcoal. He had lost motivation for the project, though he still felt a certain pride in it as he stared at it again.

It was an illuminated manuscript for the 1990s, the letters a careful synthesis of mediaeval calligraphy and graffiti lettering. The whole screen, six feet by eight, consisted of just three lines: *Sometimes I want to lose myself in faith/and Jungle is the only thing I can turn to,/because in Drum an' Bass I know my place . . .*

He had thought of a phrase which started with an "S" because it was such a pleasing letter to illuminate. It was very large, contained in a box, and surrounded by ganja leaves and sound-system speakers and modern serfs, rudebwoys and gyals, an intricate parody, the expressionless zombies of monastic art executed by Keith Haring or one of the New York Subway Artists. The rest of the writing was mostly dark, but not matt-black, shot through with neon strips and encased in gaudy integuments. In the corner below the writing lurked the police, like devils: The Man. But these days the sloganeering had to be ironic. Fabian knew the rules and couldn't be bothered to disobey them, so the devils coming up from the pit were ridiculous, the worst nightmares of St. Anthony and Sweet Sweetback combined.

And up in the top right, though not yet drawn, would be the dancers, the worshippers who've found their way out of the slough of urban despond, a drab maze of grays in the center of the piece, to Drum and Bass heaven. The dancing was fierce, but he had been careful to make these faces more than ever like those in the old pictures he was mimicking: placid, stupid, expressionless. Because individualism, he remembered explaining earnestly to his lecturer, had no more place in a Jungle club than in a thirteenth-century church. That was why he loved it and why it frustrated him and sometimes frightened him. That was why the ambiguous text as well.

He was always on at Natasha to cut a really *political* track, and she demurred, claiming not to be interested, which irritated him. So until someone would do it, he would keep on with his loving chiding. Hence the Middle Ages, he had explained. The necessary displays of opulence and style at the clubs were as grandiose and vapid as any display of courtly etiquette, and the awe in which DJs were held was positively feudal.

At first, his tutor had hummed and hawed, and sounded unconvinced at the project, until Fabian had hinted that he did not appreciate the importance of Jungle in modern pop culture, and *that* had given it the seal of approval. All the lecturers at his art college would rather have died than admit that there were any gaps in their knowledge of *youth*.

But he was unable to concentrate on "Jungle Liturgy," even though he was quite proud of it.

He was unable to concentrate on anything except his disappearing friends. First Saul, in a blur of shocking violence and mystery, then Kay in circumstances far less dramatic but no less mysterious. Fabian could still not bring himself really to worry about Kay, although it had been at least a couple of weeks now since he had seen him, maybe more. He was concerned, but Kay was so vague, so aimless and genial, that any notion that he was in trouble was impossible to take seriously. It was, nonetheless, frustrating and perplexing. No one seemed to know where he had gone, including his flatmates, who were beginning to get agitated about his share of the rent.

And now it seemed as if he might be losing Natasha. Fabian scowled at the thought and turned over on his bed, sulking. He was angry with Natasha. She was obsessive about her music at the best of times, but when she was on a roll it was compounded. She was excited about the music she was making with Pete, a man Fabian considered too weird to be liked. Natasha was working on tracks to take to Junglist Terror, the event coming up fast in the Elephant and Castle. She had not called Fabian for several days.

It was Saul's departure, he thought, which had precipitated all this. Saul was hardly the leader of a social phalanx but, since his extraordinary escape from custody, something that held Fabian's friendships together had dissipated. Fabian was lonely.

He missed Saul deeply, and he was angry with him. He was angry with all his friends. He was angry with Natasha for failing to realize that he needed her, for not putting away her fucking sequencer and talking to him about Saul. He was quite sure she must be missing Saul, but she was such a control freak she was unlikely to discuss the matter. She would only allude to it obliquely and suddenly, and then refuse to say more about it. She would listen to him, though, patiently. She always broke that social contract, the exchange of insecurities and neuroses with one another. With Natasha the offering was always one-way. She either did not know, or did not care, how that disempowered him.

And Saul—Fabian was angry with Saul. He found it amazing his friend had not contacted him. He understood that something unbelievable must be going on in Saul's life, that it would take a lot to cut Fabian off so completely, but it still hurt him. And he was desperate to know what was happening! He was sometimes afraid now that Saul was dead, that the police had killed him and had concocted a bizarre story to allay suspicion, or that he was caught up in something huge— vague images of Triads flashed through Fabian's mind, and the London chapter of the Mafia, and God-knew-what—and that he had been routinely eliminated.

Often that seemed the likeliest explanation, the only thing that could explain the deaths of the police and Saul's escape, but Fabian could not believe he would have known nothing about his friend's involvement. It seemed unbelievable. And then he was forced to consider the possibility that Saul *had* killed those men—and his father, which he did not believe, definitely—but then . . . what *was* happening?

Fabian stared around him at his room, a tip of paint and record covers and clothes and CDs and posters and cups and wrappers and dirt and paper and books and pads and pens and canvas and bits of glass for sculptures and plates and postcards and peeling wallpaper. He was lonely and pissed off.

The view was so familiar Natasha did not see it. It was a *tabula rasa* to her, a white space on which she could impose her tunes. She had gazed out at it for so many hours and days, especially since Saul disappeared and Pete appeared, that she had achieved a Zen-like transcendence of it. She transcribed its features into her mind as nothingness.

First the net curtains, a tawdry throwback to the previous occupant that she had never bothered to get rid of. They moved slightly, a constant whiteness with flickering edges. Through this veil the trees, just at the level where the boughs thrust outward from the body. Stripped by winter, black branches clutching. So a film of curtain, then the twisted knots of wood, dark and intricate, a random lattice of twigs and thick limbs. Beyond that a streetlamp.

After dark when it had rained, she would sit at her window and poke her head out from under the net curtains and stare at that lamp through the tree outside. Its rays would pass through the thicket, lighting up the inside of each branch, surrounding the streetlight with thin circles of illuminated wood, composites of a thousand tiny wet sections reflecting the light. As Natasha moved her head, the streetlight's halo moved with it behind the tree. The lamp sat like a fat spider in the center of a wooden web.

Now it was day and the lamp was nothing, just another washed-out shape beyond the curtain, a shape Natasha was not seeing as she stared at it. Beyond it the houses on the other side of the street. The child's bedroom, the little study. The kitchen. The roofs, the slate anemic, its rough red invisible inside the room. Behind the roofs the jutting landmarks, the estates that stretched up over West London, squat and huge and awe-inspiring. Behind them a sky that was all cloud, a shifting scudding mass whose details twisted and turned and decayed leaving the totality unchanged.

Natasha knew every part of this diorama. Had anything been missing or different, she would have seen it immediately. Instead she saw that it was as it should be, and therefore she did not see it at all. In her careful itemization of its qualities, it became invisible.

She felt as if she would float into the clouds, sometimes.

She did not feel tethered at all.

She thought about Saul but she thought about basslines as well, and she wondered where he was, and she heard a stunning track suggest itself in her mind. She wondered where Pete was. She wanted to hear his flute. It was time to put some layers down onto *Wind City*. She realized that she could not really think straight. She had not felt secure and engaged for some days now. But she was eager to lay down some more flute.

Pared down as it was, Natasha wanted to strip the room of all its extraneous objects, the bed, the telephone, the cups she saw by her pillow. She wanted to close the door and ignore the rest of her flat and just stare at that window, at that view, through the dilute milk interference of the curtain. She wanted no sounds except the tiny murmurings of the street and her own sequencer, weaving her tune, making *Wind City* what she wanted.

A couple of weeks ago she had mentioned the track to Fabian when he had called her, and he had made a joke about the title: about eating too many beans, or something cretinous like that. She had brought the call to an abrupt close, and when she had put the receiver down she had cursed him, sworn at him, told him how fucking stupid and crass he was. A part of her had tried to evaluate his comment dispassionately, tried to see it as he saw it, but even as she understood she saw how wrong he was. Her opinion of Fabian was shaken. Maybe he had to hear the track, she concluded charitably.

He could not hear the word Wind without remembering his little idiot jokes in playgrounds, the puerile scatology she could not empathize with. It was a boy thing. How could she make him see what *she* saw when she named that track, when she played it and tweaked it and made it work so well it made her chest hollow?

To start, a tiny piano run from some histrionic Swingbeat rubbish. She had stripped it down so severely that she had dehumanized it. This was something different from her usual approach. The piano, the instrument that so often ruined Jungle, making her think of Happy House and idiotic Ibiza clubs, here turned into an instrument that signalled the destruction of anything human in this world. Deeply plaintive and melancholy, but ghostly. The piano tried to *remember* melancholia, and presented it as if for approval. Is this it? Is this sadness? it asked. I can't recall. And under the piano she faded in, for a fraction of a second, subliminal, she laid down a sample of radio static.

She had sought it for a long time, recording great swathes of sound from all the bands on her radio, rejecting them all, until she found and seized and created exactly what she wanted. And here she hinted at it.

The beat kicked in after the piano went around and came around several times, each time separated by a severe gap, a rupture in the music. And the beat was all snares at first, fast and dreamy, and a sound like a choir welled up and then resolved itself into electronic orchestration, fabricated emotion, a failed search for feeling.

And then the bassline.

A minimal program, a single thud, pause, another thud, pause, another, longer pause . . . double thud and back to the beginning. And underneath it all she began to make those snatches of radio static a little longer, and longer still, and looping them more and more randomly, until it was a constant, shifting refrain under the beat. A chunk of interference that sounded like someone trying to break out of white noise. She was proud of that static, had created it by finding a station on shortwave and then *just* missing it, so that the peaks and troughs of the crackling could have been voices, eager to make contact, and failing . . . or they could have just been static.

The radio existed to communicate. But here it was failing, it had gone rogue, it had forgotten its purpose like the piano, and the people could not reclaim the city.

Because it was a city Natasha saw as she listened. She sped through the air at huge speed between vast crumbling buildings, everything gray, towering and enormous and flattened, variegated and empty, unclaimed. And Natasha painted this picture carefully, took a long time creating it, dropping a hundred hints of humanity into the track, hints that could not deliver, dead ends, disappointments.

And when she had sucked her listener in to the city, all alone, Natasha brought on the Wind.

A sudden burst of flute mimicking the almost-speaking of the static, a trick she had pilfered from a Steve Reich album—God knew where she had heard that—where he made violins mimic human voices. The static rolled on and the beat rolled on and the soulless piano rolled on and as the static rose and fell the flute would shudder into existence behind it for a moment, a shrill echo, and then it would disappear. Gusts of Wind sweeping rubbish off the streets. Then again. More and more often, until two gusts of flute would appear, overlaying each other. Another and another would join in, a cacophony of simultaneous forces of nature, half-musical, half-feral, artificial, commentary, an intruder in the city that shaped it contemptuously, sculpted it. A long low wail of flute piped up from behind, gusting through everything, the only constant, dwarfing the effect of the other sounds, intimidating, humbling. The peaks and troughs in the static go, they are blown flat by the flute. The piano goes, each trill of notes reducing by one until it is just a single note like a slow metronome passing time. Then that, too, disappears. The intricacies of flute are superseded and only the great single wind remains. Flute, white noise, snares and bassline, stretching off for a long time, an unbroken architecture of deserted beats.

This was *Wind City*, a huge metropolis, deserted and broken, alone, entropic, until a *tsunami* of air breaks over it, a tornado of flute clears its streets, mocks the pathetic remnants of humanity in its path and blows them away like tumbleweed, and the city stands alone and cleared of all its rubbish. Even the ghost of the radio proclaims the passing of the people, a flat expanse of empty sound. The boulevards and parks and suburbs and center of the city were taken, expropriated, possessed by the Wind. The property of the Wind.

———

This was *Wind City*, the title that made Fabian laugh.

She could not talk to him after he had made his joke.

Pete really understood. In fact, when he heard pieces of the track, he told her that it was *she* who understood, that she really understood *him*.

Pete loved the track with an extraordinary passion. She supposed it appealed to him, the notion of the whole world possessed by the Wind.

The little flat in Willesden had become the setting for Crowley's dreams. He was no longer fooled by its nondescript architecture. This flat was a dynamo. It had been turned into a generator of horrors.

He was on his haunches, looking down at another ruined face.

The little flat was becoming steeped in violence. It contained some vast attractive force luring people in to violent and bloody mayhem. Crowley felt trapped in some ghastly time-slip. *Here we are again*, he thought, gazing at the destroyed and bloody mask beneath him.

There had been the first time, when he had seen Saul's father shattered on the lawn. Not systematically pulped like this, it was true. Maybe he had been running from the flat. Maybe that was why his injuries were less severe; he had tasted it in the air, he had known that had he stayed he would not just die but be crushed. He had not wanted to die like an insect, so he had hurled himself instead from the window, eager for a human death.

Crowley shook his head. His edge was blunting, he could not help it. Here we are *again*.

Then Barker, another one whose face was destroyed, and Page, looking over his own shoulder, impossible.

And now another had been broken on this sacrificial altar. The girl lay on her back, the floor around her was vile with blood. Her face was bent inward as if on a hinge. Crowley glanced up at the door-frame. That patch of wood there, with radial explosions of blood and saliva and mucus bursting out from it on all sides, that section of the frame *there*, that was where her face had been thrust.

Crowley vaguely remembered the sense of duty which pushed him into the dark corridors at night, as he lay sleeping. He would stand in the sitting room, where he was now, looking behind him, again, again, like a dog chasing its tail, unable to stand still because he knew that if he did something would come and *smash his face* . . .

He never saw Saul, in his dreams.

Bailey entered, pushing through the perplexed knot of uniforms.

"No sign of anything anywhere else, sir. Just this, just here."

"Has Herrin got anything?" he said.

"He's still talking to the uniform who got called to the bus station this morning. A load of the buses are smashed up; and the guard, they reckon it wasn't the glass in his eye that killed him. He was hit over the head with a long, thin stick."

"Our unusual club, again," mused Crowley. "Too thin for most people's taste; they like something that packs a wallop. Of course, if you're as strong as our murderer seems to be, the thinner the better. Less surface area, more pressure."

"Our murderer, sir?"

Crowley looked at him. Bailey seemed confused, and even accusatory. Crowley could tell that he thought his superior was losing it. The extraordinary nature of the crimes had affected Bailey in the opposite way from Crowley. He had been thrust toward an aggressive, dogmatic common sense, determined to bring Saul to heel, refusing to be overawed or surprised by the carnage he saw.

"What?" demanded Crowley.

"You sound unsure, sir. Have you got some reason for thinking it's not Garamond?"

Crowley shook his head as if at a mosquito, irritated, brushing the air. Bailey withdrew.

Yes, I have ample reason, thought Crowley, *because I interviewed him and saw him. I mean Jesus look at him, he did not do this. And if he did, then something happened to change him in that night after I interviewed him, and he changed so much he is no longer what I saw, in which case I am still right, Saul Garamond did not do this, and I don't give a shit what you and Herrin think, you lumbering great pricks.*

Nothing added up. The dead guard at Westbourne Grove was clearly the victim of the same man as had killed the two policemen, and this girl here lying ruined in blood and bone. But the police had been called to the bus station minutes after the inhabitants of Terragon Mansions had reported violent shouts and bumps from upstairs. And Westbourne Park was simply too far from Willesden to be reached in that time. So whoever was shattering all that glass in those buses and pushing it in that poor man's eye could *not be* the same one who had destroyed this woman.

Of course, Herrin and Bailey saw no problem with this. Someone had been confused about the time. The people in Willesden must be half an hour or so out. Or the people in Westbourne Grove were, or both were fifteen minutes out, or something. And the fact that so many were out by the same amount, well, what did *you* think happened then, sir? If not that?

And of course Crowley had no answer.

He was intrigued by reports of music coming from the garage at the time Saul—or whoever—was destroying it. The reports were vague, but seemed to indicate a high-pitched sound like a recorder or a flute or pipes, or something. Saul was no musician, Crowley knew that, though he was apparently something of an aficionado of Dance music, the kind that his taciturn friend Natasha played. So what of the pipes?

Crowley could see the scenario being created for Saul. Saul had become a serial killer. And Saul therefore needed rituals, such as the return to this, the site of his first murder, that had unhinged him. And the playing of music at the site of a murder, such as the one at the bus station, what was this but ritualized? Perhaps he had played music also at the death of the as yet unidentified man in the underground, a crime Crowley was still sure was part of the same rampage. The public-transport connection only strengthened his conviction.

So, why was Saul no longer into Dance music? Why had he started playing what most of those who had heard it described as Folk music? None of this was airtight, of course, of course . . .

But Crowley could not help thinking it might be *another* who had played the music in the bus station. Why not? Why must it be Saul? What if it was *another* who mocked him with this music so utterly different to Saul's own taste?

Crowley straightened up suddenly. A long, thin, light club. Made of metal: the impact was clear about that. Something the murderer hung on to, used more than once. Took from crime to crime. Where he played music, it seemed.

"Bailey!" Crowley yelled.

The big man appeared, still impatient, still exasperated with his boss.

He all but rolled his eyes at Crowley's new question.

"Bailey, do any of Saul's mates play the flute?"

TWENTY-ONE

Deep underneath London, King Rat skulked and ferreted in the darkness.

He clutched a stash of food, carried it slung over one shoulder like a swag bag. His strides were long and left no sign. He stalked silently through the water of the sewers.

The rats ran as he approached. The braver souls stayed a little to spit at him and provoke him. His smell was deeply ingrained in their nervous system, and they had been taught to despise it. King Rat ignored them. Walked on. His eyes were dark.

He passed like a thief in the night. Unclear. Minimal. Dirty. Subaltern. His motives were opaque.

He reached under the dirty stream to dislodge the plug to his throne room, slid through the murk into the great teardrop chamber. He shook the water from him, and stamped into the room.

Saul came from behind him. He clutched a broken chair leg which he swung at an incredible speed and cracked against the back of King Rat's skull.

King Rat flew forward and flung his arms out with a sudden shrill bark of pain. He sprawled, rolled, clutching his head, regained his footing.

Food spread across the sodden floor.

Saul was upon him, quivering, his jaw set hard and tight. He swung the chair leg again and again.

King Rat was as pliable as quicksilver. He slid impossibly out of Saul's flurry of blows and scampered away, hissing, clutching his bleeding head.

He spun to face Saul.

Saul's face was a mosaic of bruises and blood and puffy flesh. King Rat was quite still. He eyed Saul with his hidden eyes. His teeth were bared and glinted with dirty yellow light. His breath came hard. His hands were crooked into eager claws.

But Saul hit him again, before those claws could move. Saul's hands and club came at him hard, but King Rat ripped up with his clawed hands and drew lines on Saul's stomach, below his ruined shirt.

Saul spoke, muttering in time to the blows he attempted to land.

"So what the fuck was Loplop doing there, unh?" *Slam*.

King Rat slipped inside his club. It hit the floor loudly.

"Tell him to follow me, unh?" *Slam*. "What was he going to do—report back?" *Slam*. This time the wood connected and King Rat yelled in rage.

King Rat growled and slashed at Saul with those claws, and Saul bellowed and swung the club with renewed venom. The two of them skittered around the dark room, slipping on mold and food, moving now on two limbs, now on four. Saul and King Rat moved like liminal figures, hovering between evolutionary strata, bestial and knowing.

"So was Loplop going to send a message, unh? A bird? Little *bird* going to let slip where I was, then?"

Again the attacks came, again King Rat moved, refusing to engage in battle, content to draw blood and slip away, his teeth still visible and wicked.

"What if Loplop had accidentally told someone else where I was, unh? Was I fucking *bait?*" King Rat caught the club with his right hand and bit at it suddenly and savagely, and it dissolved in a burst of splinters. Saul did not pause, but grasped King Rat's filthy lapels and carried him down into the muck, straddling him.

"Well you needn't have bothered, you fucking *shit*, because the Piper was *there* and look what he *did* to me, you shit. You just weren't ready, you and 'Nansi, so poor old Loplop had to take him on his own." Saul pinioned King Rat's arms to the brick floor and began systematically to punch his face. But even trapped like that King Rat writhed and slipped under him, and many of the heavy blows did not land.

Saul thrust his face right up to King Rat, and stared through the shadows on his eyes.

"I know you wouldn't give a fuck if I'd died, as long as I took Piper-man with me," he hissed. "And I know *you* killed my dad, you fucking shithead rapist, you piece of crud—not the fucking Piper . . ."

"*No.*" King Rat shouted the word out and convulsed, throwing Saul from him and sliding in a single movement until he stood in characteristic pose by the throne, skulking and aggrandizing, but this time with his claws bared and his teeth dangerous, coated in slaver like a wild animal. Saul moved backwards in the dirt, fought to right himself.

King Rat spoke again. "I never bumped off your dad, stupid. I killed the Usurper."

The word stayed in the air after he had spoken it.

King Rat spoke again.

"*I'm* your dad . . ."

"No you fucking aren't, you weird old fucked-up spiritual degenerate," replied Saul instantly. "I might have your blood in my veins, *you fucking rapist bastard,* but you aren't *shit* to me."

Saul smacked himself on the forehead, laughing bitterly.

"I mean, hello? 'Your mother was a rat, and I'm your uncle.' Jesus, nice one—playing me like a fucking idiot! *And . . .* " Saul paused and jerked his finger viciously at King Rat, "and, that goddamn fucking *lunatic* Piper who wants me dead only knows about me because of *you.*"

Saul sat down hard and held his head in his hands. King Rat watched him.

"I mean, I keep saying I've sorted it out, right?" Saul murmured. "And I just can't stop thinking about it. You killed my father, you rapist *shit,* and when you did that you let some fucking spirit of darkness out after me, you gave him my fucking *address,* and, what, I'm supposed to go 'Daddy!'?" Saul shook his head in disgust. He felt his gut twist with contempt and hatred. "You can fuck off. It doesn't work like that."

"So what're you after, an apology?"

King Rat was scornful. He moved toward Saul.

"What do you want? *We're blood.* It was half an age since I left, since you were a little Godfer in the fat man's arms. I could clock you getting flabby. It was time to join your old dad, the cutpurse king. *We're blood.*"

Saul stared up at him.

"No, fucker, I don't want shit from you." Saul stood. "What I want is out." He moved off behind the throne, turned to face King Rat. "You can deal with the Piper on your own. He only wants me because of you, you know? You've been *bragging* about me, you stupid shit. You don't give a fuck about family. *You raped my mum so you could have your weapon.* The Piper knows it; he called me the secret weapon. *I know what I mean to you.* I know I'm a good way of getting at him, because he can't control me.

"But he only wants me dead because of *you.* So, tell you what."

Saul moved backwards as he spoke, toward the room's peculiar exit.

"Tell you what. *You* deal with the Piper as best you can, and *I'll* look after *myself*. Agreed?"

And Saul looked King Rat in the eye, those eyes he could still not see, and he left the room.

Up above the sewers: in the sky, over the slate. Out in the air. Saul fingered the skin over his bruises and felt it stretched out taut and split. He gazed at London, spread out before him, unfolding, the underworld threatening to burst through, to rupture its surface tension. It was dark; his life was always dark now. He was becoming a night creature.

His body hurt. His head ached, his arms were scratched and stretched, his muscles burned with deep bruises. But he could not stay still. He felt a desperate eagerness to work *through* it, to burn the pain out of his body. He swung meaninglessly around girders and antennae, loose-limbed and elegant like a gibbon. He was suddenly very hungry, but he remained on the roofs for a while, running and jumping over low walls and skylights. He straddled the intricacies of St. Pancras station, and sped along the spine of roofs which jutted out behind it like a dinosaur's tail.

This was the realm of the arches. Weird little businesses waged a battle against empty space, cramming into the unlikely hollows below the railway lines. They proclaimed themselves with crude signs.

OFFICE EQUIPMENT CHEAP.
WE DELIVER.

Saul descended to street level. He was fighting to channel the force of elation which had flooded through him at his renunciation of King Rat. He was fragile, ready to burst into tears or hysterics. He was captivated by London.

Someone approached him from around a corner: a woman in heels, he could hear, a brave soul walking this area alone at night. He did not want to scare her, so he slumped against a wall and slid down to the floor, just a comatose drunk.

The associations of homelessness struck him and, as the heels clicked by him unseen, he thought of Deborah and he felt his throat catch. And then it was easy to think of his father.

But Saul did not have time for this, he decided. He leapt up and followed his nose to the dustbins of this odd realm, a world where the streets were empty of houses, where the only things that surrounded him were the peculiar businesses, Victorian throwbacks.

The bins were not rich in pickings. Without domestic rubbish there was little to them. Saul crept back toward King's Cross. He found his way to the dumping grounds of the all-night eateries, and amassed a huge pile of food. He played games with himself, refusing to allow himself to eat a mouthful until he had collected everything he wanted.

He sat in the shade of a skip in a cul-de-sac by a Chinese take-away and fondled the food he had collected, chunks of greasy meat and noodles.

Saul gorged himself. He ate as he had not for days. He ate to fill all the cavities inside him, to drive out anything that had been left behind.

King Rat had used him as bait, but the plan had gone wrong. The Piper had pre-empted his plan.

As Saul stuffed himself, he felt an echo of that surge of strength that had coursed through him the first time he ate reclaimed food, found food, rat food.

The Piper still wanted him dead, of course, now more than ever. He did not think he would have to wait too long before the Piper came for him.

It was a new chapter, he reflected. Away from King Rat. Out of the sewer. He ate until his belly felt dangerously taut, and then resumed his position in the skyline.

Saul felt as if he would burst, not from food but from something that had been released inside him. *I should be mad,* he thought suddenly, *and I'm not. I haven't gone mad.*

He could hear sounds from all over London, a murmuring. And as he listened, it resolved itself into its components, cars and arguments and music. He felt as if the music was everywhere, all around him, a hundred different rhythms in counterpoint, a tapestry being woven underneath him. The towers of the city were needles, and they caught at the threads of music and wound them together, tightened them around Saul. He was a still point, a peg, a hook on which to wind the music. It grew louder and louder, Rap and Classical and Soul and House and Techno and Opera and Folk and Jazz and Jungle, always Jungle, all the music built on drum and bass, ultimately.

He had not listened to music for weeks, not since King Rat had come for him, and he had forgotten it. Saul stretched as if waking from a sleep. He heard the music with new ears.

He realized that he had defeated the city. He crouched on the roof (of what building he did not know) and looked out over London at an angle from which the city was never meant to be seen. He had defeated the conspiracy of architecture, the tyranny by which the buildings that women and men had built had taken control of them, circumscribed their relations, confined their movements. These monolithic products of human hands had turned on their creators, and defeated them with common sense, quietly installed themselves as rulers. They were as insubordinate as Frankenstein's monster, but they had waged a more subtle campaign, a war of position more effective by far.

Saul kicked carelessly off and stalked across the roofs and walls of London.

He could not put off thinking forever.

Tentatively, he considered his position.

King Rat was no longer with him. Anansi was his own man, would do whatever made him and his kingdom safest. Loplop was mad and deaf and maybe dead.

The Piper wanted to kill them all.

Saul was on his own. He realized that he had no plan, and felt a curious peace. There was nothing he could do. He was waiting for the Piper to come to him. Until then he could go underground, could investigate London, could *find his friends* . . .

He was afraid of them now. When he let himself think of them, he missed them so much it made him ache, but he was not made of the same stuff as them anymore, and he was afraid that he did not know how to be their friend. What could he say to them, now that he lived in a different world?

But perhaps he didn't live in a different world. He lived where he wanted, he thought suddenly, furiously. Wasn't that what King Rat had told him, all that time ago? He lived wherever he wanted, and even if he didn't live in the same world as them anymore, he could visit, couldn't he?

Saul realized how much he wanted to see Fabian.

And he remembered as well that the Piper wanted to kill him precisely because he could move between the worlds. He felt a fleeting sense of loneliness as he thought about the Piper, and then he realized that the smell of rat was all around him, was always all around him. He stood slowly.

He realized that the smell of London *was* the smell of rat.

He began to hiss for attention, and lithe heads poked out of piles of rubbish. He barked a quick order and the ranks began to approach him, tentatively at first and then with eagerness. He shouted for reinforcements and seething waves of filthy brown bodies boiled over the lip of the roof, and from chimneys and fire escapes and hidden corners, like a film of spilt liquid running backwards, they congealed around him, tightly wound, an explosion frozen at the flashpoint, hovering with suppressed violence, hanging on his words.

He would not face the Piper alone, he realized. He would have all the rats in London on his side.

TWENTY-TWO

Sometimes, between putting food in her mouth and sleeping and then Jungle, seeing Pete, Natasha remembered other things.

She remembered something; she had a sense of being needed for something. She could not be sure what it was until somebody called her. She fumbled with the phone, confused.

"Yo yo Tasha!"

The voice was bizarre, muted and enthusiastic. She did not recognize it at all.

"Tash man, you there? It's Fingers. I got your message about Terror and, yeah, that's no problem. We're going to stick you on the poster, make out like you're famous. No one's gonna admit they haven't heard of you." The man on the telephone yelled with laughter.

Natasha muttered that she did not understand.

There was a long pause.

"Look, Tash, you faxed me, man—told me you wanted to spin some at Junglist Terror . . . you know, couple of weeks' time? Well, that's fine. I wanted to know what name you're under, because we're chucking out some last-minute posters. Going to do a blitz down Camden, down your way too."

What name? Natasha gathered herself, played the phone call by ear, pretended she understood what was happening.

"Put me in as Rudegirl K."

That was a name she used. Was that what he wanted, the man? Gradually she began to remember and to understand. Junglist Terror, near the Elephant and Castle. It came back. She smiled delightedly. Had she asked for an opportunity to play? She could not remember that, but she could play *Wind City*, she didn't mind . . .

Fingers rang off. He seemed perturbed, but Natasha only promised to come on the date he told her, and agreed that she would spread the word. She held the receiver against her ear for a little bit too long after he had rung off. The buzz confused her again, until gentle hands reached around her head and disentangled her from the machine.

Pete was there, she realized with a jolt of pleasure. He put the receiver down, turned her to look at him. She wondered how long he had been with her. She looked up at him, smiled beatifically.

"I forgot to tell you that, Natasha," he said. "I thought we should take the opportunity to show the world what we've been doing. So we're going to play *Wind City*. OK?"

Natasha nodded and smiled.

Pete smiled back. His face; Natasha saw his face. It seemed hurt, she saw long thin scabs adorning it, but she did not really *notice* them somehow, he grinned so happily. His face was very pale, but he smiled at her with the same wide-eyed pleasure she always associated with him. *Such a sweetie*, she thought, *so green*. She smiled.

Pete backed away from her, holding her hand until he was out of reach.

"Let's play some music, Natasha," he suggested.

"Oh yes," she breathed. That would be excellent. A little Drum and Bass. She could lose herself in that, take the tunes apart in her mind, see how they fitted together. Maybe they could play *Wind City*.

All of Saul's friends were accounted for, apart from the man Kay. As he considered the piece of paper he held, the queasy foreboding in Crowley's stomach grew. He was afraid he knew exactly where Kay was.

He felt ridiculous, like a cop from some American TV show, operating on hunches, responding to preposterous gut feelings. He had sought to cross-refer the data that had been gathered on the ruined body in the tube with the information they had on Saul's friend Kay, who had been missing now for a couple of weeks.

For a while, Crowley had played with the idea that Kay could be behind all this. It would be so much easier to attribute the carnage he had seen to the other missing man. He kept his conjectures to himself. His unwillingness to see Saul as the killer made no sense to those around him, and he could understand why. There was just something, there was just something . . . the thoughts went around and around in his head . . . it did not work; he had seen Saul; there was something else happening.

He jeopardized control of the investigation with his disquiet. He was reduced to scribbled notes to himself, exchanging favors with laboratory technicians, the usual channels too risky for his ideas. He could not sit with his men and women and brainstorm, bouncing possibilities back and forth, because they knew full well who they were looking for. His name was Saul Garamond, he was an escaped prisoner and a dangerous man.

So Crowley was cut off from discussion, the medium in which his best work was done. He was afraid that without it his notions were stunted, half-truths, soiled with the muck of his own mind that no one could brush off for him. But he had no choice; he was atomized.

Kay as killer. That was one of the ideas that he must dispense with. Kay was peripheral, not close to any of the main protagonists in this drama. He had even less motive than Saul for any of these actions. He was even less physically impressive than Saul.

And besides, his blood group matched that which had covered the walls of Mornington Crescent station.

The fragments of jaw that could be analyzed seemed to match Kay's.

Nothing was certain, not with a body as destroyed as that had been. But Crowley believed he knew who they had found.

And he still, he *still*, could not believe that it was Saul they wanted.

But he could talk to no one about this.

Nor could he share the pity he felt, a pity which was welling up inside him more with every day, a pity which was threatening to dwarf his horror, his anger, his disgust, his fear, his confusion. A growing pity for Saul. Because if he was right, if Saul was not the one responsible for all the things Crowley had seen, then Saul was *right in the middle* of something horrendous, a kaleidoscope of bizarre and bloody murder. And Crowley might feel isolated, might feel cut off from those around him, but if he was right, then Saul . . . Saul was truly alone.

Fabian returned to his room and immediately felt bad again. The only time now that he did not feel oppressed by isolation was when he got on his bike and rode around London. He was spending more and more of his time on the road these days, burning up the junk calories he got from the crap he was eating. He was a wiry man, and his hours and hours on the road were stripping the final ounces of excess flesh from him. He was being pared down to skin and muscle.

He had ridden for miles in the cold and his skin blushed with the change of temperature. He sweated unpleasantly from his exertions, his perspiration cold on him.

Straight south he had ridden, down Brixton Hill, past the prison, through Streatham, down toward Mitcham. Real suburbia, houses flattening down, shopping districts becoming more and more flat and soulless. He had ridden up and down and around roundabouts and along sidestreets: he needed to cross traffic, to wait his turn on the road, to look behind him and indicate brief thanks to someone letting him in, he needed to cut in front of that Porsche and ignore the fact that he had pissed them off . . .

This was Fabian's social life now. He interacted on the fucking tarmac, communicated with people passing him in their cars. This was as close as he came to relationships now. He did not know what was happening.

So he rode around and around, stopped to buy crisps and chocolate, orange juice maybe, ate on the saddle, standing outside the poky little groceries and newsagents he now frequented, balancing his bike next to the faded boards advertising ice-cream and cheap photocopying.

And then back out onto the road, back into the cursory conversations of the roadways, his dangerous flirtations with cars and lorries. There was no such thing as society, not anymore, not for him. He had been stripped of it, reduced to begging for social scraps like signalling and brake lights, the rudenesses and courtesies of transport. These were the only times now that anyone took notice of him, modified their behavior because of him.

Fabian was so lonely it made him ache.

His answering machine blinked at him. He pressed play and the policeman Crowley's voice jerked into life. He sounded forlorn, and Fabian did not think it was just the medium which was having that effect. Fabian listened with the contempt and exasperation he always felt when he dealt with the police.

" . . . pector Crowley here, Mr. Morris. Ummm . . . I was wondering if you might be able to help me again with a couple of questions. I wanted to talk to you about your friend Kay and . . . well . . . perhaps you could call me."

There was a pause.

"You don't play the flute, do you, Mr. Morris? Would you or Saul have known anyone who does?"

Fabian froze. He did not hear what else Crowley said. The voice continued for a minute and stopped.

A wave of gooseflesh engulfed him briefly and was gone. He fumbled, stabbed at the rewind button.

" . . . ould call me. You don't play the flute, do you, Mr. Morris?"

Rewind.

"You don't play the flute, do you, Mr. Morris?"

With an agony of numb fingers Fabian fast-forwarded, found the number Crowley gave. He punched it into the phone. Why does he want to know *that*? why *that*? his mind kept begging.

The number was busy, and a pleasant female voice told him he was in a queue.

"Mother*fucker*!" Fabian yelled and threw the receiver at the cradle. It bounced and hung from its cord, the dial tone just audible.

Fabian was trembling violently. He tugged at his bike, wrestled it through the constricted entrance hall and hurled it ready for him into the street. He slammed the door behind him. Adrenaline and terror made him feel sick. He lurched into the road and sped toward Natasha's house.

No sociability now. He wove in and out of cars, leaving a cacophony of horns and curses in his wake. He twisted around corners at sharp, sharp angles, leaving pedestrians leaping out of his way.

Jesus Christ Jesus Christ, he thought, *why does he want to know that? What has he found out? What has a man who plays the flute done?*

He was over the river now, Jesus God knew how, he realized he was risking his life at every second. He seemed to be in and out of fugues, he had no recollection at all of passing through the intervening streets before the bridge.

Blood poured through Fabian's veins. He felt giddy. The cold air woke him, slapped him in the face.

He saw a clump of phone boxes speeding into view before him. He was struck with a sudden realization of his isolation, again. He tugged at his brakes and pulled his bike up short, letting it fall to the ground and breaking into a run before it had stopped moving. The nearest box was empty, and he ransacked his pockets for money, pulled out a fifty-pence piece. He dialed Crowley's number.

Dial 999 you stupid fucker! he suddenly admonished himself, but this time Crowley's phone was ringing.

"Crowley."

"Crowley, it's Fabian." He could hardly speak; the words swallowed each other up in their eagerness. "Crowley, go to Natasha's house *now*. I'll see you there."

"Now, hold on, Fabian. What's this all about?"

"*Just be there, motherfucker! The flute, the fucking flute!*" He hung up.

What's he doing to her? Fabian thought as he ran to his bike. Its pedals still spun slightly where it lay. That weird fucker who just *appeared*, Jesus! He had thought she was having an affair with him, that this explained her weird behavior, and the obscure challenge Fabian always sensed from Pete. But what if . . . what if that was not the whole story? What did Crowley know?

He was nearly there now, speeding toward Natasha's house. London light surrounded him. He could not hear the traffic at all, he relied only on his eyes to stay alive.

Another sharp turn and there was Ladbroke Grove. He realized briefly that he was drenched in sweat. The day was overcast and cold, and his wet skin was frozen. Fabian felt like crying. He felt utterly out of control, as if he could have no effect on the world.

He turned, and was in Natasha's street. It was as deserted

as usual. The ringing in his ears dispersed and there was the Drum and Bass, the soundtrack to Natasha's house. Dreamy and washed out, a very bleak song. He could feel it creeping into him behind his eyes.

He stepped free of his bike, letting it fall beside her door.

Fabian rang the bell. He put his finger on the button and did not release it until he saw a form approach behind the smoked-glass door.

Natasha opened the door to him.

Fabian wondered for a moment if she was stoned: she looked so vague, her eyes so clouded. But he saw how white she looked, how thin, and he knew that this was more than dope.

She smiled when she saw him, and looked up at him with unfocused eyes.

"Hey, Fabe, man, how's it going?" She sounded tired, but she raised her hand to touch fists.

Fabian took her hand. She looked at him in mild surprise. He put his lips close to her ear.

His voice, when he spoke, was unsteady.

"Tash, man, is Pete here?"

She looked up at him, creased her face quizzically, nodded.

"Yeah. We're practicing. For Junglist Terror."

Fabian began to tug at her.

"Tash, we have to go. I want you to come with me. I promise I'll explain, but come with me *now* . . . "

"Oh, no." She did not sound angry or perturbed. But she pulled away from him gently and began to close the door. "I've got to play some tracks with him."

Fabian pushed the door open and grabbed her. He held her mouth closed with his right hand. She struggled, her eyes suddenly wide, but he dragged her toward the door.

His eyes were prickling, and he whispered to her. "Tash *please* you don't *understand* he's something to *do with it all* we have to get *away* . . . "

"Hi, Fabian! How's it going?"

Pete had appeared at the top of the stairs. He looked

down at them both, his body poised in mid-stride. He grinned amiably.

Fabian froze, as did Natasha, in his arms.

Fabian stared at Pete's face. It was white, criss-crossed with vicious, half-healed scratches, bloody and intricate. He affected his usual cheerful expression but his eyes were giving him away now, open a little too wide, staring a little too hard.

Fabian realized that he was very frightened of Pete. Fabian wondered how long before Crowley would be there.

"Hey, Pete, man . . . " he muttered. "Uh . . . I was wanting . . . me and Tash might split for a bit . . . uh . . . "

Pete shook his head, looking amused and rueful.

"Oh, Fabian, you mustn't go. Come hear what we've been playing."

Fabian shook his head and stumbled backwards a little more.

"Natasha?" said Pete, and turned to her. He whistled something very quickly. Instantly Natasha spun in Fabian's arms and twisted her leg, taking his feet from under him and kicking the door closed behind him in one motion. She stood to one side as he fell against the door. He stared at her, and her eyes clicked back into the focus that had momentarily deserted her.

Fabian fumbled behind him for the latch, his mouth open, his legs wobbling as he stood.

"Look, Fabe," said Pete reasonably, descending toward him. "It's simple." Natasha stood still and gazed at him as he approached. "I don't know quite what you've worked out or how, and I'm impressed, really I am, but now what? What to do with you? I could kill you, like I did Kay, but I think I've got a better idea."

An angry, frightened little noise issued from Fabian's throat. Kay . . . what had happened to him?

"So anyway, the first thing I think is that you should come upstairs." Pete motioned to the room above them, and the faint strains of Jungle that had been filtering down the stairs seemed to *swell*, the plaintive song that he had caught from outside was suddenly filling Fabian's head. And it was such a beautiful song, it completely took him away . . .

It made him think of so many things . . .

He was on the stairs, he realized, and then he was in the bedroom, but he wasn't really bothered about that, because what was important was that he should *hear this song*. There was something about it . . .

It stopped and he caught his breath, stumbled, felt as if he was choking.

The room was silent. Pete had one hand by the on/off switch on the sequencer. Natasha stood next to him, her arms by her side, the same free-floating look in her eyes. With his left hand Pete held a kitchen knife to her throat. She obligingly held her head up.

Fabian opened his mouth in horror and gesticulated toward the two of them, frozen like a waxwork scene of the moment of murder. He emitted inchoate sounds.

"Yes yes yes, Fabian. Answer or I slit her throat." Pete's voice was still measured, urbane. "Is anyone else coming?"

Fabian's eyes flitted around the room as he tried to gauge the situation. He shrieked as Pete pressed the knife to her throat, and blood welled up around it.

"Yes! Yes! The police are coming!" Fabian screamed. "And they're going to *fucking take you*, you *motherfucker* . . ."

"Nope," said Pete. "Nope, they won't."

He released Natasha and she touched her neck experimentally, screwing up her face, perturbed and confused by the blood. She picked up her pillow and pressed it to the side of her neck, watched it stain red.

Pete kept his eyes on Fabian. He fumbled on the top of the keyboard and gathered up some DATs which sat there.

"Tash?" he said. "Grab your record bag and a few twelve-inches. We're going to go to mine until Junglist Terror." He smiled at Fabian.

Fabian bolted for the door. He heard a faint whispering and his left calf burst into agony. He screamed as he fell. The kitchen knife was embedded deep in the muscle of his lower leg. He fumbled at it with bloody fingers and screamed when he had the breath.

"See," said Pete, sounding amused. "I can make you dance to my tune, but fuck it, sometimes other methods do the job." He stood over Fabian.

Fabian closed his eyes and laid his head on the floor. He was fainting.

"You *will* come to Junglist Terror, won't you, Fabe?" said Pete. Behind him Natasha quietly gathered some things. "You may not feel like dancing now, but I promise you will. And you can do me a favor."

The faint percussive thump of the Drum and Bass beat which wafted into Bassett Road was washed out, rendered nothing by the sirens. Two police cars slid to a stop outside the house. Uniformed men and women leapt out and raced to the door. Crowley stood beside one of the cars. Behind him, the residents peered out of their doors and windows.

"Have you come about all that screaming? That was quick," said an old man approvingly to Crowley.

Crowley looked away as his stomach yawned. He felt sick with foreboding.

Next to the door a bicycle lay on the pavement. Crowley stared at it as the battering ram took care of the door. The police swept up the stairs in a confused mass. Crowley saw the guns at the ready.

There was a sound of heavy feet in the house, audible in the street outside. The faint Jungle beat jerked to an abrupt halt. Crowley strode after the advance party into the hallway. He jogged up the steps and waited by the front door to the flat.

A short woman in a flak jacket approached him.

"Nothing, sir."

"Nothing?"

"They're gone, sir. Not a sign. I think you should see this."

She led him into the flat. It was thick with heavy bodies. The air was full of authoritative voices, the sounds of searching.

Crowley looked around him at the bare walls of the sitting room. By the entrance to the room was a pool of blood, still slick and sticky. One of the white pillows on the futon was stained deep red.

The keyboard, the stereo, a handbag . . . everything was untouched. Crowley strode over to the turntable. A twelve-inch single rested on it. The needle had skipped, pushed off course by the vibration of the heavy police boots. Crowley swore.

When he raised his voice it dripped bile.

"I don't suppose anyone saw how far through the record we were? No?"

Everyone stared at him in incomprehension.

"Because *that* way we could have told how long ago they left."

They looked away, surly. Next time *you* try rushing a fucking lunatic and stopping to take notes, *sir*, they said with every look and gesture.

To hell with them, thought Crowley, furious. To fucking hell with them. He looked at the blood on the floor and the pillow. He looked out of the window. The constables held back the growing crowds. The bicycle lay alone, ignored.

Fabian, Fabian . . . thought Crowley. *I've lost you, I've lost you. You were my lead, Fabian, and now you've gone.*

He leaned down and rested his head on his arms, there on the windowsill.

Fabian, Natasha, where have you gone? he thought. *And with whom?*

TWENTY-THREE

Scrawled notes were appearing on walls.

In a hand at once gothic and subliterate, they entreated Saul to a peace. They were etched into the brick, scribbled in pencil, sprayed with aerosol.

The first, Saul found on the side of a chimney stack he had decided to sleep in.

LISTEN SONNY, it read. WERE BLOOD AND BLOOD STICKS SO LETS US LET BYGONES BE. TWOS BETTER NOR ONE YOU KNOW AND IN FACT TWO CAN BE THE DEVIL.

Saul had run his fingers over the thin scratches and looked around the roof. The stench of King Rat was on the air, he could smell it clearly. The rats with him had bristled, and been ready to bite or run. He was never alone now, always surrounded by a group whose number was unchanging even as the individuals who formed it came and went.

Saul and his entourage had crouched on the roof and sniffed the air. He had not slept in the chimneys that morning.

The next evening he had woken in the corner of the sewer he had found, and painted above his head was another message. This was in white paint, paint that had dripped and slid down the walls into the dirty water, leaving the words only just legible.

LOOK YOU AINT DOING NOONE ANY FAVORS CEPT THE PIPER.

It had been written while he slept. King Rat was stalking him, afraid to speak but desperate for reconciliation.

Saul was angry. The ease with which King Rat was still able to sneak past him rankled. He realized that he was just a baby, a little ratling.

He could not think about whether or not King Rat was right. It was irrelevant to him. He had had enough of compromise. King Rat the rapist and murderer, destroyer of his family, had no right to his collaboration. King Rat had released the Piper, King Rat had made Saul what he was. He had released him, but only into his new prison.

So fuck King Rat, thought Saul. He had had it with being bait. He knew that King Rat could not be trusted.

So instead he thought about what he could do for himself.

For all that he felt liberated, for all that he felt powerful, Saul did not know what to do. He did not know where the Piper lived. He did not know when the Piper would attack. He knew nothing at all except that he himself was not safe.

Saul began to think more and more about his friends. He spent a lot of time speaking to the rats, but they were only cunning, not clever, and their stupidity alienated him. He remembered his thoughts on the night he had left King Rat, the realization that it was *his* decision whether or not his world would cross those of Fabian and others.

He wanted to see Fabian more than anything.

So one evening he bade the rats leave him alone. They

obeyed immediately, disappearing in a sudden flurry. Saul began to cross the city, alone again.

He wondered if King Rat was with him, was watching him. As long as the fucker kept his distance, Saul decided, he did not care.

Saul crossed the river under Tower Bridge. He swung like an ape along the girders which festooned its underside, convoluted thickets of vast wires and pipes. In the middle, just at the point where the bridge could split and open for tall ships, he stopped and hung by his hands, swaying slightly.

The sky was taken from him; the great mass of the bridge above him was all he could see at eye-level and above. At the very edge of his sight, buildings appeared again over the river. But for the most part the city was inverted and refracted in the Thames, a sinuous shattered mirror. Lights glinted on the water, dark shapes punctuated with hundreds of points of light, the towers of the city, the far-off lights of the South Bank Centre, far more real for him then than their counterparts in the air above.

He stared down at the city below his feet. It was an illusion. The shimmering motion of the lights he saw was not the real city. They were part of it, to be sure, a necessary part . . . but the beautiful lights, so much more lively than those above them, were a simulacrum. They merely painted the surface tension. Below that thin veneer the water was still filthy, still dangerous and cold.

Saul held onto that. He resisted the poetics of the city.

Saul walked fast, making the passers-by ignore him, being nothing to them. He strode the streets like a cipher, invisible. Sometimes he stopped quite still and listened, to see if he was being followed. He could see no one, but he was not so naive as to think that was conclusive.

He approached Brixton from the backstreets, not wanting to run the gamut of its light and crowds. His pulse was up.

He was nervous. He had not spoken to Fabian for so long, he was afraid they would no longer understand each other. How would he sound to Fabian now? Would he sound strange, would he sound ratty?

He reached Fabian's street. An old woman walked past him, bent into herself, and he was alone.

Something was wrong. The air tasted charged. People moved behind the white curtains of Fabian's room. Saul stood quite still. He stared at the window, saw the vague movements of men and women within. They milled uncertainly, investigating. With a growing horror, Saul pictured those within opening drawers, examining books, looking at Fabian's artwork. He knew who moved like that.

Saul's demeanor changed. One moment his shoulders were hunched, he was tightened into a drab stance, something to see but not notice, his disguise for the streets. Now he uncurled and sank toward the pavement. He bent in a sudden snap of motion, sidling simultaneously against the low wall. He crept through the thin strip of garden, the desultory tiny patios.

He was truly invisible now. He could sense it in himself.

He sidled along the wall, sudden bursts of motion interspersed with unearthly stillness. His nose twitched. He smelt the air.

Saul stood before Fabian's house. Soundlessly he vaulted the low wall and landed in a crouch below the window. He placed his ear to the wall.

Architecture betrayed those within. Bluff voices seeped out through cracks and rivulets between bricks.

" . . . don't like that bloody picture, though . . . "

" . . . know that the DI's totally losing it over this. I mean he's fucking well *lost* it . . . "

" . . . geezer Morris, why have a go at him? . . . thought he was a mate . . . "

The police talked in an endless stream of banalities, clichés and pointless verbiage. Their speech served no purpose, thought Saul in despair, no fucking purpose at all. He ached for conversation, for communication, and to hear words wasted like this . . . he felt like crying.

He had lost Fabian. He put his head in his hands.

"Him gone, bwoy. Him with the Badman now."

Anansi's voice was soft and very near.

Saul rubbed his eyes without opening them. He breathed deeply. Finally he looked up.

Anansi's face hovered just in front of his, suspended before him upside-down. His strange eyes were very close, staring right into Saul's.

Saul looked at him calmly, held his gaze. Then he let his eyes slide casually up, investigating Anansi's position.

Anansi was hanging from one of his ropes, suspended from the roof. He grasped it with both hands, effortlessly suspended his weight, his naked feet intertwined with the thin white rope. As Saul watched, Anansi's legs uncoupled from the fibers and swivelled slowly and soundlessly through the air. His eyes held Saul's, even as his face turned one hundred and eighty degrees.

His feet touched the concrete with a tiny pat.

"You damn good now, you know, pickney. Not easy keep track of you, these days."

"Why did you bother? *Daddy* send you?" Saul's voice was withering.

Anansi laughed without sound. He smiled lazily, predatory—the big spider-man.

"Come now. Me want fe talk." Anansi pointed with a long finger, straight up. Then hand over hand he seemed to fall up the rope, which was tugged peremptorily from view.

Saul slid silently to the corner of the building and gripped it on both sides. He hauled himself away from the earth.

Anansi was waiting. He sat cross-legged on the flat roof. His mouth worked as if he were preparing to say something unpleasant. He nodded a greeting to Saul and indicated with a nod that he should sit opposite him.

Instead, Saul interlaced his fingers behind his head and turned away. He looked out over Brixton.

There were noises all around them from the streets.

"Mr. Rattymon going crazy waiting for you now." Anansi spoke quietly.

"Motherfucker shouldn't have used me as bait, then," said Saul evenly. "Rapist motherfucker shouldn't have killed my dad."

"Rattymon you dad."

Saul did not answer. He waited.

Anansi spoke again.

"Loplop come back and him *crazy* mad at you. Him want you dead fe true."

Saul turned, incredulous.

"What the *fuck* has he got to be angry with me for?"

"You make him deaf, you know, and you done also make him *mad* again, mad in him head."

"Oh for fuck's *sake*," spat Saul. "We were both about to be *killed*. He was about to *kill* me and get fucking taken apart himself. I think the fucking Piper's done playing with us, you know? I think he just wants us all dead now, all the kings. Loplop would've fucking *died*, I saved his *life* . . . "

"Yeah, man, but him save you. Could've watch while the Piperman done kill you, but him try to save you, and you fuck up him ear . . . "

"That's a load of *crap*, Anansi. Loplop tried to save me because you all . . . *you all* . . . know the Piper can't hold me, and *you all* know I'm the only thing that can stop him."

There was a long silence.

"Well, Loplop him mad, anyway. Don't be getting too close to him now."

"Fine," said Saul.

Again, a long pause.

"What do you want, Anansi? And what do you know about Fabian?"

Anansi sucked his teeth in disgust.

"You still *green*, bwoy, fe true. You sure got all the rats dem upon you side, but you don't know what fe do with them. Rats everywhere, bwoy. Spiders everywhere. Them you *eyes*, the rats. My lickle spiders tell me what the Badman do with you friends. You ain't never ask. You not care till now."

"*Friends?*"

Anansi screwed up his face and looked at Saul disdainfully.

"Him have kill the fat bwoy." Saul's hands fluttered about his face. His mouth stayed shut, but it quivered. "Him have take the black bwoy and the lickle DJ woman."

"*Natasha*," breathed Saul. "What does he want with her . . . ? How does he *know* who they are . . . ? *How is he getting inside me?*" Saul grabbed his head with both hands, began to thump himself in despair. *Kay*, he thought, *Natasha*, he hit himself more, *what was happening?*

Anansi was on him. Strong hands gripped his wrists.

"Stop now!" Anansi was horrified.

Animals do not hurt themselves, Saul realized. There was still human inside him, then. He shook himself and stopped.

"We have to get them back. We have to find them . . . "

"How, bwoy? Be *real*."

Saul's head spun.

"What did he do to Kay?"

Anansi pursed his lips.

"Him took the bwoy apart."

They ran for a while, then there was a short scurrying climb, and they stood on Brixton Rec, the sports center. They could hear the faint thump of MTV from the weights room below. Saul stood at the very edge of the roof, a little way forward from Anansi. He pushed his hands in his pockets.

"You could have told me, you know . . . " he said. He heard himself, and hated his plaintive tone. He half-turned, glanced at Anansi, who stood quite still, his arms folded over his bare chest.

Anansi sucked his teeth in contempt.

"Cha, bwoy, you still full to the brim with rubbish. You

talk about how the Rattymon him you father? What for me want tell you that?"

Saul looked at him. Anansi was insistent.

"What for me want tell you? Hmmm? Listen, bwoy, pickney, hear me now. Me one bigass *spider*, understand? The Rattymon, him a *rat*. Loplop him the *bird*, the Bird Superior. Now you, you some strange half-ting, fe true, but what for we gwan tell you ting like that? Me tell you just what me want you fe know. Always, there you have a promise. No more hypocrisy now, you see, bwoy? No need. Animal like me no need for such ting. You leave that behind. You can trust me to be *just so* trustworthy, never no more, but never no less. Y'understand?"

Saul said nothing. He watched a train arrive at Brixton station and trundle away again.

"Was Loplop going to tell the Piper where I was? Were you all going to come for him when he tried to take me?" he asked finally.

Anansi shrugged, almost imperceptibly.

They sidled along the side of the railway, the British Rail line which rose above the market and the streets. They slid along without speaking, heading for Camberwell. Saul appreciated the company, he realized, though it was hardly what he had hoped for when setting out this evening.

"How could he find my friends?" said Saul. They sat on the climbing frame in a nondescript schoolyard.

"Him search all you books an tings. Him find some address tings fe sure."

Of course, thought Saul. *My fault.*

He was numbed. If he was still human, he realized, he would be in shock. But he was not, not anymore; he was half rat, and he felt inured.

Anansi was very silent. He made no attempt to persuade Saul to return to King Rat, or to do anything, for that matter.

Saul looked at him curiously.

"Does King Rat know you're here?" he asked.

Anansi nodded.

"Has he asked you to say anything? Get me back?"

Anansi shrugged. "Him want you back, sure. You useful, y'know? But him know you can't be told nothing you don't want. You know what him want. If you want come back, you will come."

"Do you . . . do you understand why I won't come back to him?"

Anansi looked at his eyes. Gently, he shook his head.

"No, bwoy, not at all. You can *survive* better with him, with us, fe true: And you are rat. You should go back. But I know you don't think like that. I don't know what you are, bwoy. You can't be rat, you can't be man. I don't understand you at all, but that's alright, because I know now that I will *never* understand you, nor will you me. We are *not* the same."

In the small hours, after they had eaten, they stood together at an entrance to the sewers. Anansi looked behind him, planning his route up the side of the warehouse beside them. He looked back at Saul.

Saul stuck out his hand. Anansi grasped it.

"You are the only hope, bwoy. Come back to us."

Saul shook his head, twisted, uncomfortable before the sudden intensity.

Anansi nodded and dropped his hand.

"See you around."

He turned and slung one of his ropes over an overhang, disappeared at speed over the vertical bricks.

Saul watched him go. He turned and examined where he was. The grill was in a yard littered with hulking pieces of machinery. They loomed solemnly in the dark, looking vaguely pathetic. There were no roads visible from here, and Saul enjoyed the moment of solitude. Then he reached down without looking and pulled the grill from the earth.

He hesitated.

He knew there was little point searching for Natasha and

Fabian. The city was so large, the Piper's powers so prodigious, it would not be hard for him to hide two humans. But he knew also that he could not bear to leave them in his power. He knew he had to search, if only to prove that he was still half human. Because he was disquieted by his passivity, his acceptance, the speed with which he had conceptualized their absence as inevitable, as done, as a done thing. He was becoming dulled. Kay's death was utterly unreal to him, but that was a human reaction. More disturbing to him was his reaction to the Piper's abduction of his two closest friends.

The acceptance of the unacceptable was a kind of reactionary stoicism, a dynamic that dulled his feelings for these others. He could feel it within him, a growing cunning, a hyper-real focus on the here and now. It frightened him. He could not battle it head on, he could not decide what to feel and what not to feel, but he could challenge it with his actions. He could change it by refusing to behave as if it were how he felt. He abhorred his own reaction, his own feeling.

It was an animal trait.

TWENTY-FOUR

Saul could tell something was wrong as soon as he stepped into the sewers.

The sounds, the sounds he had become accustomed to walking into, were absent. As his feet hit the trickling water, he dropped into a crouch, suddenly full of feral energy. His ears twitched. He knew what was missing. He should walk into the sewers into a barely audible network of scratching and skittering, the noises of his people. He should hear them at the very edge of his rat-hearing, and subsume them within him, make them part of him, use them to define his time in the darkness.

The sounds were missing. There were no rats around him.

He lowered himself effortlessly, sliding into the organic muck. He was utterly silent, his ears twitching. He was trembling.

He could hear the constant soft drip of the tunnels, the thick trickle of viscous water, the mournful soughing of warm subterranean winds, but his people were gone.

Saul closed his eyes, stilled himself from his toes up. His joints ceased to work over each other; he banished the sound of his blood, slowed his heart, dispensed with all the tiny noises of his body. He became part of the sewer floor, and he *listened*.

The quiet of the tunnels appalled him.

He rested one ear gently against the floor. He could feel vibrations from all around the city.

A long way off, something sounded.

A high-pitched sound.

Saul snapped to his feet. He was sweating and trembling violently.

The Piper had come *here*? Was he in the *sewers*?

Saul raced through the tunnels. He did not know where he was running. He ran to kill the shuddering of his legs, the terror he felt.

What was he doing *here*?

He sped past a ladder. Maybe he should leave, maybe it was time he left the sewers and ran for it through the streets above, he thought, but damn it, this was his *space*, his safe haven . . . he could not have it taken from him.

He stopped still suddenly and cocked his head, listening again.

The sound of the flute was a little closer now, and he could hear a scratching around it, the sound of claws on brick.

The flute slid violently up and down the scale, a cacophony of quavers chasing each other in mad directions. The flute and the claws were strangely static. They did not grow nearer or further away.

There was something strange, Saul realized, about the sound. He listened. Unconsciously he braced himself against the tunnel walls, spread his arms, one above him, one to his side, his legs slightly parted, each climbing the gentle incline of the cylindrical tunnel. He was framed by the passageway.

The flute trilled on, and now Saul could hear something else, a voice raised in anguish.

Loplop. Squawking, emitting meaningless, despairing cries.

Saul moved forward, tracking the sounds through the labyrinth. They remained where they were. He wound his way through the dark toward them. Loplop still shrieked intermittently, but his cries were not pained, not tortured, but *miserable*. Loplop's voice rose above the scrabbling—an *orderly* scrabbling, Saul realized, an unearthly *timed* scratching.

The sounds were separated from him now only by thin walls, and he knew he was there, around the corner from the congregation. The tremors had returned to Saul's body. He fought to control himself. Terror held him hard. He remembered the numbing speed with which the Piper moved, the power of his blows. The pain in his body, the pain he had managed to forget, to ignore, reawakened and coursed through him.

Saul did not want to die.

But there was something not right about this sound.

Saul pressed himself hard against the wall and swallowed several times. He edged forward, to the junction with the tunnel which contained the sounds. He was very afraid. The mad piping, Loplop's random cries, and above all the constant, orderly scrabbling against brick—everything continued as it had for minutes. It was loud, and so close it appalled him.

He looked around. He did not know where he was. Deep somewhere, buried in the vastness of the sewer system.

He steeled himself, drew his head slowly, silently around the edge of the brick.

At first, all he could discern were the rats.

A field of rats, millions of rats; a mass that started a few feet from the entrance to the tunnel and multiplied, bodies piling upon bodies, rat upon rat, a sharp gradient of hot little bellies and chests and legs. A moving mountain, replacing those that fell with new blood, defeating the urge of gravity to level its impossibly steep sides. The rats boiled over each other.

They moved in time, they moved together.

All together they pushed down with their right forefoot, then all together with their left. Then the back legs, again in time. They clawed each other, ripped each other's skin, trampled on the young and dying—but they were one unit. They moved together, in time to the hideous music.

The Piper was nowhere. On the other side of the rat mountain Saul could see King Rat. Saul could not see his face. But his body moved on the same beat as those of his rebellious people, and he danced with the same disinterested intensity, his body stiff and spasming in perfect time.

Loplop cried again and again, and Saul glimpsed him, a desperate figure before King Rat, his fists flailing against King Rat's chest. He pushed King Rat, tried to move him back, but King Rat continued with his stiff zombie dance.

And behind them all, something hanging from the ceiling . . . something emerging, Saul saw, from a shaft to the pavements above. A black box, dangling at a ridiculous angle, its handle tied to a dirty rope . . .

A ghetto-blaster.

Saul's eyes widened in astonishment.

The fucker doesn't even have to be here, he thought.

He stumbled into the tunnel and approached the seething mass. The flute was ghastly, loud and fast and insane like an Irish jig played in Hell. Saul edged forward. He began to pass straggling rats. The ghetto-blaster swayed slightly. Saul waded into the mass of rats. So many already, all around him, and he had at least six feet to walk. It seemed as if every rat in the sewer had found its way here; monstrous foot-long beasts and mewling babies, dark and brown, crushing each other, killing each other in their eagerness to reach the music. Saul pushed forward, feeling the bodies squirm around him. A thousand claws ripped at him, never in antagonism, only in the ecstasy of the dance. Under the rats he could see were layers that moved sluggishly, tired and dying; and below them were rats who did not move at all. Saul walked knee-deep in the dead.

King Rat did not turn, stayed where he was, dancing at the head of his people once again. Loplop saw Saul. He shrieked and pushed past King Rat, launched himself through the living wall toward Saul.

He was ruined. His suit was filthy, and in tatters. His face contorted, rage and confusion fleeting across it.

He waded forward two, three steps, then stumbled under the weight of enthralled bodies. He went under, drowning in the seething mass. Saul ignored him, contemptuous of him, disgusted.

But he too found it difficult to move; he pushed through the rats, killing, he was sure, with each step, unwillingly but inevitably. He swayed, regained his balance. The cacophonous flute was utterly deafening. Saul went down suddenly on one knee and the rats used him as a springboard, leapt from him, tried to fly to the dangling stereo.

Saul swore, struggled to regain his feet, went under again. He became enraged, surged to his feet, spilling rats as he rose. A few feet away he could see the pitiful sight of Loplop's body bobbing below the surface of the rats, trying and failing to stand.

Saul shook himself and brown bodies spun through the air. He could not reach the boombox. He tugged hard with his feet, which seemed stuck as firmly as in quicksand. He roared, suddenly livid, pulled inexorably through the mass of rats, stumbled again, yanked and forced his way through, past King Rat, to the point where the rats thinned out and the stereo hung six feet from the floor.

He reached up to it, and saw King Rat. He stopped moving, shocked.

King Rat stood in thrall, his face slack, his limbs swinging vaguely, stripped of dignity, a string of drool stretching and snapping from his lower jaw. Saul stared, fascinated and horrified.

He hated King Rat, hated what he had done, but something in him was appalled at seeing him so shorn of power.

Saul turned and grasped the swinging box, pulled hard, snapping the rope.

He smashed it hard against the wall.

The music stopped at the instant of impact. Metal and plastic spattered out of the broken casing. He slammed it twice more against the brick. Its speakers burst out of their housing. A tape flew from the ruined cassette deck.

Saul turned and looked at the assembled multitude.

They stood still, confused.

Understanding and recollection seemed to well over them all simultaneously. In a panic, a terrified flurry, the rats emitted a communal hiss and disappeared, scampering over each other, made clumsy by the fallen.

The mountain crumbled and disappeared. Lame and ruined rats tried to follow their fellows. The first wave was gone; then the second wave, limping after them; and the third wave, the dying, hauled themselves away, sliding on blood.

The ground was covered with bodies. Corpses lay two, three thick. Loplop crawled into a corner.

King Rat stared at Saul. Saul looked back at him for a moment, then returned his attention to the ruined stereo. He fumbled in the mud until he found the tape.

He wiped it, examined the label.

Flute 1, it said. It was handwritten. It was Natasha's writing.

"Oh *fuck*," Saul shouted and pushed his head into the crook of his arm. "Oh fuck, oh leave them alone, you fucker," he breathed.

He heard King Rat move forward. Saul looked up sharply. King Rat looked uneasy. He moved with a deferential cast to his limbs, resentment curling his mouth. He was intimidated, Saul realized.

Saul nodded.

"It's just *noise* to me," he whispered. He nodded again, saw King Rat's eyes widen. "Just noise."

With a shriek Loplop saw Saul, ran toward him flapping his rags and his arms, stumbled as he ran.

King Rat started. Saul stepped smartly out of Loplop's way and watched as the Bird Superior slipped in mud, went over in a half-controlled fall and banged his head against the wall.

Saul gesticulated at King Rat, danced back a few steps.

"Keep that motherfucker under control!" he shouted.

Loplop still shouted, still yelled his incoherent cries as he tried to stand. King Rat strode to where Loplop slithered in mud, and gripped his collar. He tugged him, pulled him along the slippery sewer bottom. Loplop struggled and whimpered. At the entrance to the tunnel King Rat crouched before him, held his finger before Loplop's face. Saul could not tell if he was speaking to Loplop, or merely holding him still with those eyes. Some kind of communication passed between them.

Loplop stared past King Rat at Saul. He looked afraid and enraged. King Rat regained his gaze and seemed to say something, gesticulated. Loplop's eyes returned to Saul, and the same rage filled him as before, but he backed away, moved away through the tunnels, disappeared.

King Rat turned back to Saul.

As he walked back through the bodies of the rats, Saul saw that King Rat had regained his furtive swagger. He had composed himself.

"Back, then?" King Rat asked casually.

Saul ignored him. He looked up into the shaft from which he had pulled the stereo. Several feet above, a grill was visible, and above it the drab orange-shot black of the city night. Something was affixed to the inside of the narrow shaft.

"So what you here for, then, chal?" asked King Rat, his insouciance wearing and affected.

"Fuck you," replied Saul quietly. He stood on tiptoe, reached up into the vertical tunnel. He could feel a corner of paper flapping in wind. He gripped it, pulled gently, but succeeded only in tearing the corner away.

He looked down briefly. King Rat stood near him, his hands held uncertainly to his chest.

Saul looked around him at the corpses.

"Another fine display of leadership skills then, *Dad*."

"Fuck you, you pissing little half-breed, I'll kill you . . . "

"Oh give it a rest, old man," said Saul, disgusted. "You need me, you know it, I know it, so shut up with your stupid threats." He returned his attention to the tunnel. He jumped up and grabbed the top of the paper, pulled it down with him when he fell.

It came away in his hands. He spread it out.

It was a poster.

It was designed by someone with Adobe Illustrator, a sixth-form aesthetic and too much time. Garish and jumbled, a confusion of fonts and point sizes, information crowding itself out and details fighting for space.

A line drawing took up most of the sheet: a grotesquely muscled man in sunglasses standing impassive behind a twindeck turntable. He stood with his arms folded, as the chaotic writing exploded around him.

JUNGLIST TERROR!!! it exclaimed.

One night of Extreme Drum an' Bass Badness!

£10 entry, it exclaimed, and gave the address of a club in the Elephant and Castle, in the badlands of South London; and a date, a Saturday night in early December.

Featuring da Cream of da Crop, Three Fingers, Manta, Ray Wired, Rudegirl K, Natty Funkah . . .

Rudegirl K. That was Natasha.

Saul let out a little cry. He bent slightly, his breath pushed from him.

"He's *telling* us," he hissed to King Rat. "He's *inviting* us."

Something was scrawled on the bottom of the poster, an addendum in a strange ornate hand. *Also featuring a special guest!* it proclaimed. *Fabe M!*

Jesus he was pathetic! Saul thought. He sank slowly

back against the wall as he grasped the paper. Fabe M! *Look, he's trying to play games,* thought Saul, *but this isn't his environment, he doesn't know what to do, he can't play with these words . . .*

It made him feel obscurely comforted. Even in the misery of knowing that his friends were in the hands of this creature, this monster, this avaricious spirit, he felt a triumph in the ineptitude with which his foe stumbled on jargon. He was trying for nonchalance, scribbling an addition in Drum and Bass style, but the language was unfamiliar and he had stumbled. Fabe M! It sounded stupid and contrived. He wanted Saul to know that he had Fabian, that Fabian would be at the club, but he was not on his home ground, and his clumsy affectation showed that.

Saul found himself chuckling, almost ruefully.

"Bastard can't play no more." He crushed the paper and threw it at King Rat, who had been hovering nervously, resentfully. King Rat snatched it out of the air. "Fucker's telling us to come and get them," said Saul, as King Rat opened out the sheet.

Saul pushed past King Rat, kicked his way through the bodies of the rat dead.

"He's operating like a fucking Bond villain," he said. "He wants *me.* Knows I'll come for him if he dangles my friends in front of me."

"So what's a rat to do?" said King Rat.

Saul turned and stared at him. He knew, quite suddenly, that his eyes were as hidden to King Rat as King Rat's were to him.

"What am I going to do?" Saul said slowly. "A trap is only a trap if you don't know about it. If you know about it, it's a *challenge.* I'm going to go, of course. I'm going to Junglist Terror. To rescue my friends." He could feel that sentiment within him which had disturbed him before, a part of him saying *fuck it, don't go, it's not your problem anymore.*

That was King Rat's blood. Saul would not listen to it. *I*

am what I do, he thought, furiously.

There was a long silence between the two of them.

"You know what?" said Saul finally. "I think you should come too. I think you will."

TWENTY-FIVE

Squadrons of rats spread out across London. Saul harangued
them in foetid alleys, behind great plastic bins. He raged to
them about the Piper, told them that their day had come.

The massed ranks of the rats stood quivering, inspired.
Their noses twitched; they could smell victory. Saul's words
broke over them like tides, swept them up. He communicated
with them by his tone; they knew they were being *commanded*, and after centuries of furtive skulking they became
brave, puffed up with millennial fervour.

Saul ordered them to prepare. He ordered them to search
out the Piper, to bring Saul information, to find his friends. He
described them, the black man and the short woman being kept
hostage by the Piper. The rats did not care about the people
being held. They represented nothing except a task set by Saul.

"You are *rats*," Saul told them, sticking out his lower lip and jerking his head back like Mussolini. They gazed at him, a shifting mass of followers, peering out from all the nooks and crannies of the building site in which they had congregated. "You're the sneakers, the creepers, the rat-burglars. Don't come to me afraid of being seen, don't come to me with fears of the Piper's revenge. Why will he see you? You're *rats* . . . . if he sees you you're a failure to your species. Stay hidden, creep in the spaces in between, and *find him*, and tell me where he is."

The rats were inspired. They longed to follow him. He dismissed them with a wave and they scattered in short-lived bravado.

Saul knew that beyond the range of his voice, the rats' fear would quickly return. He knew that they would hesitate. He knew they would slow down as they scaled walls, look around anxiously for him to shout them on, and that they would fail. He knew they would slink back to the sewers and hide until he found them and urged them out again.

But maybe one would be brave or lucky. Maybe one of his rats would scale the walls that divided the Piper's sanctuary from the outside, and pick a way through the barbed wire, scamper along the pipes and the cables, cross the wasteland, and find him.

Somewhere, squeezed into the air-conditioning housing on the top of a financial building in the heart of the City, or in a bitumen-sealed hole under a suburban railway bridge, or in a room with no windows in an empty hospital beyond Neasden, or in the high-tech vaults of a bank to the west of Hammersmith, or in the attic above a bingo hall in Tooting, the Piper was holding Natasha and Fabian, waiting out the week before Junglist Terror.

Saul suspected that the Piper would avoid the gaze of rats and spiders and birds. He was not afraid of his adversaries, but there was no point advertising his presence. He had issued his challenge, had told them the night that they would die. The Piper had issued them with invitations to their own executions.

It might be that he was only concerned with Saul, with the half-and-half, the rat-man he could not control, but he must suspect that Anansi would be there, too, and King Rat, and Loplop. They were not brave or proud. They were not ashamed to turn down challenges. But they knew that Saul was the only thing that the Piper could not control, that Saul was the only chance they had, and they knew they must be there to help him. If he did not survive, they could not.

The rats spread throughout London.

Saul was alone amidst the rubble and the scaffolding.

He stood in the center of a wide ruined landscape, a blitzed corner of London that hid behind hoardings, in easy earshot of Edgware Road. A forty-foot by forty-foot square, carpeted in crushed brick and old stone and surrounded by the backs of buildings. On one edge of the square a rough wooden fence hid the street that flanked the site, and above the fence towered the old brick walls of ancient shops and houses. Saul looked up at them. On that side the windows were surrounded by large wooden frames, rotting but ornate, designed to be seen.

On all other sides the walls that enclosed him were vulnerable. They constituted the buildings' underbellies, soft underneath the aesthetic carapace. Out of sight of their façades, he was ringed by great flat expanses of brick, windows that split at random down featureless walls. Seen from behind, caught unawares, the functionality of the city was exposed.

This point of view was dangerous for the observer, as well as for the city. It was only when it was seen from these angles that he could believe London had been built brick by brick, not born out of its own mind. But the city did not like to be found out. Even as he saw it clearly for the product it was, Saul felt it square up against him. The city and he faced each other. He saw London from an angle against which it had no front, at a time when its guard was down.

He had felt this before, when he had left King Rat, when he had known that he had slipped the city's bonds; and he had known then that he had made of it an enemy. The windows which loomed over him reminded him of that.

In the corner of the square lurked obscure building

machines, piles of materials and pickaxes, bags of cement covered with blue plastic sheeting. They looked defensive and overwhelmed. Just in front of them stood the remnants of the building that had been pulled down. All that remained was a section of its front, a veneer one brick deep, with gaping, glassless holes where windows had been. It seemed miraculous that it could stand. Saul walked over the broken ground toward it.

There were lights on in a few of the rooms that overlooked him and, as he walked silently, Saul even caught sight of movement here and there. He was not afraid. He did not believe that anyone would see him; he had rat blood in his veins. And if they did, they might be surprised to see a man striding by lamplight in the forbidden space of a nascent building, but who would they tell? And if someone were, unbelievably, to call the police, Saul could simply climb and be gone. He had rat blood in his veins. *Tell the police to call Rentokil*, he thought. *They might have a better chance.*

He stood under the free-standing façade. He stretched his arms up, prepared to scramble over the city himself, to join his emissaries in their search. He did not believe that he would find Fabian or Natasha or the Piper, but he could not fail to look for them. To acquiesce in the Piper's plans would be to abrogate his own power, to become collaborator. If he were to meet the Piper on the ground the Piper had specified, he would be *dragged* there, he would be unwilling. He would be angry.

He heard a noise above him. A figure swung into view in one of the empty window-frames. Saul was still. It was King Rat.

Saul was not surprised. King Rat followed him often, waited until the rats had left, then poured scorn on his efforts, ridiculed him in agonized contumely, incoherent with rage at the behavior of the rats who had once obeyed him.

King Rat grasped his small perch with his right hand. He crouched, his left arm dangling down between his legs, his head lowered toward his knees. Seeing him, Saul thought of a comic-book hero: Batman or Daredevil. Silhouetted in the ruined window, King Rat looked like a scene-setting frame at the start of an epic graphic novel.

"What do you want?" Saul said finally.

In a sinewy sliding movement King Rat emerged from the window and landed at Saul's feet. He bent his knees on landing, then rose slowly just before him.

His face twisted.

"So what silly buggers are you playing now, cove?"

"Fuck off," said Saul and turned away.

King Rat grabbed him and swung him back to face him. Saul slapped the other's hands down, his eyes wide and outraged. There was a horrible uneasy moment as Saul and King Rat stared at each other, their shoulders wide, their fists ready to strike. Slowly and deliberately, Saul reached up and pushed King Rat on the chest, shoved him slightly back.

His anger boiled up in him and he shoved King Rat again, growled and tried to make him fall. He punched him suddenly, hard, and images of his father raced through his mind. He felt a desperate desire to kill King Rat. It shocked him how fast the hatred could overtake him.

King Rat was stumbling slightly on the uneven ground, and Saul reached down to snatch up a half-brick. He bore down on King Rat, flailing brutally with his weapon.

He swung it at King Rat's head, connecting and sending his opponent sprawling, but King Rat hissed with rage as he fell. He rolled painfully across the shattered ground and swung his legs up at Saul, taking him down. The fight became a violent blur, a flurry of arms and legs, nails and fists. Saul did not aim, did not plan; he flailed in rage, feeling blows and scratches bruise him and rip his skin.

Blood exploded from a vicious strike below his eye and his head rocked. He slammed his brick down again but King Rat was not there, and the brick struck stone and burst into dust.

The two rolled and grappled. King Rat slid from Saul's grip and hovered like a gadfly, ripping him open with a hundred cruel scratches and dancing out of the range of retaliation.

Saul's frustration overwhelmed him. He suddenly broke off his frenzied attack with a shouted curse. He stalked away across the rubble.

Another vicious half-fight. He *could not* kill him. King Rat was too fast, too strong, and he would not engage Saul properly, he would not risk killing Saul. King Rat wanted Saul alive, for all that he was growing to hate him for his following among the rats, for his refusal to obey him.

King Rat shouted scornfully after him. Saul could not even hear what he said.

He felt blood well from the deep scratches on his face and he wiped himself as he began to run, sure-footed despite the terrain. He threw himself at one of the walls which overlooked him, scrambled up its tender surface, slipping by those unadorned windows, leaving a long smear of blood and dirt on his way up the bricks.

He stared briefly behind him. King Rat sat forlornly on the hulking piles of cement. Saul turned away from him and set out over the top of London. He looked around him as he moved, and sometimes he stopped and was still.

On the top of a school, somewhere behind Paddington, he saw harsh security lights catching on a billowing cobweb suspended below the railings that topped the building. The fragile thing was empty and long deserted, but he lowered himself to the ground and stared around him. There were other, smaller webs below it, still inhabited, less visible without the accumulated dust of days.

He lowered his lips to these webs and spoke in a voice he knew sounded removed and intimate, like King Rat's. The spiders were quite still.

"I need you to do what I say, now," he whispered. "I need you to find Anansi, find your boss. Tell him I'm waiting for him. Tell him I need to see him."

The little creatures were still for a long time. They seemed to hesitate. Saul lowered himself again.

"Go on," he said, "spread the word."

There was another moment's hesitation, then the spiders, six or seven of them, tiny and fierce, took off at the same moment. They left their webs together, on long threads, little abseiling special forces, disappearing down the side of the building.

Fabian drifted on waves.

He was stuck very deep in his own head. His body made itself felt occasionally, with a fart or a pain or an itch, but for the most part he could forget it was even there. He was conscious of almost nothing except perpetual motion, a tireless pitch and yaw. He was not sure if it was his body or only his mind which was lulled by the liquid movement.

There was a Drum and Bass backdrop to the hypnagogic rolling. The soundtrack never stopped, the same bleak, washed-out track that he had heard from Natasha's stairs.

Sometimes he saw her face. She would lean over him, nodding gently in time to the beat, her eyes unfocused. Sometimes it was Pete's face. He felt soup trickle down his throat and around his mouth, and he swallowed obligingly.

Most of the time he lay back and surrendered to the rocking motion in his skull. He could see almost anything when he just lay back and listened to the Jungle filtering from somewhere close by, twisting around him in a tiny dark room, oppressive, stinking of rot.

He spent a lot of time looking at his artwork in progress. He was not always sure it was there, but when he thought of it and relaxed into the beat, it invariably appeared, and then he would make plans, scribble charcoal additions in each corner. Changing this canvas was so easy. He could never quite remember the moment when he drew, but the changes appeared, bright and perfect.

He became more and more ambitious in his changes, going over old ground, rewriting the text at the center of his piece. In no time at all it was changed beyond recognition, as smooth and perfect as computer graphics, and he stared at the legend he could not quite remember choosing. *Wind City*, it said.

Fabian swallowed the food he found in his mouth and listened to the music.

Natasha spent most of her time with her eyes closed. She didn't need to open them at all. Her fingers knew every inch of her keyboard, and she spent her time playing *Wind City*, tweaking it, changing it in slight and subtle ways, to fit the exigencies of her mood.

Occasionally she would open her eyes and see with surprise that she stood in unfamiliar environs, that she was in the center of a dim, stinking space, that Fabian danced horizontally, lying down nearby, food drying on his face, and that her keyboard was not in front of her after all. But when she tweaked *Wind City*, it changed anyway, it did what she wanted, so she closed her eyes and continued, her fingers flying over the keys.

Sometimes Pete would come and feed her, and she would play him what she had done, still with her eyes closed.

The rats had given up in fear and confusion. The great cadres that had set out earlier in the night had dried up, had slunk home to the sewers, but here and there the braver souls continued the search, as Saul had hoped they would.

In the streets of Camberwell they searched the catacombs of old churches. On the Isle of Dogs they ran past Blackwall Basin and scoured the decrepit business park. The rats worked their way along the great slit of the Jubilee Line extension, past vast hulking machines that tunnelled through the earth.

Their numbers dwindled. As the night wound on, more and more gave in to hunger and fear and forgetfulness. They could not work out why they were running so hard. They could no longer remember what their quarries looked like.

One by one they slipped back into the sewers. Some fell prey to dogs and cars.

Soon there were only a very few rats left searching.

"Lickle bird tell me you want talk to me, bwoy."

Saul looked up.

Anansi descended from the bough of a tree above him. He moved elegantly, belying his size and weight, slipping smoothly down one of his ropes, utterly controlled.

Saul leaned back. He felt the cold weight of the gravestone behind him.

He was sitting quietly in a small cemetery in Acton. It was a tiny space that straddled the overland train line, tucked behind a small industrial estate. It was overlooked on all sides by ugly functionality, a set of grotesque flattened factories and suburban warehouses, uncomfortable in this residential zone.

Saul had wandered West London for a time and entered the graveyard to eat and rest, here amid the crammed urban dead.

The stones were nondescript, apologetic.

Anansi came to the ground silently a few feet from him, stalked past the low gray markers and crouched beside him.

Saul glanced at him, nodded in greeting. He did not offer Anansi any of the old fruit he had scavenged. He knew he would not take it.

Saul sat and ate. "Now was it *really* a little bird, 'Nansi?" he asked mildly. "How *is* Loplop?"

Anansi jerked his head.

"Him still screaming angry, bwoy. Him mad, too. Them can't understand him, the birds dem. Him have lost a kingdom again, think you take it from him." Anansi shrugged. "So we no have no birds. Just my lickle spiders and the rats, and you and me."

Saul bit into his bruised apple.

"And Loplop?" he asked, and paused. "And King Rat? They going to be there with us? They going to be there when we take him?"

Anansi shrugged again. "Loplop is *nothing*, whether him there or not. King Rat? You tell me, bwoy. He's *your* daddy . . . "

"He'll be there," said Saul quietly.

The two sat for a while. Anansi rose presently and walked to the railing in front of them, looked over at the train-line below.

"I've sent the rats to find the Piper," said Saul, "but they'll fail. They're probably all sitting stuffing their bellies right now. They've probably forgotten what it is I wanted them to do . . . " He smiled humorlessly. "We're going to face him on *his* terms."

Anansi said nothing. Saul knew what he was thinking.

Anansi had to come to the Junglist Terror, because Saul would be there. Saul was the only chance he had to defeat the Piper, but he knew it was a tiny chance; he knew that he was *walking into a trap*, that by being there he was doing exactly what the Piper wanted. But he had no choice. Because if he were *not* there, Saul's chances of defeating the Piper were even smaller, and if Saul failed, the Piper would have them all, the Piper would hunt Anansi down and kill him.

It was paradoxical. Anansi, King Rat, they were animals. Preserve yourself, that was the whole of their law. And that law would compel them to go to Junglist Terror. To their almost certain death. Because Saul had to go, because of his human friends, because Saul was refusing to act as an animal.

Saul was going to kill Anansi.

They both knew it. Saul was going to kill Anansi and Loplop and King Rat, and Saul was going to die, all in an effort to prove that he was not his rat-father's son.

Anansi looked back at Saul and shook his head slightly.

Saul returned his gaze.

"Let's talk about what we're going to do, 'Nansi," he said. "Let's make a few *plans* . . . let's not let *everything* go this fucker's way."

They had spiders, they had rats . . . they had Saul. The Piper would have to make a choice. One of the armies would be defeated as soon as they all entered the fray, but the Piper had to make a choice. Anansi and his troops had half a chance of remaining free from the Piper's thrall. And so did the rats.

A handful of rats still scoured London for . . . something . . .

They could not remember exactly what.

These were the pride of the nation. These were the bravest, the fattest and strongest and sleekest, the leaders of the pack.

As smooth as seals through the water they roamed.

One raced like a chubby bullet along the Albert Embankment.

It had come up from the kitchens of St. Thomas's Hospital, next to Waterloo, there on the South Bank of the river. It had snatched food to fortify itself, had searched the attic spaces and cellars. It had run like a ghost through the hospital, leaving its footprints in thick dust, dirtying obscure and forgotten diagnostic machinery.

It had passed through others' territories, but it was a great big animal, and it was on *royal* business. They did not challenge it.

It had found nothing. It made its way out of the building.

In the open space it scampered along the bank of the river toward the medical school.

The Thames glinted balefully beside it, oozing fatly through the city. On the opposite bank stood Westminster Palace, London's absurdly crenellated seat of power. Its many lights flickered on the river's skin.

The rat stopped.

Lambeth Bridge loomed up over the water before it, darkening the muck of the Thames.

An indistinct shape bobbed sullenly in the water beside it. An ancient barge, one of the various hulks that littered the river, untended and ignored. It heaved gently to and fro in the current, little waves slapping its greasy boards like petulant children. The corpse of a boat, its black wood leprous and decaying, a vast tarpaulin slung across it like a shroud.

The rat moved forward nervously, stopped, uncertain.

It strained its ears. It could hear something, faint and sinister. Sounds emanating from under the heavy waterproof cloth.

The barge rocked back and forth. The water was digesting it. But in the meantime, before the wood splintered and dissolved into the Thames, someone was on the vessel, desecrating it, interrupting its long death.

Two old ropes still tethered it to the bank. One dipped in an elegant curve below the surface of the water, but the other was nearly taut. Tentative, the rat stepped onto the mooring. Like a tightrope walker it scurried over the water.

It slowed as it approached the boat. Foreboding flooded its tiny brain, and it would have turned to run if it could, but the rope was too narrow. The rat was stuck with its choice, its impetuous courage.

The rope was strung like a necklace, with huge lumpy beads designed to impede a rat's progress. But unable to turn back, and dreading the water, the rat was tenacious. It hauled itself over the impediments until only a few feet of rope remained.

Stealthy now, silent, the rat continued. The sound from the barge was clearer now, a low repeated thump, a thin, plaintive wailing, the creaking of wood under moving bodies.

With the lightest of touches the rat set foot on the barge.

It crept around to the side, seeking a gap in the tarpaulin. It could feel vibrations in the wood that were nothing to do with the water.

Slinking below the boat's lip, the rat found a place where the material was rucked up, where it could creep through tunnels left between folds in the heavy canvas.

It made its way through this maze until it could hear soft murmurings. It could feel the tarpaulin opening up around it.

With a nose twitching maniacally, the rat crept forward, peered furtively up into the barge.

There was an incredible stink. A mixture of decay, food, bodies and old, old tar. The tarpaulin was stretched out on a frame to make the barge a floating tent. The rat could see by the weak light of a torch suspended from the frame. It pointed directly down and its ambient light was poor, so everything in the room was glimpsed, half-seen, noticed briefly as the motion of the boat swung the torch one way, then lost as its oscillations took it away again.

A low, very quiet bass thump pervaded the tiny space.

In one corner a man lay on the floor. He looked feverish, moved his arms and legs as if he were dancing, his face thrashing uneasily from side to side.

A woman stood nearby, facing away from him. Her eyes were closed. She nodded her head and moved her hands in abstract, exact patterns in front of her, her fingers flying, tracing intricate motions.

Their clothes were dirty. Their faces were thin.

The rat stared at them briefly. Saul's descriptions were muddled in its mind, but it knew that these two were important, it knew that it had to tell Saul what it had found. It turned to run.

A foot slammed down on its escape route, closing off the way through the cloth.

The rat bolted in terror.

It ran around and around the room, everything a dark blur, between the legs of the standing woman, under the arms of the lying man, scratching madly at the cloth all around in a frenzy of fear.

Then suddenly it heard a quick whistling, a jaunty marching tune, and it stopped running, filled with wonder and amazement. The whistling segued gently into the sounds of sex, and the slopping of rich, fatty food falling to the ground, and the rat turned and marched in the direction of the sound, eager to find all these good things.

Then the whistling stopped.

The rat was staring into a man's eyes. Its body was held fast. Frantic, it bit down, drew blood, savaged the fingers which gripped it, but they did not relax.

The eyes gazed at it with a lunatic intensity. The rat began to scream in terror.

There was a brief and sudden motion.

The Piper slammed the rat's head against the wooden floor again and again, until it had lost its definition, become just a flaccid, indistinct appendage.

He held the little corpse up to his face, pursed his lips.

He reached down for the small ghetto-blaster on the floor, and lowered the volume still further. *Wind City* could still be heard, but now it was almost subliminal.

Fabian and Natasha turned simultaneously, looked at him in confusion and surprise.

"I know, I know," he said, mollifying. "You'll have to listen really hard. I have to turn it down a bit. We're attracting attention. We don't want to do that yet, right?" He smiled. "Save that for the club. Right?"

He moved the ghetto-blaster closer with his foot. Spent batteries lay all around it, moving uneasily with the current.

Natasha and Fabian subsided into their previous poses.

Fabian sank back and began to paint.

Natasha continued to play *Wind City*. They both strained their ears a little, and heard what they were looking for.

Warily, the Piper lifted a corner of the cloth. His pale eyes scanned the darkness around the boat.

No one was passing by on Albert Embankment; Pete saw by the lights of the Houses of Parliament.

He reached out and dropped the rat's body into the Thames.

It circled, one speck of dirty darkness among many in the water. The current pulled it slowly, tugging it beyond Westminster, carrying the little cadaver way out to the east.

PART SIX

JUNGLIST

TERROR

TWENTY-SIX

Jungle night.

It was in the air. The sharp-dressed youth who congregated on the Elephant and Castle could taste it.

The clouds were low and moving very fast, ruddy with streetlamp light, billowing up from behind the skyline. London looked like a city on fire.

Police cars swirled ephemeral through the streets, streaking past those other cars that prowled toward Lambeth, stereos pumping. The strains of Dancehall and Rap, blunted and languorous, and everywhere Drum and Bass, febrile and poised, savage and impenetrable.

The drivers leaned their arms out of open windows, nodded lazily in time to the music. These cars were full, bursting with designer clothes and basslines. For the cruisers, the evening kicked in at the zebra crossings and red lights, when they could stop, engine idling, beats pounding, visible in all their finery. They drove from junction to junction, searching for places to be still.

A hundred slogans boomed out of a hundred car windows, the samples and shouted declarations of the classic tracks being played, a hundred preludes to the evening.

Mr. Loverman, came the shouts, and *Check yo'self. Gangsta. Jump. Fight the Power. There is a Darkside.*

I could just kill a man.

Six million ways to die.

They only had eyes for each other that night. They drove and walked the streets like conquistadors in Karl Kani, Calvin Klein and Kangols. In wafts of cologne the homeboys and rudegirls, the posses and massives claimed the streets south of Waterloo, striding past the intimidated natives as though they were shades.

Touching fists and kissing their teeth, the massed ranks moved in on the venue. Irish boys and Caribbean girls, smooth Pakistani kids, gangstas in huge coats muttering into mobile phones, DJs with record bags, precocious kids aping the studied nonchalance of the elders . . .

They made their way into the Jungle.

Here and there the police lurked in corners. Sometimes they were judged worthy of a contemptuous glance, a sneer, before the lights changed and the drivers moved on. The police watched them, whispered to their radios in garbled code. The air teemed with their electronic hisses, warnings and prophecies, unheard by the gathering, swamped by urban breakbeats.

The night was fraught, full of looks held too long.

In the dark streets the warehouse shone. Light spilled from its crevices as if it were a church.

Lines stretched out before the entrance. The bouncers, vast men in bomber jackets, stood with arms folded like grotesque gargoyles. Feudal hierarchies asserted themselves: the serfs in line, clamoring at the gates, staring enviously at the DJs and the hangers-on, the movers and shakers of the Drum and Bass scene, who sauntered casually past them and murmured to the guards. For the noblest of them, even checking the guest list was unnecessary.

Roy Kray and DJ Boom, Nuttah and Deep Cover, familiar from a hundred CD covers and posters, were waved in without demur. Even the proposterously proportioned bouncers showed their obeisance, as their impassivity became momentarily more studied. *Droit de seigneur* was alive and kicking in the Elephant and Castle that night.

If any of the assembled had looked up they might have caught a glimpse of something lurching across the sky, seemingly out of control. A bundle of rags as big as a man, buffeted through the air. It was not at the mercy of the wind: no wind changed direction as violently or as fast as the shapeless mass, no wind could carry such bulk.

Loplop, the Bird Superior, arced and wheeled above the streets, staring down at the dirty map below him, staring up into the night stained orange by diffuse light, falling, rising, his ears filled with ringing.

He could not hear the city. He could not hear the predatory grunting of the cars. He could not hear the *thud thud thud* emanating from the warehouse. The intricate hairs and bones in his ears had burst, and the canals were blocked with dry blood.

Loplop had only his eyes, and he searched as best he could, weaving silently between buildings, perching on weathervanes and springing into the sky.

The air was slowly thickening with birds. The few that had been awake as Loplop sped by had cried out, pledged their fealty, but he had not heard them. Confused, they had risen from the eaves and the branches of trees, had followed him, screaming out to him, frightened by his wild flight and his ignoring of them. Huge ponderous crows circled him. Loplop saw them and shouted wordlessly, clutching at the authority he had lost.

The birds wove elegantly around each other, their numbers growing. Their eyes darted from side to side in confusion.

In the midst of their slow wheeling, Loplop rose and sped and zigzagged and fell—a wild card.

The birds could not obey their general.

Elsewhere in London, other armies were also massing.

The walls and corners of houses were emptying out. From crevices and holes all over the city, the spiders streamed. They scuttled in their millions, little smudges racing across dirty floors and through gardens, descending on threads from building tops. They crawled over each other, a sudden, nervous mass of blacks and browns.

Here and there their squadrons were seen. In children's bedrooms and backstreets, the night was punctuated by sudden screams.

Many died. Crushed, eaten, lost. Ruined chitin and smeared bodies marked their passing.

Something sparked deep in the spiders' tiny brains. A sensation that was not the hunger or fear or nothingness that were previously their lot. Trepidation? Excitement? Vindication?

The city lights glinted minutely on the spiders' multiple eyes. Close set and impenetrable, as cold and disinterested as a shark's . . . except tonight . . .

The spiders trembled.

In the wilds of South London, Anansi watched from rooftops. He could feel the air shifting. He could taste the presence of his troops.

The sewers boiled with rats, incited to a frenzy.

Their Crown Prince had passed among them. Saul had spread the word. He had commanded them, controlled them, sent them forth.

The rats surged through the tunnels like a flash flood. Smaller tributaries streamed into the main branch, bodies on bodies, fat and fast.

They poured under the streets and over the skyline. Up

in the canopy of the city, in the thin air, rats bounded over walls and between partitions, scrabbled along slates and behind chimneys.

The river was no obstacle: they found their way across almost without pause.

Different dirt, different packs, a hundred different smells . . . all the tribes in London running for the south, gnawing on forgotten filth and shaking with adrenaline, ready for battle. An enormous sense of wrong had been encoded in their genes for years, eating them alive like a cancer, and for the first time they could smell a cure.

Rats spewed out of a hundred thousand holes and converged on the wastelands of South London, a scratching, biting mass, hungry and scared, trying to be brave.

Insidiously, furtively, the rats gathered around the warehouse, and waited.

The warehouse was a spark plug. It crackled with energy. It was surrounded by invisible circles, waves and cadres of rats and spiders, crowned with confused, wheeling birds, penetrated by people.

It was a magnet.

Loplop still watched from above.

Anansi scanned the rooftops.

"Where the *fuck* is she at?"

Three Fingers, wiry and cantankerous, addressed his question to one of the bouncers. The huge man shook his head. Fingers danced from side to side in frustration. The wet thumping of basslines and beats welled up behind him. He felt as if he could lean backwards on the sound without falling, cushioned, held in the air.

He stood at the entrance to the warehouse, gazing out at the crowd assembled in the forecourt. He had been on the top step for some minutes, waiting for Natasha. All the other DJs had arrived. Fingers had already had to rearrange his running order a little, in case Natasha did not appear. He trotted down the stairs into the courtyard, strode out to the split in the wire-mesh fence and looked up and down the street.

Swaggering dancers were still appearing from all over, converging on the warehouse. Looking absurdly drab in their midst, a few locals passed by, staring at Fingers and glancing uneasily at the warehouse lit up and pounding, monstrous in the dull light.

A tall figure rounded the corner and bore down on him. Close behind him appeared two figures, a slim black man and a short woman. Fingers started, looked hard. It was Natasha.

"Where the *fuck* have you been?" shouted Fingers, smiling tightly, amiable but pissed off. He strode off down the street toward Natasha and her escorts.

She looked amazing. Her hair was pulled up into a high, coiling ponytail. Her body was sheathed in a tiny bra-top, reflective red, and her trousers were so tight they looked painted onto her legs. She wore no jacket, nothing on her thin arms or midriff. She must be freezing, Fingers thought. He shrugged: no surrender to comfort in the style war. But he was surprised. Whenever he had seen her DJ before, Natasha had resolutely dressed down, in clothes that were baggy and comfortable and nondescript. But not tonight. Gold glinted in her ears and around her neck.

Fingers stopped short, waited for her to come to him.

She was approaching with an odd gait, he realized, a peculiar hybrid, at once arrogant sashay and aimless wander. He noticed that she was wearing a walkman, as was the guy next to her, Fabian. Fingers had met him once before. He was as dressed up as Natasha, and walking in the same half-lost manner. It suddenly occurred to Fingers that the two of them might be high, and he gritted his teeth. If she was fucked up and couldn't perform . . .

The tall man reached him first and proffered a hand, which Fingers stared at, then shook perfunctorily. Fuck knew where Natasha had picked this one up, he thought. An embarrassing grin, his blond hair enticed into a ponytail it clearly resented, and clothes that proclaimed his indifference to fashion. Incongruously, his face was covered in thin, half-healed scratches. If he hadn't been with Natasha, he would never have got past the bouncers.

"You must be Fingers," he said. "I'm Pete."

Fingers nodded briefly and turned to Natasha. He was about to harass her about her late arrival but, as he opened his mouth, her face passed from shadow into the dim glow of a streetlamp and his complaints died unsaid.

Her make-up was immaculate and excessive, vampish, but it could not disguise how thin and pale she looked. She looked up at him with eyes that did not properly focus, smiled abstractedly. Drugs for sure, he thought again.

"Tash, man," he said uneasily, "are you OK?"

Behind him the thumping beats of the warehouse were audible, a backdrop to his conversation.

She cocked her head, pulled the headphone from one ear. He repeated his question.

"For sure, man," she said, and he was a little reassured. Her voice sounded firm and controlled. "We're ready to go."

Fingers realized that Fabian was nodding his head slightly, in time to the beat passing through his headphones, his eyes unfocused.

Natasha followed Fingers' gaze. "You'll be hearing that later," she said softly. "You can join in. I swear you'll love it. Have you got a DAT player in there? Pete brought mine, in case." She paused and gave another wan smile. "You have to hear what I've been doing. It's special, Fingers."

There was a silence Fingers did not know how to fill. Eventually he inclined his head for them to follow him, turned and walked back toward the warehouse.

It felt like a long way.

As he walked, he heard a brief sound, a snatch of billowing and snapping like a sheet being shaken out. He turned, but saw nothing. Pete was looking into the sky, smiling.

Giddy with excitement and terror, Loplop spun in circles in the air, passing through narrow passages between buildings, searching for Anansi. He caught a glimpse of his nude torso tucked under the eaves of a building. Loplop hovered before him like a humming-bird, screeching incoherently. Anansi understood. He glowered and mouthed something.

He's here. The Piper's here.

Loplop nodded, shrieked, disappeared.

Anansi whispered into his hand, released the tiny spider held therein. It scuttled away from him down the side of the building, to the bottom of the drainpipe, where another five comrades awaited it. They caressed the newcomer with their long, powerful legs, leaned in close and gazed into one another's eyes. Then all six turned and disappeared, their paths forming an expanding asterisk, until each spider met others of its kind, waiting, and there was another brief conference, and more messengers joined the throng, exponentially, faster and faster, and word spread among the spiders like contagion.

There were a million little holes in the warehouse walls. There were passages and faultlines beneath the guttering, there were missing panes in rear windows. The building was imperfectly sealed.

Loplop circled it uneasily, seeing all the places where he could go in. He would flit toward one suddenly, ready to make his entrance, ready to attack—and then as the edifice loomed close he would balk and shy violently away, to circle again.

He cried out in anguish. A few miserable birds answered him, but they were unheard.

Loplop could lead a flock, could be the knife-point of an attacking cloud, pushed on by his ranks. With a nation behind him his fear was irrelevant.

But now he was deaf and powerless and quite alone.

He tried once more to penetrate the walls, failed again and recoiled in misery. His mind brimmed with his defeats at the Piper's hands. He remembered the stench of bedlam and the ragged pain of bursting ears, the soulless empty joy of the Piper's thrall.

With an army behind him, he might have entered. Anger and resolve might have won out as he called his troops to attention, basking in the power of command and kin.

But alone, trapped in his skull, isolated in the surge of his own blood and terror, surrounded by birds he could not command, Loplop deserted. He wailed once in miserable betrayal and arced suddenly away in a quick, shameful flight across the city, north, over the river, out of danger and into the larger night.

Directly opposite the warehouse rose a high red wall, the boundary of a long-gone factory. Behind it was a small area of urban scrub, and beyond that a thickset tower block, fabricated from gray slabs, that overlooked the warehouse and its courtyard.

On the top of the block's flat roof, something moved under a pile of old cardboard. Stealthy hands with filthy nails crept gingerly out from underneath and gently cleared a small space. Two indistinct eyes peered out as Natasha, Fabian and Pete followed Fingers up the stairs of the warehouse, past the bouncers and into the building.

The cardboard rose, then fell away as Saul stood.

He was still for a moment, breathing deeply, calming himself, slowing his heart.

His old clothes, stolen from the prison, fluttered around him.

He closed his eyes briefly, rocked on his heels, then

snapped to attention, scanned the air for any signs of Loplop coming for him.

It was partly in case of such an attack that he had concealed himself, but there was more and less to it than that. He could not speak, could not talk to Anansi, could not make any more plans. He gave an empty smile. As if they had come up with any plans.

This was the night when it would all happen. This was the night when he would free himself, or the night he would die. And he wanted to be alone in London, using the city as his climbing frame, asserting himself alone, before the night came for him.

And as he had known it would, the night had come.

It was time to move.

Saul leaned forward, grasped the gutter with both hands, shook it vigorously, testing its strength.

His legs bent a little for leverage, he paused, then vaulted over the edge of the building.

Saul swung around in mid-air, his hands leapfrogging over each other as he renewed his grip, tugged himself out of his acrobatic arc and into a sharp sideways movement, curtailing his curving passage and slithering along the gutter to the drainpipe.

He slipped down it as if it were a firefighter's pole, his hands and feet moving imperceptibly fast to avoid the bolts that tethered it to the wall.

He touched down on the desiccated earth and moved through the desultory patches of dandelions and grass into the shadow of the wall.

Saul clicked his fingers imperiously. Immediately a dozen little brown heads poked up from hiding places behind old bricks, from holes in the earth, cavities in the wall. The rats watched him, twitching in excitement and fear.

"It's time," he said. "Tell everyone to get ready. I'll see

you in there." He paused, and spoke his final words with a flat excitement, a fatalistic thrill. "In you go."

The rats bolted.

Saul ran with them. He overtook them, ran through them like a symbol of victory. He slunk along the top of the wall, invisible. He crossed the road unseen, now in the shade of a car, now flattened against a building, now as a passer-by; into the gutter and out, over the wall and along the side of the warehouse, past the waiting crowds without giving them a second glance. The air was thick with the taste of alcohol and scent, but Saul held his nose through that.

He kept his nose clean to smell his troops.

Up a low garage and across its collapsed skylight, a ramp onto the crumbling brick walls of the venue, clinging to forgotten nails and the undersides of heavy old windows. He gripped the edge of the gently sloping roof and bent his legs against the wall. He could feel the bricks vibrate with bass. Then, just as King Rat had done so long ago, on Saul's first night among the beasts, before he had eaten their food, when he was still human, Saul pushed out with his legs and swung around in a perfect circle, landing solidly on the warehouse roof.

He slithered quickly up the slates toward the massive skylights. They were cracked all over, a few seconds' work to pry open and push aside, opening the way to an attic space, a dusty wooden floor that jumped with the bass from below, as if the building itself was eager to dance to the music in its bowels.

Saul paused. He could taste a mass movement in the air. He could sense the migration of the compact little bodies, was aware of the exodus of his troops from the streets and sewers and scrub, toward the glowing building. He could feel the scratch of claws on concrete, the feverish searching for causeways and flaws in brick.

The rats and Saul left the relative safety of London's night lands and entered the warehouse, the frenzied jaws of Drum and Bass, the domain of smoke and strobe lights and Hardcore, the Piper's lair, the heart of Darkness, deep in the Jungle.

The wooden boards drummed under Saul's feet: the dust motes would not settle but hovered instead in an indistinct mist around his ankles. He crept the length of the long attic. In the corner of the great dark space there was a trapdoor.

Saul flattened himself against the floor and tugged at it very gently, raising it slowly away from the surrounding boards. Music and colored light and the smell of dancers spilled through the slit to which he put his eye.

The lights below spun and changed colors, illuminating and obscuring, bouncing off suspended globes and dissipating throughout the hall. They cut through the darkness, confusing as much as they elucidated.

A long way below him was the dancefloor. It was a hallucinogenic vision, shimmering and metamorphosing like a fractal pattern, feverish bodies moving in a thousand different ways. In the corners lurked the bad boys, nodding their heads, no more than that, no reaction to the overwhelming music. On the floor the hard-steppers, swinging their arms, loose-limbed and syncopated; and those on speed and coke, ludicrously trying to keep up with the BPM, shifting their feet like lunatics; the rudegirls, arms spread wide, winding their hips slowly to the bassline, a barrage of colors and clothes and undress. The dancefloor was tight-packed, thronging with bodies, decadent and vibrant, thrilling, communal and brutal.

As he watched, a strobe light kicked in, transforming the room momentarily into a series of frozen tableaux. Saul could investigate individuals almost at his leisure. He was struck by the multiplicity of expressions on the faces below.

The Drum and Bass felt as if it would lift the hatch out of the floor, off into the sky. It was unforgiving, a punishing assault of original Hardcore beats.

A little below him an iron walkway described the edge of

the hall. It was deserted. There was a ladder in one corner, tucked up under the walkway and secured with chains. It was designed to swing down to another, similar ledge further down. This lower level was crowded with bodies, people looking down on the dancers ten feet below.

Saul cast his eyes around the hall. There was a tiny movement in the corner opposite him.

Red and green lights swirled around a black shape suspended from the ceiling. Anansi swung gently from one of his ropes. His arms and legs were tucked up impossibly tight. His knuckles were just visible, motionless, and stretched taut from grasping.

He swayed from side to side, buffeted by sonic vibrations. Saul knew that Anansi's army was with him, around them both, invisible and ready.

Directly below Anansi, Saul saw the stage raised above the dancefloor. His breath quickened a little: there, framed by two colossal speakers, were the decks.

Behind the stage a huge graffito was hung: the same grotesque DJ who had adorned the poster, and the legend *Junglist Terror!!!* was writ very large. Dwarfed by the unlikely figure on the canvas, the DJ laboring behind the decks paced quickly to and from his record box, a bulky pair of earphones tucked against one ear. He moved with a controlled, feverish energy. Saul did not recognize him. As he watched, the man deftly segued between two tracks. He was good.

Behind him, Saul felt the tentative lick of a rat-tongue on his hand. He was no longer alone.

"Alright," he whispered, and stroked the little head without looking backwards. "Alright."

Saul opened the trapdoor. He poked his head upsidedown into the hall, breaking the surface tension of the music and immersing himself in it. He lowered himself gently to the iron grill below. The beats were overwhelming. They crept into every crevice of the room. He felt as if he was moving underwater. He was almost afraid to breathe. Out of the corner of his eye he saw Anansi notice him, and he raised his hand.

It was sweltering in the hall, as humid and heavy as a rainforest. The condensed heat of the dancers enveloped him. He pulled off his shirt. Oily dirt coated him. He realized that it was weeks since he had seen his own body. The shirt had become his fur.

He remembered the touch of the rat above, and he reached up to wedge one sleeve of his shirt under the open trapdoor's hinge. He pulled at the other sleeve until it was stretched taut, tied it to the railing which enclosed the walkway. Almost immediately, two rats scurried along this greasy canvas bridge and leapt onto the iron.

Others would be joining them, thought Saul as he watched them race away along the rampart, finding their way down.

Sweat trickled down his body, cutting channels in the grime which covered him. He felt no shame. His standards had changed.

Saul flattened himself against the wall and crept forward toward the decks, keeping his eyes fixed on the stage below him. He lowered himself as he advanced. By the time he had covered half the length of the wall, he was slithering along the cold iron like a snake. He pushed his face to the gaps in the grill, his eyes darting urgently from side to side. He crawled slowly forward.

Even through the pervasive clouds of cologne and sweat and drugs and sex, Saul could taste rat. The troops were arriving in force, waiting for his signal.

He glanced up. Anansi flickered in and out of existence in the quickfiring lights.

A door opened at the back of the stage.

Saul stiffened.

Natasha emerged from the depths of the building, into the sound and fury.

Saul caught his breath. He gripped the grill on which he crawled until his fingers hurt. She looked breathtaking. But she was thin, much too thin, and she moved as if she was in a dream.

Where was the Piper? Was she here of her free will? Saul stared at her in consternation. He saw headphones on her ears and was momentarily confused—how could she listen to a walkman in the middle of a club?—before he understood. He caught his breath, watching her bob her head, moving to a different rhythm from the rest of the dancers. He knew what she was listening to, he knew whose music it was.

In one hand she held a case full of records, in the other a squat box, some piece of electronics, trailing wires. He could not see what it was. Natasha tapped the DJ on the shoulder. He turned and touched fists with her, shouting animatedly into her ears. As he spoke she busied herself plugging the box into the sound system, nodding occasionally, whether in answer or in response to the music in her ears Saul could not tell.

The DJ removed his huge earphones and placed them over Natasha's ears, hesitating for her to remove her small walkman earpieces. When she did not, he shrugged and placed the larger ones over the top of them and laughed. He disappeared into the door from which Natasha had emerged.

Natasha rifled through the records she had brought, pulled something out, twirled it elegantly and blew dust from it. She placed it on the turntable and hunched over, spinning it, smoothing it back with her fingers, listening *through* the tune on her walkman, mixing the beats, until she stood straight, with her fingers poised, and let a burst of piano spill over from the twelve-inch she had selected into the tune now coming to an end.

It was impossible to tell where one started and the other ended, the mixing was seamless. She pulled the record back, let it forward again a little, pulled it back, scratching playfully like an old school rapper, finally releasing her hand and switching off the first tune in a smooth movement, unleashing the new bassline.

She stood back without a trace of a smile on her lips.

Saul knew that he had to get down to her, had to take the phones from her head and make her understand the danger she was in. But this must be exactly what the Piper had in mind for him. The cheese in his trap.

The door opened again and two more figures appeared. The first was Fabian. Saul was appalled, nearly leapt to his feet. Fabian was even more emaciated and exhausted-looking than Natasha. His finery could not disguise that. He was limping. Like Natasha, he wore walkman headphones. It was that beat, the tune that only he could hear, that propelled Fabian forward.

Behind him was the Piper.

As he entered the room he stopped, breathed in deeply, gave a huge smile. He spread his arms wide as if he would embrace all the dancers below him.

Fabian stayed very close to him.

Saul looked up at Anansi. He was oscillating on his rope, his sudden tension communicated violently through his body.

Rush him?

Should we rush him? thought Saul frantically.

What is to be done?

Anansi and Saul were paralyzed, caught in the gaze of a snake. And the Piper could not even see them.

Natasha turned and saw her two companions. She held out her hand and the Piper pulled something out of his pocket, tossed it across the stage to her. As it curved through the air it was transfixed for a moment in a beam of white light. It seemed to freeze, letting Saul examine it at his leisure. It glinted, a small plastic case, like a cassette but smaller, squarer . . .

A DAT.

A Digital Audio Tape. Natasha used them to record her tracks.

He screamed and leapt to his feet as Natasha's hand closed around the tape.

The cavernous space was full of sound, there was no room for his paltry screech. He could not even hear it himself in the cacophony of beats and basslines. The dancers danced on, unperturbed, Natasha turned toward the decks, Fabian continued his shambling little rotations . . . but the Piper turned his head sharply at the imperceptible sound, stared up, through the cat's cradle of light beams, past the too-cool bodies on the lower walkway, up into the shadow of the roof, gazing directly into Saul's eyes.

The Piper gave a jaunty wave, and grinned. He was burning with triumphalism.

Saul propelled himself along the gantry while the Piper laughed on the stage. The dancers were oblivious. The beats seemed to slow down, everything was slow, Saul could see the mass of bodies below him sink and rise ponderously.

He pounded along the iron toward the corner where Anansi hung, paralyzed. He stared through the floor at Natasha walking slowly toward the DAT player she had plugged in, reaching out with the hand holding the tape. Saul looked up as he drew near Anansi, who swung from side to side, around and around, a useless pendulum.

Saul had not stopped shouting. He was ululating appallingly as he ran. Anansi looked up at him. As Natasha slipped the tape into the deck and crooked one of the headphones against her shoulder, Saul grabbed the rail with his left hand and vaulted up high, moving so slowly he could stare at the faces below him, all the individuals that made up the bouncing mass. He brought his feet down together on the railing, bent down and leapt out, sending himself through the air, flying above the dancers like a superhero.

Anansi's eyes widened as Saul surged toward him, his arms flailing, legs tucked up in front of him like a longjumper. Saul spread his arms and legs wide, and crashed into Anansi forty feet above the stage.

He clutched at Anansi, hugged himself to him. He felt himself lurching crazily back and forth through the air, heard Anansi yelling something at him. The rope holding the two bodies was vibrating, dangerously taut. Saul was screaming into Anansi's ears.

"Down!" he screamed. *"Go down now!"*

Saul felt himself drop and his stomach lurched. His descent smoothened out as Anansi manipulated the fibers in his hand. Smoother than any abseiler, the spider-man and his cargo sank swiftly toward the stage.

As they plummeted, Saul and Anansi spun around their center of gravity, and the room whirled around them. Saul caught glimpse after glimpse of the dancers, frozen, gazing at the men dropping out of the air. Some looked aghast or confused, but most were laughing, enrapt at this new entertainment.

"Run! Get the fuck out!" screamed Saul, but the Jungle was remorseless, and no one heard him except Anansi.

Saul looked down, eight feet from the stage, relaxed his grip and dropped from Anansi like a bomb.

He was rigid, his quarry dead in his line of flight. Even over the Drum and Bass beats, Saul thought he heard a collective gasp. His face set as he fell, his legs straightened, but the Piper had been watching and he danced nimbly to one side, away from Saul's punishing boots, leaving Saul to slam into the wooden stage.

He staggered but remained on his feet. The decks were so well supported that the record playing did not even skip at his arrival. Saul looked on in horror as Natasha's hand tightened on the DAT player's volume control, her face furrowed over the headphones as she prepared to mix from the record to the tape, waiting for the right moment in the beat.

Saul leapt toward her, prepared to throw her away from the decks, to hurt her if need be, rage and fear filling him, but as he neared her something slammed into him from behind and he went sprawling, flying off to the side of the stage. Natasha did not even look round.

Saul rolled on the floor, twisted, and pulled himself back up.

Fabian was bearing down on him.

His friend was not looking at him, was focusing over Saul's shoulder, just as Loplop had done that night in the flat.

He moved toward Saul without pausing, his arms outstretched like a cinematic zombie.

Behind Fabian, Saul saw Anansi touch the stage, only for the Piper immediately to smack him hard in the mouth, sending him sprawling. But Saul's attention was taken by the tiniest of motions: Natasha's hand turning the volume slowly up.

Saul barrelled into Fabian, trying to run through him, overpower him, and his friend held him fast, twisted as Saul tried to run past him. The two came crashing down, Saul's hand outstretched, an inch from Natasha's shoe.

She nodded in satisfaction and turned up the DAT.

Everything froze.

There was a sublime moment. Everyone was utterly still: the dancers, the men who had jumped on stage to break up the fights they saw there, Saul, rigid with despair.

The beats that slid insidiously from the speakers were all at the high end, cymbals, no bassline. A tiny snatch of piano cried out plaintively.

But it was the flute which held the attention.

A sudden burst had heralded the song, a trill that had erupted into the room's collective consciousness and cleared the minds of the listeners. As Saul watched, Natasha removed her headphones and her walkman. No need for them now. This was the song she had been listening to. Behind him Fabian rose and followed suit.

The snatch of flute had shocked the dancers into submission, and now it faded, leaving only echoes and the sounds of radio static, the ghosts of dead stations rolling over the beat and the soulless piano. Still there was no bassline. Saul could not get up. He saw the dancers begin to shake their heads and extricate themselves from the snares of the flute, and then another burst exploded into the room and with comically precise timing, the assembled all snapped back upright, their eyes rapt.

And then again. Again.

The Piper stared at Saul, the amiable cast of his face belied by his ghastly wide eyes, ferocious with pleasure.

"You lose," he mouthed to Saul.

Saul glared balefully at the Piper. He raised his arm theatrically, and caught Anansi's eye as he struggled to his feet. Shaking, Anansi imitated him.

Together, they brought their arms down.

"*Now!*" Saul shrieked.

Floorboards and pipes boiled over with rats. Saul's crack troops exploded into the room, racing voraciously through the frozen legs of the dancers toward the stage. The walls erupted as spiders burst from the pores of the building and spilled like liquid toward the Piper.

At that moment, the bassline of *Wind City* burst into the room, pared down and simple. And riding it, sailing over the troughs and peaks of beat and bass, was the flute.

The dancers moved as one.

They moved in time, dancing again, an incredible piece of choreography, every right foot raised together, coming down, then every left, a strange languorous hardstep, arms swinging, legs rigid, up and down in time to the beat, obeying the Piper's flute. And every step aimed at a rat.

This was war.

The rats were fighting now, leaping onto bodies and backs. The dancers' unearthly unity slowly dissolved as they fought their small, vicious enemies without that dislocated look ever leaving their eyes.

The spiders had reached the stage now, with the vanguard of the rats, and both armies swarmed toward the Piper. Anansi rose behind him and lurched forward, slamming his arms into the Piper's back, but his power was diminished by the men who leapt forward to hold him. They did not look at him. They held their heads to the side to hear the music, and they did what the music told them. With a strength that was not theirs they hurled Anansi backwards into the wall. He shouted at his troops, gesticulated.

Saul slithered across the floor toward the decks, the DAT player, the source of the music. Instantly Natasha turned and stamped on his hand with her long heel. He screeched in pain, slithered away again, tried to get past her, but she stamped again and again, faster and faster, until it seemed impossible that she remain standing.

Someone behind Saul grabbed him and pulled him up and with a sudden surge of righteous anger he elbowed them in the face. The head snapped back and lolled, the body staggering but somehow kept standing by the music. Saul turned, his hands claws, and his rage dissipated in horror. His assailant was about seventeen, a chubby Asian boy dressed in his Jungling best, now spattered with blood. His nose was a mess in the middle of his face and still he tried to keep time to the beat.

Saul pushed him away hard, out of the fight.

He realized that the dancers were slowly approaching the stage, fighting and scratching, hurling rats and spiders against the walls, ripping at them with their teeth, all the while cocking their heads thoughtfully to hear the notes of *Wind City*. The fucking flute!

It was multilayered, alienating, frightening, a cacophonous backdrop.

More and more dancers leapt onto the stage, their clothes clogged with blood, rat and human, with fragments of fur, their faces shredded by tiny claws. Saul could taste the rat blood on the air. It flooded him with adrenaline.

Spiders and rats covered the stage, swarmed up the legs of Fabian and the dancers. Fabian tugged at the fat bodies of rats and slammed them underfoot where their legs and spines and skulls cracked and they crawled off to die. He slapped at himself and danced from leg to leg, smearing spiders into the wood.

Saul could hear Anansi bellowing.

Saul turned and made for the decks again. Fabian kicked him in the crotch from behind and Natasha stamped at his shoulder. He moved, avoided being impaled, but hands grasped his legs and tugged him violently across a floor slippery with rat blood and crushed spiders, slid him away from Natasha and the DAT player, slammed him into a wall. Bodies fell across him, inhumanly strong knees crushed his back, he was pinioned by a score of arms and legs.

Saul could hear Anansi shrieking.

He looked up, saw the Piper bent over Anansi, the spiderman held down by several dancers. With his head low against the boards, all Saul could see of the dancefloor was the bobbing heads of the dancers.

It was a vision of hell, rats and spiders and blood swarming over the damned.

Fabian stumbled into his view, and Saul looked up at him and back at Natasha. They were invisible beneath a second skin of spiders, a thick skittering mass. The tide of spiders spilled toward the Piper. Anansi kept shrieking.

The Piper looked up, caught Saul's eye, and looked briefly at the spiders approaching him.

"Shall I show you my new party trick?" he said. His voice sounded close and intimate in Saul's ear, whispered through the Jungle and the flute.

The Piper flickered his eyes briefly at the decks.

Something changed in the flute.

The samples were looped and laid one on top of the other, and as he listened Saul realized that one of the layers was soaring, changing, becoming staccato and breathless. Anansi was suddenly silent.

As it reached the Piper's feet, the tide of spiders stopped dead.

He's changing the music! He's changing his choice! thought Saul. *He's going for the spiders instead!*

But the dancers kept dancing, even as the spiders began to move together, incredibly, undulating with the beat. The circle of spiders around the Piper's feet expanded, gave him space.

Still the dancers did not stop dancing. The spiders coating the bodies of dancers dripped off them and scuttled onto the stage. Natasha and Fabian were uncovered, their skin covered in tiny welts and sores, dead spiders dropping from their clothes and mouths. They resumed their war against the rats.

The Piper began to leap, higher and higher, from one foot to the other, without taking his eyes from Saul's. Saul looked down at the Piper's feet. As he jumped, a little group of spiders would dance out, in time to the music, and stand below him, arranging themselves into the shape of the underside of each shoe. They would wait patiently as he plunged through the air and destroyed them exactly, the carnage of each step preempted by the spiders themselves, queuing up to die.

"You see, Saul?" whispered the Piper across the slick, stained stage. "That's the joy of Jungle. All those layers . . . I can play my flute as many times as I want, *all at once* . . . "

The dancers kept dancing, and the spiders still waited to die.

Anansi sat up, his eyes glazed with delight at the spider music in *Wind City*. An idiot's grin spread across his face. His left arm was missing at the shoulder, his side awash with blood, his shoulder a mass of ruined flesh and bone.

The Piper watched Saul's face.

"Yes, cruel, I know, to pull the legs off spiders, but this one had caused me no *end* of trouble."

He pushed Anansi's head back to the stage.

Saul's shout was drowned in the Drum and Bass and flute. He struggled violently, but was held fast by the dancers. He could feel them move slightly with the beat as they leaned on him.

The Piper leapt up, pulled his legs up hard and stamped down with all his strength.

Bones crunched and split in Anansi's head.

Saul collapsed with a howl.

The wood of the stage heaved and buckled. Something burst through the boards in front of the Piper. Saul caught a momentary glimpse of a back, of wiry arms snapping out like whipcord and grasping the Piper's ankles, then tugging sharply and disappearing back under the stage.

The Piper was gone. The music still blared, Saul was still pinioned, the rats still fought and bit and scratched, the dancers still fought back and massacred rats and danced, but the Piper was gone.

Saul could feel the vibrations of some huge battle being waged under him. He tugged at the arms holding him. They were obscenely strong but quite still. They held him tight but did not punish him for his pointless struggles.

The wood under his stomach lurched as something was thrust against it. A little to one side of him he heard a systematic pounding, something slammed again and again into the wood. Splinters of wood that fringed the hole in the stage spilled gently into the darkness below.

Spiders poured into the hole, and Saul saw the back of a nearby dancer lowering himself into the dark.

Saul pounded suddenly at the wood under his body, thrust his fingers into the tiny gap between two planks, ignoring the skin he left behind. He had no leverage, this was the wrong angle, but adrenaline gave him strength, and he tugged and ripped at the boards beneath him. His fingers shoved into the small cavity and scrabbled for purchase. He was straining, shoving upwards, feeling the board resist, then relax as old nails sprang from their moorings and the board went flying away.

He stuck his head into the darkness.

There, rolling in the dirt, his eyes frenzied and livid, his veins bulging with fury, was the Piper. And clinging to him like a limpet, the heel of his right hand shoved hard into the Piper's mouth, his teeth bared and snapping at any of the Piper's limbs in reach, his claws scratching, his old coat wrapping around the two bodies like a living thing, was King Rat.

His hand streamed with blood from where the Piper

gnawed at him, but he would not release the Piper's mouth. He swarmed with spiders. Behind him the dim shape of a dancer, bent double under the stage, flailed at him with his arms. King Rat rolled from side to side to avoid him, desperate to stay out of reach.

King Rat stared up at Saul. His eyes begged for help.

Saul saw the dancer's arms wind around King Rat's neck, begin to bend inexorably backwards.

He tugged desperately at the hands holding him, straining against them with all his strength, arching his back. They pushed him down so he suddenly *acquiesced*, rolling slightly and squeezing himself through the thin slit in the wood, being shoved through to freedom by those trying to constrain him, until he dropped suddenly and landed across the Piper's feet.

He yelled with triumph, and turned.

"Help me," hissed King Rat between clenched teeth. His head was pulled back at a grotesque angle, his arms were losing their grip on the Piper, his hand having to strain harder and harder to block the Piper's mouth. The man behind him was slowly defeating him, made preternaturally strong by the music which surrounded them.

Saul stormed through swathes of dancing spiders and punched hard at the face of the man holding King Rat.

He saw that it was Fabian just as his fist connected.

Saul had hit him hard, with all his rat-strength, and Fabian's head rolled on his shoulders dangerously fast, teeth splintered in his mouth, but he retained his grip on King Rat, and continued to pull.

The Piper was pulling free, his teeth ripping at King Rat's hand, a growl of triumph bubbling bloodily out from behind it.

"Help me," repeated King Rat. Desperately Saul grabbed at Fabian, shoved him this way and that, with all his strength, but the flute had entered Fabian's soul and nothing would move him. If that punch did not do the job, Saul knew he would have to kill Fabian to get him off.

"Help me," said King Rat once more.

But Saul had hesitated too long and Fabian pulled King

Rat free of the Piper.

"*Yes!*" The Piper was standing before Saul, filthy, scratched and quivering, spilling spiders in all directions. He grabbed Saul's collar, heaved him with those insanely strong arms, sent him flying through the hole in the stage back out into the heat and noise and blood of the club.

Saul landed awkwardly, skidded across the splintered wood.

The Piper rose behind him, dragging King Rat by the hair.

Wind City was looping, again and again. Saul was sure it covered the whole DAT, perhaps an hour long.

"*You lose!*" the Piper shouted to Saul. "You and your daddy and uncle spider and the birdman, you *lose*, because I can play my flute as often as I want now. Your friend showed me how, Saul . . . " He waved his hands at the walls where the spiders were dancing in little circles. He gesticulated at the dancefloor where the dancers jumped up and down to *Wind City*, drenched in blood, stamping on dying rats.

He released King Rat into the arms of the dancers on the stage. King Rat sagged with weakness and defeat.

Saul was exhausted. He felt more hands grab him. The Piper sauntered toward him and crouched in front of him, just out of reach.

"See, Saul," he whispered, "I'm not just going to kill you. Before you die, Saul, I'm going to make you dance for me. You think you're *so special*, don't you? Well, I'm the Lord of the Dance, Saul, and before you die you're going to dance for me. Why do you think I let your *pathetic* little army fight to the last gasp?" He indicated the dancefloor, where lackluster little battles were still continuing, where the routed rats were being systematically destroyed as the dance continued.

"You see, I wanted to *explain* to you, Saul. You see how I can make the people dance *and* the spiders? See how I did that? Well, I can make the rats dance, too, Saul. And you're the famous *half and half*, aren't you? Eh? The rat-boy? Eh? Well, I'm already playing for the people, Saul, so half of you is dancing, even if you can't feel it. So when I start playing for the *rats*, Saul, then I'm playing for both your sides. See? See, you little fucker? I didn't know what I'd found when I checked your address book, tried to find you. Just turned up at the one with stuff scrawled next to it . . . and see what I found. Your friend Natasha, who showed me how to make my flute *multiply* . . . "

The Piper grinned and patted Saul's face gently, then backed away toward the decks. Behind him stood Natasha, her clothes ruined, her face coated in blood as thick as oil.

The dancefloor still surged, but an odd calm had settled on the stage.

"I'm going to play for both your halves, Saul," he said. "I'm going to make you dance."

He looked up, raised his finger like a conductor and the music changed again.

The beat was sustained, the bassline unchanged, the static and the hesitant piano continued . . . but the flute soared.

Across the top of the mellifluous and pointillist flute lines that seduced the dancers and the spiders, a third level of sound sprang into being. An unsettling, crawling democracy of semitones and minor chords, pauses punctuated by surreal bursts of noise, music to make the skin crawl. Rat-music.

All across the dancefloor, the rats that had not fled or died were suddenly still.

Out of the corner of his eye Saul saw King Rat stiffen, his eyes glaze and focus on something just out of sight. And as he saw that, Saul felt *himself* jerk upright, *listened* to the music, heard it with a wave of amazement, stared wide-eyed at the bursts of light around him, saw through the speakers and the walls, felt his mind open up.

A long long way away he heard a high-pitched laugh, saw the Piper lying back, being borne around the room on the raised arms of the dancers, but that didn't bother him now. The hands that held him were gone. Saul stood and paced to the center of the stage. All he could concentrate on was the music.

There was something just out of his reach . . .

Just out of his reach . . . there was beautiful food . . .

He could smell it . . . he could taste it on the air, and sex, he felt his cock stiffen, his mouth was watering, his feet propelled him, he did not need to think of where to walk, the responsibility had been taken from him, he obeyed the music, two tunes at once, the rat and the man, the mellow and the frenzied, spilling around each other, filling his mind.

Beside him, he was dimly aware of King Rat, pacing from side to side, his feet ponderous but enthusiastic.

"Dance!" The command came from across the floor, where the Piper rode the arms of the crowd like a sportsman, a hero, a dictator.

Obedience came easily to Saul. He danced.

Hardstepping.

With the fighting stopped, everyone in the hall could dance, the people and the spiders and rats that were still alive, all moving in time, getting down as one, as the Piper laughed delightedly. Saul was vaguely aware of being pleased, moving in a tight circle, eager for the food and the sex and the music, proud to be part of this hall, this great gestalt.

The Piper had ridden the tops of the dancers all around the hall in his triumph, a lap of honor, and through a blissful haze Saul saw the tall figure step smoothly back onto the stage.

Saul danced for joy, opened his arms wide. This was his epiphany, he was filled with music, two strains of music, his mind relaxed and floating, his feet revelling in the dance, gazing up and around at the bobbing bodies on all sides of him, the faces of the worshippers . . . Saul was ecstatic.

The Piper smiled, and Saul smiled back.

He was vaguely aware of words being spoken, felt his feet propel him forward, across the big stage, toward the Piper, who waited for him, something long and glinting in his hand.

" . . . to me . . . " Saul heard between beats. " . . . dance for me . . . come . . . "

He stepped forward, shifting in time to the two tunes he could hear, eager to dance.

But something was wrong.

There was a disturbed moment. Saul hesitated.

The two flutelines were dissonant.

Saul put his foot on the stage and tried to dance, but a shadow had crossed his mind.

The flutes jarred with each other.

He was suddenly aware of their raucous discord. His hunger and desire burned as strong as ever, but he could not see, he was blind, pulled in different directions, shaken by the aesthetic antiphase of the two flutes.

And as he listened, standing suddenly outside the music, looking in, desperate to get back, he sensed the great cavity between the flutes.

And pushing its way through the gap, vibrating in his gut, ever-present, the foundation of the music, the beginning and the end-point of Jungle, there came the bass.

Saul stood poised, immobile, center stage.

The flute and the bass surged inside him.

The flutelines swirled around him, inveigling their way past his defenses, seducing him, urging him to dance, teasing his rat-mind and his humanity in turn.

But something inside him had hardened. Saul was straining for something else. He was listening for the bass.

The words of a hundred slogans raced through his mind, the endlessly sampled Hip Hop and Jungle paeans to the low end.

DJ! Where's the bass?

Bass! How low can you go?

R-r-r-roll the bass . . .

Da bass too dark . . .

Here's the bass.

Here's how low the bass can go.

I . . . I'll roll with the bass.

Because the bass too dark . . .

Because the bass is too dark for this, thought Saul suddenly, with shocking clarity, the bass is too dark to suffer this, the insubordinate treble, *fuck the treble, fuck the ephemera, fuck the high end, fuck the flute*, and as he thought this the flutelines faded in his mind, became nothing more than thin, clashing cacophonies, *fuck the treble*, he thought, because when you dance to Jungle what you follow is the *bass* . . .

Saul rediscovered himself. He knew who he was. He danced again.

This was different. He was fierce, swinging his arms and legs like weapons. He danced with the bassline, rolled over the beats . . . ignored the flutes.

It was the bass that set the agenda. It was the bass that made the song. It was the bass that united the Junglists, that cemented their community, that built a room full of dancers, something far stronger than this hive mind.

The Piper was still waiting for him. Saul saw a renewed smile spread across his face. He had seen Saul falter. *You wanted me to dance, didn't you?* thought Saul. *Had to have me dance my way over to you, waltz to my death . . . and now I'm dancing, you think your treble won, don't you?*

Saul danced closer and closer to the Piper. The Piper held his flute close, flush with his body like a Samurai sword. The Piper's arms were tense.

Two flutes aren't enough, thought Saul, giddy with power. He danced on, approaching his enemy. The Piper smiled and raised his right hand, the hand holding the flute, held it high, quivering, ready to strike.

Saul came close enough to touch.

"Now dance on the spot, ratling," said the Piper softly.

He swung the flute.

The strike was cocky, cavalier and ill-timed, the Piper waiting for his prey to walk into the path of the wicked silver club.

Instead, Saul stepped inside the killing blow.

He moved in a blur of rat-speed, channelling all his frenetic panic and power, burning calories from old food. He turned as he stepped forward and reached up with his right hand, grabbing the flute and twisting, spinning around in a full circle, tugging at the cold metal, ripping it out of the Piper's too-confident fingers and bringing his left arm up and around, looking over his left shoulder as he spun, and slamming his elbow into the Piper's throat.

The Piper staggered backwards. His eyes bulged and stared at Saul in disbelief. He retched, clutched at his throat, sucked at the air. Saul stalked toward him, holding the flute. The Drum and Bass was pounding in his ears. It wasn't the Piper's song anymore; it was the drums he heard, the drums and the bass.

"One plus one equals *one*, motherfucker," he said, and brought the flute up hard under the Piper's jaw. The Piper staggered back but did not fall. "I'm not rat plus man, get it? I'm bigger than either one *and I'm bigger than the two*. I'm a new thing. *You can't make me dance*." He slammed the flute against the Piper's temple, sending the tall figure spinning across the stage in a spray of blood, toward where King Rat still danced.

The Piper twirled an ugly pirouette but still did not fall.

Saul advanced on him, hitting him again and again with the flute, brutal and unforgiving. He punctuated his assault with proclamations.

"Should've just killed me. You're too strong for me, but you had to get cocky. Well, I'm the new blood, mother*fucker*. I'm more than the sum of my parts. You can't play my fucking tune, and your flute means *nothing to me*."

With the last strike, the Piper went down in the shadow of King Rat. His legs folded and he sat down hard on the floor, his back to the brick wall. He stared up at Saul, horrified and broken. His face was crushed and spoilt. Blood slid over the silver of the flute. The Piper's eyes were glazed with agony and with affront, with outrage at this man who would not dance to his tune.

His breath rattled grotesquely in his throat. He fought to

speak, failed.

Saul looked up. The dancing figures that filled the room were slowing down. The flute was mutating, folding in on itself. It could not sustain itself without the Piper's will. People's faces were confused, their heads lolling as if in uneasy sleep. The rats and spiders were twitching pathologically as the flutelines that held them imploded.

King Rat fell to the floor and twisted in agony, pulling himself out of the spell.

Always the strongest, thought Saul.

He looked back at the Piper, collapsed on the floor. With puffy lips and bloody teeth, the Piper smiled.

Saul held the flute like a dagger, raised it over his head.

There was a Stygian rumble deep in the walls. The stage shook. Saul staggered.

"What the fuck . . . ?" he said.

The floor lurched, shook violently. Saul fell backwards.

Above the Piper's head a split appeared in the wall, thin and unnaturally straight as if scored with a vast razor. The stage shook until all the dancers had fallen. It was only because it was on DAT, safe from the caprice of styluses and shocks, that *Wind City* did not falter.

The split widened and spread downwards, opening the bricks behind the Piper's back. The rent in the wall opened onto a sheer darkness.

The Piper fixed Saul with his little smile.

The darkness widened and sucked at the air in the room.

As if a window on an airplane had burst, papers and clothes and fragments of spider corpses whirled through the air into the black.

He opened a mountain once before, thought Saul urgently, he can open up a wall. He's heading for home.

The Piper was quite still as the split pulled itself open behind him, the eye in a tornado of detritus that filled the room. Saul planted his feet wide and got to his knees, adamant that the Piper would not escape out of the world.

Then, as he steadied himself and gripped the flute once

more, ready to strike, he heard a thin, desperate keening from the pit that was opening.

A child's voice.

Saul froze, aghast. The Piper was still. He did not release Saul's gaze. He did not stop smiling. The split behind his back was a foot wide now, and he began to wriggle his way into it, holding Saul's eyes all the time. The pathetic wail stopped abruptly.

And just as abruptly a chorus of terror welled out of the darkness, hundreds of tiny voices screaming, stripped raw, mad with fear.

The lost children of Hamelin could see the light.

Saul fell back in a paralysis of horror.

His mouth was stretched wide but only tiny noises burst out. He reached out to the split in the wall, powerless, useless.

The Piper saw him crumple, and winked.

Later, he mouthed, and put his hands to each side of the split, gave a little wave.

A growling thing shoved into Saul at a fierce speed and tore the flute from his hands.

King Rat gripped the flute with both hands and leapt at an impossible angle from Saul's lap to the Piper's side. His teeth were clenched, his feral roar barely contained. His overcoat whipped in the vortex of wind. The Piper looked up at him, stupid and confused.

King Rat's growl burst, became a frenzied bark, he drew back his arms, holding the flute like a spear.

He punched it into the Piper's body with an animal strength.

The Piper gave a shout of amazement, ludicrously bathetic with the music and the wails of the children behind him.

The flute punctured him like a balloon, shoved deep into his belly. His face went white under the blood, and he gripped King Rat's arms, clinging to them with all his might, holding the hands that held the flute close to him, staring into King Rat's eyes.

Everything was poised, for a moment. Everything hung in the balance.

The Piper fell backwards into the dark.

King Rat fell with him.

All Saul could see was the curve of King Rat's back, which lurched forward and stopped abruptly. The slit was suddenly closing around him; the voices of the children were more and more plaintive and distant.

King Rat's back wriggled and his arms emerged above his head, holding the great rent open for half a second more as he braced himself and shoved back from the brink, falling across Saul.

The two sides of the rip met and resealed with a faint crunch.

The Piper had gone. The cries of the children had gone.

Only the Drum and Bass could be heard.

Saul lay still, exhausted, listening to King Rat breathe.

He rolled away, crawled across the stage. He surveyed the room.

The disco lights still spun and stuttered pointlessly. The wreckage of the hall did not seem real. It was a carnage of blood and sweat, dead rats, crushed spiders, collapsed dancers. The walls were foul with a thousand different stains. The floor was slippery and vile. The dancers shuffled like revivified corpses from side to side, ruined, their eyes closed, shifting their weight from foot to foot, as the beat of *Wind City* droned on, and the flute continued to degrade. All over the hall dancers were falling.

Saul stumbled across to the decks and ripped the lead from the DAT player. The speakers went dead. Instantly, all around the room, the dancers dropped, fainting where they stood, as still as the dead. It looked like the aftermath of a massacre.

The spiders and rats still dancing when the music stopped were still for a moment, then bolted. They quit the hall and disappeared into the London night.

Saul looked around the hall, searching for his friends.

There, under the heavy body of a huge dancer, lay Natasha. He tugged her free, crooning.

"Tash, Tash," he whispered, wiping the blood from her face. She was scratched and ripped, her skin welted with the poison of a million tiny spiders, covered with bruises and rat-bites, but she was breathing. He hugged her very hard as she lay there, and squeezed his eyes tight closed.

It had been so long since he had held one of his friends.

He put her gently down, searched for Fabian.

Saul found him lolling out of the hole King Rat had pushed through the stage. He almost wept to see him. He was badly damaged, his face crushed and broken, his skin as ruined as Natasha's.

"He'll live."

Saul looked up sharply at King Rat's harsh voice.

King Rat stood over him, taking his weight on his left leg, regarding Saul's ministrations to Fabian.

Saul looked back down at his friend.

"I know," he said. "His heart's beating. He's breathing."

It was difficult to talk. His throat was constricted with emotion. He looked up at King Rat, gesticulated at the wall.

"The children . . . " he couldn't say any more.

King Rat nodded sharply. "The little fuckers whose parents clapped us out of town," he spat.

Saul's face twisted. He could not speak, could not look at King Rat. He shook with anger and disgust, clenched his fists. He could still hear the pathetic cries echoing up from the dark.

"Fabian," he whispered. "Can you hear me, man?"

Fabian moved gently but did not respond. *It's better*, thought Saul suddenly. *I can't talk to him now, here, I can't explain all this. He needs to be out of this. He mustn't see this.*

Saul could not bear the loneliness. He wanted his friend so much, but he knew that he must wait.

Time enough soon, he thought and tried to be brave.

He stood, limped his way to King Rat. The two looked warily at each other, then fell forward, catching each other's forearms, gripping each other. It was a long way from an embrace or a reconciliation, but it was a moment of connection. Like exhausted boxers leaning on each other, still enemies, but each granting the other a moment's respite, and each grateful.

Saul breathed deep, stepped back.

"Did you kill him?" he said.

King Rat was silent. He turned away.

"Did you?"

"I don't know . . . " The words lingered in the silence of the hall. "I think so . . . the flute was deep inside him, his throat was crushed . . . I don't know . . . "

Saul ran his hands through his hair, looked down at his heavy torso, smeared with the muck of combat. He felt winded by anticlimax and uncertainty. *But, then,* he thought suddenly, *it doesn't matter to me. He can't touch me. He's dead, or dying, or fucked and wounded, and if he ever comes back, I'll be whatever I am now, only infinitely more so. He can't touch me.*

"He can't touch you," said King Rat and licked his lips.

Anansi's body had gone. King Rat was unsurprised. He looked from side to side at the carpet of crushed spiders on the stage and the dancefloor.

"You'll never find him," he mused.

Saul looked at him and stared around the room. He was trembling violently. The stench of rat-blood was heavy in the air, and with every step Saul walked on the bodies of Anansi's dead. Some of the dancers were beginning to stir.

Blood decorated the walls like abstract art.

"I have to get out of here," Saul whispered.

Without words Saul and King Rat climbed to the attic.

King Rat went before him. Saul untied his prison shirt and draped it across his back before jumping and grasping the edges of the hatchway, hauling himself up and out.

He looked back once, stuck his head into the huge, silent room.

Red and green and blue lights spun on intricate axes, flashing at random now that the beats had gone. The floor was littered with bodies, a few twitching gently. Saul looked at the stage where he had arranged Fabian and Natasha. They looked as if they were sleeping peacefully side by side. Natasha moved her arm dreamily and it fell across Fabian's chest.

Saul's breath caught. He could not look on anymore.

He followed King Rat, emerged blinking from the sky-light, sucked at the cold fresh air. It seemed days ago that he had entered by this route, but the sky was still dark and the streets as deserted as they ever were.

It was the small hours, the small hours of the same night. London slept, fat and dangerous and blithely unaware of what had happened in the Elephant and Castle. The crisp ignorance of the city refreshed him. It carried on whatever, he thought. There was a great comfort in that.

King Rat and he were eager to leave these bricks behind. They moved as fast as they could, hauling themselves across the roofs, trailing their bruised limbs and wincing with pain, but high and exhilarated. When they had put some houses between them and the warehouse, Saul stopped.

He was going to call for help for those left behind in the club. God knew how many broken bones and punctured lungs and so on were lying in that hall, and he was very afraid of what they might contract from his troops. He could not contemplate that any would die. Not after that night. To live through that, crazed, possessed and dancing, only to die of ratbite in bed . . . he could not bear to think of that.

He stood a little way off from King Rat, on the flat roof of a bookie's shop. Nondescript low-rise housing surrounded them. Saul revelled in the banality of the view, the slate gray, the lackluster billboard ads, peeling and out of date, the obscure graffiti. He could hear a train pass by somewhere not far away.

King Rat faced him.

"You off, then?" he said.

Saul burst out laughing at the absurd understatement of the parting.

"Yeah." He nodded.

King Rat nodded back. He seemed very distracted.

"*I* killed him, you know," he said suddenly. "*I* took him out. Not you, you froze up. You'd have let him do a bunk, but not me! I sprung up with my sharp Hampsteads and *took* the ruffian out!" Saul said nothing. King Rat stared at him, his excitement ebbing. "But nary a rat was there to get a shufti," he said slowly. "None of my boys and girls. They saw nowt, all dancing, out of it, dead and dying."

There was a long silence.

King Rat pointed briefly at Saul.

"They'll think you done it."

Saul nodded.

King Rat began to quiver. He fought to control himself, shoved his hands into his mouth, beat his sides, but he could not contain the anguish and excitement.

He grabbed Saul's arms, his hands shaking.

"*Tell them,*" he begged. "*They'll believe you. Tell them what I did.*"

Saul stared at that dark, dirty figure. From where he stood, nothing of London was visible behind King Rat. That wiry, ill-defined face was all he could see, surrounded by nothing but the sky, the faint stars and oily clouds. King Rat was an island in his field of vision, operating under his own rules. The dark spaces in which those eyes hid were fervent, would not release him. The clouds behind King Rat's head were tinged with red, stained by the city.

King Rat begged for absolution. He wanted his kingdom back.

Saul did not want it. He did not want to be Crown Prince of rats. He was not a rat any more than he was a man.

But as he stared at King Rat's face he saw a sordid brutality in an alley. He saw a fat old man who loved him falling out of the sky in a deadly rain of glass.

Saul closed his eyes and remembered his father. He wanted him. He wanted to talk to him so much.

He would never ever speak to him again.

He spoke very slowly, without opening his eyes.

"I'm going to tell *my* troops," he said, "about how you cowered and begged the Piper for your life, and promised him all the rats he could kill, and how it would have worked if I hadn't fought past you bravely and shoved him into hell impaled on his flute.

"I'll tell them all what a craven lying coward Judas you were."

He opened his eyes as King Rat began to screech.

"*Give me my Kingdom,*" he shrieked, and clawed at Saul's face. "You little *cunt* I'll *kill* you . . . "

Saul stumbled back from the flailing claws, and pushed King Rat in the chest.

"*So what are you going to do?*" he hissed. "You going to kill me? Because you know what? *I'm not sure you killed the Piper!* And if he ever comes back he'll kill you *dead* like fucking *vermin*, and he'll make you dance and *beg* for it before you die, but he *can't kill me* . . . "

King Rat slowed down, his frantic flailings subsided. He backed away from Saul, his shoulders slumped, broken.

"See? *He can't touch me* . . . " Saul hissed. He jabbed a finger at King Rat's chest. "You dragged me into this world, murderer, rapist, *Dad*, you killed my father, unleashed the Piper on me . . . I can't kill you, but you can *sing* for your fucking Kingdom. It's *mine*, and you *need* me in case he ever comes back. You *can't* kill me, just in case." Saul laughed unpleasantly. "I know how you work, you fucking animal. Self *über alles.* Kill me and you might be killing yourself. So what do you want to do? Eh?"

Saul stepped back and spread his arms wide. He closed his eyes.

"Kill me. Take your best shot."

He waited, listening to King Rat breathe.

Eventually he opened his eyes and saw King Rat skulking, moving back and forth, toward him and away again, clenching and unclenching his fists.

"You little *bastard!*" he hissed despairingly.

Saul laughed again, bitter and tired. He turned his back on King Rat and walked to the edge of the roof. As he began his descent, King Rat whispered to him again.

"Watch your back, you shit," he hissed. "Watch your back."

Saul climbed down a curving line of old bricks and disappeared into the labyrinth behind a skip, wound his way along a tiny alley and emerged into South London.

He scoured the streets until he found a darkened arcade of kebab vendors and newsagents and shoeshops, and there at the end a mercifully unvandalized phone box. He dialed 999 and sent the police and ambulances to the warehouse. God knew, he thought, what they would make of the scene awaiting them.

When he had made that call, Saul held the receiver to his chin for a long time, trying to decide whether to act on his instinct. He wanted to make one more call.

He called directory enquiries and got the number for the Willesden police station. He called the operator and told her that his pound coin had stuck in the phone box and he had to make an urgent call. The operator acquiesced with a bored voice designed to let Saul know that she knew he was lying.

The phone was answered by a crotchety sergeant on the graveyard shift.

Saul didn't suppose that DI Crowley was available. At this time? Was Saul mad? Anything urgent the sergeant could help with?

Saul asked to be put through to Crowley's answering machine. He stiffened with déjà vu at the sound of Crowley's measured tones. He had not heard them since his rebirth, the night after his father's murder.

He cleared his throat.

"Crowley, this is Saul Garamond. By now you'll know about the fucking carnage in the Elephant and Castle. This is just to let you know that I was there, and to tell you not to bother asking anyone there what happened, because none of them know. I don't know how you'll end up writing it up . . . Fuck it, say it was a performance art piece that went horribly wrong. I don't know. Anyway, I was calling to tell you that I did *not* kill my father. I didn't kill your policemen. I didn't kill the bus guard, I didn't kill Deborah, and I didn't kill my friend Kay.

"I wanted to tell you that the main culprit is gone.

"I don't *think* we'll see him again.

"There's one more culprit for part of this, Crowley, and I can't get rid of him, not yet. But I'll be keeping my eye on him. I promise you that.

"I want to come back, Crowley, but I know I can't. Leave Fabian and Natasha alone. They don't know *anything*, and they haven't seen me. I did everyone a favor tonight, Crowley. You'll never know the half of it.

"If we're both lucky that's the last we'll hear of each other.

"Good luck, Crowley."

He hung up.

Tell me about your father, Crowley had suggested, all those weeks ago. *Ah, Crowley*, thought Saul, *that's just what I can't do.*

You wouldn't understand.

He walked into the dark streets, heading for home.

EPILOGUE

Deep under London, in a rough chamber off a tube line abandoned for fifty years, accessible from the sewers and the pipes of a hundred buildings, Saul told the rats the story of the Great Battle.

They were spellbound. They ringed him in concentric circles, rats from all over London, here a survivor of that night, licking her scars ostentatiously, another boasting of his exploits, others chattering in agreement. It was dry and not too cold. There were piles of food for everyone. Saul lay in the center and told his story, showing off his healing wounds.

Saul told the assembled company about King Rat's Betrayal, when he had abased himself in the dirt and offered the life of every rat in London if only the Piper would spare him. Saul told the story of how he himself had heard the cries of the dying and had broken the Piper's spell, shoved him into a void with his infernal pipe embedded in him, and he told them how he had stamped on King Rat in contempt as he did so.

The rats listened and bobbed their little heads.

Saul warned the rats to be vigilant, to keep a watch for the Piper, and to avoid the lies and seductions of the Great Betrayer, King Rat.

"He's still in the sewers," warned Saul. "He's on the roofs, he's all around us, and he'll try to win you over, he'll tell you lies and beg you to follow him."

The rats listened intently. They would not fail.

When Saul had finished the story, he sat up on his haunches and looked into the ring of faces. Row upon row of anxious eyes, gazing at him, demanding that he command them. They oppressed him.

There was so much that Saul wanted to do. He had a letter to Fabian in his pocket. Fabian would be leaving hospital soon and he would find it waiting for him, some tentative overtures, hints at explanation and a promise to contact him when things had calmed down.

Saul wanted to find a permanent base. There was an empty tower in Haringey he wanted to investigate.

There was shopping that needed doing. He had his eye on a very flash Apple Mac portable computer. Leaving the human world behind certainly made things easier as far as money was concerned.

But he could not operate like that as long as the rats hung on his every word, followed him everywhere, desperate to do his bidding. His revenge on King Rat had trapped him with endless ranks of adoring followers from whom he was eager to escape. And there was always the chance that the rats might start listening to King Rat. He was out there, skulking, plotting, destroying. Saul had to ensure that his revenge would last.

He had to change the rules.

"You should all be proud of yourselves," he said. "The nation scored a great triumph."

The gathering basked.

"It's a new dawn for the rats," he said. "It's time the rats realized their strength."

Excitement swept the assembly. What announcement was this?

"And it's for that reason that I abdicate."

Panic! The rats ran from side to side, beseeched him. *Lead us*, the said to him with eyes and screeches and claws, *take us*.

"Listen to me! Why don't I quibble with King Rat's right to that name? Listen to me! I abdicate because the rats deserve *better* than a King. The dogs have their Queen, the cats their King, the spiders will throw up another sovereign, all the nations fawn before leaders, but let me tell you all . . . I couldn't have defeated the Piper without you. You don't need champions. It's time for a revolution."

Saul thought of his father, his fervent arguments, his books, his commitment. *This one's for you, Dad*, he thought wryly.

"It's time for a revolution. You were led by a monarch for years, and he brought you to disaster. Then years of anarchy, fear, searching for a new ruler, the fear isolating you all so you didn't have faith in your nation." A frisson passed momentarily up and down Saul's back. He was suddenly alarmed. *Jesus*, he thought, *I wonder what I'm unleashing*. But it was too late to stop and he plunged on. He felt like an agent of history.

"So now you know what you can do, the rats will *never* kow-tow to the whims of kings again. I do not abdicate in favor of another." Saul paused theatrically.

"I declare this Year One of the Rat Republic."

Pandemonium. Rats tearing around the room, terrified, excited, liberated, aghast. And above the hubbub and confusion, Saul's voice continued, his speech nearly at an end.

"All equal, all working together, respect going to those who *deserve* it, not just those who claim it . . . Liberty, Equality . . . and let's put the 'rat' back into 'Fraternity,' " he concluded with a grin. *This way*, he thought, *maybe I can get a bit of peace.*

He raised his voice over the clamor.

"I'm not Prince Rat, I'm not King Rat. . . . Let the Betrayer cling to his outmoded title if he wants, pathetically hankering for the past. From now on there are no kings," said Saul.

"I'm just one of you," he said.

"I'm Citizen Rat."

Alone again.
   I've done this before.
   You can't keep me down.
   Watch your back, Sonny.

I'm the one that's always there. I'm the one that sticks. I'm the dispossessed, I'll be back again. I'm why you can't sleep easy in your bed. I'm the one that taught you everything you know, I've got more tricks up my sleeve. I'm the tenacious one, the one that locks my teeth, that won't give up, that can't ever let go.
   I'm the survivor.
   I'm King Rat.